MYSTIC JOURNEYS

PARANORMAL WORLD, BOOK 2

C. C. SOLOMON

CatDog Publications

ISBN: 978-1-7336259-1-3

ACKNOWLEDGMENTS

Thank you to all my friends and family who supported my dreams. Thank you to my beta readers, Judi, Krystal, Danielle, Eva, Heather, and Analisa. Your time and feedback are truly appreciated. And another Thank you to my editor, Nina Gooden, for her great eyesight, thoughtfulness, and passion. And another thank you to Yours Truly for their keen proofreading eyes and formatting.

A NOT FROM C.C.

To find information on prior books by C.C. Solomon, please visit my Amazon Author Page.

PROLOGUE

When my mother first got sick, she didn't ignore it.

She knew, as we all did, that she had caught the strange flu that many non-gifted humans were catching. The world called it the Sickness, and it hit her out of the blue. She'd survived for years after the supernatural wave had taken over our planet. With the wave came nightmarish creatures and landscapes, humans with paranormal abilities, and a disease that would kill a large portion of the world's population.

We know now that the Sickness was brought to our community by a child we'd taken into our fold. The little girl, no older than eight years old, hadn't shown symptoms at the time. Days later, the familiar pattern of the disease began to show up. A week later, the child passed away. My mother, who was serving as a town teacher, most likely caught it while teaching around the child. She then proceeded to unintentionally pass it on to my father when she was in the earlier stages of the illness.

"I know he gets on your nerves, but you look out for your brother when I'm gone," my mother said one evening. She was sitting up in bed in the house that I shared with her, Dad, and my younger brother, Charles.

She was five days into the Sickness and looked much better than others I'd seen. Although my powers could not cure the disease, I was able to stall some of the effects for a short while and at least make her more comfortable.

My mother's eyes looked tired, but the full face of makeup she had on helped cover the dark circles underneath. She wanted to look pretty for my father because they were going to have a bedside dinner date later on. Her hair was starting to fall out so she had it expertly wrapped in a colorful silk scarf that I had found during my scavenging. I'd gotten her wigs, but she didn't like any of them.

The world had changed and the supernatural had taken over everyday life, leaving electricity and technology down. Finding any mundane items were now bordering on rare as resources dwindled.

It took nine years to discover that my powers fell into the category of life mage. I was essentially a witch who could control any living and earth-based thing or element. Charles had a gift of magic over weaponry and technology, which, for obvious reasons, was in high demand. Our parents had no such gifts, which made them highly susceptible to the Sickness as "regular" or non-gifted humans. The Sickness didn't kill magically-gifted humans and, therefore, we were the ones often going on trips outside of our town to find resources or trade with other communities.

"Mom, please stop talking like that," I said, running my makeup brush over a shimmery gold eyeshadow in a palette I was holding. "Close your eyes," I instructed her as I scooted towards the bed to do her eyes.

My mother closed her eyes, and I dusted the shadow onto her lids. The shimmer brightened her honey-colored skin, much like my own. "Perfect," I said, admiring my work before putting the eyeshadow palette away in my makeup pouch.

"Amina, listen to me," my mother said, opening her eyes. "You and your brother must stay together. I don't know how long your father has if they don't find a cure for this. Not to mention, I don't know how he'll manage without me. The man can barely put on his own drawers."

I rolled my eyes. "Mom!"

She laughed and it soon turned into a long bout of coughing. I gave her a hand towel that lay on the bedside table. She continued to cough into it. When she pulled it away, I noticed a thumb-sized amount of bloody phlegm on the towel. She frowned and folded the towel before placing it back on the bedside table. I grabbed the glass of water on the table and she took it, taking several gulps before speaking again.

"Watch out for your brother," she continued, her voice hoarse. "I know he's only a year younger than you, but he isn't as mature. Don't tell him I said that." She gave me stern eyes and I smiled, nodding. "And you don't let this world steal your joy. That's one thing Charles seems to be able to hold on to. Even after all the pain he's been through."

I knew she was thinking of Jalissa, my brother's girlfriend who'd died three years prior. She didn't have gifts and she couldn't handle the new, scary world. She'd taken her own life to escape.

"You get sad sometimes, Mina," my mother continued.

"Don't we all," I muttered, picking out a deep pink blush from my pouch.

"Yes, but, honey," my mother started and touched my hand. "You are strong and you are deserving of love. You deserved it before and you deserve it still. Don't let anyone tell you that you don't have anything to offer. I've seen those movies where an apocalypse happens and they have the women be sex slaves. Don't do that."

I side-eyed my mom. The Sickness was clearly getting to her mind. "Well, I've kind of missed the sex trade so far. I'll make sure that won't change," I cracked. "The world may not need a lawyer, but I have a lot more to offer than my body."

My mom nodded. "What else? Oh, listen more than you speak. Look out for those who are weaker. Be suspicious of those who offer favors without asking for anything in return. You are more powerful than you know and don't let those nagging doubts in your head stop you from believing that. You're destined for great things, even in this world. And... Oh, just because the world isn't like it was, doesn't mean you don't make the guy wait before you give him some. He still has to treat you as a queen. That's why I named you Amina. She was an African queen, you know."

I nodded. I did know; she'd told me this several times in my life. I'd even done a report on the Nigerian queen in middle school.

"I'm putting some recipes together that are meant to be passed down. Your grandmother's famous buttermilk biscuits and fried chicken, as well as my seafood and rice dish that you loved. Oh, and my sweet potato pie. If you make macaroni and cheese, put a lot of cheddar cheese in it. Cheddar makes it better. I know you have powers to just make food out of nothing but it doesn't taste nearly as good as old-fashioned cooking. I've had frozen food with more flavor."

I nodded, no longer fighting her advice and instead trying to hold back tears. She smiled, masking her worried look as I saw beads of sweat gather on her forehead. I reached over to the table, grabbed a damp face towel and dabbed at her forehead.

"I know it was hard for you before but maybe this new world will be better for you. With your powers, you seem to be flourishing."

"I'm 27, single, and living with my parents. I think I'm in

the same place I was before." I chuckled and shook my head, putting the towel back on the bedside table. "Suck in your cheeks."

My mother did so and rolled her eyes. "You just mentioned things. I'm talking about people. You're going to find your niche here," she said after I was done with the blush. "I don't have magic like you, but I have a good feeling. This world is this way for a reason, and you and your brother have a purpose."

"I hope it's to wait out this nightmare," I muttered, shifting through my pouch to look for the right lipstick. "What do you want, red or fuchsia?" I asked her. None of the makeup I had was exactly fresh. No one was jumping up and down to make cosmetic products since the world fell apart, but I made do with what I collected over time and freshened the products up as best I could with a little magic.

When my mother didn't answer, I looked up in a panic. She wasn't—

Her eyes were wide open and she was looking behind me off into space. Except for the gentle rise and fall of her chest, which gave me great relief, she looked like a statute.

"Mom? You okay?" I asked, touching her shoulder.

She looked to me, eyes still slightly glazed. "He's going to get someone killed."

I frowned. "Who?"

"Phillip is not in control. He needs help but not your servitude."

"Who's Phillip?"

Her eyes grew desperate. "You are not a sacrifice, Amina. Stop doing that. And don't listen to him."

"Him? Who? This Phillip guy?"

She shook her head. "No, the other one. Don't let them scare you."

My mom looked away. "They can't come back." She said it as if talking to herself instead of me. "They'll kill you."

I shook my head, more than confused now. I was convinced it was the Sickness talking. The more the disease progressed, the more the victims were prone to fits of hallucinations and confusion. "Mom, maybe you need to rest."

My mother turned back to me. "Ireland will be beautiful, but be careful there. Be careful with all the places you go."

"Mom, I already went to Ireland. Remember? I went to Dublin on vacation with some friends when I graduated college."

My mom looked at me as if just now noticing I was there, blinking her eyes rapidly with a frown on her face. She looked down at the lipsticks I was tightly gripping. "I think the fuchsia lipstick would look good on me. Let's go with that."

I let out a deep sigh and nodded, tears starting to stream down my face. "Okay, Mom." I took the lipstick out of the pouch and began to apply the color.

I fought a tremble of heartache. I didn't know what to say. Really, what was there to even discuss? The Sickness took the mind, among other functions. There was no point in making my mother feel worse by questioning her about what she'd just said.

My mother's eyes widened again and she grabbed my wrist holding the lipstick. "Watch out for your brother, you hear? You're all each other has."

CHAPTER 1

My mother told me to watch out for my brother. It was odd that I didn't remember that conversation until now. I also couldn't recall her ever using Phillip's name. How had she known about him? Maybe I was remembering wrong. But I remembered doing her makeup for her dinner date with my father. It had been her last semi-good day. She could barely sit up after that.

"Amina. Amina," said a familiar male voice with a deep Australian, correction, New Zealand accent.

Erik.

I opened my eyes and bolted upright, regretting it as dizziness hit me. My brain felt like it was rattling around in my head. Recognition and the situation immediately came crashing back.

My brother, Charles, was dead. Charles was the last of my family. My mother and father had died five years after the world had gone to hell. And for almost four more years, Charles and I continued to survive. We'd escaped so many horrors that I was beginning to take for granted that we would always stay together. I should have been smarter.

David, our former captor, wanted me, but Charles had tried to stop him. I'd gotten my brother killed.

I looked up to Erik Bennet, who was standing over me with a serious look on his face. He was still wearing the clothes from the night before and he looked like he hadn't slept. I couldn't imagine he'd gotten much of any rest with me crying in his arms the whole night. His jet-black hair was messy and his beard was growing out, making him look slightly older but still not even close to his thirty-eight years of age. Paranormals rarely looked our ages. One of the perks, since our aging slowed down, giving us a longer life span.

I'd slept another night in Charles' bed. I attempted to scoot up in the bed again and was more successful this time.

"What time is it?" I croaked out. My throat felt dry from the constant weeping and my eyes were swollen. I couldn't imagine that I was visually appealing right now but I didn't really care.

"After 10 a.m." Erik said. "I was going to see Felix at the jail today. I thought you'd want to come."

I nodded. "Does Felix know?"

My brother had been dead for two days now. It seemed longer than that since David had escaped hell. David was the man who headed an organization of non-paranormal humans who kidnapped paranormal humans for our blood to make a strength-enhancing serum.

Meanwhile, poor Felix Gonzalez, who had become a best friend to my brother, was stuck in prison for killing a were pack member who had attacked Charles' girlfriend, Lisa Xu. When I'd defended Felix after the attack, Phillip Leal, the leader of the town, had detained me. Charles tried to get me out of confinement and it was at that time that David had appeared, fought Charles, and killed him.

"We told him about Charles yesterday," Erik said, grimly.

I didn't want to ask how Felix responded. I already had a good idea. Felix had a kind heart. He'd be crushed.

"How's Lisa?" I asked.

"Not good. She's not eating. Just lies in bed."

I nodded and got up. "That sounds familiar."

Erik leaned in and gave me a light kiss on the lips. "We're going to make it through this," he whispered.

I looked up at him and gave him a slight smile that I was sure looked more like a grimace. At six foot, he towered over me even if I was standing, and I strained to look up at him.

He smiled back at me and it wasn't a smile of pity, which I would hate. Instead, his smile held such comfort in it. His hazel eyes didn't betray any sadness and I inwardly thanked him for that.

I sighed and went to the bathroom to wash my face, brush my teeth, and put on some clothes. I'd taken a bath the night before. Well, Erik had drawn me a bath and, although I'd just wanted to go under the bed and hide forever, I'd gotten in to please him. Once I dressed, Erik watched over me as I choked down a slice of toast with peanut butter. We then went to see Felix.

When we got to the police station, we were greeted by the receptionist in the front; an older woman named Betty.

"I'm so sorry to hear about your brother," said the woman with sorrowful eyes. "He was a real sweetheart. I used to see him at the market from time to time. He was a funny guy."

I nodded with a forced smile. I knew she meant well but I didn't want to hear about my brother. The thought of him made my heart ache.

We got to the basement cell, and Faith Thomas was already there. Except the scene wasn't what I expected.

Faith kicked repeatedly at the bars of the cell which, I assumed, Felix was in. She cursed at each contact with her boot-covered foot. I was sure she was getting zapped by the magic ward on the cell. A guard lay on the ground, eyes closed.

"Shit, Faith, what are you doing?" Erik asked in a loud

whisper, looking behind him to the entrance of the lockup area.

"I'm breaking him out of here," she said. The tall, athletic woman placed her hands on her slender hips; her tattooed-covered arms exposed beneath the short sleeves of her shirt. Today, her lightly-tanned skin color seemed ashen and her dirty-blond pixie cut was messy. I could see she wasn't faring any better from Charles' death. She had been there with us, trying to save him. Top that with Felix, who was like a brother to her, being locked up, and she was having a tough time.

"You can't do that, Faith," Felix said in a low, somber tone.

I looked over at him. He was a handsome, friendly giant, at six-foot-six, and he was built like a wrestler. His usually kind brown eyes were full of sadness and his shoulder-length, wavy, brown hair was a frizzy nest around his head. He slouched his shoulders and sat down on his cot.

"I can do whatever the hell I want to do," she spat. "Keeping you locked up is bullshit. The trial is going to be a joke. Why would we wait around for them to just screw us over? Let's all just get the hell out of here. We've suffered enough."

"It could all work out. Maybe they'll see reason."

"They kept you and Amina in confinement for a week. I doubt it. I need you to be okay. I can't have anyone else die." Faith's voice broke, and she turned away from us, wiping her face with her arm.

"I won't let anything happen to Felix," Erik said. "Don't worry about him." He turned to Felix. "You're getting out of here. No one else is dying."

"How can you be so sure?" Faith asked, turning slightly.

"If the trial goes south, we will be prepared. I'll tell you what I'm thinking when we get out of here."

I let out a deep sigh, looking down at the unconscious

man on the ground. "If they even think of hurting you, Felix, I will kill them all," I said in a tight voice, looking up.

Erik looked over to me, his eyes unreadable. "Mina... "

"No one else in our group is dying. And I will find out if someone in this town helped bring back the man who killed my brother."

"You think it was someone from the pack?" Felix asked.

"They had motive. One of us killed one of theirs. They saw my power. I'm a threat."

"Then why haven't they just killed Felix already?" Faith asked, facing us again.

"Because her command to Seth wouldn't allow it," Erik guessed.

The three of them looked at me. I had ordered Seth not to kill Felix, right after Felix had killed the pack member who'd attacked Lisa. It was at that time that I'd exposed my ability to control minds.

"That's right, you can control fucking minds," Faith exclaimed. "Why not just tell them to let Felix go?"

"The mind control doesn't work on Phillip," I replied. "He won't let Felix out."

Phillip was the head of the town, and he and I shared some type of bond. He'd helped me escape the paranormal prison. However, in his town, I was starting to feel like a prisoner again.

"Let's just see how it all plays out. I won't let anything happen to Felix," I continued. I walked over to the cell, and he stood up and came to the bars. I grabbed his hands and looked into his eyes. Those sad brown eyes. And just like that I burst out in tears again.

I soon felt Erik and Faith come up on either side of me, placing comforting hands on my back. The connection with the three of them soothed me as it often did with us.

"We were supposed to be this special six," Felix croaked out. "What happened?"

He was right. We were told the six of us were meant to do something great. How could that happen now?

CHAPTER 2

The day of the trial filled me with dread. There wasn't an official courthouse in the town, so the hearing was held in the public library. In front of the information counter was a table set up for the prosecution with Theodore Oh, a wizard and one of Phillip's counselors. Across from him at a table set for the defendant's side, was Annie "Mae" Jenkins, a mother figure to many in the town. Seating for the audience was behind the tables of the prosecution and defense.

I walked over to Mae. "Hi, Mina," she said, giving me a tight hug. Mae was an older woman with a smooth, mahogany complexion, a short curly Afro, and a bright smile. She was also psychic. I couldn't help but wonder if she knew what would happen to my brother. I planned to ask her after the trial.

"I came to help. I have one year of law school under my belt... that I barely remember, some nine years later," I said.

"Child, if you think anything going on today will resemble what you are used to, you are going to be very disappointed. The council members are appointed to represent both sides. I volunteered for Felix."

"You can see the future. Are you going to win?"

Mae patted my shoulder. "What is meant to happen will happen. It's all going to start after today."

I shook my head. "What do you mean?"

"You should go take your seat. They're bringing Felix in now."

I sighed. Once again, I was receiving only a piece of the puzzle from Mae. It was exasperating and as an overly-analytical woman, it could very well drive me to insanity.

Felix, led by two weres, looked tired and bruised. Someone had been using him as a punching bag since just the couple of days that we'd visited him. The fact that he hadn't body slammed someone or gone all otherworldly and gotten them with his death touch was a greater testament to his character. He was allowing this to play through. I balled my fists up as I went to take a seat next to Lisa.

Lisa usually looked like a glamour girl. As a fairy, she changed her look with the snap of her fingers. Today the woman looked tired. Her ever-changing hair was now its original black color and tied back in a ponytail. Her emerald-green eyes seemed dull under puffy lids. Her face was bare of makeup.

I reached over and took her hand, squeezing it. She sniffled, and I glanced at her with a sad smile. She nodded back at me. We were in this together. She might have known Charles only for two months, but they'd seen each other every day. They had fallen in love.

Phillip entered the building and some people rose until he sat down at the information-counter-slash-judge's-bench. As much as I didn't trust him, I still found him undeniably handsome. He was the color of caramel with short, black curly hair. He had a deceptively friendly smile set between equally deceptive dimples. He was of average male height and his fit body was covered in his usual tailored suits. I looked away from him, growing more annoyed at his role in this farce of a justice system.

"Today, we are here to determine the guilt of Felix Gonzalez for the murder of Luke Brady. Theodore Oh will represent the prosecution and Annie Mae Jenkins will represent the defendant. Mr. Oh, you have the floor for your opening," Phillip announced.

And so, the travesty of a hearing began. There were alleged witnesses who hadn't witnessed a damn thing testifying false facts. Somehow the story that Lisa had attempted to put Luke under a curse, which justified his attack, came up.

Then there was the theory that Felix was jealous that Luke was flirting with his woman Lisa—clearly not knowing that she and Charles were a thing—and in a jealous rage threw Luke. Since there weren't any bites on Lisa's arm that anyone other than Felix, Carter Banks—the second in command of the pack—and I saw, our account of what happened wasn't gaining much ground.

Mae tried to paint what I believed was the truth of Luke being an angry alcoholic. She even had a couple of witnesses who testified to his history of public drunkenness, fighting, and inappropriate behavior towards women. I was actually proud of the case she made for Felix, who she painted as a friendly protector.

After both sides presented their cases, Phillip called a recess while he made a decision. There was no jury so I had no clue how Phillip would rule. He had to know that if he harmed Felix, we wouldn't let it stand. However, if he didn't find Felix guilty, it was possible that the pack would revolt and he needed them to maintain order in the town.

After an hour, Phillip entered, and the crowd hushed. I looked over at Erik, who was looking straight ahead at Phillip. I turned and looked over to Lisa and she looked back at me with a curt nod. We were all ready. If the verdict didn't go our way, we weren't going to wait around; we'd teleport out of the makeshift courtroom as fast as we could.

"I have listened to both sides, and I do not take my role as the decision maker lightly," Phillip began. "While we can all admit that Luke had some character issues, his personality and past behavior cannot be a focal point when deciding whether or not his death was appropriate. Felix, although new to town, has shown himself to be a valuable member, but again we cannot look to that when deciding innocence or guilt. The only thing we can look at is if his actions were warranted. We have the testimony that Luke bit Lisa and there was blood on his teeth, but we cannot verify if it was hers, as he was bleeding from the mouth from the impaling." He paused and looked around at the audience in the pseudo court.

Just another negative of the apocalypse. No one was going around doing DNA testing.

"In any event, there is no proof or evidence that Luke intended to kill Lisa, which would be the only justification for his death. Felix could have reacted to the alleged behavior a number of ways, but killing Luke was not the correct option."

I did not like where this was going.

"Therefore, I find Felix Gonzalez guilty of the murder of Luke Brady. Because I do not believe it was premeditated and that this was a heat-of-the-moment action, he will not be sentenced to death. Instead, he will be sentenced to blindness."

The crowd erupted in a mixture of shouts of shock and cheering. Some were satisfied with the ruling, others thought it was too lenient.

I looked over to Lisa but she was gone. I quickly turned to Felix and he too was gone. She worked fast.

The room went insane.

Seth McIntire, the leader of the town's were population,

rushed towards us and Erik, who was recently made Seth's third, jumped up.

"Where did that bitch take him? He has to pay!" Seth spat.

I was enraged. I knew Phillip wouldn't do the right thing, but it was still hard to see it happen. I somehow had hope that he would let us go. Letting Felix live would have made him look weak but to blind him was unacceptable when Felix was innocent. The pack, led by a crazy brute, wanted vengeance even if it wasn't logical.

I got up and moved past Erik. Seth reached out to grab me and I threw my hand out, psychically sliding the tall, muscular man on his heels, away from me. I had no more patience for his antics. I stormed towards Phillip, who was standing looking at me in confusion.

"That trial was bullshit and you know it. You never had any intention to do what's right. You just want another victim to exert your control!" I shouted.

"And yet, he got away," Phillip replied in a calm voice. His honey-colored eyes looked down on me with almost robotic coldness. "So, who will take his place?" He looked past me. "Maybe his friend, Erik, will do what's right."

I felt Erik's presence behind me. "I'm not doing shit," he stated.

"Not surprised." Phillip looked over to Faith.

"Don't look at her," I demanded. Faith joined Erik and me in front of the counter.

From the corner of my eye, I saw Raya Ortiz, Seth's fifth in command. The brunette stood with legs apart, ready to fight. Seth wrapped a hand around a fist and glared at us. A few vampires I did not recognize stood behind him, and the small group slowly began to approach us.

"This doesn't have to get ugly. Just let us leave this town," Erik stated.

"No one's leaving until Felix comes back to get his punishment," Seth stated with rage-filled green eyes. The weretiger was built like an athlete. He had short, blond hair and a wide mouth that was typically set in a cocky grin. Today his usual grin was set in a scowl.

Phillip looked at me and smiled. "Erik's going to stand in for him. Here." Phillip's lips moved, but I could not hear what he was saying. A second later, he opened his hand, and a butcher knife materialized in his palm. "Erik, take this knife and cut out your eyes."

Seconds later, Erik walked around me towards Phillip.

"Erik, stop!" I demanded.

He stopped in his path. We had to get out of here. We could teleport. But when I turned, I saw that Faith was being held by were police. I couldn't leave her.

I turned back towards Phillip in time to see him give the knife to Erik. "Erik, stop!" I screamed. But he took the knife and raised it over his left eye.

Phillip sucked his teeth, giving me a fake pity look. "Right, I told him to ignore your command."

I ran to Erik and grabbed the knife from him in mid-motion to his eye, trying to prevent it from lowering. He held tightly to the knife but he was slowing down, as if resisting the blade.

"Please stop," I cried, tearfully.

He looked down at me from the corner of his eyes, his face scrunched in discomfort. "I can't," he said through a strained voice. The blade was only an inch from his right eye now. Panic gripped my stomach.

Still grasping the knife, I took a deep breath and closed my eyes. I pictured the knife in my hand. A prickly heat stabbed at my fingertips but when I opened my eyes again, the knife vanished from Erik's hands into mine. I turned and Seth was suddenly in front of me. He backhanded me across the face and I stumbled to the ground, momentarily dazed. The knife fell out of my hand.

Well, that was enough to snap Erik out of Phillip's

control. He turned and right hooked Seth in the face, shouting out in a spine-stabbing growl.

Phillip moved around the counter.

"Stop where you are, Phillip," I shouted, getting up. I touched my soon-to-be swollen cheek from where Seth slapped me and winched. "No one is dying or losing their sight. Let this go. You won't lose control of your people."

"Not happening and there won't be any more discussion," Phillip replied in a deep voice. His eyes were fully black now, no white could be seen.

I took a hesitant step back. What was happening?

A sharp pain came to my other cheek as if I had been slapped again.

Phillip's hand was out in a stop motion, the other hand touching his cheek. He frowned.

Oh, he wanted to play witchcraft beat down, eh? I threw out a mental punch to his stomach but I was the one who keeled over in pain. I was certain that I had done the attack on him, not myself. What was going on here? I looked up and saw that he was clutching his stomach as well.

Erik grabbed me. "What's going on, Mina?" he asked.

Phillip lifted a pointer finger and sliced the air. I screamed as a searing pain went across my forehead. I touched the pain spot, feeling wetness and a stinging cut. I brought my hand down and saw blood.

"What's happening to you?" Erik shouted in a confused tone.

I had a horrible feeling I knew. My magic was ricocheting back on me.

"The hell?" I heard Phillip cry. I looked up and saw that he had a long horizontal cut across his forehead, much like I expected my own appeared.

I knew where this was going and when I got out of here, I would appropriately freak out. But now I had to fight. I picked up the knife and quickly slashed my forearm, clenching my teeth at the pain.

Phillip cursed and rolled up his sleeve, a matching cut appearing on his forearm. He looked wide-eyed at me, stumbling back to the counter.

"Stop what you're doing or you won't like what I do next," I demanded, pointing the knife to my crotch area. I wasn't sure if I was really going to go that far, but I was hoping he wouldn't call my bluff.

"Mina, what's going on?" Faith asked behind me, her voice careful.

The room had grown quiet and everyone paused their arguing and fighting, eyes focused on Phillip and me. "I'm not scared of you. Whatever you do to me will come back to you. So, let us go."

Phillip scowled. "We were supposed to be partners. Don't do this." His voice didn't match his angry face now. He sounded almost pained, but also like himself again.

"Then let the others go."

Phillip shook his head. "No."

I put the knife to my throat and froze the room of people with my powers, raising my left hand in a fist. I didn't want anyone to play hero or jump me, especially Erik. "You let us go or we both die."

Phillip cocked an eyebrow. "You wouldn't do that."

I pressed the knife harder to my neck, drawing blood. Phillip winced and touched his neck, finding blood on his fingers from the psychic nick. I had no death wish. I wasn't ready to die, and I was hoping he wouldn't call my bluff. I just needed him to let us go. Despite how crazy this world had become and the gut-wrenching loss of my brother, I still wanted to stick it out. But Phillip was too dangerous to keep me under his thumb. I'd already been a prisoner helping some egotistical asshole get more powerful; I wouldn't do it again. Never.

I looked over to Erik. "I'm sorry," I whimpered, holding back tears of pain and fear.

"No, Mina, don't!" He shouted, unable to move due to my magic.

I began to cut slowly. The others in the room, who I called friends, cried out in protest.

"Stop!" Phillip shouted, grabbing his neck.

My freezing magic broke, and before I could recast the spell, a male were punched me in the face. I felt a searing blinding pain on the right side of my face and I stumbled to the ground. I vaguely heard Phillip curse.

"Sorry, boss, I had to stop her," the brute said before things went momentarily dark for me.

I opened my eyes and fought off the feeling of nausea. Erik stood in front of me, guarding me as he tossed pack members to the side. Faith punched a female vampire, knocking her on her behind. The vampire sat up and spat out blood. Faith's eyes were already blood red now and she meant to kill. That would only make things worse. As a succubus, she would drain her victims dry of their life force. We didn't need more death on our hands. We had to get out of here.

I threw out my hand to stop Faith's attacker, but a brick force knocked me sideways to the floor. I struggled to move under the heavy pressure and managed to see that it was Raya, her eyes were wolfen blue, and she snapped her teeth at me, scraping my arm.

I punched her in the face and kicked her in between the legs. Crawling backwards from under her, I clapped my hands together. "Inferno!" I shouted. A ball of fire appeared in my hand but I felt no heat from it.

I threw my hands back as if to pitch it like a baseball. A hand grabbed my wrist.

I looked up, enraged. It was Erik, his face neutral and stoic. "Don't. Let's just get Faith and get out of here."

Faith backed up to us. I looked over to Phillip, who stared at me with curious eyes. They were their normal light brown again.

"Let them go. For now. She lost her brother. Perhaps we should consider that an eye for an eye," he said in a neutral tone.

Faith spat in his direction. I gave him my middle finger before grabbing Erik's and Faith's hands and teleporting away.

CHAPTER 3

Felix stood over Charles' cloth-covered body, shoulders shaking with his cries. "He was a good man. He was my friend," the large man said through tears.

We were now in the Hagerstown hospital, in their basement morgue. We'd sent my brother's body here in anticipation, prior to the trial. Lisa and Erik moved him out of Silver Spring, in case we were going to really break out. We'd packed a few things prior as well.

I looked down at Charles' body. Lisa had magically given him a new set of clothes. He looked like he was simply having a peaceful sleep. It'd been four days now since he'd passed and he hadn't shown signs of decay. I'd assumed it was because he was paranormal and this was just another part of that power. We'd have a funeral for him tomorrow.

I slouched on a stool near the table where Charles lay. I was exhausted and sick. Felix had healed me from my battle at the library, but I wish I had kept the wounds. I'd rather focus on that pain over what I was feeling now. Charles was all the family that I had left. While I realized that most people weren't lucky enough to have close family still with them these days, I started to take for granted that Charles and I would remain together. Charles kept me going. I didn't want to go on anymore.

Lisa got up. "I feel like I'm going to be sick," she said before running out of the room.

I didn't go after her. I was starting to feel numb.

Upon her exit, Mae entered the room with Bill Locklear, her partner and Silver Spring's best medical mage. They were silent as they walked over to Charles' body. Felix moved away and Mae touched Charles' shoulder, closed her eyes, and prayed.

"Did you know?" I asked, looking across Charles' body to Mae. "Did you see it in a vision and just not tell us? Maybe you didn't want us to worry or do something differently. You said it would all work out for us. How is this working out?" My voice was restrained, but I wanted to shout and kick chairs.

Mae turned and looked at me with sad eyes. "I knew things would change for you all. I knew things would become difficult. I thought the six of you had to be together to make a difference. There had to be six to stop what's coming." Her face looked genuinely distressed.

"But you didn't know if it was the six of us, exactly," Felix stated.

For the first time since my limited exposure to Mae, I found her looking unsure. "I'm so sorry, honey. My visions have never failed me, but perhaps I misinterpreted something."

I shut my eyes and sighed. I couldn't blame Mae for this. She didn't kill Charles. I looked at his body again. My breath quickened and fresh tears ran down my face. I got up and ran out of the room, struggling to breathe. Mae rushed after me and gave me a tight hug. I didn't think I would ever get past this. I thought of my mother and father and cried for them too. I was overwhelmed and I didn't have the fight in me anymore.

"I know, honey. I know this is hard. But you are not alone. Don't forget that. The others will help you." She rubbed my back as she spoke.

"I need to know what's going on!" I cried out. "Who helped David escape? What is this power that Phillip and I have over each other? Do you know? Is Phillip a threat to me? Did *he* help David?" I could feel my heart beat faster. I was on the verge of a nervous breakdown. I struggled to maintain my composure and wrung my hands together.

Mae sighed. "He would never want to hurt you. Helping this David man would not be something he'd do."

"Can he be killed?" Faith asked, standing near Felix, hand on his arm.

Mae shook her head. "You can't kill him."

"Why not?"

I pulled away from Mae. Also confused.

"If Phillip and Amina hurt themselves, the other gets hurt. If they hurt each other, they, themselves, get hurt," Mae explained.

"What? So, if Amina cuts herself, Phillip gets cut too? And if Amina cuts Phillip, she still gets cut?" Felix asked, shaking his head.

Erik nodded. "That's what we saw at the library."

"Yes. So, you see, you can't kill him or Amina gets killed," Mae said.

"What if someone else kills him?" Faith offered.

"I was punched by one of the pack members and Phillip felt it," I stated. "A lot of this is new. When I was locked up, Phillip was never hurt and I didn't have mind controlling abilities. I didn't really have body controlling powers either. At least not over humans. Now I do."

Mae put a finger to her chin and squinted her eyes. "It's because you've begun to connect with him now. Before, you were just in each other's dreams. But when you met, that's when your individual powers really grew. And they'd continue to grow if you had stayed together. It would also make you more vulnerable to each other, as you saw."

I sighed and threw my head back, staring at the ceiling. "What is he?"

Mae clasped her fingers. "What are the *both* of you? When Phillip spoke to me about you, I knew. You are soulmates."

Nausea took hold of me again, but this time, it wasn't because of pain. I leaned against the cold hospital wall to steady myself. My head rested against the cool tile.

Mae looked at me and frowned. "I know that isn't what you want to hear. And I don't mean to insinuate that you two are lovers meant to be together. That is only one definition of soulmates. It's the one we came to understand in the Pre-world, and it was true for people we used to call power couples. That was a pairing that would make one or both very successful in life and career. In this new world, soulmates are beings filled with powerful magic. They are extremely rare and fated to meet. I've never met any others in this new world but I met some in the Pre-world. I've had visions of soulmates of the past. My hope was that Phillip would come to Good and the two of you would reach your full potential. You need to be strong in this impending fight."

I rolled my eyes. "If this is true, why didn't we know of each other earlier? It's been nine years."

"That's a good question. I honestly don't know. Either you weren't tuned in to your magic well enough then or something was blocking your connection."

"What kind of power do I have now?"

"You're both life mages but have your own soulmate magic too, that connects and makes your individual gifts even stronger. You can never hide from each other. He will know where you are," Mae explained. "If you open yourselves up, you will be connected in ways you never knew. Shared thoughts, shared pain. Telepathy. Energy. Which he already did to help you get free. You can make him better."

Erik walked to my side. "I'd rather us spend our time finding a way to kill him without hurting her."

Faith ran a hand through her hair, her face scrunched in frustration. "Mae, it sounds like you want us to help Phillip. Why?"

"He was not always like this," Mae stated. "I don't know what happened but something changed him. For some reason, whatever happened to him is being mentally blocked from me. But Amina might be able to find out with her pow—"

"Right now, I don't give a fuck about him," Erik stated. I could feel a growl threatening to erupt from his chest. "This soulmate thing sounds dangerous. She needs to stay away from him."

I heard Mae sigh again. "He already knows where she is. We have to look past our likes and dislikes for the greater good."

I felt a dull and persistent headache attack me. I couldn't hear any more about helping Phillip. He had made his own choices; I had no sympathy for him and didn't want to help him in any way.

"My brother's dead, and Phillip tried to sentence Felix to blindness. I could give a shit about the greater good. Who is he to you? Why do you care so much about us helping him? Why do we need him? What do you know that you aren't telling us? I'm tired of you giving us pieces. I want the whole truth, dammit!"

Mae looked away.

"Tell her, Mae," Bill said in a gentle voice. The silver-haired man walked over to Mae and placed an arm around her. "It's time to tell everything now, Mae."

Mae shook her head, her eyes closed and lips placed tightly together. "Phillip is my godson. He is more like my son. His mother and father died when he was fourteen and I took care of him after that. His mother was my best friend.

Phillip's mentor I told you about, the one who was killed by humans, was my husband, his godfather. I know Phillip to be better than he is. He isn't the son I see now."

"You lied to me!" I cried, throwing my hands out. The ground shook under us, but I kept talking; not caring if I was the cause. "You brought us here and you knew what he was. You made Lisa trust you. You didn't tell her your town was run by a sociopath who had mind control powers. I tried to let it slide because I thought maybe you really needed our help, but he's practically your son." Erik gently lowered my hands and grabbed my right hand in his. I felt my temper, which was verging on out-of-control levels, lowering. The ground settled. "Is there even a big evil really coming? Or did you just want someone here to help Phillip be the man you used to know? It's a new world. It changes people. Accept it."

"I'm so sorry, Amina. It's not that way. I never lied to you," Mae said, eyes watering. "Helping Phillip was not my main objective in getting you here. I admit that I hoped you could help him. But without you helping Phillip, I don't know if the group will be strong enough to fight what's coming."

"Screw this soulmate shit," Erik stated.

"I agree. We need to stay here and focus on figuring out what's coming for us. None of us are going back to Silver Spring," I stated.

Erik sighed.

That didn't sound like he supported me. "What's the sigh for?"

He looked down at me. "I have to go back, Mina. Seth and Phillip are dangerous. I might be all there is to help the pack. When things die down, you can come back. It's a good town and they need us. A lot of the people we freed from the prisons are there. We can take down Phillip and Seth and make it something good. Hagerstown doesn't need us."

"So, you're leaving us? Because I'm not going back."

"I really want you to come back. I want us all back."

"You gotta be kidding me. You can't be a hero to every-one, Erik," I spat.

"I know it's hard now, Amina," Mae began. "But you are all meant to be in Silver Spring. I think you can do good, not only for the town there but for the world. If left unchecked, Phillip could do real damage in this world. Having Erik return would help but you all need to come back."

I shook my head. "It's not safe for Felix there, or Lisa, since she teleported him away. It's definitely not safe for me since Phillip is clearly threatened by my power."

"We can help settle things and then have you come back," Mae reasoned.

"What about me? Am I'm expected to go back with Erik now?" Faith asked with a tone of unapproving surprise. "Screw that."

Erik shook his head. "Faith, since you've befriended Blake, she can give you knowledge about Phillip."

I was fuming. All I wanted to do was bury my brother, mourn, and seek out those who helped David escape hell. Going back to Silver Spring and trying to resolve their prob-lems was a distraction I didn't have time for.

"Where's Lisa?" Faith asked, looking around.

"She's not here," Felix replied with a frown.

"I know she wasn't taking this well. Maybe she went to lie down," Faith guessed.

Felix shook his head. "She's not here. She's not in town."

"Did she teleport somewhere?" Faith asked, her face in a patient question.

Felix shrugged. "In a way."

Faith rubbed her temples. "Felix, please, this is not the time for riddles. Where did Lisa say she was going?"

He looked at her with wide eyes. "She didn't speak to me. I've been beside you this whole time. I just know." He raised a hand before anyone could ask. "She's not here anymore."

"How could she leave us?" Faith asked, visibly hurt.

I understood. Lisa was like her sister now. My heart hurt. I was no one's sister anymore. Somehow sensing that renewed pain, Erik squeezed my hand.

"Her boyfriend was just murdered in front of her. What was there to stay for?" I asked in a strained voice.

"But what about the visions?" Felix asked, eyes wide with a mixture of pain and confusion.

"Charles is dead. The Power of Six is over. We lose. Let her be." I looked back over to the morgue doors. A wave of exhaustion swept over me.

Bill, who I was beginning to understand was not a man of many words, spoke up. "We don't lose. It's not over," he said in a quiet voice. "We keep moving, we keep fighting, we keep the faith. We've made it this far, and we still have work to do. Through the pain, we have to still believe."

Tears welled in my eyes, blurring my vision. I wanted to give up, but I gazed around at the faces of everyone in the hallway and thought about those who still needed our help. I thought of the children back at Silver Spring. The children who would grow up in a world of magic and the supernatural, many of them orphans who needed people in their lives they could trust. They needed protecting, but I wasn't in a space to help. I couldn't emotionally or physically move myself to be a hero now. I was done with loss, pain, and the unfairness of it all. I just wanted to lie down and forget.

CHAPTER 4

The next morning, I awoke to an odd call from the morgue. We were set to have Charles' funeral, so I didn't need any problems. They wouldn't tell me on the phone what the problem was and insisted I come to the hospital.

Erik, with his superior were hearing, heard the caller, and got dressed with me. As I got ready, I heard him make some calls to the others to tell them that something was going on at the morgue.

When we arrived, Mae, Bill, Felix, and Faith had beat us there. It made sense, as they had stayed in an apartment building near the hospital. Erik and I had settled into the apartment I used to share with Charles when we first stayed in Hagerstown.

"What's going on?" I asked. The four turned and exposed what they were facing.

I looked over to see a cold steel table where my brother lay. Only, he wasn't in the peaceful, almost-sleeping position from the night before.

Instead, he looked like a toppled, grotesque statue. He was frozen, with a deeply arched back, head still on the slab, hands clawed up and legs bent. His eyes were open but unblinking.

I gasped in shock, knees buckling. "How long... has he been like that?"

"We aren't sure," Bill replied. His dark-brown eyes looked tired and I wondered if he and Mae had even gone to sleep. "The mortician came down here around 8 a.m. and alerted me. Mae and I stayed late at the hospital to get to know people and help where we could. We went past the morgue again at 8 p.m. so he could have moved any time after that."

That meant he could have been like this for almost twelve hours. "Is he... is he alive?" I whispered. I didn't want to allow myself to have any hope, but it was the obvious question.

Bill shook his head. "I checked his pulse," he replied with worried eyes.

My heart plummeted.

Faith rubbed her hands over the lids of her deep-blue eyes as if attempting to erase the image of my brother from her mind. "Could this be... rigor mortis?" She looked away from Charles' body, visibly uncomfortable, which was an unfamiliar look for her.

Bill shook his head. "Not like this."

If it wasn't rigor mortis, what was it? I'd seen people with magic die before and this didn't happen.

I walked went over to the table. "Charles!" I shouted at his body. Reason told me he was still dead, but he had moved at some point! His whole body had shifted, and his eyes were open. This was a new world, controlled by the supernatural, and I had to believe that maybe things weren't as they seemed.

But Charles didn't move. I put a hand to my mouth and leaned over to get a better look at him now. His eyes were fully blood red, with just a black iris in the center. I hadn't seen that from the door. "Why are his eyes red like this?" I asked to whoever could answer.

I slowly reached out to touch him.

"Don't!" Bill shouted, walking over to me.

I turned to him. "Why?" I frowned and narrowed my eyes. "What do you know? What's happened to my brother's body?"

Bill glanced over to Mae. Mae gave Bill a sympathetic smile and nodded her head. Looked like she had more secrets than I thought.

"Charles can come back."

The room filled with gasps and sounds of confusion.

I turned to Bill, glaring. "What are you talking about? You just said he's gone. He has no pulse. We were just here yesterday, and no one said anything. I don't want him back as a zombie." Bringing someone back to life basically made them a simpleton controlled by a mage of the undead or necromancer. That wasn't what I wanted for my brother.

Bill raised his hands in surrender. "I wouldn't dare do that, Amina. That's worse than death and it's not within my power."

"Then how can he come back?"

Bill sighed. He was drawing this out and I was getting angry.

Erik placed a comforting hand on the center of my back and my anger subsided a bit, slowing my pounding heart. "Bill," he stated in a caution-filled voice.

"Mae had a vision that something bad was going to happen to The Six," Bill started. "We didn't know if it was going to be death, but we knew we couldn't risk losing any of you. There have to be six. You're all too important. So, we took some precautions for those we could get to. We had a vampire that we trusted help us. At different times this week, we served everyone but you, Amina, the vampire's blood. And the only reason we didn't get to you was because you were under Phillip's eye. We also didn't think anyone would dare hurt you because of Phillip."

"I had tea with you," Faith stated, scratching her head in frustration. Her eyes held a look of disgust and irritation.

"You came to the prison and gave me some homemade soda," Felix said, face in shock. "It was good, too."

"I came to talk to you, Bill, and drank your coffee," Erik added.

The older couple nodded.

"Vampire blood stays in the system for about a week. You don't need a lot," Bill explained.

Mae clasped her hands together and gave a sympathetic look. "Charles and Lisa came for dinner, and they each had a glass of red wine."

"So, they all drank blood? Then what?" I asked eagerly.

"Vampires weren't just made from the change. They're still being made. Just like weres, who can be made from a bite or birth from a were parent. If you die with vampire blood in your system. You don't always stay dead," Bill replied. "You can come back. As a vampire."

"Charles is going to be a vampire?"

We all looked to my brother's unbreathing, unmoving body.

Bill nodded. "I thought it would happen last night, but I didn't want to get your hopes up. It can take as long as seven days. The fact that his body hadn't decayed was a good sign, but that isn't always due to vampirism. Paranormal beings are slow to decay in death, just as their aging is slowed down in life. This—" he waved his hand towards my brother's awkward form "—is a good sign that he will change. When we saw this, we knew you'd have to be here if he woke up."

Erik let out a low growl. "Why didn't you tell us before doing all this?"

"Would you want to be vampires, honey?" Mae asked from across the room. She was perched on a stool looking more than exhausted.

None of us answered. Vampires were glamourized in the

movies, but in our new world, they weren't all like Blake Devlin, the head of the Silver Spring Vampires. She was beautiful and alluring. However, vampires ranged in appearance and behavior.

In general, vampires didn't need to eat food. They couldn't be out in the sun. Even the strongest ones would get sunburned and the weakest would be set ablaze against the sun's rays. They had to drink blood to survive and although they were hard to kill, there was no proof, at least not yet, that they were immortal. Then there was the whole not being able to have kids thing. The living vampires made as a result of this new magical world could still procreate, but if you were made by blood exchange, you'd be sterile.

Lastly, there was the bloodlust. This typically affected weaker vampires and meant that they became scary monsters completely ruled by their hunger for blood. None of us were certain we would have agreed to that kind of life and Mae knew that much.

"The six of you must survive," Mae insisted again, her hands balled into fists. Passion wrapped around her voice and I saw in her eyes real fear. It unsettled me how close to desperate she sounded. Her visions of this terrifying future that only we could stop from happening had really scared her. "I'm sorry that we withheld this from you, but... we must make sacrifices to save the world. We can't afford to lose anyone."

I crossed my arms. I wanted to be mad, but ultimately, there was hope. My brother had a chance at life again. I wouldn't have let my mother down. I wouldn't be alone and he wouldn't have lost his life being in a place he never wanted to be. He'd be a vampire but he'd be alive-ish.

He would hate me for allowing this. Or maybe he wouldn't. I needed to see his smile again. I need to hear his jokes and smart-mouthed quips. I needed his hugs and reassurance that things weren't all crazy in this world.

It would be a while until night, but I wouldn't leave him. "I'll wait until he properly wakes then," I stated in a soft voice.

No one left for any long period of time. We took bathroom and food breaks, but remained in the morgue otherwise. We spread out in the room like a morbid party.

The group passed part of the time discussing how to find Lisa. In this world, that would be close to a hopeless endeavor. We didn't have cell phones working, just some communities with landline phones. Felix emailed her, which assumed she had access to the internet wherever she went.

I hoped that wherever she was, it was of her own accord. I tried not to think about the possibility of her being kidnapped, but I couldn't ignore it. I'd have to do a locator spell when I left here.

If Lisa never returned and Charles didn't come back, I'd just have Faith, Felix, and Erik. What if they all left or died too? Would I turn into a pile of mush and give up on the world? I was ready to now and I didn't think I had much strength left to survive any more loss.

I realized now how much I'd depended on Charles to be there for me emotionally. Even before, in the Pre-world, I called him whenever I had a bad date or when I wanted to chat about the latest TV show that we both loved. Just the thought of the memories made me tear up again. If we were thinking of fighting Phillip and his henchmen, it was very possible that we wouldn't all make it out alive.

How would I hold up if I lost Erik?

I looked over to him sitting next to me on the floor. His head rested against the stark white wall; eyes closed. He hadn't left my side since Charles was killed, practically following me to the bathroom. I sighed. I couldn't get used to his presence. It would hurt too much if he left or died. Leaving to go back to Silver Spring was dangerous to me and Erik seemed to entertain that danger with no fear. Sure, he was a former military man and bodyguard, and as an alpha werejackal he was strong, but he was still human to me.

I'd had bad breakups in the Pre-world that'd left me on the couch in a puddle of tears and comfort food. And then a friend or a family member would swing by or call to cheer me up. But they were all gone now. I had no one.

Sure, Faith was nice enough but she wasn't exactly a cheery sweetheart. Felix was sweet but he was also struggling with his own issues. He had lost his memory and a bit of his mind the day the world changed.

Suddenly, I didn't feel so strong. I felt emotionally exhausted and overwhelmed. The ties that I was beginning to form with the others were starting to feel like weighted burdens. The thought of losing Erik made me almost sick to my stomach. I was getting too vulnerable and my prior naiveté had cost me dearly. If I was going to be a match for Phillip, I needed to be cold and calculating like him.

"I had another vision last night," Mae stated, breaking the silence. "I have a better idea of what the six of you are meant for."

"What?" I asked in a soft voice.

"Something... important is coming. Smaller things will happen before then but those things will build your strength."

"What is this something?" Erik asked, eyes now opened.

"My images of the future shift to different possibilities. Some good, some bad. I don't know what the outcomes will be, based on certain actions you take. What I know is that another shift will come about. It is already happening."

"What's the new shift?" I questioned.

Mae looked at me with fearful eyes. "Humans as we know them will no longer exist. Only the gifted. But war and new sickness and division will come to the gifted. Certain groups will die out on a massive scale, much like the ungifted humans. Other groups will become their more primitive selves."

"What does that mean? Like a werewolf would stay in wolf form or, no, still look like humans but just walk around on all fours like an animal, hunting and eating people?" Felix joked.

Mae gave him all too serious eyes. "Yes, and yes. I've seen very similar things in my visions. Think of the worst aspect of all of your groups."

"Too much of a good thing," Faith murmured, hanging her head.

"Exactly, my dear," Mae said, pointing to her. "Balance is what we need. And before you ask, I don't know when or how this will happen. Or even how you can stop it. I just know that you six are key to preventing our world from falling apart. Everyone is important, even humans without magic."

"Shit," Faith cursed, throwing her forearm over her eyes. "Like we need another damn thing to add to our list of to-dos. If Charles doesn't come back and we can't find Lisa, are we screwed?"

Mae shook her head. "I honestly don't know. I always dreamed of the six of you. I don't know what happens if you aren't all together."

Part of me wished she'd kept her premonition to herself. She'd basically stated that we were in big trouble as it stood now.

~

5 p.m. hit. We canceled the funeral for anyone planning to attend. There were questions but we kept the real situation a secret for now.

7 p.m. came. It was getting darker outside the last time I'd

taken a stretch break but not yet dark enough. This was the 24-hour mark. Still nothing.

By 9 p.m. I was slowly giving up hope and believed that his composure, which had not changed, was some supernatural post-death rigor mortis, despite what Bill said.

At 10 p.m. I looked over at Charles' body. His pose looked painful, but Bill was adamant that we not touch or move him. Bill assured me that since Charles would be the undead, unlike the humans turned to vampires from the initial magic hit, he wouldn't be harmed by the stiff pose. Charles' body would no longer work like a regular human.

"What if Charles doesn't come back, Erik? I mean, it's already after ten," I whispered, looking at his body with worried eyes.

"Night's not over and we have tomor—" Erik stopped, mid-response.

The sudden sound of movement came from the table where my brother lay.

Charles was now flat on his back, legs down, hands at his side, and his chest was moving up and down at a rapid pace. His eyes were blinking.

He was alive.

CHAPTER 5

"Charles!" I shouted and jumped up, rushing to him.

"No!" I heard Bill shout behind me. "Wait, Amina, don't touch him. He's not fully aware yet, and he could hurt you."

I paused, already a few feet from the table. "What do I do?"

"Wait," Bill replied. He walked over to me with a syringe full of dark-red liquid in his hand.

"What is that?"

"A special kind of sedative. He won't go to sleep, but it will calm him." He injected the liquid into Charles' right arm.

"Why does he need that?"

"So, he won't bite you."

I looked back to Charles. His breathing was off. His chest rose and fell at a startlingly fast rate, as if he were hyperventilating. His red eyes were still staring up at the ceiling. He was definitely not alright and so I wouldn't test Bill's words and instead, remained in place.

"Speak to him, Amina. He needs to hear a voice he knows," Bill stated, remaining by my side. I felt Erik come up to my other side and the movement of the others behind me.

"Why is he breathing like that?" I asked.

"He is breathing only because that is what he remembers to do. He doesn't need to but his mind is not all the way back. He doesn't recall the regular way to breathe. Speak directly to him. It'll help give him clarity."

"Charles?" He didn't look at me. "Charles, it's your sister, Amina." Nothing. I looked to Bill. "Can I touch him now?"

Bill nodded. I could hear the others around me stir as they watched me.

I looked back down to Charles and reached out to touch his hand nearest me. I braced myself for him to do something. Attack me. I didn't know. He stayed the same. I placed both my hands around his hand. He didn't look up at me, just up at the ceiling, a pained expression on his face.

"Charles, remember when we were kids? I think I was ten, so you were nine. You wanted a puppy, and Mom and Dad weren't having it. So, I prepared a case for us to get a dog. I had note cards and pictures. I put you on the stand, which was just a dining room chair, and Mom was the other side. Dad was the judge. Remember, I had the stuffed animals to the side as the jury. It was so silly. But I won the case! I got the bug for being a lawyer after that. I don't know if I was really good enough to win the case for a dog or if Mom and Dad already changed their minds and just wanted to make us work for it. But I remember you smiling and looking at me like I was your hero. I tried my best to always be there for you and have your back. I'm sorry I couldn't help you this time." Tears flooded my eyes and I tried to blink them away to no avail.

Charles' breathing slowed down, and he looked over at me with those scary red eyes.

"Mina? Mina," he croaked out, his voice hoarse. I nodded my head swiftly and his face scrunched up. He closed his eyes and began to weep silently. Watery, red liquid dripped from his eyes down his cheeks.

I looked over to Bill, alarmed.

"Vampire's tears are mixed with blood," he explained in a calming voice.

I'd never seen a vampire cry before. I turned back to Charles, bent over, and hugged him tightly. He slowly wrapped his arms back around me. He felt shockingly cold but I didn't care.

"Mina, I saw them. I saw them," Charles cried. "I see what they're doing."

I heard Mae gasp behind me.

I pulled away slightly. "Saw who?"

"They're strong. I don't know what they are. People bow to them like they're gods. They turn people into monsters."

Mae moved to Charles' other side and touched his free hand. "My premonition."

"They were looking for us, but now they've found us," Charles said, his voice cracking. "They're waiting to get stronger, but when they do, we're all going to die."

"Who is looking for us?" Erik asked.

He shook his head. "I don't know. I could barely see them."

Erik narrowed his eyes, leaning forward. "Where were you?"

"I don't know. It didn't look familiar. It was like here but it wasn't. It was dark and there was destruction everywhere at first. Buildings were on fire; bodies were on the ground. There were beasts and they were crying out. Then things changed. The world looked different. It was sunny, clean, and beautiful. People had smiles on their faces but they weren't really happy. I didn't understand it."

"It's the beginning of it all," Mae whispered. "My visions. Charles, where are they now?"

Charles tossed his head from side to side. "I don't know," my brother said with a tinge of frustration. "They have people everywhere though."

He'd just survived coming back to life. I needed my brother to be calm and comfortable. "Let's give him some time to adjust. We can ask more questions later."

Charles looked around the room. "Where's Lisa?"

I really didn't want to tell him that right now but he wasn't a child. I couldn't delay the truth. "She thought you were dead. She couldn't handle it and... left," I explained. "She didn't know that there was a possibility for you to come back. We all only learned that today."

Charles looked up at the ceiling. "She left me?"

"We'll get her back, don't worry."

Charles suddenly winced in pain as he clawed at his shirt. "What's wrong with me? My stomach hurts."

I looked to Bill. "Why does his stomach hurt?"

Bill, who I hadn't noticed move away earlier, came back to the table with a mug. "He needs blood," he explained. "I was able to secure some."

Charles sat up, Erik helping to lift him upright. "What am I supposed to do with that? I feel like I could eat a house," Charles asked.

"This will help," Bill said, handing him the blood.

Charles took the mug and looked down at it, his face twisted in disgust. He looked up at us, then looked around the room once more. "Why are we in a morgue? Why did Lisa think I was dead... " He paused and soon full awareness entered his eerie red eyes. "That fucker stabbed me. Did you—"

"I killed him. He won't be coming back." At least I hoped. I made David explode, so I didn't think he could put himself back together again.

"Was I in a coma all this time? How long have I been out?"

"Six days. And, no, you weren't in a coma. You were, you were—"

"Transitioning," Bill cut in.

Charles frowned. "Into what?" he asked. He looked down

at the mug again. "Into someone who drinks blood. Shit, I'm a fuckin' vampire?" Charles looked to me with angry eyes. "You let them turn me into a bloodsucker?"

I raised a hand to calm him down. "I didn't know they gave you blood but I also didn't want you to die when I found out. Don't look at me like that. You would do the same if the roles were reversed. I love you, get over it."

"I can't drink fucking bl—"

Mae slapped her hand on the table. "All right, vampire or no vampire, that is enough cursing, young man," Mae shouted. "Now, this situation may not be ideal but no one here was going to let you die. You are loved and way too important. I am sorry we tricked you. However, you will find that your life as a vampire won't be so bad. You will still have your tech powers, so you'll be stronger. Everything's going to be okay. Now drink the blood so your stomach will stop hurting."

Charles froze and looked at her for a beat and then proceeded to gulp down the red liquid from the cup. I grimaced and looked away, then sighed as he asked for another cup.

My brother was a vampire, I didn't think this is what my mother had in mind when she'd told me to look out for him.

CHAPTER 6

"Alex, if you pull Briana's hair again, you'll get detention," I said sternly to the ten-year-old boy in my classroom.

Alex was an elf with brown hair and large, blue eyes that made him look innocent and cute, but he was sneaky. He loved to pick on Briana, a human girl with a head full of tightly-coiled hair. Alex pouted and then looked over to Briana with sad love-sick puppy eyes. She stuck her tongue out at him and rolled her eyes. She pretended to be annoyed with him, but I had overheard her tell her friends she thought he was cute during recess one day.

They both lost parents at different times during the supernatural change. Briana's parents died of the Sickness, and Alex's mother died during his birth in the Pre-world. His father was killed two years ago by an ogre during a scavenging and hunt. Most of the children and teenagers at the school in New Hagerstown were orphans.

A month had passed since Charles' resurrection and I had poured myself back into teaching, mostly because I needed to make a living. I also enjoyed teaching and felt I was making a difference. It amazed me to think that these children would only know this life. They'd hear about the Pre-world and watch the old movies and shows in amazement. Alex would only know life as an elf, and Briana would know a world full of all types of magical humans. In a community like ours, divisions of race and nationality would seem silly when you shared space with vampires and were-creatures.

The bell rang, signaling the end of the day, and I dismissed the class, reminding them of the paper due Monday on their favorite person in history. I stayed later to run the drama club. The arts weren't on everyone's mind nowadays, but we could not survive and thrive on just the basics. Sure, now arts were all after-school subjects, but at least we got to have them. We had an art club, band, and chorus. We also had sports.

The town was growing larger every month, growing to well past two thousand in population, and that meant our school was expanding. Right now, we were doing a production of a Broadway show I had tickets to see with my mother before the supernatural had taken over and turned society into a nightmare. I still carried some bitterness about never getting to see that musical, but I'd found the lyrics and script from the play and decided to live out my dreams through a bunch of thirteen- to eighteen-year-olds.

It felt good to be normal for a bit. No fighting, no human locking me up and draining me of blood, no one mind controlling a town. Sure, some of these problems still existed, but I needed this down time. I deserved this time.

I worked, joined a jogging group, met friends for happy hour, and searched for Lisa... She was still missing.

I'd tried every location spell in the book to find Lisa. I even reached out in secret to some of Phillip's people to help, but no such luck. It was as if Lisa had been wiped off the face of the earth. There was simply no trace of her on the planet. It had kept me up many nights. I didn't know if she had willingly hidden herself or if she'd been taken by someone who'd hidden her location by magic.

In the meantime, I honed my magic, which consisted of me meditating, meeting with a witch group, playing with my powers, and reading and searching through even more supernatural books and websites than I had before. If I were stronger, I could find Lisa, find David's ally, and fight Phillip. Although he hadn't sent anyone to come for Felix or myself, I wasn't naive enough to think that meant we were in the clear. I was going to be ready to kick his ass. Nice girl Amina was a thing of the past.

According to Erik and Faith, Silver Spring had become even more big brother-ish. Townspeople were doing everything short of praying to Phillip, which included bowing and kneeling when he was around and addressing him as 'Master.' I knew better than to think that after trying to help my brother live and letting me go, Phillip would have turned over a new leaf. Seeing that my power matched his had probably made him paranoid.

Also, I still wasn't certain that he knew Charles was alive again. We certainly had not spread the word. Better Phillip and his cronies think we were defeated. If they believed that Charles was still alive, Seth would come around seeking retribution for the pack member Felix killed.

Thinking of my brother drew a deep sigh from me. I hadn't seen much of him. He was a new vampire—albeit a strong one, since he was a technology mage—and he still needed his daylight beauty rest. It worked out for him, since tech work wasn't a job that was relegated to just day time.

However, beyond his need for rest, he was not the old Charles I loved. It wasn't just the becoming a blood-sucking undead that changed him, but also what he saw when he was in the state of returning to life. He believed that whatever evil we were going to face was already on earth and roaming the planet growing followers. And those followers wanted

Charles to join them. It had scared him, and he continued to have nightmares about it. His lack of sleep and depression over Lisa's absence, coupled with coping with his new self, left me with a very different Charles.

That Friday evening, after school, I went home to get ready to meet the others at the town pub. This had become our regular routine on Fridays. Dinner, then sometimes going back to one of our apartments in Hagerstown plotting our revenge and building our Power of Six connection, sans Lisa. It wasn't always the five of us. Sometimes Chelsea Samuels, our friend from the paranormal prison, and Henry Butler, the head of the Hagerstown vampires and close friend to Felix, came.

Chelsea despised Phillip for killing her human boyfriend, and Henry had an interest in supporting his pal Felix in the fight. In the meantime, Henry and Chelsea mentored Charles in the vampire way.

As for Phillip, I knew he wasn't going to let me live my life as I pleased for long. Phillip knew we were soulmates, and he'd clearly expressed to me that he had no plans to ignore our connection. He was still making appearances in my dreams, trying to communicate with me, and I tried my best to fight him and wake up but I couldn't. Most dream communication rotated between him trying to convince me to join him and just plain taunting me. I'd wake up exhausted, searching unsuccessfully for dream protection spells. I had no doubt he was zapping my powers from our dream connections. He'd done so while I was locked in the prison, although he claimed it was by mistake.

Phillip didn't visit me every night, but it was sporadic enough to make me feel as if sleeping were a risking endeavor. Even when I napped during the day, he found me. Then he would also talk to me telepathically. It had been comforting when I was escaping David, but it was annoying now.

There were only a few people I told about my Phillip hauntings. I told Felix because, as an amnesiac, he didn't remember much of what you said and therefore could keep a secret. I also told a nurse named Joanie, who worked at the hospital because she'd become a wise friend.

She'd used to be a nurse in our prison hospital, but I didn't blame her and made sure she was protected when she'd joined the Hagerstown community. Without her at the prison, we'd have probably been treated even worse. I might have died. She hadn't had the power to help us escape, but she'd had the power to keep us alive.

I also told my magic mentor, Shayla Winans, witch and partner to Henry. She worked tirelessly to get me strong enough to repel Phillip.

I did not tell anyone else, including Charles, who had enough on his plate. With the others, I was embarrassed that I was so weak and vulnerable. I feared they wouldn't trust me if they knew I still had a link to Phillip. I told them that Phillip being my soulmate, wasn't going to compromise me, but then I'd see something in their eyes, uncertainty or suspicion, that led me to believe they weren't buying what I was selling. So, no, I wouldn't tell them about my nighttime Phillip visits.

I continued to get ready for our gathering and threw on some jeans and a black halter top. It was September and the heat was still thick and unyielding. Since the supernatural had taken over our world, nothing was as it had been, including the weather. Now our seasons were pretty much winter and summer. We would go from high seventies to low forties overnight. In some years, we would even go from 80-degree weather to 30-degree weather in the span of a few days. This shift usually happened in November. Then we would go through six months of cold with barely any rain. We'd get a lot of snow most of those months, sometimes blizzards, and March would bring powerful windstorms.

Then May would come with instant heat, along with a month of rain and recurring thunderstorms, sometimes carrying with it, hurricanes, hailstorms, and tornados. Now, even countries where it never got cold got some type of drastically cooler-than-normal temperatures.

Although it was still hot, I grabbed a matching cardigan in case the cold air conditioner inside the bar got to me. I pulled my dark-brown curls into a high ponytail and put a bit of makeup on.

A witch had opened up a beauty shop in town, and the former makeup junkie in me had gone a bit crazy in her boutique. It was mostly powdery makeup potions, some organic products, and even a few illusion spells. I'd gotten a brownish-red powder that I used as lipstick, blush, and eyeshadow, a kohl liner for my eyes, and a black, inky potion that somehow made my lashes long and full when applied.

I heard a knock at my door just as I was spraying perfume on my neck. I left my en suite bathroom and headed down the short hallway to answer the door. I noticed my brother's bedroom door was open and he wasn't in it. It was around 8 p.m. and dusk outside, so it wasn't shocking for him to be out. He was probably at work. Or biting someone. I tried not to think about that last possibility.

I looked out the peephole. Erik. Shit. In the past month, I'd tried my best to keep a healthy distance from Erik. I hadn't stopped caring about him, but I was angry at him for leaving and I just needed to protect myself. Erik seemed set on risking his life by going back to Silver Spring. He'd stayed with me for a few days after Charles "woke up" before heading back to Silver Spring with Faith to be a superhero. I tried to understand but I couldn't. It just seemed that he put those strangers ahead of us.

I was petrified of something happening to Erik and how I would handle it. I cared too much for him, too fast, and that worried me as well. I wanted to have my head clear so that I could focus on learning more about the Power of Six, how to break my own connection to Phillip, and finding out who helped David escape hell.

Erik didn't like our distance and was still very resistant to it all. Seeing Erik every Friday was an exercise in willpower. Each time I saw him, it didn't get easier. At least not for me.

Now he was here at my door, which was not part of our routine. I didn't see him until I got to the bar or restaurant. If he was here now, something had obviously happened, and he was the only one who could get to me.

My heart sped up as I opened the door, and a round of nausea hit me as I contemplated any number of things that could be wrong.

Erik stood there with a neutrally cold face. He looked different. His beard was gone, and his hair was a little longer. He looked like he should be on the cover of a magazine; he was so damn handsome, even with his angry face. My heart gave an involuntary flutter.

"What's wrong?" I asked. "Who got hurt?" I looked around him to see if anyone else was with him, but he was alone.

He walked into my apartment. "Nothing's wrong, at least not with any of the others," he replied in an annoyed growl.

I cocked an eyebrow and closed the door behind me, thoroughly confused.

"Is something wrong with you?" I asked.

"Not me. You look tired."

I rolled my eyes. "Thank you."

He shook his head, leaning against the wall in the foyer. "You've been going through something, and I've tried to give you your space, but at some point, we have to make a decision about us."

I nodded. "I know."

"You want to call it quits?"

I shrugged. Did I? I wasn't ready to say that aloud now. My heart wasn't ready to consider that option. "Maybe this was all magic between us. Maybe I subconsciously controlled you into falling for me."

He knitted his brows together. "Do you really believe that?"

"It's possible."

"The thought did cross my mind, but then I thought it really wasn't a stretch to care about you. Don't sell yourself short."

There he went being sweet again. It just made things more difficult. "Can you give me a little more time? Just a little. When all this Phillip stuff is over, it'll be better for us. I don't want anyone to get hurt because he's my stupid soul-mate. Especially if you insist on staying in Silver Spring, where I can't have your back. In fact, maybe it's better that I separate myself from everyone to keep you all safe."

"Woman." Was all he said, looking up at the ceiling.

"Is that why you came by? To tell me I look old and talk about our relationship?"

He scowled in annoyance. "No, smartass. I came to tell you that I'm going to challenge Seth at some point."

My heart gave a quick jump. I didn't like this talk. I knew that was the ultimate plan, but a challenge in Seth's pack meant a barbaric, mixed-martial-arts-style fight to the literal death. Erik already had to kill a man to get to third ranking. He wouldn't touch Seth's second, Carter, who was a good man.

I knew Erik was strong, especially as part of this powerful six that Mae foresaw us being. However, nothing was certain, and I didn't think we needed to jump to a fight. Seth and Phillip were dangerous, but I still wasn't sure Seth was a threat. The only reason to take him out was to have one less person fighting on Phillip's side if or when it came time for me to confront Phillip.

"But you aren't going to challenge Seth now, right?" I asked.

He shook his head, and I sighed in relief. "Not now. I want to be at my absolute full strength. I'm not there right now."

"You'll get there. We all will." Something was up. He didn't come here just to announce something we knew was coming but not anytime soon.

"Seth has five wives. But one of them is his actual mate. No one knows which."

I shrugged. "Why'd he bother getting a mate?"

"Because there's strength in having a mate. Just like a soulmate."

I bristled when he said that. Soulmates was a sore subject with us. Understandably. Learning that your significant other was bound to another person and then having her distance herself after learning this news wasn't exactly a fun state of affairs. As mad as I was at Erik for returning to Silver Spring, I was the jerk in this situation; that was clear.

"If I challenged him, there would be a good chance he would beat me. I would need something to get me to his level. Our Power of Six practice can only take me so far until we find Lisa, and even then, we don't know if it will make me powerful enough, alone, to win a fight against someone as strong as Seth. He's got enhancements beyond his mate. Magic infusions or something, I heard." He shook his head, looking confused. "He wouldn't play fair, and I'm sure Phillip would help him."

He went quiet and stood there, hands at his sides, staring at me. He was struggling with something he didn't want to say.

"What do you need, Erik?" I asked quietly, knowing what he was going to say.

"I have to get a mate."

I felt like my heart would burst through my chest, and my legs went slightly weak. I frowned. I couldn't help but feel a little hurt and jealous. Was he doing this as payback for me having Phillip as a soulmate? I hadn't chosen it. Fate had. Now Erik was going to run off and find some woman to become his mate.

The thought of him mating, and whatever that entailed, with another woman made me physically sick. I was sure there were tons of women who stood eagerly in line to get a chance at Erik. I could see Raya now, jumping at the chance to be his mate. Raya was Seth's fourth in command, and on paper, she was a better companion for Erik; matching her werewolf to his werejackal. She was also beautiful and didn't have an evil soulmate attached to her.

"I'm assuming you didn't just think of this. Do you already have someone in mind to be your mate?" I asked, trying to hold the bitterness from my voice and failing miserably. I turned from him and bent down to put my black sandals on so that I wouldn't continue to stare daggers at him. Had he come here to emotionally stab me with this news? Did he think I'd backed off from him romantically because I'd stopped caring about him? I was just trying to do what was right for us all right now.

"You, who else?" he replied.

I turned to him and straightened up. He looked at me as if I'd asked the dumbest question in the world, his eyebrows raised.

"I thought you had to be a were to be a mate," I stated, crossing my arms.

Erik gave a quick shrug. "Who says? The whole point is that I'm bonded with someone. And if that someone is paranormal, it will enhance my strength. Weres, especially canine ones, don't believe we should be alone. We're still learning about ourselves, but the idea of wholeness is very strong with us. That's why we jump to be a part of a pack, just like our counterparts in nature. Being a lone wolf is not a good thing, and we are our best with companionship. So, I need a mate with power, and you have power. A lot of it."

Erik's hazel eyes still looked cold, and there was no feeling in his voice. This was not a declaration of love or a proposal for marriage. He was suggesting a business arrangement.

"Don't I have to be a pack member?" I wasn't saying yes, but I needed to know the facts. Part of me thought he deserved my help. He'd saved the other paranormal humans from that prison and protected me from David when he attacked me during our search for the prisoners. Erik was stubborn and grumpy, but he was a good man.

Erik tilted his head from side to side. "Technically."

"Seth won't let me in the pack without you turning me into a were and, no offense, I'd prefer not to be turned. And I'm not ready to go back to Silver Spring. Not sure I'll ever be. So, I don't even know what that means for us. And what if Phillip finds out Charles is still alive? Won't they come for Felix then?"

"Mina, you can come back. It'll be safe for you. They already know about Charles."

I widened my eyes in a panic. "What? Then why hasn't Seth attacked?"

"The pack leads asked him not to. Even Raya. We all know that Luke deserved to die for biting Lisa."

I looked away. "No one could say that before we went to the freaking trial and Felix and I were locked up? Do you think Phillip also had anything to do with stopping Seth?"

"Fuck if I care," Erik spat, his hazel eyes darkening. "I honestly don't care what he thinks or does."

I raised my eyebrows in alarm. Of course, he had a right to be angry at the mention of Phillip's name, but the rawness in his voice still surprised me.

I nodded. "Okay. Fair enough. So, in theory, what does turning me into your mate include, exactly?"

"You just do an exchange of blood and flesh and some meditative words that will focus your mind and mentally connect. I've seen it done a few times. Most recently, last month with two members of the pack who got married."

I scrunched my face up. "An 'exchange of blood and flesh.' What do you mean, exactly? I have to drink your blood and eat part of you?"

Erik nodded slowly. "You can mix it with food if you don't want to taste it. That's what I've seen done. And it's not much blood or flesh we'd have to consume of each other."

"Maybe if you put it in a quiche, it wouldn't be so bad," I cracked. Who was I kidding? Even if I didn't taste it, I'd probably still gag.

Erik chuckled, the first laugh I'd heard from him in weeks, directed towards me. I missed seeing that smile, and my heart hurt again. "I could make that happen," he stated, slight grin on his face.

"So, when a person's a mate, is it for life? No un-mating?"

He lost his smile, and my heart sank a little. "I don't know. I've never seen an un-mating done. It's for life, as far as I know."

"Besides strength, what do mates have?"

"We'd know when we were in danger. We'd have a mental connection. We could share strength and power."

"And if one died?"

"The other could still live. But in full disclosure, it may not be a good life. When one loses a mate, the surviving person might die of a broken heart or even go loupe."

Loupe was the were version of going crazy. It was very similar to when vampires went bloodlust. The were was no longer human and became almost a rabid animal. Loupe weres were extremely dangerous, and usually, there was no going back.

However, I was human, so that wouldn't happen to me. Or could it? A crazed, super-powerful mage was a risky possibility; assuming such heartbreak could lead to me going crazy. I wasn't were. There had to be differences.

I pondered it for a moment.

"You don't have to give me an answer now, Mina. I know this is asking for a lot. Especially because you wanted to keep your distance from me, so you don't get hurt." His voice sounded very deadpan to me, and his eyes confirmed his total annoyance at the situation. He was doing this out of necessity, not desire.

I shrugged. "For a bond that might be tighter than marriage, I'd like to feel it's more than just a good business transaction."

Erik crossed his arms again and cocked an eyebrow. "You're the one keeping me at arm's length, Mina. I've been giving you your space because I know you're dealing with a lot. It was hard enough for me to come here to ask you this."

"Erik, I wasn't trying to push you away. It's just that I'm—"

"Angry at me for leaving you, and you want to be on your own so you can focus on yourself. Apparently, caring about people makes you weak."

The hell? I dropped my mouth open.

"I'm not weak!" I sputtered. "This isn't me being selfish!"

Erik walked to the door, then paused and turned slightly back to me. "You had a month, Mina."

He didn't say anything more, but I knew what he meant. I had a month to get my act together and come back to him.

"Perhaps because he's in your head so much you can't think about anyone else," he said in a low voice before opening the door.

I stiffened in shock and telepathically closed the door with my magic, preventing Erik from leaving. "How'd you know?"

"Phillip isn't trying to keep it a secret, like you are," he replied, turning to face me, his eyes dark with anger. "Why didn't you say anything? Have you fallen in love with him?

He is your soulmate, after all. Maybe that's really why you've been keeping your distance from me."

I looked down at my feet and balled my hands, which were now shaking, into fists. His assumptions were pissing me off. He had no idea what I was going through. "I thought you wouldn't trust me anymore; that's why I didn't tell you. I was ashamed I wasn't strong enough to keep Phillip out of my head and scared all of you would look at me as the enemy. I've tried everything. I don't even sleep that well anymore. Which is why I look so damn tired, as you so eloquently pointed out. It's not easy to look this bad." I gave a weak smile, looking up at him.

"Mina, you look beautiful. I was just being an ass." Erik's voice was softer. He looked down at my hands. "I didn't realize."

I opened the door with my magic. "It's cool, don't worry about it. I'll meet you at the bar," I stated in a rush of words. I felt like my heart was twisted in knots. I massaged my chest as if that would resolve the internal pain I was feeling. I didn't want him to see me break down. I couldn't be weak anymore.

CHAPTER 7

I walked into the Irish pub, which was one of only two places open past 11 p.m. in town. Although it was only 9 p.m., the pub was packed full of townspeople. The other late-night spot was an Italian restaurant that they'd converted into a nightclub with a DJ.

The atmosphere at the pub was lively, illuminated with recessed lighting and lit candles on the tables. In the far corner, a band played rock music on a wide platform, and there was a standing room only space in front of the stage where patrons gathered dancing and talking. Across from the stage was a long bar, crowded with more patrons. Tables and chairs were placed around the walls of the space, and waiters and waitresses moved about taking food and drink orders to the seated customers.

It was sometimes hard to believe that nine years ago, Hagerstown had been a suburban community just like any town in the country. Then the world changed, and we were reduced to small, self-sustaining communities with no proper federal government, the world population cut in half, no electricity without the help of magic, and fighting off creatures we'd only ever seen in movies and our nightmares.

With the help of magic, in particular witches and technology mages, many communities were able to get electricity and the internet going. Then up popped what we call "government towns," which were communities, like Hagerstown, with a leader pushing to get our former government back. The leaders worked with other government communities, and those leaders all formed a type of congress. The towns had yet to elect one overall leader or a president.

In this apocalyptic world, Hagerstown was a pretty good community. It was ever-expanding and was currently at about five square miles. A magical ward surrounded the town to keep out scary creatures or any unapproved guests. The government towns had also developed a way to detect if someone had the Sickness before letting them in the community and had, therefore, avoided any outbreaks for a few years now.

Everyone had a role or a job in which they were given credits to get things. Some jobs warranted more credits than others, like healthcare, farming, policing, and teaching. In this world, there were no menial jobs. Now, the rock stars were those who could bring back electricity, heal the sick and injured, provide food, build, and protect.

Chelsea was the first to greet me with a wave when she saw me approaching the group table.

She had thick, strawberry-blonde, shoulder-length hair and greenish-hazel eyes set against ivory, freckled skin. With her beauty, she'd had no difficulty in catching the eye of a guard while we'd been locked up. And, against all understanding, they had fallen in love. When Charles and I rescued our fellow prisoners, it was an all-out battle between our side and the guards. During the battle, Phillip had cruelly killed Chelsea's love.

"I'm going to the bar to get a drink. We'll wait forever for someone to come," Erik announced, standing up. "Mina,

Jack, and ginger ale?" He gave me sorrowful eyes, and I knew he was trying to apologize for his sharp words to me earlier.

"You know me so well," I said, giving him a smile that didn't reach my eyes before taking a seat. I could get through tonight and remain cordial. I didn't want to make the others uncomfortable.

He nodded and headed to the bar.

When he was far enough away, I turned to the others. "Erik asked me to be his mate."

Felix frowned. "I thought he just asked you about your drink."

I shook my head. "Earlier. He asked me to be his mate back at my place."

Chelsea tilted her head with a questioning gaze. "He came to your place? I thought you two broke up?"

"He just showed up," I replied. "And it's not a breakup. It's just a time out so I can focus on growing in strength and figuring out who helped David escape."

Faith sat back in her seat, an unsurprised look on her face. "He told me he was going to talk to you about it."

"He presented it like a business deal."

Faith rolled her eyes. "You broke up with him, honey." She threw out her hands in mock surrender. "I'm sorry, you put him on a time out. How else should he have proposed it? If you hadn't dumped him, I'm sure he'd have gotten down on one knee and all that, but now he's probably afraid you'd kick him in the face."

I gasped. Did they think I was that evil? "Why are you making me out to be the enemy here?"

"You aren't the enemy. You're just silly."

I opened my mouth to object, but Chelsea interjected. "What'd you say when he asked?"

"Nothing. Well, he just told me to think about it," I replied.

"Think about what?" Charles asked, suddenly appearing

at the table with a short glass of clear liquid in his hand, probably vodka.

"Erik asked Mina to be his mate, which sounds like a marriage proposal to me, but Mina said it was actually a business proposal," Felix answered matter-of-factly before taking a swig of his beer.

Charles sat down. His typically expressive eyes were now lazy. This had become his usual face, and it was difficult to tell how he was feeling. His emotions seemed to appear sparingly and carefully.

Charles didn't say anything for a long moment, and we all sat quietly, waiting for a response. "You need him; he needs you. I approve," he said in an indifferent tone before sipping his vodka.

And that was it.

Erik came back to the table with our drinks and was greeted with knowing smiles. He looked over to me, and I took my drink, avoiding his eyes.

"Okay, let's focus on where we are now," I said. "Anything new over in Silver Spring?"

"Business as usual. I've been accepted into Blake's clique," Faith replied. She was a succubus, but she functioned like a vampire except that she needed life force, not blood. There were several succubi and incubi in Silver Spring, and Blake, the vampire leader, was appointed their leader as well. "She told me that she doesn't actually agree with the things Seth and Phillip do, but she is super loyal to Phillip. And I found out why. He healed her sister, who was dying from cancer. She didn't want to become a vampire, and Phillip was able to help her."

"I didn't know she had a sister," I stated.

Faith nodded. "Yeah, she's no longer in Silver Spring. Moved to the Virginia government town. Even though she's human, they were going to let her stay, but she fell for some other non-gifted and decided to leave."

"How does that son of a bitch heal someone but then go and kill innocent people?" Chelsea asked, a heavy scowl covering her delicate features.

"Blake and Mae keep saying he's changed. Maybe he's possessed?" Faith guessed.

"Whatever it is, we still have to act," Erik said. "He's growing stronger and more dangerous every day. If I can get control of the Weres, I'd be in a better place to stop him. We're the largest group there."

"Phillip may not need their support," I started, looking down at my hands. "He can probably control everyone on his own now. He may not even need to make the regular announcements to refresh his control over the town. Once might be enough for good."

"How do you know?" Charles asked, an eyebrow raised.

I didn't look up. "Because my powers have grown too."

"How?"

I looked up now. I guess it was time to share my secret. Eventually, I had to tell them, and it was only cowardice that was holding me back now. "Everyone hold hands."

They did so without question. I grabbed Erik's hand, and Faith's on the other side of me. I looked around at the darkly lit pub. "Stop," I commanded.

Everyone in the pub went still except the six of us. The band stopped playing, people stopped dancing, no one spoke. It was as if we were in a bar full of mannequins. The only signs of life were the rise and fall of the patron's chests and the slight sound of breathing.

"I used to only be able to stop only the people I concentrated on. But now, I don't have to focus, except if I want to be specific. Like now, I don't want you guys to be controlled. Holding your hands keeps you exempt from being frozen. I can also do two types of magic at once, maybe more, which I couldn't do before." I looked across the room to the dark fireplace with a stack of logs settled inside. A group of frozen people sat in large, leather-and-upholstery-covered chairs and couches in front of it, in mid-conversation. One of the people, a shorter man with black hair, walked over to the fireplace, took a lighter from the mantle, and lit the logs. He then turned and sat back down, eyes glazed and dead. I didn't even break a sweat to move him while maintaining the frozen status of everyone else.

My friends turned and looked at the bright light coming from the fireplace. No one spoke.

"I could only think that if these things were happening to me, they were happening to Phillip too. Or it could just be because I'm part of this six that Mae told us we were, but without Lisa around, I don't know."

"How'd you find out that your powers grew?" Felix asked, staring around at the people on pause. "This freaks me out, man."

"Go," I stated. I let go of Faith and Erik's hands, and the crowd around us came alive with movement and sound as if nothing odd had happened. I'd done that too. I hadn't just controlled their bodies. I'd controlled their minds and made them want to pause their bodies and thoughts. It was easier that way, for them not to know. There wouldn't be any questions or fear, like before.

"I accidentally found out at school that I could do this. The fourth and fifth-grade kids were being really rowdy one day. They just weren't listening. It was after recess, so I guess they were still hyped up. I got overwhelmed and kindly told them to be quiet. Okay, I yelled it, actually. They all shut up. At first, I thought that maybe they were just listening to me and decided to be good. But they weren't." I drew an imaginary circle around the rim of my glass as I spoke. "I started to go back into my lesson, and I asked them questions, but they couldn't speak to answer. Some of them began to cry, but no sound came out of their mouths. They were like mimes. I begged them to speak. And they did. Twenty 9 to 11- year olds crying and screaming at once."

"Why didn't we hear about this?" Felix asked. He worked at the school with me as a math and science teacher.

I shook my head. I really hated telling this story because it didn't make me look good but it necessary that I be open with them. "The principal thought it best we keep it under wraps as long as I kept my powers in control."

Erik twisted in his seat to face me, his eyes dead so that I had no idea what he was thinking or feeling. "How'd you get the kids not to talk about what happened?"

And this is the part I'd tried to forget. I tried to keep this quiet because it made me less innocent than I wanted to believe I was. It made me like Phillip, no matter how I tried to justify it.

"She wiped their memories," Chelsea guessed with a squinty-eyed smile. How she found this amusing, I couldn't figure out.

I nodded, biting my lip.

Erik sighed. I wondered if he was angry or disappointed. He was full of judgement, I was sure. Living up to his standards was probably something I could never maintain.

Felix adjusted in his seat, lips twisted to the side. "When did this happen?" Felix asked. His voice didn't betray any disgust or disappointment. He was a kind heart, and I'd confided in him before without his judgement, but this part I just hadn't wanted to share. Instead, I kept my head down as I answered.

"Two weeks ago. I was embarrassed and scared to tell you all."

"You didn't mean for that to happen, honey," Faith comforted me with a pat on my hand. For a woman full of tattoos with an anger problem, she was amazingly understanding and kind when it came to her friends.

I looked up, and she gave me a sympathetic smile.

I looked to Charles, who was leaning back in his chair with a slightly bored expression. That was disturbing. He seemed unfazed by the whole situation but, then again, that seemed to be his current state of emotion. "Those kids probably needed to shut up. I don't see the problem. You fixed it. All's right with the world," he said, crossing his arms.

I felt a squeeze of my knee and turned to Erik, who looked at me with uncharacteristically softened eyes as he gave my knee a light pat. "You did the right thing," he stated. "Just maybe not make a habit out of it."

The others nodded, and I let out a sigh of relief.

"It's good that you're growing in power. We can use that. There are more things about Phillip that we didn't share with you because we thought it would make you worry," Erik started.

The hell? Seems I was right about my fears after all. "Do I look like I'm so fragile that I can't be told things?" I asked, leaning back in my seat.

Charles gave a snort. "Do you want an honest answer? Because we can test it out by mentioning your dark circles and your couple of premature gray hairs."

I narrowed my eyes. "Tell me lies. Tell me sweet little lies."

Erik shrugged, lifting his drink to his mouth. "Okay, I won't tell you."

"Seriously?"

"Phillip's imprisoning more people. People he thinks are betraying him. He's still maiming people for disobedience."

Chelsea slapped the table with the palm of her hand. Our drinks shook slightly. "I'm killing him. As soon as we find a way to unlink him to Mina, he's a goner."

Charles balanced back on one leg of his chair "He'll kill you before you get close enough." He raised his hand and snapped his fingers, looking around the room. "Where's the waitress?" Can they be any slower here?" Charles muttered as he rose. "I'm going to go get a beer with a shot of blood. I hope it's fresh."

I raised my eyebrows. "Do they sell blood here?" I asked.

Chelsea smirked. "No."

I jumped up and raced to follow Charles, but he was already hidden in the crowd. He was super-fast. A mixture of vampire and witch, he was much more powerful than his former status of just being a tech mage. He was also dangerous, and I couldn't ignore the fact that maybe Chelsea's influence on him was partly to blame.

Since being freed, her dealings with humans were becoming tenuous. Hagerstown was a human and paranormal government town, which meant they did not allow for paranormal-only groups, except for special occasions. Therefore, there were no were packs, vampire kisses, or witch's covens. So, I was surprised she liked it so much here. Sure, we had paranormal leaders or liaisons to parts of the government to keep communication and control, but government towns focused on growth and the overall human connection and not division, magic, or otherwise.

I began to assume that the only reason she was at Hagerstown was to get in on the action of taking revenge on Phillip. It wasn't exactly that she hated non-powered humans, her murdered boyfriend had been one of them, but he seemed to be more of an exception now. Currently, she stuck to just other paranormals in her free time. At work, she was a cashier in the grocery-store-slash-farmer's-market and was friendly to everyone.

I hadn't thought she wasn't being genuine until I saw her snacking on the necks of a few humans. She didn't kill them. That would get her killed. She healed them and wiped their memories of the encounter. However, those weren't the rules. If she drank human blood, it had to be donated.

I didn't approve of her actions, but there weren't many humans offering up their blood unless they would get credits for it. The town was over two thousand in population, and about three hundred were vampires, that we knew of. Most people were still a little fearful of them and the weres, so not everyone was jumping up and down to self-identify. Although the town had found a way to test for the infection, they couldn't test for the paranormal gift.

Colonel Robinson, the leader of the town, had to make a few announcements about remembering to treat everyone, including the paranormal humans, with dignity and respect. Not everyone listened, and any day now, a fight between the different groups would happen.

However, for now, I had to find my brother and make sure he wasn't going to do something reckless to start the fight early.

I reached the bar, hoping Chelsea was wrong about the pub not serving blood. I didn't see Charles. Not good. I didn't see the point in asking the bartender if blood was on the menu. If Charles wasn't there, that was a good indication they didn't. I turned around and searched the room.

Where could he be?

He hadn't headed towards the front door. I headed towards the back of the bar and outside to the patio area. There were tons of people outside enjoying the last of the warm September evening. The space was lit with colorful string lights, and wooden picnic benches covered some of the cobblestone ground.

No Charles.

I pushed through the crowd and went through the metal gate leading to the street. I looked to my left down the back-alley parking lot. Nothing. I looked to my right towards the main street. I spotted two figures under an unlit lamppost. One was a woman, the other a man. They looked like they were making out. They weren't.

I walked over to them. "Charles, stop it. Now!" I shouted,

clapping my hands with each word. "Stop it!" I patted my thighs when he didn't move away.

Charles pulled away from the neck of a woman. She was plump and appeared to be in her 40s with dark-blonde hair and bangs.

Charles sighed, rolling his eyes. "What, Amina? I'm not a dog. This is consensual," Charles said in an exasperated tone.

I looked to the woman. Her eyes looked glazed over. I didn't doubt that all my handsome brother had to do was flash a smile to get her to consent if she were lonely or intrigued. Several people still believed that the old, Pre-world fairy tale of handsome vampires still existed. The fact that vampires often used their glamour and compulsion power only helped that myth.

"What's your name?" I asked her.

"Laura," she said in a tight voice, narrowing her eyes. I was sure she was annoyed I was cutting into her and Charles' time.

I reached up and hovered my hand in front of her neck, pouring healing energy out to close the puncture marks that Charles left. "Go back in and grab a glass of wine on me, Amina Langston," I stated, throwing my magic into my voice.

Laura nodded and headed back through the gate into the pub.

Charles crossed his arms. "Way to be a hypocrite, sis. It's bad if I do what's in my nature, but you can go around controlling every man, woman, and apparently child, and it's all good."

Well, that one stung. I turned to Charles, who was taking a pack of cigarettes out of his pocket. I watched in open-mouthed horror as he took out a cigarette and lit it with a word spell of fire. "You guys said it was okay. And really? You're smoking now?"

Charles cracked a smile. "First, we said that one time was okay, but then you go around doing it over and over again.

And second, this is weed. And I think I'm okay, what with me being dead and all. I'm sure I won't get cancer, and it won't age me."

I stepped back and did an over-exaggerated wave of my hand to break up the smoke. "Okay, you're right. I can't just use my magic any way I want. It's very irresponsible. I was just shocked to see you like... this. And you can go to Joanie for a donation." Joanie, feeling guilty for her role in the prison, offered her blood to Charles regularly as atonement.

Charles turned his head and blew out a ring of smoke. "Eh, that woman was closer. Stop acting like my mother. She's dead."

I put my hand down and frowned. We were both quiet for a moment, letting his last sentence sit in the air. It was true, our mother was gone, but it was still hard to hear. She'd been gone almost five years now. It still hurt.

"I know that. Look, Charles, I just want things to be the way they were. Like—"

"Well, they aren't, are they?" Charles took another puff of his joint. "I'm dead. You're the soulmate to an asshole, and Lisa is gone. Nothing is the same."

"I'm sorry."

Charles shook his head. "Not your fault, Mina. Stop apologizing."

I threw out my hands. "So, what do you want me to do?" I was frustrated and scared that I was losing the old Charles I knew, forever.

"Just let me be!" he cried. He rubbed his joint against the lamp pole and put it back into his cigarette pack. "Let's go back in."

He turned and walked away. As I looked at him go farther and farther from me, I wondered how I could make things right again. Did I even have that kind of power?

CHAPTER 8

I was in a club. It was dark with colorful strobe lights moving about on the dance floor. Smoke emanated from the corners of the large space, and people danced to a sexy R&B tune blaring from speakers. A DJ stood on a wide stage on the west end of the room, surrounded by more dancing people.

I passed a wall with a floor-to-ceiling mirror and caught a peek at myself. I was dressed in a red halter dress with a plunging neckline and a slit going thigh high. On my feet were silver, open-toed heels. My hair was big and curly. I didn't look like me. This was not an outfit I would feel comfortable going out in, not even to the club.

Why was I here? Where was I? Where were the others?

I didn't know where to go from here. I looked behind me at the velvet-roped entrance that led to the outside and began to walk that way. Whatever was going on, I didn't think the answers would be in here.

"Buy you a drink?" came a deep male voice.

I knew that voice. I spun around and came face to face with Phillip Leal. A smile covered his handsome face, and for a fraction of a second, I allowed myself to find him attractive.

But I came back to myself, having fallen for his deceptively kind eyes before.

The mystery was solved. I knew what was going on and grimaced. "Pass," I replied. I turned to leave. I had to get out of this dream. I hoped maybe if I walked outside of the club, I could disconnect from him.

Phillip reached out and grabbed my wrist.

"Please," he begged, his voice uncharacteristically vulnerable. "Don't leave."

I tried to yank my hand away, but he held on tight. "Let go."

His light brown eyes softened. "Don't leave. We need to talk. I've tried to give you time, but we can't ignore each other forever. We're soulmates."

I tried to yank at my hand again but was still unsuccessful. "What do you want from me? I'm keeping my distance, so I don't upset your power base. Faith and Erik haven't caused you any trouble."

"You look beautiful," he said, still smiling. It was as if he was unfazed by my mood or anything I said.

"Did you dress me in this?"

He gave a quick shrug. "I can't help what my mind wants. But if you don't like this... "

I turned away again, and the scene began to change. The walls of the club melted, the music fading, and people disappeared. In its place came a dusky, blue sky. The floor was now white sand, and in front of me were lit beach bars and far-off silhouettes of new people, laughter, and reggae music. Behind me, I heard ocean waves. I looked down at my feet, and they were bare. I looked farther up and saw that I was now wearing a flowery, off-the-shoulder, knee-length dress that blew gently in the wind.

Turning to the ocean, I saw Phillip again, but this time he was wearing off-white linen pants and a pale-yellow button-down shirt. I wanted to curse at him, but the view distracted me. The sun was setting, a half circle beyond the water. Colors of purple, orange, and dark blue shaded the darkening sky. I had not seen the ocean in ten years. I stood still as I watched the sun seemingly disappear into the water.

I walked to the edge of the water, letting my feet get splashed by the cold ocean.

"We're in Jamaica, and one day I'd like to take you to the real thing," Phillip said behind me in a low voice.

I tried to ignore him but I couldn't. I wanted this moment, this dream, to myself. He was turning it into something else.

"I don't want you taking me anywhere," I said, my back still to him. "If you want to do something for me, how about you turn yourself in to us? We can lock you up so you can't hurt anyone else. You're dangerous. I'm sure you caused Wilford to cheat in Erik's challenge, Luke to bite Lisa, you killed Chelsea's boyfriend, and then you charged Felix to blindness and locked me up. Not to mention, you were controlling people and maiming those who disobeyed you."

Phillip chuckled and stood beside me. "You think I'm the cause behind all your troubles. Do you blame me for David coming back as well?"

I'd thought about that but killing me never seemed to be a part of Phillip's agenda. "Not yet. So, you're denying your role in the other stuff?"

He looked down at me with amused eyes and threw out his hands. "You got me. How'd you find out?"

"I've been in your dreams. Your subconscious isn't as much of an asshole as you are."

"I'm not a bad guy. I just believe in order."

"You locked me up when you saw my powers matched yours. You later attacked me when we got Felix out of that bogus trial." I turned to face him. "You don't care about me or order. You care about power. If we join as soulmates, it won't do anything good for the town. It won't do anything good for me. You have to be stopped."

Phillip chuckled again. I wanted to slap him. "You're not going to stop me, *mi corazón*. You're going to fall in line. I have plans. I have to expand. I have to make it ready for them."

"What are you talking about? Who's 'them?'"

"You'll see. Silver Spring is just the beginning, but I need your help."

"You want to rule this country like some psychotic tyrant with a bunch of crazy followers? Screw that. And there is no way I'm going to allow you to take your barbaric show on the road."

He gave me a patronizing smile. "I knew you wouldn't come willingly. You're stubborn. So how about we try something to fairly settle this?"

"What would that look like?" I asked, squinting my eyes.

"A sort of magician's battle."

I crossed my arms, waiting for him to further explain.

"We would compete in a series of tests. Five, to be exact. The person who wins the most is the winner and makes the decision on what to do with the loser. And if there is a tie, we'll have a bonus."

"What are the tests? And where do they come from?"

Phillip put his hands in his pockets. "One of the witches in my town found an active Wiccan website where witches schedule competitions to sort of show off; prove who's the strongest. I don't think these tests are new. They seem to be a combination of tests made from different groups all over the world, over time. Even during the Pre-world. This set of tests is what many magical covens use to pick their leader. Makes perfect sense for us to do this."

I raised an eyebrow in interest. "Go on."

"First, you use magics on top of one another. The one with the most spells going at once and still standing wins.

Second, break a difficult ward. The quickest to break it wins. Third, you break a curse. Fastest to break it wins. Fourth, follow a certain potion that only a few witches have ever been able to make work. It's a potion to give life. It only works on animals... for now. Fifth test, you make up your own spell to create something never done."

That "for now" part was scary. Sure, I'd like to prevent death, but the negative possibilities of bringing people back to life gave me the chills. Charles coming back as a vampire was different but still scary. He was going through a process that led him to be reborn. The thought of him coming back any other way was chilling. He would be something else. So would an animal. I bit my lower lip and turned back to the dark ocean.

Sensing my hesitance, Phillip spoke up. "They wouldn't come back as zombie animals, if that's what you are concerned about. I can get you the website I looked at so you can become familiar with it all, out of fairness. We can both pick the witches who will put together the ward spells and the curses. They'll have to have time to find some difficult ones. Ones even they aren't strong enough to break."

I had to admit, on the surface, the test sounded fair, but I had no idea if I was strong enough to beat Phillip, and that was nerve-racking. We were soulmates, but it didn't mean that we were equal in strength. Phillip was surrounded by magic. His mind was always searching for ways to be more powerful. It made sense now why he hadn't come for me all this time. He was preparing.

Sure, I'd been practicing, but I spent a lot of time doing other things like teaching kids. While I'd spent most of the last nine years surviving and dabbling in magic to help me survive, Phillip had been focused on building an empire. He'd been helping to lead Silver Spring for five years.

"What happens with the winner and the loser?" I asked, not turning around to face Phillip.

I heard him sigh. "If you win, I will bow down to you and whatever you choose to do with me. Lock me up. Make me follow your command. I'll step down from running Silver Spring. I'll put Seth in check. It's up to you. But if I win, you join me as my partner. As my real soulmate. Not exactly my equal. You will go along with my initiative, and you will help me reach my goals. Your friends will stop whatever they are doing and obey me."

I shook my head and turned to him. "My friends aren't doing anything."

Phillip gave me a look of disbelief, his lips twisted. "I don't believe Faith and Erik are staying in Silver Spring just because they like their apartments and jobs."

"Erik believes he has a duty to the pack as the third in command, and Faith has found a family in Blake's vampire group. Hagerstown doesn't allow for paranormal groupings. It's emotional."

"It's bullshit," Phillip spat. He usually kept his cool, and this show of emotion made me more than uncomfortable because he was unstable. "I only let them stay because of you. I don't trust them. There are very few people I trust. I'd like you to one day be one of those I do trust."

"What if I didn't want to take this test?"

Phillip raised his eyebrows and smiled but it was anything but friendly. "Well, then I win by default. And it would not be pretty. I'd lock up your friends. Or maybe even kill them. Oh, who am I kidding? I'll kill them. And then we'll head to Hagerstown and kill your friends there, too. And no one's coming back like your brother, Charles, because I'd take their heads. And I will keep you in a coma. I gotta be honest, I freakin' hate that option."

My blood ran cold. He would do all of this. I had no doubt. Suddenly the reality of my situation hit me hard. I was not a strategist, and I was taking our situation for granted. A mash-up of thoughts entered my mind, but I was too afraid to separate them out. He would possibly know. We were soulmates, and I, foolishly, hadn't considered that he could read my mind. I wasn't safe to think anymore. No one could tell me their plans until I figured out a way to effectively block Phillip. The others would hate me, especially Erik.

Phillip tilted his head and touched my cheek with the palm of his hand. I tensed up, but I couldn't move. It was clear to me that he controlled this dream. Or rather, I wasn't focusing my powers enough to match his strength. I would change that.

"I don't like to threaten you, *mi corazón*. I don't want to fight you at all. If you don't want to do the challenge, then just give in to me. If you'd just agree with what I am doing, everyone would be okay. I'd maybe even allow you to take out Seth. Carter and Erik are more civilized and could run the pack just fine. Let Erik go be with Raya." He looked at me with mock pity. "They are a better fit, you know that. And you and I can be together. We have chemistry. Remember our first kiss?"

I wished I didn't. When we'd finally seen each other in person, it had been an almost animal attraction. I'd had to fight to stay apart from him. Now that memory made me sick.

"It would be perfect," Phillip continued. "I would treat you so well. Give you everything you'd want. Your brother could even join the vampires. Blake would like him. We'd be one big, happy family. We'd make this country, this world even, a better place. With paranormals at the top."

He leaned in as if to kiss me, and I stepped back into the water, finally breaking free from his control.

He moved closer to me again. "So, what do you say?"

I looked away from him, to the glowing lights of the island bars in the background, wishing I was really on vacation sipping a rum punch and dancing to a reggae tune. Maybe one day it would be possible again.

I looked back to Phillip, and his honey-brown eyes gazed at me in amusement. "I agree to the battle," I stated.

Phillip nodded. "We can meet in two weeks. In the real world. We'll have a dinner with your side and mine, and then battle the next day, either in Silver Spring or a place in between. We can agree to that later."

I grew panicked. No way would I be ready in two weeks. "I need two months to prepare."

Phillip tilted his head again. "Amina... I can't."

Of course, he could. He just wanted to battle me while he thought I was still too weak.

"Six weeks!"

He shook his head slowly.

"One month, then!" I cried. I knew showing my fear would only motivate him to stand his ground, but I had to fight him.

"Well, no one can say I'm not a generous man. One month."

I stifled a sigh. That was better than two weeks, but I had no power here. It was either go for it or let Phillip do what he wanted and kill my friends. Hagerstown wouldn't be able to beat Silver Spring. Although Hagerstown had more people, Silver Spring was a paranormal-only city, while Hagerstown was a mixture of non-human and paranormal, with the numbers towards non-gifted humans being in the majority.

I nodded, accepting Phillip's offer.

"Let's seal this deal with a kiss, and I'll follow up with a proper offer via email tomorrow." Phillip smiled.

I lifted my upper lip in disgust. "Absolutely not."

Phillip gave me a lazy smile, eyes half-closed. "Can't blame a guy for trying."

I backed farther into the dark water, going deeper until the water was at my waist. I wanted to hide in the ocean and disappear or wake up. I gave him the middle finger with both my hands.

Phillip remained where he stood, looking on at me with that self-satisfied smile. "This is going to be fun, Amina," he shouted.

I turned from him and continued on until I could no longer walk and had to swim. I closed my eyes in the darkness and then pushed my head underwater, letting the ocean overtake me.

CHAPTER 9

"You can't battle him, Mina," Erik stated the next morning, pacing back and forth in my living room.

I heard a knock at the door, and I got up from my gray suede couch and walked to the apartment door. I looked out of the peephole and saw Chelsea and Henry, both wearing sunglasses, and let them in.

Chelsea was carrying a plastic bag of something. "I brought donuts from the bakery," she announced.

"Please tell me you got the apple crumb one," I stated, feeling my stomach rumbling.

"Of course, my dear," she stated, walking to the glass dining table near my kitchen, and putting the bag down.

I went over to it and found my beloved donut. "I might as well eat all the delicious donuts while I can." I bit into it and moaned inappropriately.

"You talk like you're going to lose," Felix observed, bending over and grabbing a red velvet donut from the bag before sitting back down at the table.

"You talk like you're going," Erik glowered from across the room.

I sighed, chewing the donut before speaking. "Erik, we don't have a better option. And I thought you'd be behind me since you like to battle all the time."

Erik rolled his eyes. "That's different. We can maintain the course—"

"It's not different, and we can't!" I cried. I coughed suddenly as a piece of donut caught in my throat. I refused to think about the possible karma there since I didn't need to raise my voice.

Charles sat up at the sound of my shouting. Clearly, he'd been sleeping. He'd been slouched down in the red love seat near the couch, sunglasses on, trying to stay awake, since this was his usual bedtime.

"You all don't get it. Phillip knows what's in my head," I continued. "He knows we're trying to take him out. He's been letting this go on out of amusement! And so he can ready himself for this stupid challenge he's only giving me a month to prepare for." I sat back down on the couch and put my donut in a cloth napkin on the dark, rectangular coffee table.

"Why didn't you tell us you were still communicating with him via dreams?" Faith asked, her eyes neutral. I couldn't tell if she was mad or disappointed, since her body language seemed at ease. She was sitting backwards on a dining room chair, resting her arms on the back of the chair.

"Because there wasn't anything anyone could do about it. I didn't want to worry you even more."

"You could have jeopardized everything, Mina," Erik stated.

I nodded. "Yep, I know," I replied. "I'm a liability. Maybe I should just forfeit and turn myself in. Give him what he wants."

"So he can lock you away forever?" Charles said, sliding back down in his seat. "Fuck that, sis, he's not getting what he wants. He's not going to lay a hand on you."

I sighed and smiled at him. It was good to know Charles

still cared about me. I was beginning to wonder. I looked around the space. "If you're going to try something, you have one month to do it, and you can't let me know about it."

"Maybe I can help you put up some type of block against him," Felix offered, mouth full of donut.

Most of the time, Felix was in another mindset when he was at his full strength and didn't even remember what he did. He had a guardian angel, Azrael, who only spoke when he or she wanted to, and barely gave Felix any information.

Felix, sensing my doubt, spoke further. "If you're soul-mates, that's spiritual. That's my arena. At least, I think so. Maybe I can do something to build a psychic wall. I know I couldn't break your bond, but maybe I can help weaken it. I'd have to ask Azrael because I have no clue how, but they said they liked you and will do what they can to make sure The Six stays together. And that includes locating Lisa."

"Felix, do what you can, please. But if we don't come up with a plan that is guaranteed by the end of today, I'm continuing with this deal." I turned, looking at everyone. "I can't hide from Phillip because of our bond, so there is no running. You guys can, though, and as long as you stay away from me, you'll be fine."

Henry put out his hands and smiled. "I may be new to the gang here, but I'm pretty sure no one's going to leave you," he said in a soft southern accent. He was a good guy, always seemingly on chill mode. He was a shade under six feet, with long dreadlocks that he mostly kept in a low ponytail. I placed him at early- to mid-30s, with a constantly pleasant and smiling face. Because he was paranormal, I knew he was much older. "You've got the vampire support here, that should count for something. Let my guy Felix help you, and we'll right this whole thing."

Felix then spent the better part of an hour trying to help me build a wall against Phillip. At some point, Mae and Bill showed up. I tensed when they appeared. I hadn't seen Mae since Charles had been brought back. Her betrayal still bothered me. Having lost my mother to the Sickness, I suppose I had imprinted that affection onto Mae. I'm sure many people did. She just had a motherly way about her.

Mae looked at me. Her eyes were pained, and she gave a sympathetic smile. I gave her a half-hearted smile in return, and then grimaced as Felix continued to psychically dig into my head. Dig might be too great of a description. I felt no invasion or pain. He put his hands on my head, and the only thing I felt was stupid.

Spoiler alert, nothing Felix did worked. As soon as my mind purposefully wandered to Phillip, it felt like he came to attention. I would see him in my mind's eye doing something, and he would look up and out, as if staring into space, but he was staring at me. And he would smile. He knew I was connecting. At one point, he even waved hello. I felt nauseous. He could have been doing this to me for the past month, and I'd never known. How had I never felt him?

The reality was, I had. I'd felt something but was too scared to acknowledge that the feeling of being watched was coming from him.

Felix sighed. "Azrael says it can't be done," Felix said, dejected. "They say you and Phillip are joined at the soul. There's no end and no beginning. They tried to build a wall, but it's like there's no ground to build it on. They said maybe in the old world they could have separated you both, but now the magic rules and nature won't allow it. You are him, and he is you."

I growled and put my head in my hands.

Mae took a seat at the dining table. "The best you can do is to start being sensitive to his presence, just like he is to you. Contain your emotions, including worry and stress. Be in the now."

Charles, still wearing his sunglasses, chuckled. "Yeah, good luck with that."

I glowered at him. "I'm a type-A worrier," I grumbled.

"Just don't talk for a while and... " Felix began. Sitting on the floor in front of me, he looked around the room and then grabbed a decorative pillow from the couch. "Squeeze this when you feel stress and just focus on it. If you don't let your emotions overtake you, you'll be able to sense him."

Henry raised his hand. "Can I ask an obvious question?" He was now sitting at the table with Mae, Bill, and Faith. He didn't wait for a response. "How do we know we can even trust Phillip for this challenge? This could all be a setup. Or he could break his word if he loses the challenge. We already know the guy has a shaky grip on morality."

It was a good question. One, I knew we were all thinking. I had no assurances that Phillip would acquiesce if I won. I had no assurances that he wouldn't cheat. But then again, what choice did I have?

"I know all about this challenge of Phillip's. He's been thinking of ways to subdue you since the trial," Mae stated.

Faith nodded. "We told Mina that. That's why we've been trying to come up with ways to break their bond," she explained, crossing her tattooed arms.

"That isn't the thing to do."

"I don't want to be his soulmate," I said.

"I understand, honey. But you have to be soulmates so we can—"

"Fight the big bad coming," I interrupted her, rolling my eyes. "I thought it was the six of us who were supposed to do that."

"With his help. The power boost you'll have by being soulmates with him will help you in this fight. We need you at your fullest strength."

I hated that full strength meant I had to be bonded to someone I despised. "And that's tied to your psychotic godson."

Mae nodded. "Actually, yes. And until he has his senses again, this challenge is the best option."

Erik leaned against the wall, eyes narrowed in suspicion. "Was this challenge your idea?"

"He was so fixated on getting you back. I had to talk him down from killing Erik and attacking this place. A challenge was the compromise," Mae answered.

"What if I lose?" I asked.

"Don't worry about that."

A hopefulness rushed through me. "So, you've had a vision that I'll win?"

"Not exactly. Something's going to happen, and things will work out. I had a different vision. You will become a leader in Silver Spring and not one who is second to Phillip."

"How will that happen?"

She placed a hand on her cheek with a sigh. "I wish I knew. I just saw a vision that this would come to pass if a certain line of events happens."

Erik swore under his breath. I could since his growing agitation with every minute that passed. "And those events are?"

Mae glanced at him, her eyes worried. "One of them is her accepting this challenge. Then I saw a town surrounded by green that I wasn't familiar with and a man of fire. And there was a man with an arrow as well."

Charles chuckled. "A lotta men hanging around."

"I also saw a woman with a sword." Mae smiled. "There are other things involved, I'm sure, but so far, that is what I saw in my vision. Those things happening will lead to good both for you and Phillip. Your leading will be because whatever has a hold on Phillip will be gone."

While I wasn't certain I was a leader, I knew Phillip staying in power wasn't the best option either. I squinted my eyes. "You really think he's possessed?"

Mae sat back in her chair and sighed. "I don't know for

sure. Possessed or maybe even cursed. And he is getting worse. I know that it's because you two are separated. He's become irrational."

"Well, we can help him out by putting his ass in a coma," Faith muttered.

"Are these magic tests legit?" Erik asked.

Mae looked to Bill, who was more in tune with the witch community since he was a mage. He nodded. "I've never seen the full challenge done, but I knew of some of the tests. We have a witch committee who will supervise the challenge. Out of fairness, we convinced Phillip to allow you to bring two witches you trust to join in overseeing the challenge for a total of four judges."

Erik shook his head. "I still don't like this. Phillip's too powerful. If she loses... "

Charles gave a wave. "It's bye, bye girlfriend."

I shot eye daggers at him, but I couldn't tell if he was ignoring me behind those sunglasses.

"Amina's strong enough to beat him," Felix cut in with an assured voice that didn't match his questioning eyes.

Erik, whose face looked uncomfortably tense, pushed back from the wall and began to slowly pace again. "I think it's better if we get control of the vampires and weres. We can use magic to get people to fight the mind control. And we lock Phillip up. Contain him somehow. Probably with a ward from Mina," Erik stated, looking around. "We keep him in a coma until we can find a way to get rid of him without hurting her. Then I challenge Seth and get the weres behind me."

I turned to Erik and frowned. "I already agreed to the challenge. If I don't go, it'll be war. The goal was to find an alternative to war by the end of the day. And you can't risk fighting Seth until you're fully powerful. The Six aren't here, so we can't effectively help you."

Erik nodded. "Then we should be mates. It'll match my

strength to Seth's. It might make you stronger against Phillip too. Maybe it'll even detach you two."

Charles snorted, and I wanted to run over to him and wrap my hands around his throat.

"So, you think a were mate could trump soulmates?" Chelsea, who was seated beside me, asked with thoughtful eyes.

"That won't stop things," Mae stated, shaking her head. "Erik, you care deeply for Amina. I feel for what you are going through, and I can understand why you would believe that being mates would change things between Amina and Phillip, but it will not. You should know what you are getting into by becoming the mate of someone who is already bonded to another."

I can't lie. It hurt to hear her say that. I secretly hoped that Erik and I could move forward with whatever was between us without worrying about Phillip. At least one day.

She paused and looked at me. "Do you want to have this conversation here and now?"

I nodded. "Everyone here is family. They can hear it. Besides, if The Six are bonded, then I would think that this might affect them too."

Mae nodded. "Fine. I've been doing some research, speaking to others in the spiritual and magic community. The internet really is a wonderful invention. Anyway, I've learned a great deal more about mate bonding of all types and magic. When you are mates with Erik, the benefits the two of you will share from being mates will expand to Phillip. So, it won't just be you and Erik who will have this strength. Phillip will grow stronger. And I suspect that whatever bond you and Phillip have, part of it might spread onto Erik. It will be that the three of you would become bonded. I don't know what that would look like exactly. What I am certain of is that mating with Erik will not break your bond with Phillip. It may not even weaken it."

Erik let out a curse word in a low growl.

"What do you advise?" I asked, a feeling of devastation growing. I hadn't realized how much I'd wanted mating with Erik to be my salvation.

"I advise that you become mates if it is in your heart to do so. It could even be that your combination could help Phillip heal. It certainly would be advantageous to Erik having, possibly, two mates in one. You could beat Seth in a pack fight."

"So, what's the deal, Amina? You going to be a threesome or no?" Charles asked me, an amused look on his face.

This time I did get up to strangle him.

CHAPTER 10

$\mathscr{A}$fter Erik pulled me back down into my chair, the rest of the meeting was productive. Bill shared as much knowledge and guidance as he knew on the tests. I went to my mentor, Shayla, afterwards, and she agreed to train me every day.

For a month after that, my life became a mind-numbing cycle of practicing magic, eating, and sleeping. I wasn't even teaching right now. Everyone seemed to know the importance of this fight, even if they hadn't met Phillip.

So far, I'd broken a ward, followed a challenging spell, and had three types of magic going at once. However, making a spell was an entirely different matter. What useful spell that hadn't been invented could I create?

I was still holed up in my room studying, a week before the challenge, when I heard a knock at my door. I tossed the notebook I used to collect spells to the side and got off my bed. I had no idea who it could be, but I welcomed a break. I was a touch close to pounding my head against the wall just to get away from the growing panic keeping me in an off and on state of nausea.

I went to the front door and looked through my peephole.

Erik stood there holding a canvas tote. I opened the door and lifted an eyebrow.

"Hey?" I said in a questioning voice.

He raised the bag in the air. "I made dinner," he said. He gave me the barest smile, and I let him in, suddenly realizing how hungry I was.

He walked in and headed to the dining area.

"Sooo, you made me dinner? Out of the blue. Even though we barely talk anymore," I stated, following him.

Erik started taking wrapped dishes out of the bag. "Mae made you a lemon ice pound cake," he replied, ignoring my suspicion. He placed the dessert dish on the center of the table. "And I made us steak and grilled vegetables. I'll have to heat it up again in your oven, since I'm sure it's grown cold after a two-hour drive from Silver Spring." He turned and walked to the kitchen, turning the oven on.

"You didn't have to do all of this," I replied, watching him put the food in the oven.

"I've been a jerk."

I crossed my arms. "You've been yourself."

He turned and glared at me. "Are you saying, I'm regularly a jerk?"

I slowly raised my shoulders in a shrug but smiled. "I've been a jerk too. I pushed you away and didn't tell anyone the truth of what was going on. I've also used my mind control powers on people, which is bad."

"Namely for the people getting controlled. I've been your puppet twice, now."

I looked down at my feet. He wasn't wrong but I hated to be reminded of it. "I'm really sorry. I don't know how to make it up to you."

He didn't look too appeased. "Just don't do it again."

I raised my hands in surrender. "Fine, fine... but what if—"

"Grab some glasses," Erik said, walking back to the dining room obviously done with that part of tonight's discussion.

I decided to let it go to maintain the peace, silently grabbed some glasses from an overhead cabinet and entered the dining area again with a curious look. "I don't have anything fun to drink. Charles drank it all."

Erik held up a glass jug filled with a clear liquid. He had a coy smile on his face.

"Dude, is that moonshine?"

He nodded with a mischievous grin. "Apple flavored. There's a guy in our pack who makes it. All kinds of flavors. All natural, no magic."

"I love the hell out of you right now," I replied, matching his smile.

"And I love you always." He gave me a wink, took the glasses, and poured the liquid in.

I widened my eyes and then looked away. This man, how could I give him up? He didn't run from his emotions. That was a rare breed. Yet, still, I feared falling into such love.

I took a seat, feeling spoiled. We chatted over dinner like old friends, and we didn't discuss Phillip, Seth, Lisa's disappearance, or my crazy brother. For just one evening, we only wanted to talk and be normal.

After dinner, we moved to the couch with the moonshine and talked some more. I should have been more responsible and gone back to studying and practicing. I should have just sent Erik home, but I didn't want to.

"When does Charles usually get in?" Erik asked, turning to me on the couch.

I twisted my lips. "It's a Saturday night. He may not get back until dawn," I sighed. A heavy weight pressed upon my chest, and I leaned my head against the back of the couch. "I can't believe I tried to strangle him a few weeks ago. He's just not like he used to be. He used to be so sweet. He was the nicest brother a girl could have. Now he's like a—"

"Asshole teenager?" Erik raised an eyebrow, and I quickly nodded. "In a way, he is. He was reborn. Most of us changed on the day the supernatural came in one quick moment. He died and he came back as something supernatural in a different way than us. How was Charles as a fourteen-year-old?"

I grumbled. "A jerk. He was cool before middle school and then got better in college, but for about seven years, I wanted to dropkick him. He was always trying to prank me and had a smart-ass comment for everything."

Erik put a hand behind his head; his bicep flexing as it held the weight of his head. "He was reborn as a fourteen-year-old vampire."

I chuckled lightly. "That actually sounds very dangerous. He's not happy. He's just existing. That's not a good combination."

Erik yawned and closed his eyes. "Do they have a spell to bring peace of mind or happiness?"

I scrunched my face and thought for a moment. I'd never looked for such a spell, so I wouldn't know. "Not sure, but if not, that might be a good one to make. I could give the spell to Charles to use if he wants and pass one of the tests all in one!" I grinned at Erik. "Look at you, being more than a pretty face."

Erik grinned, eyes still closed, and I fought the desire to lean over and surprise-kiss him. His smile grew wider, and I wondered if he knew what I was thinking. "So there, two of your worries are solved. What else you got for me?"

Ah, yes, the other part. His proposal. If you could call it that. "I don't think we should be mates." I bit my lip. I'd been thinking about that ever since he proposed it but being challenged by Phillip, and Mae's warning that being Erik's mate might make things more complicated, made me all the surer.

Erik opened his eyes and looked at me coolly. "You're serious?"

"I don't want to expose you to Phillip. It's not fair to you."

He sat up, a coldness clouding his eyes. "You must like staying this way with Phillip because, to me, the benefits of being your mate, outweigh the risks."

I rolled my eyes. He really thought I liked Phillip. Didn't he realize how dangerous the guy was? "Of course, I don't want things to stay the way they are. I just don't want you to resent me if you end up being attached to Phillip. He will find out, and he will make things very... uncomfortable for us." I could consider the countless ways in which Phillip would poke the bear that was Erik. Phillip entering Erik's dreams. Phillip reading Erik's mind. Erik might escape being mind-controlled by Phillip, but he wouldn't be free of him.

"Let him walk into my dreams. I'll make sure it's a nightmare for him," Erik growled.

I smiled.

He relaxed his shoulders. "Stop carrying this stuff alone, Mina. Let me help you."

"How would being mates work with us? We aren't even together."

"We should be together," he stated, grabbing my hand. The chill in his hazel eyes died away, and something warmer replaced it. "I want you as my mate, but I want more."

He lowered his eyes and ran his thumb lightly over the palm of my hand, sending chills over me. "Mina, you are so damn stubborn. You said I could have you, and I haven't given up but if I'm the only one feeling this way, then put me out of my misery and just say something. And not because you think Phillip might hurt me if we stay together. If I need to move on, I will, but I don't want to. Do you want me to?" He looked down at me, and there was a vulnerability in his eyes that I had never seen before.

I cared deeply about Erik. Yet, I had to focus on the challenge. I couldn't let this distract me. If we were together and

I lost, we would both be devastated. My distance from him was the only protection I could give him right now.

"I just have to focus on this challenge right now," I said with bitterness. My words felt hollow and stale. I wanted to wrap my arms around Erik and tell him that I needed him. That I hadn't stopped caring about him and that he had been on my mind every day. But I couldn't. Not now. It would just confuse things for the both of us. "Can we have this discussion after?"

I didn't look at him when I spoke, which was the coward's way out.

"Sure," he said and let go of my hand.

My heart plummeted, and a coldness spread over the hand that he touched.

"You know, it's supposed to be The Six, not just Amina." He stood up. "I should go."

The Six. He was right. Mae clearly stated that we were better together. Relying on the others made me panic. To be so tied to another, to several others, that their living or dying could affect me so overwhelmingly scared me. Erik scared me. But I was a woman who, perhaps foolishly, never let my fear stop me. Why was I doing so now? I couldn't figure that out, but I would defeat at least one scary thing now. Baby steps and all.

"Wait!" I grabbed his hand to pull him back down on the couch. "Okay, okay. If you can handle it, let's be mates. If the offer still stands."

He nodded. "Are you sure?" He searched my eyes.

I was already tied to a man I despised. Being mates with Erik, a man I deeply cared for, would be a cakewalk. I nodded vigorously. "Yes. As long as you're completely okay being tied to someone in my circumstance."

"I wouldn't have suggested it if I wasn't."

"How will the pack handle me? I assume people know I'm connected to Phillip now. Will they accept me? Will they try to turn me? I'm not sure I'm cut out to be a werejackal. Maybe a werecat." I gave a slight smile. "Like a domestic long-haired cat. I think they're really beautiful."

Erik gave me a lazy grin. "No one is going to hurt you or turn you. There are a couple other non-were mates in the pack, and they even live in our building. You would just have to come to events and be cordial."

I bit my lip, pondering the life I was getting myself into. "I'm not sure I could be cordial to Seth. I'll be your mate, but I don't want to be part of your pack."

Erik sat down. "I understand how you feel. I'm asking you to play the game for a while, like I do, until we don't have to anymore. This is just a means to an end."

I sighed and then nodded again. "I know, you're right."

Erik clapped his hands together looking unusually excited. "Okay, do you want to know what this entails?"

I shook my head quickly. "No, I don't want to be scared away if it's gross."

Erik raised an eyebrow again. "Smart."

Turns out it *was* gross.

It involved Erik cutting a small sliver of his flesh and mine, maybe half a centimeter long, and us eating it. He put the skin in a bite of cake to make it easier. I found myself wondering if Mae's making that cake was a coincidence.

"I feel like this is not sanitary," I said, staring at the miniature cake ball I'd made to mask the flesh.

"I don't think I can say anything that will ease your mind," Erik replied. He'd had no trouble consuming his and I'd wondered how many times he'd done this before. I'd heard that the process was very similar for joining a pack.

I swallowed the cake concoction down like a pill with the moonshine but I still gagged from the thought.

After the cannibalism, Erik did what appeared to be some meditation, which was him actually just channeling his pack magic through a series of chants.

"Do you feel any different?" he asked me, hands gripping mine.

Yes, sick. "Just queasy from eating human flesh," I replied with a slight shrug.

Erik shook his head and went back to chanting. Several minutes later, something did take over. A tingling, or rather, itchiness. It started in my hands and then spread throughout as if ants were crawling all over me. I wanted to rip my skin off. The last time I'd felt this way was when the supernatural had taken over and I'd gained powers as a life mage. My body was changing and becoming something magically different all over again.

I rubbed at my arms and grimaced. "This is horrible," I grumbled.

Erik scooted close to me on the couch and wrapped his arms around me. The itching sensation slowly began to fade. "You're feeling a connection with each member of the pack. It's like they're all touching you at the same time, and you are touching all of them. It's essentially the same way you would become pack, except it would be Seth's skin you had to eat. But through me, you're also now pack. It's a two-for-one deal," he explained with a playful note in his voice.

I puffed out my cheeks in disgust. "Fun," I whispered, wiggling in his arms from the psychic touching, wanting to escape my own body. "So, what next?"

"We go back to Silver Spring and face some music."

I sighed. "Right, for the challenge."

"That and... Seth will know you're my mate now and part of pack. He'll want to meet with you."

I rolled my eyes and pulled away from him. "I don't have time for Seth. I need to practice."

Erik opened his mouth and squinted his eyes as if trying to find the right words to say something. This was unlike him.

"What am I missing?" I asked.

"Because you aren't a preapproved mate, he'll want to talk to you as soon as possible to avoid conflict. And you'll have to move in with me until the challenge because mates must live together."

I pursed my lips together tightly and glared at him. "I have to practice."

"Which you can still do. You can teleport back here or Shayla can teleport to you every day."

"Are you kidding me?"

Erik frowned. "Looking at your face, I wish that I was."

I looked up at the ceiling and clasped my hands together. "Please, heavenly Father, help me not to also strangle the werejackal sitting next to me. Amen."

I didn't have time for this.

rriving back in Silver Spring felt odd. Erik stopped his black SUV in front of the twenty-foot steel wall that surrounded the town, and a car-sized portion of the wall rose to let us in. New Silver Spring was not a town that let in just anyone, nor were they advertising for more people, like the government cities. They were a selective group, and the steel wall kept out anyone wanting to be nosey. Well, the wall and the protective wards.

The city was slightly larger in square miles than the Hagerstown government city but had half the population. That was mainly because Phillip only allowed those with gifts to live there. The town was set up in the downtown district of the Pre-world Silver Spring, compromised of high-rise apartments, an entertainment area full of repurposed bars, shops, and restaurants, an urgent care clinic that served as the hospital, a gym, movie theater, school, library, police station, and a park and wooded area that was also used as a farm.

It was a hot afternoon, and people still walked about enjoying the safety of daylight, dining al fresco, exercising, and drinking at the few bars in the town. Phillip did an excellent job capturing his own little normal world within the steel walls, much like Hagerstown. Before I'd found either city, I'd been living in smaller communities consisting of collections of neighborhoods with houses repurposed for a myriad of uses, but they'd never had the feel of the Pre-world.

Erik drove us to the pack apartment and parallel parked near the side of the building.

"Should I wait in the car until you get things sorted out?" I asked, watching Erik unclick his seatbelt and open his car door.

"No," he said and got out before grabbing my bag from the back seat.

I sighed, suddenly feeling super nervous. I got out of the car and slowly walked up to the high rise, following Erik inside.

A man sat at the front desk and brought a walkie-talkie to his mouth when he saw me. His eyebrows were raised, and he had a look of worry on his face. Erik stopped at the concierge station. I looked onto the desk spotting several monitors and buttons connected to the top of the man's desk as he watched the comings and goings of the residents in the shared spaces. There would be no privacy outside of Erik's apartment, and I'm sure the desk staff reported everything to Seth, who would then report it to Phillip. A pang of fear gripped my insides. I'd have to see Phillip again in real life. I didn't want to.

"Sir, he wants to see you both in his penthouse now," the wide-eyed man stated.

Erik gave a curt nod, and we took the elevators past the front desk to the top floor. We walked down the hall and Erik knocked on the door, still holding my duffle bag. I was dismayed that we couldn't even get settled first but kept my mouth shut.

A white woman with deep red hair answered the door.

She was wife number something or other. Seth had five wives, diverse beauties that showed he had wide-reaching taste, although that still made him a chauvinistic jerk.

"Hi, Erik," the redhead greeted him with a breathy voice and leaned in to kiss him on both cheeks. Before I could tingle with slight jealousy, she turned to me and greeted me the same way. "I'm sure you forgot my name. I'm Brittney. It's good to see you again, Amina. Welcome to the fold."

I gave her a genuine smile. She seemed authentically welcoming. Maybe it stood to reason that not everyone in the pack would hate me.

We walked into Seth's three-bedroom apartment. The space held dark hardwood floors and a full, granite-countered, open kitchen, with stainless steel appliances. He had a separate dining room and living room as well as a balcony that ran the length of the apartment. We walked through the foyer area and past the laundry room and kitchen where two women were whipping up a delicious-smelling dinner. Seth also had the apartment across the hall where three other wives stayed, for a complete family-sized harem home.

We entered the living room space where Seth sat relaxed on a black recliner. A white, blonde-haired woman sat on the floor in front of him, rubbing his feet and a black woman with long, honey-blonde dreadlocks, stood behind the seat, rubbing his shoulders.

I pursed my lips, trying to hold back a disapproving look.

Seth had his eyes closed, smiling as he tapped his hand to some country music blaring through his stereo. His other hand held a large glass of what appeared to be beer.

Seth opened his eyes and smiled. Laugh lines adorned his bright-blue eyes, showcasing a man who had many wins in his life and still, in this new earth, continued to stay on top. I wanted to knock him down. "Erik, Amina, good to see you." He snapped a finger. "Get our guests something to drink."

Brittney turned and went to the kitchen before I could object. He was such an asshole.

"Take a load off," he said, gesturing to his large, matching leather couch.

Erik motioned for me to go sit down, and he followed suit, dropping my bag to the side of the couch. I sat at the end of the couch farthest away from Seth.

I looked over to Seth, who was still getting his spa treatments. He was in good shape. Before this, he'd been some sort of mixed martial arts fighter. I began to wonder again if Erik could really take him in a fight.

Brittney came back with our glasses of beer. They'd originally come from the town distillery, which someone had revitalized a couple of years ago. She disappeared from the room again, and I didn't blame her.

"So, Erik, I see you went off and sort of eloped. Made this beauty here, your mate. I had no idea you were planning to do that."

"We didn't plan it," Erik replied. "Just felt like the right thing to do."

Seth closed his eyes again. "I see. I'm assuming, Amina, that you've gotten over our little problems of the past."

"You mean when you attacked me?" I spat.

He opened his eyes. "All's well that ends well. We haven't even come for our revenge over Luke's death. He was always such a hothead. Let's just begin again, yes? Erik got a right hook in on me, and we're still cool. Just us weres letting off some steam."

He gave me a teeth-baring smile, and I tightened my lips, remaining silent.

His grin widened. "Is that a yes or no? Answer me."

He was testing my sincerity. He appeared to play the part of a dumb jock, but he was no fool. He couldn't have an openly defiant pack member. If I did defy him, he'd make me hurt, and there wouldn't be anything Erik could do that wouldn't end up getting him killed or hurt too.

"I'm all for new beginnings," I replied in a tight voice.

"Awesome. And are you planning to become a were, Amina?"

"No," Erik answered for me.

Seth turned his smiling face to Erik. "Well, your name isn't Amina, is it?"

Erik gave a deep sigh and sat back.

"What he said," I replied, touching Erik's knee.

"Hmm, not sure how that's going to go with the pack. Someone ranked so high with a non-were mate. Especially a controversial one like you. You might want to reconsider. Being were ain't so bad."

"Actually, I think Helen's mate is a nymph or something," the blonde at Seth's feet stated. "They seem to get on well, and people like Ryan."

Seth looked down at her and shoved his foot out, knocking her in the shoulder. She toppled to the side onto her bottom.

"Jesus," Erik cried. He jumped up and headed over to help her.

"Leave her," Seth demanded. "Sarah, the next time I need to hear your opinion on something, I'll ask for it. Otherwise, keep your mouth shut."

Erik, ignoring Seth, helped the woman up and sat her on the couch beside me.

"Your shoulder okay?" I asked. Seth was a strong were, a shove like that, even to another were, could be damaging.

The woman looked to Seth, who was busy drinking his beer and rolling his eyes, then looked back at me with scared eyes. "I'm fine," she squeaked out and then got up to tend to Seth's stinky feet again. He waved her away and she got up, and stood near the window awaiting his next order.

I looked back at Seth, my eyes in slits. "Loving way to treat your wife," I stated, fist tightening.

"That's just how we are. She's not hurt, right?" Seth replied with a lazy grin. "If you're going to be a mate of a were, you've got to toughen up."

"Amina's fine," Erik cut in, sitting back down next to me. "She won't have to worry about me hurting her."

Seth ignored him and continued to look at me. "Ever been around your guy when he changed? How about on the night of a full moon?"

I didn't answer. I'd seen Erik in jackal form, but he made it a practice not to show himself changing or to visit on a full moon night. I had no misunderstandings that Erik was a dangerous being. I'd seen him kill, but he was always protective of me.

"Didn't think so," Seth cracked. "Have you had sex yet?"

This guy was ridiculous. I didn't see how Erik could follow him, even if it was for a bigger purpose. "Are you kidding me?" I cried.

"Relax, it's a legit question. Weres are strong. You may be a witch, but you still have a fragile human body. Maybe sex before was fine but mate sex or sex near a full moon?" He shook his head. "He could break you. We don't know our own strength when it comes to bonding with our mates, especially as it gets close to a full moon. Things get really primal. I love it."

Weres got in heat the closer it was to the full moon. Erik and I had made love before the breakup but it had not been painful. Of course, it hadn't been on a full moon and we weren't mates then. Visions of me with a crushed pelvis made me involuntarily cringe.

Erik reached over and rubbed my knee. He always had a light touch with me. I didn't think I had anything to worry about. I didn't think.

As if sensing my discomfort, although my face surely gave

it away, Seth snorted. "Yeah, you might need to get turned into one of us if you want to keep up. Might be cool to have a were-witch anyway."

"I'll think about it," I lied through clenched teeth. *Keep the peace, Amina, keep the peace.*

Seth, being able to use his weretiger nose to sniff the truth, knew that I had no intention of thinking about it. "Well, how about we let Phillip decide after your challenge? Although he didn't seem to be a fan of this arrangement." He gave a bull-crap sympathetic smile.

"You're talking as if I'm going to lose," I said stiffly, putting my glass of beer down onto the glass coffee table.

Seth shrugged. "If you knew better, you'd just avoid wasting your time and do what Phillip says, but I guess it makes a good show. It's just no fun fighting a losing battle, ya know?" He looked over to Erik.

That wasn't a casual look. His sentence and stare at Erik meant something more, beyond my challenge with Phillip. Did Seth know of Erik's plan to challenge him? This meant all the more that I had to win my battle against Phillip. We had to get rid of Seth.

"Well, I get that battles aren't fun, but I'm confident Amina will win," Erik replied with a smile, baring his teeth in a less than friendly way.

Seth chuckled. "Good for you." He looked at me. "You're one of us now, Amina. The mate of a third. You have to stay in line. Even if you should somehow win against Phillip. I still have rules you gotta follow."

"I get it. I'm not here to challenge you, just Phillip." I gave him my best Erik, teeth-baring smile. I didn't have fangs, so I'm not sure how intimidating it was.

"I hope you're telling the truth. Hard to sniff out the truth with you, witches. However, I'll tell the pack to welcome you with open arms. Not that anyone would harm you, since you're Phillip's girl." He said that to get at Erik. And to prove my point, he looked to Erik with a slight grin. "Sorry about that, pal. She's also your girl." He chuckled again, and I tensed, ready to jump on him like a wild cat.

But I calmed myself, feeling Erik's fiery energy next to me. While I couldn't really physically go at Seth, Erik could, claws and all. Yet, that wouldn't do us any good. I gave him a look with forced calm in my eyes. He looked down at me, and quickly, the rage in his eyes started to subside. I think I was going to like this being mates thing. If I could make a spell that could do what we could do with our eyes, life would be great. It would certainly shut up folks like Seth.

"How about a welcome celebration Friday before the challenge, at the bar? Might be your last bit of fun for now," Seth implored. "You should invite your friends. Including your brother and Felix."

I wanted to say no, but Erik spoke up. "Fine, we'd be glad to attend."

That was not how I wanted to spend my night before the challenge. I needed to put all my energy on the tests, and I had to admit, I was getting less and less confident of my ability to win.

~

I practiced even harder the final week and barely slept. Erik had a spare bedroom, and I stayed inside it like my own little self-imposed prison, trying my best to ignore that I was so close to the man I cared about. When I heard his shower run, my mind always went to naughty places. I began to wonder if it was better to spend my nights back in Hagerstown. Erik said it was against practice for mates to live apart, especially in the first five days of being mates, but I wondered if he was really telling the truth. I tested it out one night by staying in Hagerstown at Shayla's place after a practice session. He ended up knocking on her door and sleeping on the couch.

By the time Friday evening came, I had developed a spell I had thought anyone could do and I'd used multiple magic at once. Everything else, the ward, the curse, and this mysterious potion, I wouldn't know about until the actual challenge, but I practiced enough to feel competent. I was as ready as I could be, and still, I didn't feel ready enough.

I sat on the edge of my bed back in Erik's apartment in a black fit-and-flare dress with small cutouts on the sides, exposing glimpses of my waist. It was a bit risqué for me, but when I saw it at a boutique back in Hagerstown, owned by an elf with amazing clothing talents, a cheerful voice in my head that sounded much like Lisa's said to get it. I then started crying when I got it, and the elf told me that I could think about it if I wasn't ready to purchase it with my credits. I shook my head, bought the dress, and ran out of the store embarrassed.

On my feet were strappy black heels, the only fancy shoes I owned. I straightened my curls, and my hair hung loosely down my back. I felt pretty. It might be my last time to look so snazzy. Lisa would have approved. My heart ached again at the thought of my missing friend.

I left my room, and walked to Erik's bedroom door. It was open and Erik stood at his door, heading out to the hallway. He paused and looked at me. There was something behind those eyes. Longing or lust or love? "You look beautiful," he said in a low voice.

I smiled. "So, do you," I replied, still feeling nervous.

He looked dapper in a tailored black suit and pale-blue shirt with a matching tie that seemed to play up his golden, hazel eyes. I fought the urge to jump him, sure it would just confuse things.

We looked like we were going to go see the New Year's ball drop, not go out to dinner at a bar filled with a good number of people we didn't like. However, we had to present a showing of confidence in my ability to win the challenge.

To add to our support, I invited the whole gang. Shayla and Henry wouldn't be a problem but the others were more concerning. Seth promised no harm would come to Felix, and Chelsea promised to be on good behavior, but there was no certainty.

When we arrived at the pack bar, it was far from neutral territory. Most of the pack was there as well as Phillip and Blake. Mae and Bill were also present, along with several witches and vampires. There was a buffet of meats, cheeses, breads, fruits, desserts, and vegetables. A live band played on the small stage area in the back of the pub, and people danced in front of them in a cleared-out space. Memories of the last party we had in the pack bar two months ago played in my head, giving me a feeling of déjà vu. Only this time, I hoped no one got bitten or killed.

I turned to Erik. "I showed my face; can I go now?" I asked.

"Yo!" Seth shouted from near the bar. "Amina is here. Our guest of honor! Welcome to the pack!"

People clapped, and a couple of pack members came over to shake my hand and congratulate me like I'd won some sort of prize. While it was nice to know the pack and the rest of the town didn't hate me, this was not what I expected.

Mae and Bill walked over to us, and Mae grabbed my hands, smiling. "Are you ready for tomorrow?" she asked.

I shrugged. "I guess so," I replied, with a less than confident smile.

She squeezed my hands. "Don't you worry. Things will work out the way they are supposed to."

I sighed, not sure if I believed her, but she did want Phillip better, so having him win wouldn't be a gain for her.

"Thanks for the pound cake. Did you know I was going to be his mate?" I eyed her suspiciously.

She gave me a knowing smile and released my hands. "I did. This is a good thing."

"You didn't make it sound like that earlier."

"Well, something like that should be your decision."

"Is Erik part of the whole soulmate thing now?"

We'd considered it. If Erik was now in the mix, I was sure Phillip wouldn't be jumping to provide that information to us. Erik tried to connect with him mentally as a test without any luck but that didn't mean that Phillip wasn't just hiding from him. I knew I was hiding from Phillip now. I'd grown strong enough to prevent him from entering my dreams, and I wondered if being Erik's mate had given me the boost to be able to block Phillip now.

"He has a connection but not the way you and Phillip are. He's safe."

I sighed in relief.

Carter came up to me and gave me a hug. The bald, mahogany-colored man was actually a shapeshifter, but the pack had welcomed him as one of their own. It didn't hurt that he could turn into just about any living creature on earth.

"Can't believe this guy talked you into this," Carter stated, giving Erik a greeting handshake.

"Are wedding bells next?" Raya asked, walking up to us. She raised a perfectly arched eyebrow and placed her hands on her non-existent hips. She looked beautiful in a short, teal, body-hugging dress that showcased her athletic figure. Her brown hair was in a loose, wavy bob.

I could imagine she'd done a spit take when she'd heard that Erik had made me his mate. That thought did please the petty part of me.

"Damn, Ray," Carter chuckled. "You sound like somebody's mama. Let them marinate in this first."

"Just saying, if she's good enough to be your mate, she's

good enough to be your wife," Raya replied, her lips were smiling, but her brown eyes were anything but friendly.

"Right now, I'm focused on the challenge," I replied coolly.

She gave a quick chuckle. "Phillip's my leader, so you'll have to excuse me for not rooting for you. But hopefully, Phillip will be merciful to you and your... union." She looked over at Erik with disappointed eyes.

I glanced up at Erik beside me, and he actually looked uncomfortable. He gave a light cough in his fist and looked away.

I then looked over at Carter, who raised his eyebrows, glancing back and forth between the two of them. "So, who wants a celebratory shot?"

We all replied in the affirmative and headed to the bar. My super-powered female intuition was blaring again. Erik and I had been in a semi-long-distance relationship, if you could call it that, for two months. I'm sure many women pounced on the opportunity to ease his lonely nights.

A jealous rumble formed in the pit of my stomach as I wondered if Raya and Erik were more than just police partners. Had I sent him to Raya? But if I had, why did he want me as his mate?

"Did I miss something between you and Raya?" I whispered to Erik, a tightness in my throat.

He glanced sideways at me. "No," he said firmly but said nothing more.

I nodded, not comforted at all by his answer.

After swigging down a shot of the town vodka, I turned and saw Felix, Faith, Henry, Chelsea, and Charles heading over to us. They all looked spiffy. For some reason, Charles and Chelsea had on sunglasses.

"Why are you wearing sunglasses when it's night?" I asked.

"We just had a feast and our eyes are a bit... tired," Chelsea explained with a nonchalant shrug.

"What does that mean?"

"They gorged out on blood," Henry replied in a disapproving tone. His eyes were fine.

I turned to them. "Let me see your eyes."

Chelsea sighed and shook her head, but she did remove the large glasses. Her eyes were red as blood, with a small black pupil in the center. I dropped my mouth open. "Why do your eyes look like that?!" I cried.

"We thought it would be good to drink up before getting here. You know, so we could be at our strongest in case shit went down," Charles explained.

"We got carried away," Chelsea added, putting her sunglasses back on.

"You almost went bloodlust! That's past getting carried away," Henry growled in a tight voice. I rarely saw him get angry, but he was serious about his role as a vampire leader, especially in a town full of non-gifted humans. "You do that again, and you're going to get kicked out of the community. We don't want to make the humans nervous."

Charles gave an exaggerated sigh. "We're cool."

"You're drunk on blood," I cried. Even now, I could see that Charles was a bit unstable on his feet, wobbling a bit.

"Get your shit together, man," Henry said, slapping him on the back.

Charles threw out his hands. "Look around, sis, we're not the only drunk ones."

I glanced around me, and he was right; the place was packed with partiers, many of whom were clearly intoxicated.

I looked back at Charles, and although I couldn't see his eyes, I knew he was giving me a glare. Just as I was contemplating giving him the finger, Phillip walked over to us. My heart started beating quickly. He scared me more than I cared to admit.

Phillip must have had the same idea about peacocking to show he wasn't afraid because he was dressed to impress. He wore a well-tailored, cobalt-blue three-piece suit, with a white button-down shirt underneath. A patterned handkerchief hung neatly out of his jacket pocket.

"You look amazing, Amina," Phillip stated, shaking his head in admiration.

I smiled tightly, trying not to draw attention to us, but everyone was looking anyway.

"Are you ready for our little challenge tomorrow? I'm pretty excited. Should be fun," he said with a wide grin.

I bit my lower lip to control my annoyance. Erik reached over and grabbed my hand.

Phillip glanced down at our interlocking hands. The smile in his eyes faltered slightly but he quickly recovered and put his fake happy face back on. "I hear congratulations are in order. The two of you are now pack mates. That's cute." He chuckled. "I'd have done the same thing if I were you. I'm sure it helped you with your powers." He paused. "Because it sure did help me."

I kept my face neutral. Mae feared that would happen. If I was so connected to Phillip, it stood to reason that he would have shared in the powers that resulted from Erik's and my union.

"Well, that's fine," I replied. "Guess we're still on even playing fields then." That wasn't fine but I didn't want him to know that.

Phillip lifted an eyebrow. "You think we're even? *Corazon...*" He glanced over at Erik when he called me that, a careful smile still on his lips. I felt Erik vibrate a growl. "We aren't even now. But we can be one day. If you want that now, we can skip this whole unnecessary challenge thing and start working together."

"I'm good, see you tomorrow," I said, letting go of Erik's hand and turning my back to Phillip to face the bar. I ordered a whiskey. I needed something strong to mellow me out.

"Am I dismissed?" Phillip asked, sounding too amused.

"I don't think you two need to talk," Erik stated. I felt him stand between me and Phillip.

"You're a good dog, I mean jackal. When I win, maybe we can have you as a guard for our home."

Before Erik bit or I could drop some unpleasant magic on him, Charles cut in. "Why are you even here? This is a celebration for Mina and Erik. You're not a friend, and you're not pack," Charles sneered, standing beside Erik.

I peeked slightly behind me. Carter stood beside me, he had to play it neutral, but Felix, Chelsea, Henry, and Faith stood beside Erik and Charles to serve as a wall between myself and Phillip.

He shrugged, not intimidated. "I support pack celebrations. Seth's my friend as well. And I'd like a little fun before the test."

Chelsea took a step forward. "I can give you some fun."

I knew her fun for Phillip involved her ripping his throat out with her teeth. Assuming she got close enough to do that. She wouldn't.

"Be easy," I whispered.

Phillip looked over and considered her for a moment. "Do I know you?" His voice sounded bored.

That only angered Chelsea. I turned around again, this time a drink in hand.

"You killed my boyfriend, you son of a bitch," she spat. I touched her back, trying to calm her, but it wasn't working. She wasn't one of The Six. Touch was not something she needed.

Phillip responded to her anger with an unbothered look.

"Sorry, sweetheart, I don't recall, but I'm sure I had good reason to do it."

Chelsea raised a hand as if to strike, and Erik threw out an arm to block her. Phillip chuckled again and walked away.

Chelsea turned to face us. "Sure we can't just group attack him tonight?"

I shook my head. "Not if we want to live."

"Starting trouble already?" Blake announced, appearing next to Carter. She gave us a squinty-eyed smile. "This is a celebration. Have fun."

Her green eyes were full of interest to match deep-red pursed lips. She looked pretty as usual with a magically-colored—that was the only way now—platinum-blonde bob that barely contrasted against her fair skin tone. She rocked a tight, metallic jumper and looked like she should be on a stage singing a pop song instead of walking around a grubby bar. Her eyes rested on Chelsea and Henry. "It's always nice to meet new vampires. Aren't the both of you beautiful?"

Henry threw out a hand and gave her one of his charming smiles. "Henry Butler. Hagerstown Head Vampire."

Her eyebrows raised. "Oh, lovely. I'm Blake Devlin, Head Vampire here. We must chat." She looked back to Chelsea. "What did our Phillip do?"

"He killed a human I cared about during the prison rescue," Chelsea answered, still scowling.

"Oh, I'm so sorry," Blake replied with a genuinely sympathetic expression. "Perhaps it was an accident. That was a very hectic event, and humans were behind that horror, after all."

"It was no accident," I stated in an even voice.

Blake turned to me, her face neutral. "It's better for everyone if you believe it was. Enjoy your evening, everyone. My cabaret club is open for anyone wanting a late-night show. And Amina," She looked back at me. "Good luck."

I wasn't sure if she actually meant that, since by default,

she was supposed to be Team Phillip, but it felt real, and I'd take all the luck I could get.

I put in another hour and then begged Erik to take me back to his place. I needed to get away from Seth and Phillip and their people. Erik understood, and we said goodbye to Charles and the others, who were staying local so that they could attend the challenge the next day.

We were almost at the entrance of the pub when we heard some commotion off to our left. A man was poking his finger in Phillip's chest and yelling. He looked a little unstable, stumbling a bit as he talked. Phillip stood unmoving, arms crossed and face neutral.

Felix walked up to us. "What's going on?" I asked.

"Carter mentioned that this guy's wife is locked up for treason. Phillip thought she was part of some plot to take him out. He's been locking up suspects," Felix replied.

"Let her go! Linda is innocent, you piece of shit!" The man shouted.

Obviously, some folks were no longer drinking the Phillip punch. Two men, I assumed pack henchmen, surrounded the man and grabbed him by the arms to drag him away. The man spit at Phillip, and the glob of fluid landed on Phillip's left cheek. The band on stage stopped playing and everyone froze in fear of Phillip's response.

Phillip's neutral mask fell, and he wiped the spit from his cheek in disgust. "I should have locked you up with her as well. That can be easily fixed. You're lucky your wife is even alive. For plotting to overthrow my rule, she could be killed. Instead, I simply subdued her." He looked to the henchmen and nodded for them to take the man away to whatever gloom that would not reunite him with his wife. "Oh, and Mark. The next time you want to spit at me, you'll find you won't be able to."

The man's face went into a painful scowl and he opened his mouth screaming. He stuck his tongue out and leaned forward, struggling against the guards. Blood gushed out of his mouth as he keeled over farther. Seconds later, what appeared to be his tongue fell from his mouth to the floor. Screams erupted around the bar as the henchmen dragged the bloodied man out of the space.

Phillip turned around to face the crowd. "Let this be a lesson to anyone who challenges me. Be prepared for the consequences." He looked over at me. "Enjoy the rest of your night, everyone."

Workers rushed to clean up the blood and severed tongue, and the band slowly started to play again. Most of the patrons obeyed Phillip's orders and went back to their revelry, seemingly unaffected by the savagery only a moment ago. Such was the way with Phillip's mind control magic.

"What kind of shit is this?" I heard Henry whispered, forgetting that this was his first time witnessing the Phillip experience.

"Welcome to the jungle," Charles muttered.

I looked up at Erik, a cold fear wrapping around me. Phillip was a monster and he could not get any more power. I needed to stop him. "If I don't win tomorrow, I need you to do me a favor."

CHAPTER 12

The challenge was to occur at 12 p.m. on Saturday. I got up at 6 a.m. from a restless night. I left my bedroom and walked to the kitchen for a glass of water. Standing in the open kitchen, I noticed a figure on the balcony. I squinted. Erik. I put the glass down and walked past the living room space to the outside.

It was already light outside, as the last few weeks of early days held on before the darkness of late winter took over.

Erik was dressed only in his sweatpants. His back muscles flexed as he balanced his hands on the railing. I was dressed in only a T-shirt and shorts, but it was at least 80 degrees out this early, so I'd be comfortable.

I opened the sliding-glass doors. "What are you doing out here?" I asked.

He didn't turn towards me. I looked down to his lower right side, at the bullet wound in his back he'd received in the Pre-world, probably during battle as a soldier.

"I thought about your request," he said in a low voice.

I tensed, waiting for his answer. "Yes?" I said, my voice barely audible.

"I can't."

I sighed. "I can ask someone else. Maybe Faith."

"She's not as tough as you think." Erik straightened up and turned around to face me.

His body was distractingly defined. All hardness and cuts of muscle, marred only by the bullet wound and four-inch claw marks on the left side of his stomach.

"Henry maybe," I replied.

"Amina, if you lose, no one is going to kill you. I won't let them, and I don't think Charles would either."

My shoulders slumped. "Then we're screwed. He tore someone's tongue out of their mouth with just his mind. Erik, if I have to bow down to Phillip, with our combined power... he could do anything. Be anything." I shivered, thinking of the possible horrors Phillip could do. My imagination knew no limits, thanks to years of horror movie watching.

"It's the only way to stop Phillip." I wrapped my arms around myself. It was too warm to be cold but there was an uncomfortable chill spreading inside of me. "He's a monster, but he can't keep going. If you kill me, you kill him. If he wins, this is all for nothing."

Erik shook his head. "There are other ways. Mae said some other things were meant to happen."

I gave my head a hard shake before pushing my fingers through my curls and scratching my scalp in frustration. "Yeah, and she didn't say when. She didn't say who else would get hurt until those other things occurred. If I lose and you fight him, he won't hesitate to kill any of you, and you won't be able to get close enough to him to do anything."

Erik sighed. "I can promise not to fight him, for now. But the other thing... no."

"What if he hurts some other innocent person?"

"But that person won't be you, according to Mae, and it won't be the Six. That's all I can afford to care about right now."

"I don't believe you. You care about other people. That's why you moved back here. Are our lives more important than anyone else's?"

"If we kill you, then no one wins."

"Then put a sleeping spell on me, like the fairytale. Only your kiss can awaken me. Who knows? Maybe me being in a coma will put Phillip in one, too, or at least make him weaker. But you won't ever have to kiss him."

Erik turned and looked at me. His eyes held no humor at my weak attempt at a joke. "You aren't funny. Do me a favor and stop talking like you are going to lose. If you don't have faith in yourself, you won't win this. Didn't I say you were a badass? When are you going to believe it?"

I was scared. There was no doubt about that. I believed in my abilities, but the evil in Phillip seemed overwhelming. All I knew was that Phillip had to be stopped, even if it meant I had to die.

I pounded my chest again with a closed fist in an attempt to hold back silly tears and slow my constricting heart. It wasn't helping.

Erik opened his arms. "Come here," he said.

I remained where I was, shaking my head. I couldn't hug him. I would never want to let go because then it would be that much harder if I lost him. I backed away, re-entering the living area.

"Woman, stop running from me," he ordered in a low voice.

"I can't. I can't. I have to focus. I have to win." I closed my eyes and covered my face with both my hands.

"Come here," he said again. His voice was still gentle.

I uncovered my face, ready to argue, but paused. His arms were open again, and he smiled at me with soft eyes. My heart tugged once more, and I let out a deep sigh before walking over to him. As much as I tried to push him away, I couldn't. I really didn't want to even though I knew it was the right thing to do.

I moved my arms around his waist and laid my head on his bare chest. He was warm, and his skin felt hard and yet smooth. I missed the feel of him. He wrapped his strong arms around me, and I felt so protected. It made no sense to me. He couldn't stop any bad from coming my way, but his presence made me believe he could. Instantly, my heart began to slow down, and the itch of uneasiness that constantly plagued me faded away.

He inhaled deeply. "I missed your smell," he whispered before kissing the top of my head. "It's not too late to change your mind. I can sa—"

"Save me?" I cut him off. "You can't rescue every female you come across." I tried to push away from him, but he held me to him. I barely put up any resistance. Despite my words, I wanted to be in his arms.

"You aren't a victim, Mina. Never were. I forget that sometimes. I just want to protect you."

I looked up at him. For the first time since I'd agreed to this challenge with Phillip, I noticed real fear from him. He was scared for me.

"Erik."

"You aren't the only one who doesn't like getting hurt. I've suffered loss before. Men in my unit in war. My daugh...
"

He trailed off. He'd never told me about his daughter. However, Lisa had shared that he'd once had a seven-year-old who hadn't survived the shift into a werejackal. Yes, he knew pain and he'd still opened himself up to save Lisa when she might have been killed by weres and saved me when David tried to kidnap me again. And now, he still wanted to save me. Me, with all my psycho soulmate baggage.

"Mina, I know this is all a lot for you. Have you considered that maybe you might have some PTSD from all that's happened to you? You don't have to do this challenge."

"You think I'm not stable?"

I felt him shake his head above me. "No. That's not what that means. I do think you are really stressed, maybe even traumatized, and you're making some rash decisions."

"I have to do this. I really don't have time to talk to some therapist, even if we had one in town." I leaned into him. "I'll win and things will get better for me. I'll be fine again. It's just a little stress from the challenge. And then... " I stopped speaking. And then I would tell him I loved him and everything would be okay.

Erik had called me naive when we first met. Somedays, I thought he was right, but hope was all I had to keep me going.

~

The challenge was held in a high school gymnasium that now housed all grade levels of education. It seemed an innocent place to host such a dark battle, but our magic had to be in a contained space.

We had an audience of witches and specially invited guests who sat on the bleachers near the west side of the room. In front of the bleachers were four desks. Our judges, all witches, were seated there. Two judges were from Silver Spring and two were from Hagerstown. I knew the Hagerstown judges well and thought they were good people. One was a forty-something woman named Danielle and the other was a fifty-something man named Brad. The Silver Spring judges looked vaguely familiar but I didn't know them. To the left of my judges was a woman with a short bob. I couldn't tell her age. Maybe thirties or forties. Next to her was a man in his late fifties or early sixties with balding, gray hair.

Behind the judges, I spotted Charles and the others. I also saw Raya, Seth, Blake, Carter, Mae, Bill, and Grace Sarin. Grace was someone I could call a friend in Silver Spring. She was also a siren who could control people with the melody in her voice. She was not susceptible to our mind control. The beautiful Indian woman with tailbone-length, dark-brown hair and enviable thick, well-shaped eyebrows, gave me a sympathetic smile.

Suddenly, nerves hit my stomach hard. I turned slightly and fanned a hand in front of my face as if to swipe the growing nervous nausea away. Erik, who had been standing beside me, leaned over and whispered in my ear. "It's not too late to change your mind," he stated.

I turned to face him as we stood at the entrance of the gym. "Yes, it is," I replied. I patted his arm. "I'll be okay. It's just hot in here."

"If it looks like you're losing, don't do anything crazy. Promise me that." He scrunched his eyebrows together and gazed at me intently.

I didn't answer.

"Welcome, everyone!" cried a voice. It was Phillip.

"We've got to go in." I walked forward, but Erik caught my wrist.

"Promise me."

"Is Amina Langston here?" Phillip shouted through a microphone.

"She's here!" I heard my mentor shout. A look of pure irritation spread across her cocoa-colored face, and she crossed her arms as she stood to the left of the room.

I turned to Erik. "Fine, I promise." I won't kill myself, but I won't fall in line with Phillip either.

Erik's eyes seemed to droop. He knew I wasn't telling the truth. I could never deceive him, especially now as his mate. However, he let my wrist go and we both headed into the gym. Erik climbed the benches to join the others. I stopped beside Shayla.

"God forgive me, but I do not like this man. I don't know him but I don't like him," Shayla said in a harsh whisper. She frowned in anger and the wrinkles between her eyes marred her deceptively-youthful face. She was just shy of forty years of age, which I only knew because she told me. Actually, she looked almost a decade younger. Her long braids were piled to the top of her head in a bun and she was dressed in workout clothes, as if she were going to compete in a marathon.

I had on dark-blue capri jeans, a black, short-sleeved T-shirt, and red Converse low-top sneakers. I wondered if I'd mistaken how I should have prepared for today.

"I know, Shay," I replied. "Listen, I want to thank you for all that you've done to prepare me for this."

She shook her head. "Oh, girl, not a problem. Now, let me give you my pep talk." She grabbed me by the shoulders. "You got this. You are strong, powerful, smart, and an overall good person. You envision kicking his behind, and you will. Don't think about anything negative. Just believe in yourself. You got a slew of folks who believe in you too. So, with all that, this should be easy." She wrapped her arms around me in a tight hug. "Go kick his ass."

She seemed as emotionally invested in this as me. She'd never been to Silver Spring, but during the time I'd spent training under her, I'd shared a lot of stories of my short time here and of Phillip.

Shayla patted my shoulders again and ran to the bleachers to sit with Team Amina.

I turned back to the center of the room and looked at Phillip. A male in his thirties with shoulder-length, brown hair stood next to him and was now holding the microphone.

"Good afternoon, ladies and gentlemen," said the man. "For those who don't know me, I'm Ron."

"Ronnie, Ronnie, Ronnie," called some people in the crowd. Apparently, this dude was popular.

"Settle down now, folks. I'll be your host for our first-ever witchcraft challenge. The goal of this is to establish the top witch in the area. There will be a series of five timed challenges. The one who passes the most challenges or passes the most challenges first, wins. To help ensure the integrity of the process and to measure success, we have four judges experienced in magic. To the far left is John. Beside him is Tessa. Then joining us from Hagerstown are Danielle and Brad.

"Our challenges will be, in the following order: One, multiple magic use; two, break a ward; three, break a curse; four, follow a potion that gives life; and five, create a spell on something no one has done before. You will only be given fifteen minutes per challenge. There will be no cheating. We will sense it. In addition, you will not see what the other is doing for most challenges. We will put up a visual barrier spell between the two of you that you will not be allowed to break. You will also not know how much time you have left for each challenge. When I call stop. You will stop." Ron looked at us. "Good luck to you both."

Seeing as *Ronnie* was a member of Silver Spring, I didn't think he meant me any luck.

"Now, this first challenge is open, so you will be able to see each other. You have fifteen minutes to get as much magic as possible going. If you've both reached your capacity before the conclusion of time, then we will end there." Ron looked to a blue-haired woman with glasses who sat in a chair near the judges. I assumed she was the time and scorekeeper.

I looked back at Ron. He gave a curt nod to the woman. "Begin."

Phillip and I walked to separate parts of the gym and began. The space had a few items we could work with for our magic. A trash bin, desk, containers, and utensils. I stood in front of the trash bin and closed my eyes, not wanting to distract my energy with any use of senses that I did not need.

I pictured the trash bin in my mind and muttered a spell of fire. I pictured the papers inside burning. Seconds later, I felt a warmth in front of me. I opened one eye and saw the fire. I smiled. Shayla taught me that staying positive and remaining calm would keep me at full strength. She believed that anger and nervousness would require too much energy and take away from my power, so I wouldn't be getting in my head today.

I closed my eyes again and whispered another spell. Soon, I felt drips of cold touch my arms, and the crowd whispered, "Ahh."

I'd made snowflakes fall from the ceiling, not disturbing my fire. I dropped to my knees and touched the floor. I heard more murmurs from the crowd from what I assumed was Phillip's magical showcase but did not get tempted or distracted by opening my eyes.

For the next display of magic, I wouldn't need a spell. This would be of my own life mage magic. I splayed my fingers wide on the floor and a slight rumbling shook the ground under my hands. The floor tile broke and I brushed rubble away with my hands. Soon I felt dirt and quickly smoothed a patch of ground two feet wide. The feel of grass and flowers splayed through my fingers. I adjusted and crossed my legs yoga style. I smiled as the sound of birds chirping filled the room. I had no idea where they came from but they were part of nature, life, and they would come when I wanted them.

By now, sweat prickled my skin and dripped down my back, however, I hadn't reached my limit and continued on.

Next, the smell of baked apple pie filled my nostrils. I

inhaled deeply, a memory of my grandmother playing in my mind. She was in the kitchen baking and humming an old jazz tune. Charles and I were sitting at the kitchen table laughing and eating pie. The buttery crust and sweet cinnamon baked apples came to my tongue.

I heard a few confused voices in the crowd murmur about the taste and smell of pie. It wasn't real but humans, like the birds, were of nature, and I could control their minds to believe that what they were smelling and tasting actually existed. All the fun without the calories.

I stood up on shaky legs and opened my eyes. I heard what sounded like a bear and the crowd went into excited screams. My bonfire briefly wavered but I caught it before it disappeared.

I had five bits of magic going right now. I looked at my creations. A small patch of the gym floor was a garden of roses. Snow continued to fall and birds fluttered over our heads. A few people ducked as the birds flew too close.

I was sweating and feeling nauseous. I had never gone past five before but there was something in me that pushed for more. It told me I had to try to get out one more bit of magic. At this point, I was struggling to remain standing.

I closed my eyes and let out a deep breath. I had never had six bits of magic going at once. Whenever I tried to go past it in practice, I had a nice little fainting spell. That could very well happen now but I still had the five.

If this was the edge I needed to beat Phillip, then I wouldn't hold back. I threw my hands up and tilted my head back. Large booms filled the room, and I opened my eyes to see fireworks play above me. Again, they were merely false images to the eyes of the audience that I controlled but they sure were pretty.

I smiled as my legs gave out, and I dropped to my knees. I stayed upright and looked around to make sure all my other magic was still working. The snow had stopped and I grinned to calm my nerves and pushed forward. Snow began to fall again through the colorful explosions.

A loud alarm buzzed. "Stop!" Ron shouted.

I exhaled, and my magic disappeared. The birds flew out of the gym, the fire and snow died, and illusions left. All that remained was my miniature garden. I panted, wondering if I had made enough of an effort to win. I also hoped that I hadn't exhausted myself too much since I had four more challenges to go.

"We have taken notice of both magic occurrences and have determined that this round goes to... Amina!" Ron called.

The crowd did a polite clap. I didn't expect them to cheer. I wasn't exactly in friendly territory. I looked over to my group and Charles gave me a thumbs up, his eyes behind sunglasses. Erik grinned at me and mouthed, "Yes."

There was a small cheering section, screaming and whistling. Shayla stood up with her fist in the air and the rest of my support around her whooped it up as well.

Let's not get too confident, I thought.

"For the rest of the challenges, we will have a visual barrier. Moving on to challenge two. We have two boxes which my assistant will provide you with. Each box is warded. You must break the ward to get the box to open."

Blue-Haired woman walked over to Phillip and then to me.

Wards. It should have been an easy one for me. I escaped the prison, which was surrounded by a ward. I put up my own strong wards all the time. This should have been a piece of cake. And because I was so cocky, the fates decided to have Phillip break the ward before I could even determine the type of ward I was trying to break.

I panicked. It hadn't even felt like five minutes! I had wrongly assumed that because we had fifteen minutes for each challenge, the tests would be difficult enough to require that full time to succeed. How else would that make one a top witch?

"Phillip wins this round," Ron announced. "Phillip, that was amazing. Our witch who made that ward has said that the fastest anyone has ever broken it was fourteen minutes. For most people it takes around thirty to forty minutes. You broke it in six minutes!"

The crowd erupted in a loud cheer. I looked down, not wanting to meet the eyes of my supporters. I knew they wouldn't be disappointed in me, but it would still hurt to see their faces.

"Okay, now we are at challenge three. Breaking a curse. We have two people. Both cursed to blindness. You must each break the curse, which will restore their sight. The first to do so wins."

Who volunteered to do this? I wondered. Two men entered the gym, one with a limp being escorted by the blue-haired woman to Phillip. The other man walked with a stick towards me, unassisted.

"Both men were cursed with dark magic by someone who is not a part of this town. This witch is extremely powerful, and we do not expect this to be an easy endeavor. These men understand the risks of volunteering for this and will be compensated well for their participation, regardless of the outcome."

Clearly, these guys were in desperate situations to volunteer to be blinded for compensation of some sort. I wondered how they were being rewarded? I also wondered about this witch they happened upon who could cast a dark curse and then decided to split town. An edge of doubt and distrust of this competition played at the edge of my mind. It had always been there, and with Phillip's seemingly easy win of round two, I was now more suspicious. However, I wasn't so sure I had any real ground to contest anything.

"Round three begins... now," Ron shouted, and we began.

I had no time to ponder the fairness of this challenge. I moved to face the man I'd been given to help. "What's your name?" I asked. It really didn't matter, I knew, but it felt important to know him.

"Sam," The man stated in a quiet voice. He was a young man, maybe early twenties, with cropped brown hair.

"I suppose you can't tell me anything about the person who cursed you," I said.

He shook his head. "I don't know anything, actually. Sorry."

I didn't have any more time for chit-chat, not that it was helpful anyway. I reached out and touched his shoulder and employed my witch's sight, unfocusing my eyes. A deep black smoke outlined his form. This was dark magic for sure. I was no expert in that arena. Shayla made me learn some for the challenge but we'd never practiced because that went beyond our boundaries. We were too afraid we'd open the door to something dark.

I also just assumed we would stay away from it because it usually consisted of some form of sacrifice. If you were cursing someone, the sacrifice usually required a death. I hoped that the death was not a human one, although I would never put it past this group. If the curse was based on a human sacrifice, then it would usually take a sacrifice to break it. That could take the form of killing someone. It could also take the form of cutting off a body part of a particularly strong being.

I frowned. The idea that this challenge could result in something so dark concerned me. Perhaps that was the point. Maybe Phillip knew that I would never hurt anyone to win.

But he would.

"I need an assistant to break this curse," I heard Phillip announce. "May I be allowed to seek help from the audience?"

Seconds later, I heard Ron answer in the affirmative.

Shit.

"Xander. Can you help?" he asked in a neutral tone. Like Xander would say no.

A man who appeared to be in his late 20s, with curly blond hair and glasses, moved down the bleachers without hesitating.

I knew where this was going. I was sure I could mind control someone in the crowd to help me too, but if that help meant killing or maiming them, then I wouldn't do it. I could heal but growing back an arm or even a finger was beyond my magic. I wasn't willing to hurt anyone to win. That wasn't the way I wanted to succeed. Of course, the idea of grabbing Seth and breaking the curse with his sacrifice didn't sound so bad.

Then again, I'm sure that wouldn't do much for what Erik was trying to do with the pack and no one would believe Seth had volunteered of his own free will. They would never follow Erik if I took out their leader.

The only other option was for me to cut myself. Blindness was serious but I wasn't experienced enough to know if it was take-a-life kind of serious or cut-off-a-limb type of serious. I didn't want to cut off a hand, only to have really needed to kill someone.

There's a sentence you don't think of often.

I suddenly heard commotion from the crowd and looked up. Charles was standing near the judges and pointing at me. "I'm her volunteer," he said. "Phillip gets one, so does she."

"She didn't ask for you," Ron stated.

I shook my head. What was Charles up to? I suppose having someone by my side wouldn't hurt. "Charles, will you be my volunteer?" I cried.

The judges agreed, and Charles jogged over to me.

"What do you need me to do?" he asked, lifting his sunglasses to the top of his head.

"It's dark magic. I need a sacrifice or a limb," I replied, sighing and shaking my head again.

Charles shrugged. "I'm already dead. Use me. As long as you don't cut off my head or damage my heart, I'll come back. Or cut off my arm; I think it'll grow back."

I raised my eyebrows. "You think? I can't risk that."

"Then you're going to lo—"

He stopped as the crowd gasped. He ran around the invisible barrier, grimaced, and came back to me.

"What happened?" I asked.

"The fucker sliced off dude's arm with a machete," Charles answered. "He didn't even attempt to heal the guy, just went back to his table with the bloody arm. You have to do something now before you lose."

I grimaced. "It's dark magic, Charles. I can't mess with that. You use it and it's like a stench you can't get rid of. Once is enough. It opens you up to do more bad things and lets evil get inside you. Real evil, not figuratively. I don't want to open that door."

He frowned. "Then you'll lose."

I sucked in a breath. "I think I'll have to be okay with that for this rou—"

"I can see!" shouted Phillip's blind volunteer.

I could have vomited.

Perhaps he was lying.

Ron walked up to the man and tested him. He asked him how many fingers he was holding up and what certain people in the audience were wearing. The man got every answer right. Doubt crept into my mind again. I had no proof the man had actually been blind in the first place. Perhaps this was all a set up.

"The winner of round three is Phillip!" Ron shouted.

The crowd erupted in joy again.

I let out a sigh and my shoulders slumped. I looked to my

blind guy. At least he had the decency to look sad. Although I'm sure it wasn't for the same reason as me.

"It's okay, you've got this next one!" I heard Felix shout out.

I looked over to him and gave him a sad smile as some in the crowd booed him. Erik smiled at me and nodded. I glanced over at Mae and she gave me a neutral look, as if she were watching a play. I wasn't really sure who she was rooting for now. She certainly didn't look bothered that I had just lost two challenges in a row.

"Okay, everyone, just two more challenges left. So far, it's Amina one, and Phillip two. It's still anyone's game," Ron announced. "For challenge number four, each of you will be given ingredients and directions for a potion that brings life."

Two people walked into the room, pushing carts towards Phillip and me.

Ron went on. "This may sound deceptively easy, but it is not. Not just anyone can make the potion work. In fact, as of now, no one we know has succeeded in making it work. We believe it requires a certain level of power already in the witch. However, since you are both life mages, this might be a piece of cake. You know the drill. Whoever gets this to work wins. Clock starts... now."

We were life mages, but we couldn't bring life to something dead, only control anything living. I looked down at my tray. There was another wooden bowl, a motor to crush powder, a spoon, several unlabeled containers of ingredients, directions typed on a sheet of paper, and something the size of a large male shoe under a cloth. I lifted the cloth and grimaced. It was a dead, gray kitten with a white underbelly and paws.

There was a special place in hell for these people. Who were these monsters?

They must have killed the animals this morning because the kitten wasn't yet decaying. That made it a little better.

Zombie cat was creepy enough on its own without looking like it. Its eyes were closed and it looked like it was resting peacefully. I decided to name her Poppy, thinking naming it would bring it some identity or life on its own.

I picked up the directions and read.

One teaspoon each of the following:

Juniper

Fennel

Pine

Thyme

Ivy

Ginger

Clover

Sandalwood oil

Adders tongue

Angelica leaves

Burdock root

I cocked an eyebrow. Where were they getting all of these ingredients? Even in the Pre-world, it would have been hard to find some of these things. I couldn't imagine who was growing them. But then again, if you were a witch who relied on potions and spells, these would be things you'd want in your backyard just as much as vegetables. They'd also make great items for selling at the market.

I started dumping the ingredients into the bowl. I had to say I was a wee bit disappointed that there was no eye of newt, dragon claw, or batwing needed. The herbs listed made magic seem so... practical. Which it was. Of course, the recipe highlighted even more that magic really was in the person who used it.

I took the motor and began to grind the powders, leaves, and oil together into a paste. This took some time, but when done, I scooped some out and dropped it onto Poppy in a few places. I pursed my lips and rubbed the concoction into the stiff, furry animal. I would have loved some gloves, but magic was in my skin, and if this was going to work, I had to do it right. If I failed, there would be no round five. Phillip would be the automatic winner, having won three in a row out of five.

I massaged the animal and pushed my magic through my fingers. I envisioned the animal waking up and running around, but when I looked down, poor Poppy was still stiff as a board and unmoving.

"Come on, Poppy," I whispered. "If you wake up and don't become a flesh-eating zombie kitty, I'll get you all the fish you can eat."

Poppy apparently wasn't impressed because the kitty remained dead. I put more paste on the kitten.

I leaned in a bit, still giving the kitty a massage with my fingertips, rubbing the paste further in. "Look, Poppy, don't embarrass me in front of these good people. This is your time to shine. Don't let them beat us."

I sighed and straightened up. This wasn't good. Charles and Erik would fight before they'd let Phillip take me and they would die with no coming back this time.

I started to pat the cat with gentle strokes. "I promise we'll be best friends forever if you wake up," I told the kitten.

I felt movement under my fingers. The skin under the fur rippled and I fought the urge to take my hand away. It was creepy and kind of gross, but I had to toughen up.

Soon, the kitten's body moved up and down, breathing in and out. Poppy's eyes opened. They were covered with a film at first, but the kitten continued to blink, and soon, the eyes were regular yellow with large, black pupils. I heard some of the crowd that was close enough to see, gasp.

I smiled. "Come on Poppy, show off."

As if she understood, Poppy the Kitty, stretched her whole body in one long line and then rose to her paws. She began to purr, and she brushed her head against my hand before licking my fingers. "Oh, good girl, Poppy. We're besties now."

The crowd cried out.

I leaned over and picked up Poppy. The adorable cat, who I now decided was my new pet regardless of the outcome, snuggled her head into my neck and continued to loudly purr. I figured since she hadn't bitten me, she wasn't a zombie cat, so all was well. Of course, if she had, I'd have been done for.

Note to self: don't let the cuteness fool you. I should have learned that from Phillip by now.

I walked over to the judges with Poppy, and they looked on in awe. I placed her down on one of the judge's desk as they crowded around and inspected the kitten. Poppy was none too pleased with the poking and prodding and swiped little kitten paws at them. She cried out and scratched at my jeans for me to pick her up. I smiled and picked the cat back up. One of the judges looked to Ron and nodded.

"Although it looks like Phillip just woke up his puppy. The winner for challenge four is... Amina!" Ron shouted.

My crew jumped up, and shouted and a few others in the crowd gave polite applause.

"Okay, everyone, we now have a tie," Ron stated on his microphone. "This is the final challenge. Whoever wins this one wins everything and will have final rule and the title of most powerful witch."

I looked at Poppy. "Okay, kitty, let me give you to someone. I've got work to do," I stated. I walked over to Charles, who raised an eyebrow. I shoved the kitten in his face. "Watch Poppy for me, please."

"Poppy?" he asked, taking the cat, who sniffed his face. Deciding that she preferred me, Poppy wiggled out of his grasp and raced to my feet. She rubbed up against my ankles lazily.

"Poppy, listen to me. Go with Charles. I'll get you as soon as I'm done. Okay?"

The kitten looked up at me and meowed before jumping into Charles' lap.

"Did she actually listen to you?" he asked, patting the kitten on the head.

I shrugged.

"You're doing good out there, Mina," Erik said. His eyes were uncharacteristically soft and he gave me a slight smile.

"Thank you. Promise me you'll both be good, regardless of how this last challenge ends."

"Amina, are you ready?" Ron called in an impatient voice.

Erik pointed his head back to the center of the room. "Better get back there."

I looked back at Poppy. "Make sure they behave, Poppy," I stated, pointing at her.

The kitten meowed in response. I arched an eyebrow. Maybe she could understand me.

I walked back to my position.

A sudden wind blew through the gym, knocking me forward a few steps, and I struggled to stay on my feet. The hair from my ponytail blew forward, and I turned around to see the origin of the wind.

A thick cloud of smoke swirled near the back wall beside the doors between Phillip and I. Soon it dissipated, revealing the outline of a petite figure.

As the smoke cleared, I was able to see the figure more clearly.

"Lisa!" I cried.

CHAPTER 13

*L*isa, to my relief, looked healthy and strong. Her black hair, with hot-pink tips now, hung to her chest and her bright, emerald eyes appeared energized. Her petite frame was covered in a robin's-egg-blue ruffled sundress, exposing tan but unusually-sparkly skin.

"Hey, Mina!" She exclaimed, waving at me with a bright smile.

She looked like she'd just come back from vacation, while all this time we thought she was captured or worse. I was more than peeved. "'Hey, Mina?' Where have you been?"

She lost her smile. "I'll tell you one day. I promise. But for now... Don't hate me, okay? I'm really sorry, but I have to do this."

I frowned. "Huh?"

She put out her hand, palm up, and blew. And, I kid you not, glitter appeared. Or what looked like glitter. Little sparks of colorful lights moved in swirly lines towards Phillip and me. The lights wrapped around our bodies like a confetti explosion. I wrapped my arms around myself and squinted my eyes in confusion. Phillip batted at the swarm of glittery lights, but it was useless. This colorful parade was not budging.

I tried to shout but couldn't hear myself. There was no sound blocking my voice; rather, it was as if I'd lost my ability to hear. Through the glitter, I could see an odd commotion all around me. Erik ran towards me. but it seemed as if he were moving in slow motion.

My feet levitated off the ground, and the floor quickly evaporated into white nothingness. Everything, except the glitter swarm and Phillip, was beginning to similarly fade to white. Outlines of bodies disappeared, until we were no longer in the gym or around the others. We were nowhere. We were now surrounded by a bare-white space with just the two of us and the damn glittery lights.

And then, as suddenly as everything had disappeared, a scene grew around us. Only it wasn't the gym.

Pavement appeared under my feet, buildings grew on either side of us, and a cloudy evening sky spread above us.

We were now in the middle of what appeared to be a city, surrounded by tall buildings. They were mostly shops, restaurants, bars, and offices. Tall grass grew in front of establishments and some of the buildings looked dilapidated, with boarded or broken windows and graffiti covering the outsides. Ahead, I spotted a short pedestrian bridge crossing a long canal littered with boats and debris. The area was filled with the stench of waste and decay, and I grimaced as I took further inspection of my surroundings. A few cars and bikes were pushed against the sidewalk in random directions as if people haphazardly tried to clear the streets to go forward. The street was also full of trash and plant life that had broken through the asphalt.

This didn't feel like America. There was something old about it. I looked for street signs but they didn't appear familiar. Although I couldn't see the signs too clearly in the dark, the shape, drawings, and writing on the signs seemed off.

Still, I felt like I'd been here before. I looked behind me and spotted a light rail or tram overturned in the middle of the street. The asphalt was broken up around the tram as if a strong earthquake had knocked it off course. The back end of the tram dipped into the pavement where the ground broke up underneath it.

It was quiet, and I saw no people, none living anyway, or lights on the street. Wherever we were, it was abandoned.

I looked over to Phillip, who stood a few feet in front of me, looking around. He suddenly spun towards me, eyes wild with anger.

"What the fuck did you do?" he shouted at me.

I took a step back. He'd never cursed or yelled at me before. I was a bit shocked. "I didn't do anything. Did you not see Lisa blow that fairy dust?"

"You asked her to do it. You knew you would lose, so you had her step in when things weren't going your way." He pointed at me, walking closer.

I stepped back again. "I just won a round; why would I need her? Not to mention she has been missing for two months."

"I don't believe you didn't have her help you!" He thundered.

I threw up my hands. "I didn't do this. I had no role in Lisa doing what she did. We can go back and straighten this all out."

Phillip actually sneered at me and then closed his eyes, throwing out his hands. I stood stiffly as I watched him attempt to teleport himself back to Silver Spring.

Nothing.

Minutes passed, with him cursing in frustration as he attempted to disappear.

He finally opened his eyes. "Why can't I teleport?"

I shook my head and shrugged. "I'll try."

I poured my energy through my hands and envisioned the gym as I chanted the teleportation spell, but I felt nothing. Not a tingle in my stomach where my body would shift and change for the location move. Instead, as I strained, it felt like I was pushing against a brick wall.

I sighed and dropped my shoulders. "It's not working. And before you start yelling at me like a maniac, I didn't have anything to do with this. Lisa surprised me, too. If I were a part of this, then why am *I* here?"

Phillip frowned at me, eyes narrowed. "You love sacrificing yourself. Maybe this was part of it. The only way to send me away is to send you too."

I tilted my head. That was practical. "Yeah, that's a reasonable guess. It'd be a pretty smart thing to do, but you're going to have to trust me on this. I didn't have anything to do with it. If I did, I'd just tell you. You know when I'm lying, after all." I smiled sweetly. I wasn't exactly happy to be here, but I did enjoy seeing Phillip pissed off.

Something not too far away groaned loudly, and I heard what sounded like a large flag flapping, but there wasn't any wind.

That sound was the sound of wings. Very large wings.

"It might be a good idea to have this conversation inside before whatever is above swoops down and gobbles us up," I stated, looking upwards at the full moon.

"We should go into one of these buildings," Phillip stated, the anger in his voice relaxing. I was hopeful that he believed me about not sending us here, but I knew better. Regardless of that fact, our hatred for each other would take a backseat for bigger, scarier monsters.

"We might want to pick something that's not on this street. Doesn't look so people friendly," I replied.

He growled. "I don't think we have the luxury of being picky right now."

I shrugged and walked away from the commercial buildings, towards the pedestrian bridge. He could stay in an office building. I wanted a house and away from him. Phillip, followed me, muttering, which I found both amusing and annoying.

We crossed the pedestrian bridge, looking ahead for shelter. We went a block farther and found a five-story apartment building.

I hesitated, but Phillip blew open the door with his magic. It was good to know we still had power. Apparently, we were only hindered in teleporting.

"You didn't want to knock first?" I asked, standing behind him.

"Who was answering?" he replied, stepping inside. "It's a building, and there was no ward."

"Still could be people in here, and maybe they are asleep."

"Well, they're awake now."

I couldn't see his face well in the dark, but I was sure he rolled his eyes.

"We can't check this whole place, so we should just ward the building and pick an apartment to stay in for the night," he continued.

"We?" I asked. "I'm going in my own apartment, and then I'm going my own way in the morning." And if I found a way back home, I'd just go on without him and leave him here to rot. And I wouldn't send a recovery team because I didn't even know where we were. I moved around him and headed up the front steps of the building.

Phillip reached out and grabbed my wrist. "Wait. I don't think it's a good idea for us to separate."

I shook my hand free. "I'm already sharing a building with you. I really don't want to share a room with you."

"We can find a two bedroom."

"That's still too close." I strained to look around. I did a spell of light and a ball of fire levitated in my palm.

Phillip shut the front doors and warded the doorway as I looked around. We were in a small front entrance. The floor was dirt-covered and cracked with age. To the right were rows of rusted metal mailboxes covered in a thick layer of dust. To the left was a wall with ripped up, faded flyers. In front of us was an elevator and stairs.

We climbed the steps to the first level. We had no need to stir things up by trying to get the elevator to work.

When he was done warding, Phillip turned to me. "We'll stay on this floor. And we're sharing an apartment. There's no point in us separating until we figure out what's going on. I'm no threat to you."

My eyes widened. "Are you kidding me? You are always a threat. You threatened me a month ago, saying you'd murder my friends if I didn't do the challenge, you hurt me at that sham of a hearing, you maim people. You are dangerous," I cried.

Phillip raised an eyebrow but didn't respond for a moment, as if contemplating my words before speaking. "Fair enough. But hurting you at the trial was a mistake. I apologize. There are things about my power that I'm still learning." His eyes softened, throwing me off as I wondered if he was being sincere. "You're too special to me to hurt, Amina. I know you don't believe me and I get why, but we're both here and we might as well work together until we get back home."

To trust Phillip was foolhardy, but seeing as he couldn't kill me and we were both stranded, I could at least use his power to help me figure this mess out and prevent some scary creature from eating me. "Fine, pick a damn apartment," I grumbled.

Phillip didn't seem too picky and choose the apartment nearest the stairs. When we opened it, a stench of death hit us. Phillip shut the door quickly. "Let's find one with no dead inside."

I didn't disagree with that and moved in front of him, going farther down the hall to another apartment a few spaces away from the one we'd originally opened. I opened the door this time. No smell. At least not of a decaying body, long dead from the Sickness or some awful supernatural attack.

The place didn't smell like vanilla either. There was a staleness in the air with a hint of rotten food or trash and maybe urine. I coughed and opened the hallway closet. A litter box was on the floor. It was filled to the brim with poop and other things I didn't want to investigate.

"Shit!" Phillip shouted from somewhere in the apartment.

I walked down the hallway, unrushed. Maybe whatever it was would eat him. Then, of course, I might die too. I walked a little faster.

"What the hell is the problem?" I walked into the first bedroom and saw Phillip standing on the other side of the queen-sized bed, looking down at the carpet.

"Nothing," he said, bending down. "Dead cat."

"This is going to be your room." I turned and walked to the room next door. It was the master bedroom and had an ensuite. I did a cleansing spell and watched in never-ending amazement as dust vanished, pillows fluffed, and dirt disappeared. When the room was fit enough to sleep in, I flopped down on the bed, stretching out.

A minute later, I heard Phillip come into the room behind me. "Seriously? You can sleep now?" he asked in an incredulous tone.

I shrugged. "I'm not sleeping. I'm just laying down."

"We need to figure out where we are."

I got up, walked to the window and stared out at the dark street. "It looks like we're in Ireland. Dublin, to be exact."

"How do you know?"

"I vacationed in Ireland several years ago. This feels like a neighborhood I visited. I'll know better at daylight."

"She sent us to Europe! How the hell can we get back?" Phillip punched a wall, and I jumped.

I turned around and looked at him. "We can find a boat and someone who knows how to sail or even someone who can fly a plane. I'm sure there are communities that survived over here. Or maybe we can find witches who can teleport us back, since we can't."

Phillip walked over to the bed and sat down. "Why would Lisa do this?"

"I said I didn't know. She's been missing. That's the first time I've seen her in over two months."

"And she comes back at that exact moment and then sends us away. She knew you were losing."

I shook my head. "I'm sorry, I thought it was a tie. We're equal."

Phillip wasn't looking at me. "This bed is actually nice. Since we have a plan for the day, how about we spend the night having a little... fun?" He patted the space next to him on the bed.

He was clearly not focused on the important issues. "I know in your egotistical, psychotic mind you think things are cool between us, but they aren't. Maybe you've forgotten, but we were just in a challenge against each other."

Phillip smiled, probably meaning to be flirtatious but it just pissed me off. "Well, for the time that we're here, let's let bygones be bygones. We're in this together. And what happens in allegedly Ireland stays in Ireland." He wiggled his eyebrows at me.

I clasped my hands together tightly and steadied my breathing. I had to remember that this man was a monster. He would not see or think the way a normal person would. "What happened to you? I can't imagine you were always this way for Mae and Blake to love you so much."

Phillip tilted his head and considered me. "Fine, you want answers?"

I nodded my head. I was bordering on panic inside; discussing his internal craziness would be enough of a distraction to my growing stress.

Something flashed beneath his eyes. Confusion? Remorse? Sadness? He quickly regained his mask of a smile, showing me his teeth. But it was too late. I noticed it. Mae had alluded to something having happened to him. It was beyond the hurt that most of us encountered with the loss of loved ones or our former selves. No, something more sinister affected Phillip. Perhaps it was still happening.

I frowned. "Are you possessed? Or cursed?"

Phillip stood up, dead eyes not matching his smile. "Now, wouldn't that be fun?" he whispered, before turning and leaving my room.

"Ok so you really aren't going to answer my question?" I called after him.

He hadn't exactly said no. I was on to something.

I spent the next couple hours trying every way I could to teleport or communicate with my friends, but nothing worked. I was interrupted a few times by unrecognizable sounds from outside. It was now fully dark, and something flew past my window. I couldn't tell what it was behind the curtain, but I saw the shape of a large, eagle-sized bird. Only it was not an eagle because it had pointed ears and a long, thin tail. Nine years in, and this new world was still creepy, especially at night, and for the first time, I was alone.

I cursed and I kicked the furniture. I was enraged. I was mad at Lisa for doing this when I had a real shot at winning. She could have talked to me beforehand about the banishment. We could have planned it together. I would have gone for it. It was much better than dying if I didn't win. However, she'd taken the choice from me and treated me like a threat. Maybe we weren't as close as I believed.

I wondered if the others were forcing her to get us back. We'd only been gone a few hours, but that would have been enough time for them to have her bring me back and yet, I was still here. Were they unable to get her to bring me back? Or did it mean that they agreed with what she'd done? Maybe they were too scared that I wouldn't win that final round, and Erik, knowing that I'd asked him to kill me if I lost, thought that this was a better option.

My heart hurt when I thought of that. I'd left Erik without telling him how I felt about him. I had barely been kind to him. He'd been good to me, and I'd treated him like a stranger.

What if I couldn't return any time soon? Would he give up on me? Find another mate? Marry Raya? What if by the time I returned, he had moved on?

I rubbed at my eyes. I thought of Erik's handsome face, his scowl that I found so annoying but cute. I willed my thoughts to him. Thoughts of how much I cared about him, perhaps even loved him. That part hurt the most. He might live the rest of his life never knowing the truth.

I didn't know how the mate bond worked. Would he eventually be able to find me? Could we share a psychic link like Phillip and I?

I waited in agonizing silence for anything of Erik to press into my mind, but there was nothing.

Eventually, my little bit of energy dried up, and I grew tired. I dragged a chair from a desk across from the bed to the door and rested it under the doorknob. I didn't trust Phillip, and if he tried to come in while I was sleeping, I wanted to be ready.

～

I woke up to immense pressure on my chest, and my breath trapped in my lungs. I was sure I was having the heart attack that I had been eluding before drifting off to sleep. I opened my eyes in a panic, thinking I was dreaming, but it was no dream. I was trapped beneath a great shadow. It was more translucent, as I could vaguely see the ceiling past it. The mass was large and human-shaped. I tried to move my arms and legs, but they would not bulge. I was paralyzed under the grip and weight of this shadow figure. I tried to cry out, but no sound was released.

I was helpless. My heart began to race as panic grew. I let out a soundless whimper, still trying to move, but my body refused to cooperate. Closing my eyes tightly, I focused on my magic, envisioning the mass being thrown off of me. But it did not budge. In fact, the pressure only increased as the dark, translucent figure tightened its hold on my wrist.

Suddenly, I heard a thudding on the door.

Pounding.

"Amina!" Phillip shouted. "You okay? Open up!"

Hope surged through me. Times were hard if I was wishing for Phillip to save me. I couldn't respond, and I feared he would give up.

The door burst open, and I could make out part of him behind the figure.

"Get away from her!" he shouted.

The figure shifted, then dispersed in an explosion of dark smoke, but not before turning and hissing at Phillip, spitting out his name in a thick whisper.

I gasped for air, and I could hear myself now. The pressure was gone from my chest, and I was able to move.

Phillip raced over to me and grasped my arms. "What the hell was that?" he asked me, a genuine look of concern on his face.

I moved away from him and noticed then that my chair was no longer near the door and it wasn't knocked to the ground when Phillip burst in. It was upright in front of the desk where I'd originally retrieved it.

"The hell?" I whispered.

A door slammed from somewhere in the apartment and I jumped, taking Phillip along with me.

"Someone broke the ward," I stated.

Phillip shook his head. "I didn't feel it break."

We waited for footsteps, but nothing came.

The sound of something breaking. Perhaps a dish or a lamp. I couldn't tell.

"I don't think anyone's in here," Phillip stated in a careful voice.

"Then what in the world is going on?"

"Let's get the hell out of here."

Phillip grabbed my hand and I didn't fight him as we ran out of the apartment, down the steps, out of the building, and onto the vacant street. Dawn was approaching, thankfully.

"Haunted house," I heard Phillip mutter. "I should set that place on fire."

I looked back at the apartment building. All of the windows were now filled with light, looking deceivingly inviting in this barren city. The front door slammed shut. Soon other doors on the block began to open and shut.

"Let's get away from here," Phillip stated.

I nodded and followed him as we headed to the end of the street and off the block.

"Now we know why this area is vacant," I said.

"That was a ghost," Phillip said, looking around as we walked. "You're sure you're okay?"

I frowned and shivered; not answering. I hated ghosts more than anything. They were one of the few supernatural entities that I couldn't understand. My magic simply didn't work on them. They required spells and incantations and a lot of energy to banish.

We walked on a few blocks in silence, passing more dilap-idated houses and a few boarded-up businesses, pubs, and restaurants. All vacant. It seemed that the locals left the city like many cities in America. Large cities were the most heavily-populated with the paranormal, the good, bad, and scary.

Phillip walked over to a silver SUV and opened the front passenger door. He looked in then motioned me over. "Get in," he ordered, leaving the door open.

I frowned. "Why?"

"Because we're both tired, and it's still dark out and risky. I'm assuming the creepy crawlies come out more at night here, like in the States. I'm hoping these cars aren't haunted," he replied, walking over to the driver's side door.

I got in and closed the door. Made sense. He was an ass, but he was a smart ass.

He got in the car and closed his door. "You okay?"

I sighed. "Stop asking me that."

"I'm just saying you sounded kind of upset back there?"

"A ghost tried to kill me and all it took was you yelling like some angry dad for it to disappear. Did you send it to scare me?"

He sneered. "That would be childish. That wasn't me. But, I'm talking about before all that."

I bristled. Of course, I knew he heard me having a fit, but it was still embarrassing to be confronted with it.

"You're upset about more than just our predicament, right? If you want to talk about it, I'm here."

I gave him a sideways glare. "In what upside-down world would I ever confide in you? I'm fine."

He snorted. "You're not. I've been where you are. You feel like the hits just keep on coming, and you can't get control of anything."

"No, seriously, I'm not going to share my innermost thoughts with you so you can skip the therapist routine."

"Fine. Let's talk about something else."

"Must we?"

"You seriously aren't behind us not getting home?" He rested his head on the headrest, looking weary.

"Are you really going to keep asking me that question?"

He didn't say anything.

I shifted in my seat and turned my back to him. "How'd you know I was in trouble?"

He pointed to his head. "Soulmates, remember?"

"And you came to help me."

He looked over at me. "I never said I didn't care about you, *mi corazón*. Besides, if you die, then I die, and who wants that?"

Didn't he want me gone?

CHAPTER 14

I woke up with a start. For a moment, I didn't know where I was. I looked around and realized we were still inside the SUV. I squinted and shielded my eyes with my arm as daylight spread through the windows.

Phillip snored lightly beside me. For a moment, in that peaceful state, he looked innocent and good. Like the man that I had first fallen for in my dreams. I knew better now.

I leaned over him to look at the watch on his wrist. It was after 9 a.m. My stomach rumbled, and my throat felt dry. We needed food and water.

I opened the car door and felt a hand on my wrist. I turned back to face Phillip, who looked at me with sleepy eyes.

"I need to find a bathroom and get food and water," I explained, yanking my arm away. He had one more time to grab me before I kicked him in the privates.

"We don't separate," he replied in a groggy voice before opening his door and getting out.

"I'll do what I want."

I got out of the car and stretched, raising my arms to the

sky and looking around. In the daylight, the area looked less scary, well, outside of the destruction and eerie quiet. I wondered if the whole city was abandoned. It would be a shame. I'd really loved Dublin the last time I visited. It held a cheerful people and old-world culture I found charming.

We walked a few minutes in silence and then found a small café. The door was closed and the front window was still intact. We could assume one of many things when we entered a building that wasn't too dilapidated. First, it could be safe because there was no damage by the supernatural. Second option, it could be empty, and there wouldn't be anything of use inside because people weren't in a rush and had taken the time to close the doors. Or third, it could be haunted.

I frowned, suddenly recalling something. "It knew your name." I stopped walking, standing at the entrance of the café.

Phillip walked into the building and began to inspect the surroundings. "I think there's food here. Maybe the town was functioning for some years after the Event then. Something more recent must have run them off. You can use a spell to make rotten food good again, right? That was never my thing," he said, standing behind the counter.

I walked in towards the counter, passing several small circular tables and chairs. There was a narrow hall behind the counter off to the right that I assumed led to a kitchen and bathroom. "Did you hear me?" I asked, hands on my hips.

"The ghost knew my name. Yeah," Phillip replied with a bored tone, continuing his inspection of the café.

I shrugged. "You don't care?"

He turned on the sink faucet in a preparation area behind the counter. No water came out. He cursed under his breath.

"I care," he replied.

"Maybe that ghost wasn't coincidental then."

"I came to that conclusion as well. Just because I didn't bring it up, doesn't mean it hasn't been on my mind. You didn't seem to really want to chat with me earlier. I can only assume that monstrosity knew you as well."

"Yep, since it was trying to kill me and all. I could see a ghost coming for you but why me? And why did it leave so easily?"

Phillip turned to me with a frown. "Why *me?*"

"I'm sure you've killed innocent people."

Phillip shook his head. "Actually, no."

He walked past me and headed down the hall. I followed.

"Mae told you about the big bad that's coming?" Phillip asked, turning his head slightly back to me.

I nodded as we entered a small kitchen area. "She mentioned something coming, but she wasn't certain what."

"Wouldn't be surprised if that ghost was related to the big bad. Here we are, isolated from our support. We're easy prey. Tell Lisa, good job." He opened the large industrial refrigerator and stifled a gag before covering his mouth.

"I will. So, you think they, whoever *they* are, know we're here and they sent a ghost to scare us?"

"I know I look smart, but I actually don't have all the answers." He crossed his arms. "I think we have enough to put together a meal with magic. After this, we need to drive and find people who can help us."

We magically cooked up a meal; spinach quiche. It was slim pickings, unsurprisingly. I packed a bag of jelly sandwiches I made, with the hope that we'd find a water source soon.

We got back onto the street and began to return to the SUV.

"We should stop in a bar and get some whiskey," Phillip thought aloud.

"We aren't on vacation," I muttered. "We need to be sharp."

Phillip looked unconvinced. "I'm less inclined to annoy you if I can get a drink. Not to mention we need hydration."

"I don't think alcohol will help with that." I rolled my eyes as I followed him across the street to a small pub. He headed to the barely-stocked bar and threw out his hand towards me, keeping his back turned as he looked over the limited stock. "Pass me the extra tote." He ordered.

I dug through my tote for the folded up additional one, then paused. "Say please."

He turned to me with a smile. He winked. "Please, *mi corazón.*"

"Don't call me that," I grumbled, passing the tote to him.

"Why? Does it bother you?"

I sighed. "Get that one last bottle of whiskey so we can keep moving. We're burning daylight. After all this time, are we even sure that what's in there is even what's labeled?"

"We'll find out. More than likely, they made their own and just reused the bottles. Still Irish whiskey, so I'm fine with that." He took the tote and raised his hand. A dusty bottle of whiskey floated off the top shelf towards him. He grabbed it, then magically grabbed the bottle of vodka and placed them in the bag. "Got to have options."

"Great, the bar is officially dry." I shook my head and walked across the room and out of the pub.

There was a man in the street, and he was looking at me.

I stopped suddenly at the door.

He had toffee-colored skin with deep-brown eyes. His jet-black hair was short, and he was maybe five-foot-nine, with an average frame covered by a tailored black suit.

"We have company," I said.

Phillip walked up behind me. He paused momentarily, seeing the man, and then he walked around me; stopping in front of me.

I moved partially from behind him. "Sir, do you live in this area?" I called.

The man looked at me and then Phillip. He squinted his eyes. "Phillip and Amina," he replied in a sophisticated, British accent.

Part of me hoped he was sent here to help us. Most of me knew he was sent here to hurt us. There was an energy about him that did not register as friendly. I received quick confirmation when he threw his hands up to the sky, and a strong wind from seemingly nowhere lifted us off our feet and then dropped us on our behinds.

"I'll take that as a no," I grumbled, getting to my feet.

"Tell us who you are and stop attacking us," Phillip demanded. His voice was laced in his mind-controlling magic.

The man gave us saddened eyes but said nothing. How odd. He was the one attacking us, why would *he* be sad?

Phillip stood beside me silently, his face visibly straining, veins in his neck pronounced. Soon his face relaxed, replaced with a worried look. "He isn't controlled by us."

"Maybe he has mind control abilities as well," I replied. "It would cancel our power out."

"But even my body control powers aren't working."

The ground shook, and I held tightly to my tote as if that fabric full of food would steady me to the ground. Phillip placed his tote on the ground and stood up on shaky legs, feet wide apart to remain balanced.

He shot out his arm and psychically pushed the man, who slid back, tumbling to his knees.

The ground stopped shaking. I put my bag down as well and stood up in time for the mystery man to regain his balance and push out wind magic with his hand. This time, Phillip was ready, and the gust of wind hit an invisible wall in front of us. We felt not even a breeze. Impressive.

I looked at the man on the other side of the wide street, his face unmoved. He took in a deep breath and then exhaled. A thick cloud of dark smoke came from his mouth. It grew in size as it surrounded us.

It seeped into Phillip's invisible box, turning our safe zone into a smokehouse. Phillip let down his magic, coughing in fits.

I covered my nose and mouth and dropped to my hands and knees, pulling at Phillip's jeans for him to do the same. He came down and I looked ahead, seeing what I assumed was the mystery man's expensive-looking loafers slowly approach us.

I shot my right hand upward and pushed the smoke out in the shape of a tunneling tornado.

The smoke flew past the man, separating all around him as if repelled. His eyes were no longer deep brown but fully engulfed in fire. I thought he was another witch, but this eye thing threw me.

Man with fire. Mae's premonition rang in my head. He clearly wasn't on our side. What was his role in me getting to power in Silver Spring?

Eyes of fire, what was he? More importantly, how could he see?

Could he have been a fire mage? If so, he'd be tough to beat. As a witch, I could create fire, but it was basic compared to what a fire mage could do. Mages were the experts in whatever they had the natural power to control. A fire mage could walk through fire and not get burned. They could turn fire into the shape of weapons without the use of a spell. They could keep a fire going far and wide, long after they'd gone on to new ventures. This was true of all mages and their specialties.

Of course, that wouldn't explain why he wasn't affected by our body control magic. Every creature or life form on earth, natural and supernatural, could be under our control, according to Mae. She could be wrong, and there was a limit or... this man was not of earth.

I didn't have time to figure it out. Scary dude was probably going to shoot us with his laser beam eyes. Then we'd be toast. Fire would not be my weapon of choice.

I pushed my hand onto the street. The ground rumbled and broke apart. Several golf ball-sized pieces of asphalt rose up and shot out at the man, pelting him in a barrage of rock until he was knocked to the ground, bloodied and unconscious.

Phillip jumped up and helped me to my feet. "Good job," he complimented me. "I can see how you won your round." He honestly looked impressed as he eyed me with intrigue.

"Yeah," I said simply, not wanting to make this a bonding moment.

He bent down and picked up our totes. Miraculously, his tote of liquor was still intact.

I looked over at the man. "Who was he? How did he know our names?" I wondered aloud. I tentatively walked over to the man. He was still unmoving, eyes closed. "Is it silly to wonder if he has an ID on him?"

I kicked the man's foot like a curious little kid and jumped back. He didn't move. Maybe I had already killed him. I grew sick at the thought. Killing people was the last resort for me. I didn't want to pile up a count of those I'd murdered. Even if it was for self-defense.

"I shouldn't have to tell you this, but please stop playing with the dead body," Phillip called from behind me. "Now, let's go see if we can find others to get us home."

I turned halfway to Phillip. "I'm checking to make sure he's out before I search his pockets. Maybe he has some type of ID on him. Who was this guy? What did he want from us? Why try to hurt us?"

"Amina, run!" Phillip shouted.

I didn't look behind me. Instead, I tried to take off in a sprint but my legs wouldn't move. My limps were frozen.

Phillip dropped the totes and ran to me but was blown back towards the café by an impossibly strong wind. It felt hot, like the inside of an oven. I twisted my upper body around and saw the mystery man sitting upright, hand clawed out towards me as if he were gripping an invisible object.

My left leg snapped and I cried out, dropping to the ground. There was no doubt that he had broken my leg at the shin. Tears welled in my eyes as throbbing pain overwhelmed me. I didn't have time to whimper too much because my body was sliding back towards the man. My jean-covered bottom burned against the asphalt and I clawed at the pavement in a futile attempt to stop my movement.

Suddenly, the pulling stopped.

I twisted to the man and saw him clutching his eye, an arrow sticking out of it. He didn't scream. Another arrow pierced his chest, then another. I looked around. Phillip was struggling to his feet, hunched over. This wasn't his doing.

I turned back to the man and threw out my hand to attack, but he was now surrounded by a cloud of black smoke. I called out a paralyzing spell, but it seemed to do nothing. His shape was gone. There was no man now. Only a fire burning on the street where he'd once sat. I closed my fist and the fire dissipated. No burned corpse remained.

Phillip raced to me and hovered his hands over my broken leg, healing me with his magic.

"Where'd he go?" I asked. I winced at the pain of my broken bone reconnecting as it healed.

"Back to hell. Who helped us?" he questioned, still healing my broken leg.

"Well, aren't you lucky? You only shattered one bottle," we heard a male voice say behind us in a thick, Irish accent.

We turned to the voice and found a man hunched over, going through our totes. He was fair-skinned with short, orangey-red hair and a long, matching beard. He wore dingy jeans and a black T-shirt, which partially covered an arm full of tattoos that led up to his neck. On his back was a case of arrows and a sling.

So, he was the mysterious arrow man.

Man with the arrows. So far, Mae's words were all falling into play. I had to find out who this guy was.

He grabbed our totes and stood up, looking at us. He was maybe in his late 30s or early 40s. Heavy living covered his face, making him possibly younger than he appeared, as there was a youthfulness in his eyes. He had a lined forehead and crow's feet surrounded his steel-gray eyes. I noticed he was also wearing a holster with a gun and a knife sheath.

"If I were you two, I'd get out of here before your friend returns," the man stated.

"Those are our bags," Phillip thundered, helping me get to my feet.

I kicked out my left leg. Good as new. I kind of loved magic.

"And you're welcome," said the red-haired man.

I sighed. "Sorry for our lack of manners. Thank you. You saved my life." I smiled genuinely.

Redhead winked at me.

"Everything all right over here, Ed?" Another Irish voice shouted.

Soon several people, men and women of differing ages with masks covering their noses and mouths, appeared. Their clothes were slightly frayed and dingy, just like Red's. They were carrying weapons ranging from guns to swords to knives. All weapons were aimed at Phillip and me.

I raised my hands in surrender. Phillip kept his hands low with a look of annoyance.

"Everything's all right," Red, now known as Ed, replied. "They got us groceries."

Phillip grumbled.

"They got weapons, yes?" asked one woman with chin-length, brown hair. She had slightly-crazed, smiling, emerald eyes and was athletically built. She also had two handguns aimed at me. Not cool.

"No weapons, but they got powers," Ed stated.

"One of *them*, huh?" said another man, closing in on us, sword in hand.

"We aren't going to hurt you. Your friend, Ed, saved our lives." I assured them.

"You got here, how?" the woman asked, circling me; still smiling eerily.

"Can we have this discussion somewhere else? Before that man who can't be killed comes back." Phillip asked, an impatient edge to his voice.

The woman did a little jig. "Oh, let him come back. I want to kill him. Ed, you always have all the fun."

I decided something was off about her.

"We don't let your kind in our village," said another man with short black hair. He glared at us in disgust.

Phillip looked down at me with raised eyebrows. "So, with all that is going on in the world, these guys are racist too? That makes sense?" He crossed his arms, looking back at them.

"No, we got no quarrel with colored people," shouted an armed man with a bald head.

"Colored people?" I said, scrunching my face.

Ed sighed. "This is really not where this conversation should be going. Please excuse Mac. He should really just look and not speak," he said loudly. "We may not have a lot of black people in Ireland, none in our village, but we certainly aren't racist. We were talking about people with powers."

I nodded slowly. "Your village is just full of regular humans?"

The others, about five of them, nodded. Then that

explained the dingy clothes. They'd probably run out of detergent a long time ago, and if they didn't have electricity, they were doing laundry by hand. The masks were probably to keep themselves safe from the Sickness.

"Well, that's a little hurtful," Phillip said, with a frown. "We would never be part of a village that was so exclusive. We are all human."

I turned my head slowly to him, struggling to keep my face neutral. He ignored my gaze boring into the side of his face.

"You people always bring destruction," shouted Mac, clearly not getting the warning that Ed gave him. "You're the reason all this mess started. You brought the Sickness!"

"We are just as innocent as you," I said back. "I had no control over becoming what I am. My parents didn't change. They died of the Sickness as well. I'd give anything to go back to the way things were."

The group went silent.

Ed, who I was beginning to believe was the leader, spoke up. "How'd you get here?" he asked, eyes slit in suspicion. "You sound American."

"Long story. But let's just say magic and against our will."

Ed raised an eyebrow. "You were banished?"

I scratched my neck, feeling awkward. It was hard for us to look like the good guys when we were kicked out of our home. "No, we have people at home who want us back. But we were sent away by magic we can't break or we'd just tele-port ourselves back."

"We were hoping we'd find someone who had a boat or could fly a plane, with magic, to get us back," Phillip added.

"Where do you magic people live?" asked the crazy woman. She lowered her guns now but I knew she could put a bullet in me faster than I could say a spell.

"America. Near Washington, D.C."

The group grew silent again. Then burst into laughter.

Phillip looked back at me. "Did I say something funny?"

I shrugged.

"No one here has the capabilities or the time to get you to America. At least, not right now." Ed crossed his arms and considered us. "So, you'll have to stay here."

Phillip opened his mouth to speak, but I spoke first. "Can we stay in your village until we can get home?" I threw up my hands. "I realize you said no people with powers, but we can keep our gifts under wraps. We're witches, so it'll be easy. Or we could use our magic to make things better for you. Heal the sick. Ward your town. We won't cause any trouble. We're good people." I looked up to Phillip. "Right?" And if Mae thought it important enough to refer to this Ed guy, I had to stay close to him. If I didn't, it was quite possible her premonition wouldn't be realized.

Phillip slowly nodded, lips pursed together.

The group gathered together and whispered, shooting suspicious looks at us every once in a while, except the crazy-eyed woman who waved at us from the huddle.

Phillip turned to me. "They aren't going to want a bunch of strangers in their town. Besides, they don't have the means to help us. We should just keep going."

"And go where? We don't know this country. We don't know how long it might take us to find other people. If we stick with them, we might have a better chance of meeting people who can help us. Regardless, we need to be part of a town to survive."

"But a town of—" he lowered his voice even more "—non-gifted humans? How can they help us?"

"Well, they survived this long, and Ed just took out a magic being. There are a lot of strong ungifted humans out there. I live with some in Hagerstown. It's time you see things differently, as well."

"Fine," Ed called. "You can help us in town. Heal some of our sick, grow food, get our electricity working. You can stay with us on a trial basis. You do anything funny and you're out, unless we decide to kill you."

"Thank you," I said.

"And you can tell us more about you on the way." He handed one of the totes back to us. The one with the food. He kept the one with the liquor.

CHAPTER 15

We headed back to Ed's village in our SUV. They came in two cars but were all too happy to have us use our spells to get other cars working. So much for not liking our kind. Gas was a hot commodity nine years in. No one was exactly importing and exporting it and most of our gas was taken from what was left at gas stations we scouted and cars on the road. That was just about gone now, and most mobile cars were electric or hybrid cars that were magically powered. Gas based cars could still run if powered by magic but not for long.

"I see you aren't out of gas here," Phillip observed.

"We use electric cars. Ran out of gas options a while ago," Ed explained while walking to our SUV before we hit the road.

"I thought you were anti-paranormal humans," I stated. "How'd you get cars to work?"

"We used to know a tech mage. He got a load of cars running before we parted ways. We also work with a village in Galway that has a lot of your kind there."

"I guess we aren't all so bad," Phillip muttered.

Ed shrugged. "The pretty lady rides with me," He stated,

looking over at me. "You go with Peter over there," He said to Phillip, pointing to an older blond-haired man.

Phillip moved closer to me. "Or, just a thought, I go with Amina."

Ed gave him an amused smile. "Or I can leave both of you here. We don't know you and, honestly, don't trust you. If something goes down with one, at least we have the other as insurance."

I frowned. I wasn't exactly jumping up and down to stay with Phillip, but I didn't want him causing a fight if we were separated either, especially if that resulted in me getting hurt. I was in no mood to talk about the whole soulmate linking just yet.

"That's fine," I said, eyeing Phillip.

He raised the corner of his upper lip in a silent snarl and then proceeded to speak to me in Spanish. Now, my Spanish comprehension game was severely lacking, but for some reason, I understood everything he said to me.

"Be careful. I don't like the way the red-headed guy looks at you. Kill him if he tries anything. Be safe," he said in Spanish.

I cocked an eyebrow and without thinking, replied in perfect Spanish. "I'm better off with him than you."

His eyes widened then narrowed before he turned away and went to the other car. Well, that was curious. How had we just communicated in Spanish when I only knew the bare minimum? On my best days, all I could do was read it. And yet, here we were talking normally as if it were nothing. Phillip, although raised most of his life in the U.S., was origi-nally from the Dominican Republic, so Spanish was natural for him. Could our bond even stretch so far as to include knowledge? Did I know what he knew and vice versa? Again, I wondered how deep our bond went. Could he read my thoughts? If he could, he hadn't given it away.

"Come on, darlin'," Ed called, honking the horn of the car,

unfazed by our exchange in Spanish. I got in the front passenger seat, continuing to look at Phillip as he got in his assigned car.

"He your boyfriend?" Ed asked.

My eyes widened, and I shook my head quickly.

Ed snorted. "Well, he thinks he is."

Ed mentioned that they lived thirty minutes outside of the city, but it would take closer to an hour due to the state of the roads. So, there would be plenty of time to tell our life's stories.

Ed drove us out of the city into a suburban area, which was a longer but safer route to their town. He mentioned that although their highways were much quicker, they were a nightmare to get around. Apparently, there were still many abandoned cars there from attempts to flee the city when vampires and ghosts attacked, and the Sickness came. Highways were now graveyards that attracted those who fed on the dead and anyone simple enough to go there. He was surprised we were still alive, but when I mentioned that we were run out of an abandoned apartment due to ghosts, he gave an "A-ha."

"You seem pretty all right but, your mate seems like a bit of an arse. Can we trust him?" he asked, giving me a quick side-eye.

"Sure, you can... most of the time. He's just a bit... uptight."

He grumbled something unintelligible. "I must say, this magic you lot have is amazing. You can turn rotten food into edible food and restart technology. How did you learn about these spells? You say you weren't a witch before all of this, right?"

I withheld the fact that we were actually life mages. I didn't think it would go over well to tell them that Phillip and I had power over anything living. Anyway, mages were a subset of witches, so I wasn't lying. "Correct. I found spell books at specialty book stores, met other witches who shared their knowledge, and then there's the internet."

He looked quickly at me with a frown. "You still have bloody internet access?"

I nodded. "Yes, if it weren't for witches and mages, America would have a hard time getting back together. I mean, it's still having problems, but now we can at least communicate with each other without having to leave our towns, at least with others who have internet. Makes it much easier to coordinate efforts."

"Guess you're having an easier go of it," he grumbled, shaking his head. "We've visited some other villages that have the internet as well. The tech mage we met didn't stick around long enough to get the internet working. He was only passing through and fixed a few of our cars and got our electricity going in exchange for food. That was almost three years ago. But when anything breaks, we're out of luck. The only other way to keep electricity working is to have a steady source of magic around."

"And since you don't let magic humans live in your town, until now, you can't keep things working."

Ed scratched his beard. "We'd let some folks from a town in Galway live with us but they aren't too keen on coming to Dublin and we aren't too keen on moving to Galway. I like our town. It's got many resources nearby and they aren't scarce yet. Plus, their leader is an arse."

"Do you have computers or laptops in your town?"

"Yeah, as decoration."

"We can help get them working. I can try to reach my people in America, too. And we can try to fix anything that's broken."

"So, you Americans are doing well?"

I gazed back out of the window at streets filled with abandoned houses and closed businesses. I knew not all of Dublin city was forgotten but we seemed to be taking the quiet route. "Not everywhere. It's still a divided country. The government's trying to start up like it used to be but there are still a bunch of independent towns. I'm sure there are many towns like yours in America. Places that have essentially gone off the grid because they don't have a tech mage or witch near them. Or maybe don't even want to be bothered with technology and electricity anymore. Simple life might be easier."

"It has its charms. I have no idea what's going on in my country and not sure that I care. I raced out of the city when people started getting sick. The best way to survive is to isolate yourself from strangers. The suburbs are the safest. Countryside is best from the Sickness, but then you get more of the hard-to-kill monsters."

I lifted a brow. He certainly had a point and from what I knew of the state of Ireland it had taken a heavy hit with the return of magic. It was a magnet for supernatural events and creatures.

"Also, the suburbs have fewer supernatural packs. If we just get a random stray magic, like a selkie or a goblin, we're lucky."

"Selkie?"

"We're near the water, so we get a few creatures of the sea wandering over to us from time to time. Selkies are like seals that can become human. They aren't a bother, but some have gotten into our village. Caused a bit of mischief is all."

"Oh, like mermaids?"

He nodded. "Something like that. Now, the fairies... bloody bastards. The changelings, in particular, are a dangerous lot. They love stealing little children, especially the babies."

I opened my mouth in shock. "My friend who sent us here is a fairy."

"You understand what I mean then. She's not your friend. Once our wall is fully up, it'll be easier to fight against them."

We fell quiet for a while as we left the suburbs and headed into the countryside. Fields of lush, tall grass below a now gray and cloudy sky filled my view. With the country's population reduced to half its size and no signs of life as we drove, the cloud-covered sky only added to a gloomy atmosphere.

A town of green. More of Mae's vision played in my head. By green, had she meant plant life? This area was full of vibrant nature. I could only assume that Ed's town was part of that as we headed farther from the city. A bubble of excitement grew in me. What if this was the start of the chain of events leading to Phillip's defeat?

"At least your nature looks nice and healthy," I observed.

Ed scoffed. "A quarter of the plant life here will eat you alive, darlin'."

I grimaced. "What happened to your town that made everyone agree to ban paranormal humans?" I asked, still gazing out of the window.

He grunted. "Early in our first year as a town, almost four years ago now, we were more vulnerable. We didn't have as many people or weapons. Many times, we fell under attack by fairies. We eventually had to move. I don't think the Fae were ever human. They probably just came here from the fairy world or some shite."

"The fairy world?"

"They have a whole different dimension where time passes differently. We only know this because someone was actually able to escape after being kidnapped by the Fae. She was maybe a ten-year-old girl when they took her but thirteen when she returned. They took some of our children and adults. Killed a few as well. I still have battle scars from that fight."

"Why?"

"Their population is small. They like to build their ranks by finding people to have children with. And they have this fascination with children. Easily pliable, so that they can become future mates when they're old enough, I suppose. The ten-year-old, Maddy, is the only one to ever come back. She claimed she'd only been in the fairy world a few months. But we knew she'd been gone almost three years. And she still looked ten, not thirteen like she should have been. Her mother had died a year after she was taken. Some say of a broken heart. She just went to sleep one night and never woke up. And here was her little girl, as if no time had passed."

"Geez."

He shrugged. "So, you see, we aren't too keen on magic. It hasn't done us much good. Except for the cars."

I stopped myself from asking what made him change his mind about allowing Phillip and me to come back with him. Suddenly the answer seemed very clear. Nothing had changed his mind. *Someone* had. I would have to choke Phillip when I saw him.

On the one hand, using his magic to convince them to let us come to their town was doing the very thing they hated us for. On the other hand, if he hadn't, we'd still be roaming the Irish streets looking for help.

I'd kick him in the knee cap and get him under control as soon as we had a private moment. I decided not to bring up the subject to Ed. If he even suspected we were using magic on him, he'd kick me out of this car while it was still moving. I didn't want to press my luck with his kindness. He didn't seem like the type to randomly give it.

I looked back out of the window and squinted my eyes. There was a person waving his or her arms, standing on the side of the road farther up.

The car in front of us slowed down in front of what I could now see was a man and then sped up, driving on.

Soon our car passed but did not slow down. I looked out at the man as he stared at us with pained, watery eyes. He looked older, perhaps in his late 40s, with thinning hair and a frail frame. His lips were cracked and dry, and his skin was just as dehydrated and splotchy.

"He looks like he has the Sickness. Is that why no one stopped?" I asked.

"Correct. Could be something else, but who wants to risk it nowadays? I feel for the poor bastard but I can't take any chances. We just had to send out a man who caught the Sickness while on a scout. Some arse we ran into sneezed on him."

"That doesn't mean he caught it. If he doesn't show signs in a week, he's fine."

"And during that week, he could have spread it to others. We aren't monsters. We have a house outside of our village that we put the sick in. They get exiled a week until we are sure they don't have the Sickness. Then they can come back. He didn't."

"Phillip or I could have given the man food."

"And how do you know that just because you don't get sick, you aren't carriers? That poor bloke touches you and you come back to my town and spread the Sickness. Everyone who isn't immune dies and you come out without so much as a cough. I can't place that kind of risk on my people."

He had a point. His people had only survived this long by being careful and diligent. I hadn't come across many human-only towns. They were the most vulnerable but the smartest. They took no unnecessary chances and remained on high alert, putting in systems to ensure the safety of their people from the supernatural and the Sickness. They didn't have the benefits of wards and other magic. They only had their own strength and intelligence. I was very curious how Ed's town existed in this world.

"Are you the leader? I assume you are," I stated.

"Of sorts."

"What did you do before this?"

He gave a quick shrug. "A little of this, a little of that. Mostly construction. Look, people just followed me in the beginning because they thought I was the scariest looking. They figured I'd protect them. When those monsters appeared, my mates and I were able to fend them off. We're good with weapons. Probably why I did a tour in prison."

"For killing monsters?" I raised an eyebrow with a smirk on my lips.

He smiled. "For robbing a bank."

"I see." I nodded slowly and adjusted in my passenger seat.

Ed glanced over at me. "I didn't hurt anyone, if that's what you're wondering. You're safe with me, darlin'." He looked back at the road. "I don't profess to be a good man but I've kept the others safe. We have maybe 300 people in our town. We're surviving. We even have a farm and go fishing when it's safe. Even without magic or technology, we're living."

"Clearly," I replied as I gazed out of the window, continuing to enjoy the beauty of the Irish countryside.

～

Once we arrived at the suburban community, Ed parked the car and offered a tour of the town.

Phillip jumped out of the car in front of me and cursed. "This woman cut me!" He exclaimed to whoever was listening.

The crazed woman with the brown bob exited the backseat with a disappointed frown. "I wanted to see if he could heal fast. It's a massive disappointment that he does not," she said, looking very let down.

"You could have asked instead of slicing me in the back of my neck with a damn knife, you crazy *puta*!"

She gave him a confused look. "Well, what's the fun in that? And what did you just call me?"

Phillip gave her an incredulous look. "Keep her away from me."

"Is that any way to treat our guests, Mercy? Now you have to keep your distance," Ed chided her with a look of full amusement. "You'll have to excuse her. She tends to get a bit... stabby, when she likes someone."

She pouted. She had to have been in her mid-to-late-20s, but she behaved as though she were a spoiled teenager. "Aww, but he's so cute. I don't see many like him, except in the old shows. Can I keep him?"

"Fuck, no!" Phillip shouted before turning to me. "Can you heal my bloody neck, please?"

I nodded and then paused. "I didn't get a cut on my neck."

He frowned. "What?"

I looked at the small surface cut on his neck and then touched my own neck to confirm what I already knew. "If you got cut, I should have been cut too, but I wasn't."

Phillip deepened his frown. "How?"

I smiled. "I've gotten stronger." I didn't know for certain, but maybe when I was able to finally block him from my dreams, I was able to put up more of a barrier than I thought. I wondered if that barrier was strong enough to separate us if one died.

"It won't," Phillip stated, lips twisted. "Unless you want to try."

"You could read my mind?"

"I can read your face. You want me dead that bad?"

I narrowed my eyes. "Wouldn't you, if you were me?" I didn't wait for him to answer. "How do you know anyway?"

"There are logical limits on how much we can separate. Unless we split the soul we share, I don't think it would work."

"What are you two going on about?" Ed asked, squinting his eyes as he walked over to us.

"How much he gets on my nerves and that sometimes I

want to kill him." All of that was true. "Turn around, jerk, let me fix your neck."

After I healed Phillip's wound, Ed gave us a walking tour of the town. It was actually a village made up of a collection of streets lined with houses, a couple of corner stores, one café, and fields used as gardens and farms for cattle. It was all surrounded by a wall, built of various housing materials, which went up two stories. There was also a covered tower where someone stood watch.

There were gardens that held arrays of vegetables, fruit, and wheat, while a fenced-off field held a few cows, several chickens, goats, and pigs. In another section of the village, there were also a few horses, which appeared to be the main mode of transportation, along with bicycles. Most of the houses were residences but a few were converted to a school, a hospital, and other needed businesses. There were also vacant houses that they would use as the town grew. Ed mentioned if they needed, they would build more houses or extensions to existing houses.

"How high are you trying to build your wall?" I asked as we walked down the center of one of the streets.

"Tall enough to keep out a giant," he answered.

"If you want, we can ward this village."

"What does that do?" Mercy asked, suddenly appearing beside me.

Phillip snorted. "You don't know what a ward is?"

She peeked around me to smile at Phillip. "That's why I asked, silly."

I rubbed my forehead. "Phillip, please. If someone is covered in a ward or surrounded by a ward, then either she can't get out of the surrounding, or nothing can get into her surrounding. It all depends on the type of ward. There are many types. It's the best tool you have against the supernatural. Even if we leave here, the ward can still hold up unless someone breaks it."

"We had a ward up when we were attacked by Fae before. Didn't keep them out," Ed stated.

"Then it just wasn't strong enough," Phillip surmised. "Amina and I can make you a good one."

"We don't need magic. We've been doing much better since we got the wall up," Mercy said, crossing her arms and glaring at me.

Why was she angry with me? What was her problem? I hoped she didn't think I was a threat to her little crush on Phillip. She could have him.

"You say that now, until some giant troll wanders by and kicks your wall down. Or a vampire leaps over it. Or something swoops in from the sky. Or another witch teleports in," Phillip replied. "You can't fight the supernatural by natural means."

Mercy frowned, her face giving way to worry.

"Well, it certainly can't hurt to have it," Ed replied in a low voice. "And you say it'll last even when you're gone?"

"Until someone breaks it or the maker of the ward dies," I answered.

"Well, then, let's keep you alive."

Phillip and I separated again as I worked on the ward. I didn't trust him to do it, so I sent him to help heal people who were ill. He wasn't too excited about that job, but he was rational enough not to fight me on it.

Only a small handful of people had a problem with us being there and bringing magic. Most of the town, however, seemed to have no problems with getting back to where they were before the world crashed. They were trying to survive and abided by the no-magic rules. However, most of the village residents came after the fairy attack and weren't as rigid about keeping paranormals out, especially if they were willing to help the village.

We were rewarded with a big dinner and an empty

cottage to stay in. Phillip and I had to share and I was not too happy with that, but was too exhausted to make a fuss.

Before my head hit the pillow, we tried to contact our friends via email. If we couldn't get to them via magic or the old school way, maybe they could get to us. I sent emails to Erik and Charles on the desktop computer we found in the cottage's living room.

The emails came back undelivered. Phillip tried as well. Same result.

"Something is beginning to tell me that even if we found a boat or someone who could fly a plane, it wouldn't work," I surmised. Real despair was starting to crash into me. I couldn't be stuck here.

Phillip kicked the computer desk, cursing.

"Easy, man," I stated, throwing a hand out to steady the small metal desk. "Maybe this fairy banishing magic can wear off. Ed says there are lots of fairies in Ireland. Maybe we can find one and they can break the spell."

Phillip looked down on me with a face twisted in anger. "If I see your friend again, I'm going to kill her." He walked past me and headed for the stairs.

If he thought he was going to spend this time threatening me, he had another thing coming. "Hold up, dammit! Come back here! Let's stop this right here, right now." I was tired as hell, mind, body, and soul, but I didn't know how long we had here. If I was stuck with him, we were going to fix this once and for all.

He stopped and turned around, biting his lip. "I kind of like it when you yell at me. Turns me on."

I scowled, giving him the very reaction I knew he loved.

"What do you want to do? The final challenge?"

"Screw the challenge. We're soulmates. It's fair to say that neither of us is more powerful than the other, but we need to stop working against each other."

He crossed his arms. "All I ever wanted."

"Stop threatening my friends and family. Stop being a dick. I know you controlled these people to get them to accept us. Don't do that anymore. They treat us good; we'll do the same."

"They're just humans."

"So are you!" I paused and collected my nerves. I put my hands together in prayer and moved them up to my lips. "I know you aren't possessed. If you were, you would be pure evil. I sense the regret in you and even kindness. Sometimes. Mae believed you could be healed."

He gave me a bored look, eyes lazy. "I told you I wasn't possessed."

"And you weren't always like this either."

"I feel like we've had this conversation before. Correct me if I'm wrong."

I crossed my arms and tilted my head. I was coming to something in my mind. I was beginning to get what was going on now. "You aren't the great evil Mae spoke of. You aren't possessed. But you hate ungifted humans. Maybe you really are cursed. Or did something happen with humans that caused you to change? What did they do to you?"

"What did they do to *you*?" He spat back. "They held you as their slave for half a year. How can you think of them as your equal? If you let humans, no, if you let anyone who isn't as strong as you take control over you, then you're a fool. I use my abilities because I can. Why wouldn't I? Before, I was kind to humans. Our former leader was kinder and because we had powers, he got a little too comfortable. We traded with a group that said they came from Fredericksburg, Virginia. One day, they took advantage of our kindness and kidnapped some of our people. They wanted to use them as slaves. Not in the way those humans did you. They had no formula. They really wanted to use them for magic labor. Since we weren't willing to live with them, they just took."

"Didn't they know you'd come for them?" I asked.

He gave a grimace. "Of course, they did. That's why when we went to the town, it was cleared out. It wasn't a large one to begin with. A quarter of our size. They had planned for this."

"How'd you know it was really them and what they were planning?"

He looked at me with cold eyes. "We found them several months later. Got some revenge. Don't ask what kind."

"That greatly affected you."

His smile returned. "Are you my psychologist now? You want to fix me? I'm not a head case, *mi corazón*. I didn't just wake up and change because some bad guys did some bad things. In the Pre-world, I was getting my MBA. I've got my head on right." He laughed. "I grew to decide that I would never allow myself to be weak."

He could joke around all he wanted, but he'd broken inside and became this new hardcore man. I stood up. "I call bullshit."

He scratched his head. "I am a complex man. Can't it just be that?"

"I'm going to get to the bottom of this whole thing with you," I began. "I won't waste this time that we're here together."

He walked over to me, but I stood unmoving. He brushed my cheek with the back of his hand, and his eyes were large and sincere. For a millisecond, I thought of the man that I'd first met, but that man was a master of lies and deceit. "I wouldn't want us to waste this time alone together either," he said in a low voice.

I moved my head back. "That isn't what I'm talking about, and you know it. You can't even tell me what's happened to you."

"Nothing happened to me. Can't you accept that?"

"If I did, then I would always hate you."

He looked visibly pained by what I said, which I couldn't

reconcile. How could he be so heartless and at times be so sensitive?

"What can I do to change your mind?"

I thought of my friends back home and of all the people he'd hurt. There was nothing. "I don't know that you can. But you could start with lifting your spell on these people."

He frowned. "What? Then they might kick us out of here."

"Then we'll be kicked out. I know it's what you're used to, but we can't control people. We take our chances just like everyone else does."

"But we aren't everyone else. We're better. They are just humans."

"And that, right there, is the reason I could never love you. The man I love is a protector of all people." I pointed my finger at him. "If you do anything to hurt these people, I'll stab you in the eye."

Phillip raised an eyebrow. "That's a very specific threat."

I gave a sinister smile. "Well, I know I can do it without hurting myself now. Break your spell on the villagers!"

He tilted his head, considering me. "I'd like to, *mi corazón*, but I can't. However, you can. I won't stop you, as long as the villagers don't pose a threat."

Why couldn't he do it himself? I wanted to ask but decided not to look a gift horse in the mouth. If he was willing to give in this much, then maybe there was hope for him and I wouldn't have to kill him.

CHAPTER 16

A month later I found myself back home in my apartment in Hagerstown, sitting on the edge of my bed. The sun's rays shone through my window, bathing the room with light. I felt a warm breeze through the open window, informing me that summer was not ready to end. I leaned back onto my hands and sat still, feeling the slight wind on my skin.

"I tried every night to reach you in my mind," I heard his voice say from behind me.

My heart jumped, and I turned to see Erik's back as he sat on the opposite side of the bed facing my doorway.

"I didn't know if weremates had the same type of power to communicate in dreams like soulmates. Everyone said we didn't. But I figure between us being this special Six and you being a soulmate; maybe it would work. So, every night, I went to bed and pictured you in my mind before I fell asleep. Most of the time, the dreams I had of you were just dreams. This is probably the same, but I just... I can't give up," he continued.

I shot up and raced to the other side of the bed. I lowered

myself in front of him and grabbed his face with my hands. "I'm here, Erik."

He searched my eyes, a look of peace in his own. "I search for you every night. For a month, I've been searching."

"You found me. This isn't a dream. Well, it's not a regular dream. We're communicating."

He frowned. "How do I know the difference?"

I shrugged. "I don't know." I let go of his face and sat down beside him.

"Where are you, Mina?" he asked. His eyes looked almost pained now.

"I'm in—" I began to say, but the word wouldn't come out of my mouth. It was as if I had lost my speech. "I'm in— I'm in— I can't say. It's the spell."

Erik seemed to ponder this before speaking again. "Are you in America?"

My body froze. I couldn't so much as shake my head or nod. "I can't say. The spell won't let me."

He cursed under his breath. "I'll work on Lisa. I'll find a way to make her bring you back."

My heart sank. She really didn't want me to return. She had purposefully sent me away. I tightened my hands into fists.

Erik grabbed my hand and brought it to his lips to kiss. "I don't know how I did this or if it's even real, but I'm happy to see you at least. Wherever you are, are you at least safe?"

I nodded. "Yes, we're in a good place. You don't have to worry."

He frowned. "Phillip's still with you? Is he causing trouble?"

"No. He's been on his best behavior. Erik," I looked down at our now entwined hands. I didn't know if I'd see him again. I couldn't waste it. "I miss you. I'm so sorry I pushed you away. I thought I was doing the right thing."

"You weren't," Erik cracked, giving my hand a playful squeeze.

I lightly slapped his chest with my free hand, and he grabbed my wrist. I looked into his hazel eyes, which were filled with something I'd never seen from him before: Heartbreak. He was in pain because of me and there was nothing I could do. "I love you, Mina, you know that? I'm in awe of you," he replied in a whispered voice. "I wanted to say that before."

My vision blurred from the tears that were filling them. "I love you, too."

Erik leaned into me, and I closed my eyes as I felt his lips press onto mine. It had been so long since I kissed him. I didn't want it to end. I scooted closer to him and wrapped my arms around his neck, cherishing the moment as his tongue parted my mouth. I moaned, pressing even closer, and nipped his bottom lip, which sent a growl from him. His lips felt like butter on mine and I craved more.

Erik slowly pulled back, resting his forehead on mine. "I think I have to go."

I grabbed his shirt by the sides, not wanting to let him go. "No."

I felt him chuckle. "If I could snatch you through this dream and bring you home, I would. I just need to say a proper goodbye before I wake up. I'm going to find you, Mina. Stay safe. I don't know if we'll be able to dream meet again, but I'll try. I'll—"

~

I woke up. Afternoon daylight hit my eyes. I lay horizontally on my bed, blinking my eyes as they adjusted to the light, and smiled. This was the first time we'd connected. Usually, dreams of Erik were nonsensical or nonlinear, skipping settings, leading me to believe that they were just my subconscious. However, this was different. This was more like my dream communications with Phillip.

Finding a way to connect with Erik had been a challenge. We were six hours apart, time-wise, so sleeping at the same time was tough. Trying to reach his mind during the day like I could do with Phillip was unsuccessful. Our mate bond just wasn't as powerful.

Connecting with Erik that day had been a complete surprise. It appeared that my Saturday afternoon nap had overlapped with his regular night sleep. I'd tried it before with no success, but now it'd somehow worked.

I got up and did a little two-step in celebration. I still couldn't tell Erik where I was, but this was encouraging.

Perhaps getting home would happen sooner than I thought.

During our stay, we tried everything we could to communicate with home. We even had some town people send emails on our behalf. Their emails went out, but any email mentioning Phillip or myself and being in Ireland just came right back as undeliverable.

I'd never dabbled or encountered Fae magic, outside of Lisa's, and it was proving to be a very challenging magic to overcome. It was actually quite humbling. I had to admit that I was beginning to get a bit cocky with my magic; believing that maybe I *was* super powerful.

A month in, and that confidence had disappeared. So, when I found Erik in my dreams, a spark of hope ignited in me again. I wanted to tell Phillip but decided against it. He'd been suspiciously pleasant the past month, although that didn't mean he wasn't plotting and scheming. I'd come to believe he would never physically hurt me, but he would knock me out of the way if I came between him and his self-interest. Right now, that interest was getting back home, so he could continue his reign of terror. However, if Mae's visions were true, I'd be ending his reign.

The only reason I suspected he wasn't setting up roots here was because he had no interest in running a town of non-paranormal humans. That would be a demotion to him. Although, in a way, he was still running things. The more good he did, the more admiration he gained from the villagers. Even Ed seemed to take to him, and Mercy had actually gotten into a fight with a woman she saw flirting with Phillip. She continuously greeted me with dirty looks when she saw me stand too close to Phillip and I assumed the only reason she hadn't stabbed me was because Phillip had asked her not to.

That Sunday, after my dream communication with Erik, Ed invited us to go fishing. I was looking forward to leaving the small town, just to explore and see what else was out there. After our initial attack in Dublin city, I thought it best to lay low and not venture around. We didn't want whoever that man was, to find us and wreak havoc on the village, but I was getting restless. I figured one lone venture outside of the community might be okay.

We stopped our cars in an open, grassy space that led to a rocky beach and choppy waters under another cloudy, gray sky. People got out and commenced putting together their fishing gear. A nearby group scouted for land animals, seeds, and such. I followed the other group to the water. I'd never been fishing but I figured my magic could aid in collecting fish.

I walked to the edge of the water in my bare feet; my cargo pants rolled up to my calves. Phillip pulled off his shoes, shirt, and pants, revealing swim trunks before walking into the water.

"You don't want to get in the boat?" I asked him, pointing to a few people hopping in a fishing boat tied to a large boulder at the shore.

He shook his head and kept walking, then swam until he stopped abruptly, moving to a floating doggie paddle. I sighed. For a moment there, I was worried he was trying to drown himself, although I hoped he hadn't planned to take me out.

He placed his hand out and slapped the air in front of him. He moved his hands farther out, as if miming, but I knew he wasn't. He was touching a ward. Crap.

He turned to me with neutral eyes.

"Can you break it?" I shouted.

He shrugged and turned back to the ward.

Mercy walked up beside me. "What's this about?" she asked, scratching her head.

"We're warded in," I explained.

"Well, that can't be right. We've sailed these waters loads of times."

"Maybe someone recently warded it."

Mercy shook her head. She pointed out diagonally. "Tell that to the boat rowing past him now."

My eyes followed her hand, and I saw a small boat carrying three people rowing a short distance from Phillip farther into the ocean. Phillip moved horizontally to follow the direct path of the boat. He met the invisible wall again, pushing with seemingly great effort against nothingness.

"Bloody hell," Mercy cursed, running her hands through her short hair.

All hope drained from me. "It's not a ward. It's the magic over us. We can't sail out of here," I stated. My knees betrayed me and I sank to the ground, suddenly devoid of any energy.

"Lucky you found out by water instead of flight first. Can't imagine you both are indestructible. I couldn't have anything happen to my Phillip."

I grimaced, a tightness in my heart growing and stealing my breath. Was I having a heart attack? I was too young for that, right? I poked at my chest in a futile attempt to try to massage the dull pain away.

"You okay?" Mercy asked.

"Just a bit of heartburn. I'll be fine," I replied, hoping that was true.

"Maybe you should lie down in the car."

"Maybe I should." I wiped a bead of sweat from my forehead and stood up on shaky legs. I didn't have time for this, whatever this was.

A loud horn interrupted my pity party. "What is that?"

Mercy ran to the shore. "Get out of the water, Phil!"

The boats turned and headed back towards us as I ran to Mercy. "What's going on?"

"There's danger somewhere. The horn sounds when paranormal danger is round. Someone saw something. We need to take cover. Phil!" She jumped up and down and waved her arms.

Phillip was midway back when he suddenly went under water as if something had snatched him. The backside of a translucent, pale-gray beast rose above the water. Its skin appeared thin and tiny lights presented a glow from within its body like a jellyfish or firefly. Even its internal organs and veins seemed to glow with light. Except it wasn't a jellyfish. It was the size and shape of a whale. Only it wasn't a whale either, because it had a long, thin tail that fanned out at the end. It also... flew. Breaking free from the water, the large beast, which I could see looked like a cross between a seal and a whale, expanded its gray wings and took off several feet in the air with Phillip riding on its back.

"What the fuck?" I wondered in awe.

Phillip clung tightly to the back of the beast, a terrified expression on his face. I didn't know whether to be scared or laugh.

The large beast changed directions and flew low towards

the shoreline. Mercy took a step back and took out her gun, aiming.

I frowned. "No, don't hurt it!"

"It's going to kill my Phillip!" she whined.

I wasn't so sure. It had an opportunity to eat him by now and it chose not to. "Is it?"

The beast gently lowered to the beach, collapsing its wings back into itself. It let out a cackling sound, like that of a dolphin. Its beady eyes looked friendly and unassuming. Phillip slid off the beast and took off towards us.

I walked towards him, and he grabbed my hand as we faced each other. "Come on, let's get the hell out of here," he cried. "I almost died."

I shook my hand free. "I don't think you did. He'd have eaten you if that were true. Instead, he brought you back."

"It's a he now?" he asked, eyebrows raised.

I walked forward, carefully, to the beast. "Don't you think that it's a he?"

"Amina, what are you doing?"

"We have powers over the living. We shouldn't be scared of him." I stopped several feet away from the beast. He looked at me, still resting on the shore. I could see now that he had whiskers and a snout more like a seal. "What are you?"

He made his cackle noise again as if to answer, but of course, I had no idea what he was saying.

I walked to the shore and lowered down, thrusting my hand into the water. A minute later, fish appeared around me, responding to my magic call. I picked one up and walked over to the large beast with my catch.

The beast sniffed the fish and then opened his mouth slightly. I placed the fish inside, praying he wouldn't snap down before I could pull my fingers out. He didn't close his mouth until I took a few steps away, and then he proceeded to eat the fish.

Once done with his mini bite, he cackled again as if in appreciation. "Oh, you're a friendly beast, aren't you? You didn't want to eat that crazy man back there, did you?" I carefully reached out to touch the beast on the snout. He let me without movement. His skin was smooth and thin and the sparkling color in his body danced and shone like carnival lights. I began to stroke the animal on the face and he gave a gentle, rumbling sound.

"So, we don't kill it?" Mercy shouted from a distance.

"No, we don't. He's our friend. I'm sure if you are kind and give him some fish whenever you visit; he'll look out for you when you go fishing. Not all supernatural wildlife is bad."

Phillip gave a disgusted grunt. "You've never seen this thing before?"

Ed, who had gone hunting on land, appeared next to Mercy. "No. This is the first time. Guessing it swam here from another part of the ocean. Probably looking for food."

I continued to pet the beast. "Well, you have a new friend. Andy. Be good to Andy, and he'll be good to you," I stated.

"Andy?"

I gave a curt nod, and smiled at the water beast, finding him oddly relaxing to touch and look at. "You're going to be my new friend. I'll come and visit, okay?"

"Really?" Phillip said with a quizzical tone. "Andy tried to drown me, and now he's your best friend, huh?"

I gave him a wide grin but didn't answer.

Phillip raised an indignant eyebrow and turned away.

Our trip to the ocean proved to be a fruitful one. Other than finding out the final stage of how trapped we were and me making a new animal friend, we also caught a ton of fish, mussels, and clams. Phillip seemed especially excited about the impending seafood fry and not the least bit disturbed about our banishment. More and more, I began to wonder if he had a bigger plan he wasn't sharing.

While Phillip seemed content, my dream visit from Erik helped me to move past devastation and into rage again. At Lisa. She didn't even give me the option to agree to banishment or even say my goodbyes. She disappeared and then came in just when I had a chance of winning. She ruined everything. And now I knew that she was refusing to right her wrong, even with someone she loved, like a brother and the woman who saved her life. I remember seeing in Erik's eyes the pain and anger he had at our separation. How were they handling Lisa all this time? Was she locked up? Did she leave again?

Phillip patted my hand, seated beside me in the back of the jeep as we headed back to the village. "Don't let that anger control you."

I wanted to stab him from the hypocrisy of it all. "What are you talking about?" I spat, moving my hand away.

"I can feel your energy, remember? You're burning so hot with rage, I'm sweating," he cracked, a slight smile on his lips.

Something about his new, calm demeanor worked to soothe me, and I let out a deep sigh as I stared out of the window.

"If it's meant to be, we'll be back. Mae said we had work to do," Phillip stated.

"I didn't think that work was going to be done in Ireland," I muttered.

"For a while, would that be so bad?"

I didn't answer him, just gave him a glare. "A month ago, you hated being here; now it's a vacation."

"I didn't say all that." He shook his head and looked away. "It's just calmer here. Well, outside of almost getting eaten by some ocean beast. I just feel more like my old self."

When we got back to the village, there was an announcement for an impromptu dinner party that sent the village buzzing with preparation. I tried to avoid being a downer and helped prepare food.

The overall celebration was actually a fun one. The Irish, as I recalled from my last visit, knew how to party. The gathering took place inside the local café and spread outside. It was the last few days of the summer months before the November cold would blast in unapologetically. We wanted to make the best of the days left. I could only imagine what an Irish winter felt like since they were already cooler in their summer months, when compared to the U.S.

In front of the café, there was a large bonfire on the street. Most of the people gathered around the fire as they listened to music. We blared some songs from old music players that Phillip and I revived. In between a few songs, a band made up of some of the residents played with musical instruments they had collected over time.

The spread of food consisted of our day's gathering, French fries, or chips as they called them, assorted vegetables, and desserts. Of course, there was booze, beer, and whiskey that they'd learned to craft.

I leaned against a tree, slowly sipping on a glass of whiskey with a plastered smile on my face.

I looked on at Phillip dancing in front of the bonfire with a curvy, red-headed woman. He had a joyful smile on his face and looked genuinely happy. I just didn't get it. He'd been enraged a month ago, and now he was having big fun. This was starting to seem like a punishment just on me.

"I'm going to roast that woman alive," Mercy grumbled, appearing next to me.

I chuckled. "I'd like to see that," I replied. I looked over at her angry face. "You really like him?"

She shrugged. "He's cute, don't you think? And he has that cocky confidence about him that I quite like."

"Then why'd you cut him when you first met him?"

"I was just trying to mark my territory. It's what we did at my old camp."

"What?"

"Before I came here and met Ed, I stayed with a camp back in Belfast for about six years. It was hard, but we were safe. Some people were real dicks there, though. They'd make certain people subservient."

"Where'd the cutting come from?"

"The top people would find men and women they liked and mark them with their initials or some symbol as theirs. No one else could date or have sex with them."

I opened my mouth in surprise. "Are you kidding me? They branded people?"

Mercy nodded before taking a swig of her beer.

I sighed. "Were you marked?"

She nodded again. "Twice. The guy who cut me second, killed the first guy."

"Oh, my God. What kind of barbaric place was this? And you were there for six years? How'd you meet Ed?"

"He had a run-in with the guy who ran the place. They were always fighting each other over things. One day, the fight got bad and Ed's guys came at our guys. Our guys lost. Then we were free to do what we wanted. I followed Ed. He didn't even want to mark me. He said I could stay with his people as long as I contributed. I like it here best."

"How old were you when the world changed nine years ago?"

Mercy scrunched her face in thought. "Well, I'm twenty-five now."

"So, you were sixteen when you were with that camp?"

"Yeah, I guess so. I was almost twenty-two when Ed came."

I shook my head in disgust. If they were branding people, I could only imagine what other horrible things they were doing to people. It explained a lot about Mercy's violent behavior. Who knows how she was in the Pre-world. She'd only been a teenager.

"I'm sorry that you went through all that, Mercy."

She waved her hand at me. "It's all right. I survived the Sickness and not getting eaten by a werewolf or something, so all things considered, I lucked out. Anyway, I was putting my initials in Phil's skin so the other women would know he's mine. Maybe that wasn't the right thing to do, but now look at all the women coming up to him. I'll have to fight them."

"Oh, please don't."

"Then how can I get him to like me?"

"I'm not sure he's worth it. He's an arrogant asshole."

She smiled at me. "I like arrogant assholes."

I cocked an eyebrow. "Well, then, be persistent. Never let him out of your sight."

"You think he'd like that?"

Of course, he wouldn't and that would bring me much pleasure. I shrugged. "I'm not sure he has a heart to like anyone other than himself, really. He's a waste of time, if you ask me."

Mercy shook her head. "I'm just going to make my move. Thanks for the talk, Mina. You aren't so bad. Maybe you aren't my competition."

I gave her an incredulous look as she headed away. I was definitely not her competition.

Ed walked over to me and leaned on the tree. "Look at that face. What got you all bothered? Maybe if you drink more, you'd be a little happier. Nothing that a bit of whiskey can't fix."

I glanced over at him. "I don't think alcohol is going to fix my problem. I'm stuck here."

"For now. Maybe the spell will wear off. And we're not such a bad people," he replied. He gave me a wink. "I see you're bonding with Mercy. She's taking a shine to you, looks like."

"She told me about where she was before she came here."

Ed frowned and nodded. "She's a fighter. Was an athlete

in school before all this. I think rugby. And that disrespectful shithole she was in did show their folks how to fight. She's a tough one on the outside but all mush inside. She watched her parents and siblings die of the Sickness. That and whatever they did to her at that camp, which she doesn't talk too much about, gave her a bit of PTSD. Least that's what the head doc says here."

"I can see that. I couldn't imagine losing everyone. I thought I had."

"You still have family?"

I raised my eyebrows. It was a seemingly odd question to ask someone so young, but in this world where loved ones could die of so many more things, it wasn't uncommon. "I have my brother back home. And a man who loves me."

"Lucky him. He must be going mad with you gone."

Before I could respond, the sound of a loud explosion surrounded us, and a blaring alarm scattered the villagers.

"We got visitors," Ed shouted.

Phillip ran over to us. Mercy followed behind him with an excited look. I wondered if this was another supernatural creature, like earlier today. Perhaps it would be friendly, too, but I wouldn't hold my breath to find two good creatures in one day.

"They're saying Fae are outside the wall. They're trying to break the ward," Mercy announced, practically jumping up and down with delight.

"Good luck with that," Phillip grumbled.

"The ward will hold up," I stated.

Ed began to walk, and we followed. "Even so, everyone has their places."

"Do the Fae attack often?"

Mercy shook her head. "We haven't had a Fae attack in years."

I glanced over to Phillip. "It's because of us, maybe. We should leave."

"You'll stay. Just help us fight," Ed barked ahead of us.

"You got it."

Fae. We were going to fight Fae. Would they know Lisa? Could we get one to help us break her magic? This just might be our ticket out of here. For the first time ever in my life, I was looking forward to a fight.

CHAPTER 17

We walked to the source of the explosion, where the wall was first built. People were in place throughout the perimeter of the village, but most were centralized at the front. I could only assume that was because our attackers were mainly at the entrance of the town. It appeared that Ed had the villagers well prepared for action when the alarm rang out.

"They know we're here. We should talk to them," I stated.

Mercy and Ed exchanged concerned glances.

"They'll take you as soon as you step beyond the ward," Ed explained. "Besides, we don't know for sure it's you they want."

"So, we won't step past the ward. We'll talk to them from your tower."

"We can hold our own, don't worry," Phillip added.

"You didn't hold your own with that guy in the city," Ed countered, as we walked to the tower.

A bang against the ward shook me, and I inadvertently grabbed Phillip's arm, who steadied himself, looking down at me. "That's not good. They're weakening it," I gathered, letting go of him and straightening up.

"So, we strengthen it," Phillip replied, expression confident. He looked over to Ed and Mercy. "We could have handled that guy. Just was taking longer than expected." Phillip walked towards the tower, which was a few feet ahead of us.

Ed didn't look convinced. "Amina, be careful up there. The Fae, they aren't like your friend. They are manipulative."

I nodded. No one in the village knew the full extent of our powers. Since mind control was part of our gifts, we weren't susceptible to it from others. However, I wouldn't underestimate the strength of Fae magic, especially with our current banishing spell.

The four of us climbed to the top of the tower after the current guards descended the ladder upon Ed's orders. "Make sure no one shoots," he told one of the guards.

"It'll either ricochet off, weaken, or even break the ward," I explained. "We're fine right now."

The guards nodded in understanding and took off. We'd explained this to the villagers already, but it didn't hurt to send a reminder out.

I turned to the ground in front of us and maintained a neutral face as I gazed at about fifteen beings standing on the pavement in front of us. A guard from below shouted that there were just as many in the back. Clearly, the Fae were outnumbered but I could only imagine their power made up all of the difference.

The beings did not look like Lisa. I had no experience with Fae other than her and what I learned in books and movies as a child. It was a hit or miss, regarding whether any of our supernatural understandings from the Pre-world were really valid. Some were very true, like witches using spells. Some were mostly true, like vampires not liking the sun but not all of them burned to a crisp. Some myths were totally not true. You did not become the undead if you were bitten by a vampire or a zombie. There was more that needed to happen.

Fae, in my Pre-world knowledge, were glittery, with wings, and usually small in size. They carried wands and made wishes come true. Lisa was barely over five feet and petite, so I figured that was close enough. Evidently, I didn't know a damn thing.

Even though I was several stories above them, I could see that they were tall. No one was below six feet. They were like a co-ed basketball team. They were all pale in color, almost iridescent, with varying hair colors, ranging from blond to black to even green and blue. The Fae were dressed in regular street clothes and there were no wings on their backs or wands in their hands; not very exciting.

"They don't always look like that," Mercy muttered. "They're using glamour. Sometimes they look like the monsters they are."

"What do you want from us?" Ed shouted down.

The fifteen Fae looked up at us in unison. Creepy.

One spoke. A woman with waist-length, deep-red, wavy hair. "Edward. We mean your village no harm. We would simply like Phillip and Amina, please," she replied in a deep and powerful voice laced thickly in an Irish accent. She sounded educated and wiser than the years she appeared, which couldn't have been more than thirty-something.

"Why?"

"That is our business."

Ed gave a lazy smile, hands on his hips. "I'm sorry, but it isn't. See, Phillip and Amina are our guests, and they only leave if they want to leave. Now, I'm sure if they were going to consider leaving, they'd want to know why."

"They are the soulmates; we need them."

Ed crossed his arms and smiled. He looked over to us. "Soulmates? What is she talking about?"

I sighed. This was not the time to go into this matter and

I really regretted keeping our full powers a secret now. We'd essentially tricked them into housing us and I hoped we didn't get kicked out because of it. However, perhaps it was for the best. "Basically, we're super strong witches. We can go into detail later, if you don't mind."

Ed looked deceptively amused and shrugged. I was certain he wouldn't let this go and was probably rightfully pissed.

"What do you need us for?" Phillip called down.

"Your power," the female Fae replied in a neutral tone.

Of course.

"Do you need us to help you with something in particular?"

I shot Phillip a look. These people weren't here to ask for help. They were here to take.

"We need you," the female answered, eyes dead.

"Sorry to hear that, ma'am, but we're going to have to pass. We appreciate you, though," Phillip replied with a smile.

She shot her hand outward, and the ground shook.

Not good. If she kept at this, it was very possible our ward would break. If I didn't know before, I knew now; the Fae were strong.

I grabbed the railing. "We need to go down there. No use starting a fight and risking the lives of other people," I said to Phillip.

"You sure, darlin'?" Ed asked, eyes filled with concern. "Fae are dangerous. Their magic goes beyond making themselves look pretty. They affect time, they can make you fall into a deep sleep, they can—"

"Banish a person," Phillip muttered. "But we'll be ready for them. I refuse to believe the Fae's magic can beat ours."

I side-eyed Phillip. I was glad he was so confident, but I sure as hell wasn't. Nothing in the past nine years of magic made me believe that I was invincible.

"Got to give the people what they want," Phillip stated

before grabbing my hand and whispering a teleportation spell.

A second later, we were standing at the edge of the ward. Teleporting within Ireland was no problem; getting out was another thing.

"Just so you know, we have no intention of leaving with you. Not without a fight. But no need to bother these good people," Phillip announced.

"One of my best friends is Fae, you know. I don't think she'd appreciate you coming for us," I reasoned. This was my last-ditch effort before a complete fight.

The red-headed fairy, who I now decided to call Fae Lady, narrowed her otherworldly pink, yes, hot-pink, colored eyes at me. She considered me for a moment and then relaxed her face. "Lisa," she stated.

I raised my eyebrows. How did she know? No time to figure out Fae magic now, but I'd file it in the memory bank for later contemplation. I nodded.

"She sent you away. She is not your friend," Fae Lady stated.

I was beginning to think that myself, but it didn't make it any less difficult to hear. Phillip lightly elbowed me, and I was sure that was his way of saying, "I told you so."

"She's just confused on a few things. In fact, maybe if you could send us back to where we came from, we can resolve everything and work out some sort of deal," I offered. It certainly sounded reasonable in my head. I had no idea how they would get whatever they wanted from us but I figured one step at a time.

"No, we take now," said Fae Lady. She didn't even bother to consider my very sound offer.

"Why? Why go through fighting when we can maybe work out something mutually agreeable?" I was getting panicky and frustrated now.

I looked up to Phillip, who was glaring at the Fae with narrowed eyes and tight lips. He was ready to pounce.

"That is not the plan. The soulmates must submit," the Fae Lady continued.

"Submit to what? We can help!" I shouted.

She gave a bored sigh and raised a hand, inspecting her nails. "Our masters are coming. You are to follow."

"Who are your masters?"

"They have plans for you, but it is not ours to tell."

Phillip swore and shifted in his stance. "We aren't going anywhere without knowing anything."

She glanced at us and tilted her head.

This was going to turn into a fight. Sacrificing ourselves wasn't a good idea. Whoever, her masters were, I didn't want any part. "Look, we are trying to protect the world. So, if that isn't your master's objective, we aren't going."

She glared at me. "You submit or die. You have no other options."

What the... If I weren't afraid of zapping myself, I would have banged my head against the invisible ward wall. Why weren't they willing to at least talk this out?

"We're soulmates; we don't submit," Phillip called.

She shook her head and frowned. "You know nothing of your power. You know nothing of soulmates." Fae Lady scoffed. Her cronies remained still during this exchange, like creepy statues. "Well, I shall educate you. Soulmates are enhanced souls. Born on the same day of the same year at the same time. When you were both born, you were born with only part of your own soul but part of the other's soul. You have this gift and have not been trained on how to use it. You are the most destructive of any pairing. Our masters can teach you."

If we were that powerful, why would these masters just give us the blueprint on how to reach our full potential without wanting something in return? No, these masters wanted to either use us or subdue us.

"What if just I come with you?" Phillip stated in an even voice.

I looked up at him, mouth open. Was this arrogant asshole actually trying to be selfless? Nope, there was a catch somewhere.

"Send Amina home and take me. It's as good as submitting, since we won't be together. We won't be a danger that way."

"Phillip, you can't," I said in a lowered voice. While I wasn't in full forgiving mode with him, I didn't think him walking into the hands of the mysterious enemy would do our overall cause to fight these evil masters any good. In fact, it would probably make it worse. "You aren't going to sacrifice yourself. We don't even know if anything they are telling us is true."

He looked down at me with softened eyes. "Aww, will you miss me?"

"Wha—"

Fae Lady spoke up. "No. We take both."

"Fuck that," Phillip said evenly.

"Bloody bastards!" I heard Ed shout from behind us.

I turned slightly. He stood behind us, aiming his bow and arrow at the Fae.

"Ed, this isn't your fight. Your people don't have to get involved."

"Oh, darlin', any chance to kill fucking fairies is something we welcome. And with your help, we have a better shot," he replied with a menacing smile aimed at the Fae. "Let's fight!"

I looked back to Phillip. He winked at me then stepped beyond the ward.

CHAPTER 18

I followed Phillip over the ward. Ed and several of his people soon did the same. Anyone who did not want to fight would be safe behind the ward. That left nearly a hundred humans joining us in the fight.

One of the Fae, a male with spiky, silver hair, disappeared. I frowned and did a full spin searching for him. He soon materialized above me with a sword in his hands. It was framed in a glowing blue light and had a gold-trimmed hilt. The weapon came towards me, but I jumped back before he could land the sword into me.

I widened my eyes in shock, surprised at the speed of my movement and the distance I'd cleared. I'd never been that mobile. How had I done that?

I didn't have time to think as the silver fairy raced towards me. I moved out of the way, lightning fast again, and circled behind him. I pushed my hands onto his back, and the fairy arched forward away from me. He let out a high-pitched cry and I watched in horror as his skin shriveled and grayed where my hands connected to his back. Soon, the decay expanded over his entire body. His hair thinned and his body became frail. He was aging. He dropped the sword and fell to his knees.

As he appeared to weaken, I began to feel renewed and energized. I felt like I could jump over trees. How could I physically feel that strong?

Ask how later and focus on what you're doing, woman! I heard Faith shout in my head.

Faith, is that you? How am I hearing you?

She doesn't listen. She never listens. I heard Charles grumble in my mind.

What the hell is going on? Am I going crazy?

No. We're having visions that you're in trouble, so we're just lending some help, Faith replied telepathically.

But how? How can you send me your power and talk to me?

Phillip had spoken to me and lent me strength telepathically when I was locked in the paranormal prison, but now I understood that to be due to the soulmate connection. How had Faith and Charles done this?

Could be due to the Power of Six. I heard Felix chime in. *Mae said we could do stuff like this, so we're trying now.*

Right, we all felt you were in trouble. I guess at the same time. Lisa stated.

I bristled at hearing Lisa's voice but tried to move past that unease for the time being. *Where's Erik?* I asked.

Right here, baby. Pay attention. We can figure out the how later. Erik said in my head.

I nodded. *You can see everything I see?*

A chorus of voices answered, "Yes" in my head.

Phillip clapped his hands together, and the grass grew under the feet of an orange-haired, male fairy. The blades of grass wrapped around his body in milliseconds, covering him like a mummy and drawing him down to the ground. His peers did not stop to aid, focused on their own fights with the villagers.

The fairy struggled against the grass, which seemed

impossibly strong, and soon his body sank into the ground, covered by dirt. The process took less than thirty seconds.

"Can he dig his way out?" I asked Phillip.

"The thousands of ants eating his body won't allow that to happen." He looked at me with emotionless eyes. "That's why he was struggling. I can't imagine it felt nice."

I grimaced. "I thought it was because of the grass."

He looked away. "That helped."

Phillip was clearly taking no prisoners.

"I'm sorry. But we can't be nice."

As if he could ever be nice, Faith grumbled.

For once I agreed with him. "No, we can't, but we need to keep at least one alive to help us get home."

That's smart. Fae sent you there; Fae can get you out, Erik stated.

Mina, I'm sorry, Lisa said in a soft voice. *I'm trying to get you back, but it's harder than I thought.*

Fae Lady let out a high-pitched scream that stabbed at my spine. She charged towards Phillip, who stood his ground.

Another fairy, closer to me, walked with purpose in my direction. Her face changed, growing more angular before my eyes. Her skin took on a sickly, yellowish tone, and her long, forest-green hair whipped around her face like snakes. Her limbs appeared thinner and longer, hanging unnaturally to her knees. She was now over six-foot-five.

The hell is that? I heard Charles cry. *Get out of there, Mina!*

I looked past her as the Fae and humans charged each other. The Fae had begun to strip all glamour away and were now in full warrior forms, representing various shapes and sizes of goblinesque creatures. Not exactly Cinderella's fairy godmother.

The green-haired fairly ran straight for me and then disappeared mid-run. I spun around, meeting her claws. Her hands sank into my chest easily, as if I were not made of skin and bone but, rather, water. However, I felt no pain, only pressure as her fingers moved around in my chest. I was frozen. Paralyzed, really.

Teleport, Amina. Lisa cried in my mind.

I can't.

Tears welled in the corners of my eyes from the pressure, and my breath stopped. She was reaching for my heart. My mind clouded. I couldn't focus on magic to push her away.

And then the digging in my chest stopped.

She screamed out, and the hand that was pushed into my chest was now without a body. She backed away with fury, now missing a right arm and hand. I looked over to Mercy, who was holding a sword.

A woman with a sword Mae had told us. Was that woman Mercy?

She swiped again, but the fairy stopped her with a wave of her hand, sending Mercy back onto her bottom.

I yanked the hand out of my chest, and this time, it did hurt. It felt like ripping a blunt object out of me, only no blood spurted out. Hopefully, that meant no internal damage. However, I didn't have time to whimper. The green-haired fairy was about to turn Mercy into body parts. I magically burned her detached arm, now lying on the ground. The fairy cried out an inhuman shriek. Could she really feel that?

She bent down and reached for her burning arm, and I kicked her in the face with a strength I'd never had before. Her green, bushy eyebrows narrowed in rage. Her right cheek and nose were now misshapen, bloody, and bruised from my attack.

Before I could send another kick her way, Green Fairy pushed out her remaining hand and a ball of ice flew from her palm into my stomach. Ice cold spread within me, freezing my insides.

I needed iron. That was like kryptonite to Fae, from what the books said. I whispered a spell of healing to stop the cold spread, but it didn't stop, only slowed. The fairy smiled at me as the cold reached down to my legs, leaving a dark, opaque film resembling frostbite as it paralyzed my body once again.

I'm trying to slow the freezing, but my magic isn't working, Felix called in my mind.

"Toss me your sword!" I shouted to Mercy, who looked ready to swipe at the fairy again.

She raised an eyebrow at me but didn't ask questions. She threw the sword and then reached into her holster for a handgun, firing immediately. The bullet hit the fairy in the chest and she fell back, but I suspected she wouldn't stay down.

I caught the sword and focused my magic on it, but I was weakening under the fairy's cold magic.

I need help, guys.

You'll need fire to fight her, Lisa said. *I can help with that.*

Soon, fire tinged the sword like a torch. I focused on the element of iron, and the sword grew heavy in my hand.

I knew we could control various aspects of life, including plants and elements that made up life forms. Iron, being a large part of the earth's core as well as a part of various plants and vegetables, was one of those elements.

My new and improved iron sword wouldn't do much for swinging and attacking quickly, but if it touched a fairy it would do all it needed to do. This would especially come in handy, since Faith's life-draining magic was ultimately impractical for me. A sword could reach a lot farther than my arm. The fire, in the meantime, was disguising the transformation so the fairy wouldn't know what hit her.

One-armed Fairy rose back up off the ground and walked over to me. Mercy shot at her again, but the fairy moved on, ignoring the bullets as if they were only minor annoyances. She withdrew what appeared to be an actual wand from her pants pocket. It was thin and black, with a tiny blue light, like you'd find on a keychain or cell phone, emanating from the tip.

I was pretty sure she wasn't going to turn my old jeans and T-shirt into a pretty, blue dress with that. I didn't want her turning me into a mouse or anything either. She pointed the wand at me and I waved the heavy sword in front of me, blocking whatever magic she sent my way.

I'm not sure I can work well with this sword. The iron is too heavy. I thought to myself and, perhaps, my friends.

I got your back, mama. Felix called in my head.

The sword suddenly felt as light as a plastic toy as I channeled Felix's strength.

However, I still couldn't move. If the cold reached my heart, it'd be game over. Right now, it was mostly focused on my knees and thighs.

The fairy, probably realizing I wasn't able to go anywhere, walked closer to me. She disappeared then reappeared; toying with me. I just needed her to move a little closer so that I could tap her with the iron sword.

She disappeared again, then reappeared on the side I wasn't holding the sword on. The giant woman towered over me. "Now I take your soul," she said in a low, deep voice.

"No, ma'am," I shouted and swung the sword with all my might at her, twisting my body to the left.

She threw out her arm to block the sword and the fire died, leaving the iron to connect with her skin.

She screamed as the iron burned her arm, and I swung again, this time impaling her in the stomach. The blue light in her wand died, and she dropped it as she backed away, looking down at the sword. Her arms hovered over it as she tried to pull it out, but her hands were burned each time she tried to touch it.

The cold in my body stopped spreading and dissipated as her magic broke. The fairy tried to disappear, but only went translucent; unable to teleport.

Another fairy, a purple-haired male, came at me screaming but Mercy shot him in the head, killing him instantly. She then retrieved a butcher knife from her sheath and ran, screaming, in warrior mode, to the purple fairy in case he could come back. She brought the knife down on his neck. She then began the work of decapitating the fairy-like a madwoman. Blood squirted up and splashed over her. Mercy seemed unfazed at the gore as she hacked at him with amazing speed.

When she finally stopped, she looked up at me. "Fun," she said, giving me wild eyes and a teeth-baring grin beneath the mask of blood.

I gave her a curt nod; slightly terrified. This crazy human was saving my ass today.

I looked back to the green-haired fairy, who was now yanking at the sword in her stomach and screaming as her hands burned and smoke seeped beneath her fingers.

"Oh, hell no," I shouted. My legs were now thawed out, and I moved to the fairy and pushed out magic. The sword sank deeper into her stomach, appearing to melt.

She coughed, her eyes wide. Green tears streamed down her yellow face, and dark-black liquid poured from her mouth. Iron.

The fairy bent forward as the iron melted into her stomach and poisoned her system.

The green tears soon turned to thick, black liquid, which was now also pouring from her nose. She dropped to her knees and hands, vomiting liquid iron.

She was suffering, and I didn't care to draw it out any longer. "Mercy!" I shouted, not looking behind me as I stood over the dying fairy.

Mercy reached my side in a second.

"End it," I ordered.

Mercy shot the fairy in the head, and the fairy dropped sideways to the ground. I moved my hand in a come-hither motion, and the sword slid out of the fairy's dead body, no longer iron coated. It hovered in the air above the body.

"Do you want your sword back?" I asked Mercy, still looking at the body.

"Hell, yes," Mercy shouted, grabbing the sword and then swiftly decapitating the green fairy.

I turned around to see if there were any other scary Fae to take down. The grounds were scattered with humans fighting grotesque monsters. The humans were armed with swords, knives, guns, axes, bow and arrows, and even grenades. They couldn't use the tower to shoot down the Fae from the vantage point because it would break the ward. However, the humans were strategic in their fighting. Several villagers would attack one fairy at once, moving fast and purposefully.

A female fairy with long, stringy, silver hair and a wide body, perhaps six hundred pounds on a six-foot frame, stood in a wide stance. Her body looked muscular and hard but smooth. Suddenly, she charged at a black SUV that was speeding towards her. For her size, she moved impossibly quick. I shouted a protection spell to wrap the car from the damage they were sure to face. The car smashed into her and took her down without so much of a dent to the SUV.

A male leaned sideways out of the passenger seat of the car seconds later. He held a rifle and shot the fairy monster in her head just as she was struggling to her feet. Half of the fairy's face blew away. He shot again until the fairy was missing a head.

Effective.

I turned around to find Phillip but couldn't see him.

"Where's Ed and Phillip?" Mercy asked, standing beside me with sword out; ready for attack.

I closed my eyes and saw Phillip in my mind's eye. "The back."

Leave him be, Faith grumbled.

"If I do that and he gets hurt, then I could die."

"What's that?" Mercy asked.

I shook my head before grabbing her hand and tele-porting.

At the south end of the village, we found more fighting, as well as Ed and Phillip battling a fairy giant.

It, or rather, he -he was not clothed- must have been well over seven feet tall. He was hairless and blueish-gray in color, with large, bulging muscles covering seemingly rock-hard skin. His face was still very human, only modified with lime-green eyes and a very thin, long nose. His lips were almost nonexistent, and his teeth were rows of razor-sharp canines.

At the moment, Phillip was trying to electrocute it with zaps of lightning that poured from his fingers. However, the blue fairy was resistant.

I cracked the ground under the fairy, and he faltered and fell to his knees but not before swiping Phillip and Ed out of the way with both of his hands. I ran up to it and poured mag—

Blue Fairy disappeared.

And then reappeared behind me, lifting me in the air by my waist, wrestling style. Mercy sliced at its back, but her sword ricocheted off his stone skin.

"Shit," I heard her cry.

The fairy monster lifted me above his head, and a night-marish vision of him cracking my back across his knee entered my mind. I tried to teleport out of his hands but couldn't. Suddenly, my body bulked in energy. I felt muscles harden and stretch.

You won't be hurt if you fall, Erik mentally stated. Appar-ently, I was taking on his were strength. I hoped that didn't mean I was going to change into a were jackal, but if it meant I survived, I'd take the help.

An arrow shot out and landed in Blue Fairy Monster's eye. I looked down and found Ed shooting. The next arrow bounced off the skin, but the blue fairy was already slightly off balance and lowered me a bit from the damage to his left eye.

Phillip cracked the ground under us wide enough to sink a car. Ed shot an arrow into the fairy's other eye, blinding him. I screamed along with the fairy as we fell into the open earth.

The fairy let me go and tried to reach for the ground and missed, falling into the opening and a seemingly-endless pit. I reached for the edge of the open ground before I fell into the earth as well, but also had no luck. Phillip lunged over the edge of the cracked earth, touching my fingers, and we disappeared.

When I reappeared, I was lying on top of Phillip; his arms around my back and our faces less than an inch from each other's.

"I believe there are better places for this than here, friends," I heard Ed say above us.

I heard a distant growl in my head that I knew belonged to Erik.

Phillip opened his arms, seemingly reluctantly, a disappointed smile on his face. I quickly moved off of him and got to my feet. He got up as well and stood beside me as I surveyed our temporary battlefield.

Mercy and Ed walked over to us.

"Is it over?" I asked.

"I think—watch out!" Ed shouted towards Mercy.

Phillip knocked Mercy to the ground and swung his hand outwards. "Inferno!"

I turned to the source of his power word to see Fae lady erupt in flames. She spun around as fast as a whirlwind, putting out the fire. When she slowed to a stop, she looked totally unharmed. Whoa.

"You are good fighters, but this was just a taste of what we have in store for you," she sneered, patting a leftover spark of fire on her arm. "You are but children." She then snapped her fingers and disappeared in a mist of what appeared to be black smoke.

I heard Phillip grunt behind me. I turned to see him clutching his stomach, face twisted in pain as blood surround his hand. He dropped to his knees and fell face-forward into the ground.

CHAPTER 19

The battle was over. We'd killed many Fae but taken no prisoners. Somehow, the humans won, but not without casualties. Looking down at Phillip in the town infirmary, I was beginning to wonder if he would be another casualty. In his effort to save Mercy, he'd sacrificed his body and gotten hit by Fae Lady's magic. That magic sliced into his stomach and his insides looked like he'd fallen on a grenade. He would have died if he'd been a normal human. I tried to pour healing magic him as soon as he fell to the ground, but the damage was too intense for a quick healing. It would take work and time to get Phillip back to health. Perhaps this was the answer to our problems. Although I did feel guilty about not minding his death. I was better than that.

Pain suddenly twisted my insides as if I was having ghost pains from some nonexistent injury. I didn't understand where it was coming from. I scrunched my face as I keeled over in my chair, next to his bed. I had to continue to heal him, but I could barely sit up straight. What was going on?

He *would* die if I didn't use my magic. I didn't need that on my consciousness. If I was going to off him, it was going to be when he was up to something evil not because he hurt himself saving an innocent person. I placed a shaky hand back over his stomach and poured out my magic, ignoring my own stabbing pain. He began to heal, but very slowly, and I wasn't sure it was fast enough to prevent his death. He was starting to grow cold from blood loss and he'd passed out earlier. I was beginning to feel woozy myself.

"This would go a lot faster if you guys helped me out," I stated to the friends in my head.

Let him die, Erik stated.

"He just risked his life for someone else and saved my life. Can we give him a pass for now?" I grimaced as another round of sharp pain twisted my insides.

Perhaps this is a gift, Faith said.

"What if I die?"

Are you hurt? Erik asked.

"I feel like something is trying to rip its way out of my stomach." I'd thought I gotten strong enough to separate our soulmate bond to the point I wouldn't get hurt if he got hurt. However, I was now realizing that wasn't the case, at least not for major injuries.

Shit, they are *connected,* Charles replied. *On it, sis.*

You've got the pack's magic, baby. Hold on, Erik stated.

I heard Felix and Faith agree.

I'll help too, Lisa said. A tiny voice in my head. *And, Amina, I am trying to get you back.*

Soon after, I felt the cool power of Lisa's fairy magic, coupled with another tingling power that I knew to be Felix's healing gift.

We combined our magic and poured it into Phillip and myself. Moments later, I began to see Phillip heal rapidly, and the gripping pain in my stomach subsided. I remained with him until he was mostly healed, but he stayed asleep.

"Is he going to be okay?" Mercy asked, standing above me.

I nodded. "I think so."

She let out a sigh. "He saved my life. He's a good man."

I stood up and asked Mercy to keep watch over him for a while, which she eagerly agreed to do. Phillip would have an even harder time shaking her now.

I went to the other injured townspeople, and the others assisted me in healing them. Once done, I felt heavy, longing for bed. There weren't any free spots in the repurposed cottage, and I didn't want to leave the medical house, in case I was needed, so I sat on a loveseat in the living room.

Thanks, guys, for helping me today. I still don't know how this is all happening.

Honestly, we don't either, Mina. Felix replied. *Mae said the Power of Six would evolve with Lisa back.*

We didn't think we could tap in like this. We don't have that kind of control yet. But, I guess, when you're in a high level of danger, it alerts us. Erik added. *It's all hit or miss. Just like reaching you in a dream.*

Do you know where I am? I can tell you I'm in— My head pounded in pain, forcing me to shut my eyes and bend forward.

Mina, don't try to tell us. The banishment won't allow it. Lisa stated. *I'm really sorry I had to do that.*

"Had to?" I asked aloud, the pounding in my head subsiding.

There's a reason I had to do this. It'll be better if I explain to you in person. I'll get you back.

A sleepy weariness grew over me.

I want to stay up and talk to you all but I'm feeling very tired.

It's okay, Mina. Erik began. *We'll figure out a way to get in touch with you. Hopefully, without you having to be in danger.*

"Love you guys," I whispered before my mind went black with rest.

I heard the chorus of their voices reply that they loved me too in the darkness of my mind.

~

he next day, we had a mass funeral for the villagers who'd bravely fought with us but hadn't survived. Ed gave words of hope and encouragement. He made a point of saying that those who'd died helped defend the village, and that the Fae who'd escaped would now know what kind of warriors they were. I had to admit; they were amazing fighters. They strategized and optimized their own human abilities in the face of defending themselves against magical beings.

The village tried to move forward after the battle; helping those who'd lost loved ones and backfilling certain jobs of the deceased. My mind, however, was filled with more questions. It was clear to me that the Fae were working with or controlled by whoever this big bad was that Mae feared. First the ghosts, then the strange man, and now the Fae. The big bad seemingly couldn't get to us directly, but they had no problems with finding others who could.

I still held out hope that I could return home. A week had passed since the battle and I studied everything I could on soulmate magic and the Power of Six. Needless to say, there wasn't much on the internet about either. However, I had to get prepared for the next attack, which I was sure was imminent.

It was now November, the start of winter. The temperatures were already moving towards chilly, and we were entering our six-month supernatural winter. I left the makeshift infirmary where I spent most of my days and dragged my feet on the cold walk home.

Home.

This was not my home. Not without Charles or Erik. Phillip was no substitute. Although he'd been on his best behavior, I still didn't trust him, nor had I forgiven him for his actions in Silver Spring. I had no doubt that if we returned, he'd be his same old, sadistic self.

Before I could touch the doorknob to the cottage, the door opened. I raised an eyebrow and walked inside. Phillip was home, so I was sure he was behind the door opening magically. I walked through the entrance and the door closed behind me. No sign of Phillip.

The smell of marinara sauce filled my nostrils. Pasta? I walked to the left and peeked in the tiny kitchen. The gas stove was off but there were no longer any pots on the stovetop. I stepped back out of the kitchen and looked down the hall towards the dining and living rooms. Across from the living room, I could see light emanating from the sliding glass doors leading to the backyard.

I stared outside with an open mouth, sliding open the glass door.

The backyard, barren before, was now a miniature garden full of rich plant life, roses, daisies, tulips, and various vegetables and herbs. How had I missed his working in a garden all this time? I had no doubt he'd used his magic to make this garden.

I stepped out onto the cobblestone space that spanned the entrance. In the center of the garden was a grassy patch with a metal table and two seat-cushioned chairs. The spaghetti dinner I smelled in the kitchen sat on top of the table, along with a bottle of what I assumed was whiskey, and glasses. Above me, balls of fire hung in mid-air, illuminating and warming the space.

I looked to my right and found Phillip playing with an old MP3 player and speaker system sitting on top of a closed grill. He settled on what sounded like acid jazz and backed away smiling.

"What's this all about?" I asked, voice full of suspicion.

He turned to me. "I made dinner. I owe you my life, we've been here almost two months, and we haven't tried to kill each other. You pick," he replied, waving his arm, implying I should have a seat.

I cautiously walked to the table, eyeing the food. It looked good and I was hungry but my trust of Phillip, even after all this time, was still low. "You put something in the food?"

I heard him sigh, walking behind me. "I've cooked for us many times; why would I do that now?"

I side-eyed him as I sat down. "And what's with this romantic atmosphere? I'm just gonna make a plate and head to my room. Nice flowers, thanks for the grub." I began to put the pasta on my plate.

"Stop!" Phillip demanded.

"That power doesn't work on me and I'm going to test this food for magic before I eat it," I stated, continuing.

"Please," he added, his voice softer.

I paused and looked up at him. Now he was trying to sound nice. What did he want?

"Let's sit and pretend to be friends for one night, please. I know you don't owe me anything, but would you mind doing me this favor?"

"Why? We called a truce, but I don't see why I have to do any more. Eventually, you are going to go back to who you were before, and I'll feel like a fool for having ever trusted you."

He grabbed his head, frustrated. "You used to be much nicer. What happened to you?"

I tapped my chin and looked up at the sky. "Hmm, I was imprisoned for six months, attacked several times, my brother was killed then came back as a vampire, some crazy people hate me for no reason, and the guy I thought was cool turned out to be a dangerous jerk." I gave him a pointed look.

Phillip nodded slowly. "This jerk you're talking about, is it—"

"It's you."

"I figured, just wanted to be sure. I apologize, Amina, for my role in... darkening your life. I'm not a good person.

You're right not to want to eat with me or trust anything I say or do." He lowered his head and turned away from me.

I rolled my eyes. "I'm not coming to your pity party, dude, so don't waste your time. But if you want me to pretend we're friends for one night, I guess I can do that. I don't have anything better to do," I grumbled.

Phillip didn't say anything for a beat and then finally walked to the table and sat down across from me. "Fine," he muttered before pouring whiskey in our glasses.

We filled our plates and began to eat in silence.

"Can we at least try to have a conversation?" he asked.

I shrugged again, wrapping my fork with the spaghetti.

"Do you miss home? Is that why you're grumpier than usual today?" he asked.

Why did he care? I nodded. "Don't you?"

"To a degree. I miss Mae and Bill. That's it, really. Here, I feel like my old self again."

I raised an eyebrow. "You keep saying that. So, you're admitting you're not the person you used to be. What was your old self like? I mean in the Pre-world."

He looked away, a thoughtful expression on his face. "I was a smart-ass, but I was dedicated. I liked sports. Dated a lot of girls. Drank too much, partied too hard. Mae used to say she saw a better man in me. She said my time was coming. Then the world went to shit. And I thought, 'Well, this was my time to be a better man. I can be a hero.' I got on the right track. Helped those in need with my gifts. Then when Tim, the former leader of Silver Spring, died... I struggled some. When I found you in my dreams, I thought you could help me. I'm still hoping you can. I just wish you could forgive me. I don't want to keep being that jerk who I was back in Silver Spring. You don't have to believe me Amina, but... I'm tired. This time here has been... refreshing. Attacks and all."

I didn't speak, still suspicious. Either he was a very good

actor, or he was sincere. I could actually see the exhaustion in his eyes. I'd thought all this time it was because he was getting sick of this place. What was he going through?

"Sometimes I feel like I'm fighting myself," he continued. "I want to say things but I can't. I mean to not do something, but I do it anyway. It's like I can't stop myself from being this monster." He looked down at his hands as if his frustrations were held there.

"Well, you haven't been a monster since you've been here, for the most part. So, I'm not sure I'm buying that," I muttered. I sipped my drink in contemplation. I couldn't reconcile the man in front of me with the one who had sentenced an innocent person to blindness, killed Chelsea's boyfriend, locked me up even after knowing what I'd gone through in the prison, ripped a man's tongue out, and controlled the minds of innocent people.

Then there was the man who'd helped me escape that prison, shown such kindness to the villagers, saved Mercy's life by risking his own and kissed me like he did when we'd first met. Maybe this was a game. Was he really being sincere? Was Mae right about him? Perhaps he really was possessed or even cursed. Suddenly, an idea came to my mind.

I put my glass down and sighed. "I'm going to try something. And you're going to sit there and take it."

He raised an eyebrow. "Does it involve pain?"

"No."

"Okay, that's good."

"At least, I don't think."

I didn't wait for his response. I grabbed his hands and closed my eyes, whispering the spell that I'd made for the challenge. I had no idea if it would work on him, but it was worth a try. I repeated the sentences again and again, tightening my grip on his hands.

His eyes grew wide with confusion. "What are you doing to me?" he whispered.

"My spell. For the challenge. I originally made it for Charles, to help him deal with what was happening to him; being a new vampire and all. It was to settle his mind and find peace for inner turmoil."

"Did you try it on yourself?"

"No, I'm fine."

He snorted.

"How do you feel?" I asked, opening my eyes.

He smiled at me, his eyes growing soft. "Good."

I chuckled. "Well, I expected more of a description. I guess time will tell." I let go of his hands and stabbed my fork back into the spaghetti. "This is really good, by the way." If hadn't sensed any magic over it and if he was trying something on me, it had failed.

He touched the corner of his eyes with his index finger and then looked down at his finger. "What is this?"

I looked over at the clear liquid on his finger. "Phillip, tears. Tears, Phillip. There, now you know each other."

"I don't cry." He wiped at his face.

"You mean you used to not cry. Look at that. Now you have emotions. Long time no see, huh?"

He frowned and rolled his shoulders back. "Yes, and I'm freaking out here because I feel like an actual physical weight has been lifted off of me. How is that possible?"

I looked up at him. "Maybe you really were possessed."

He shook his head. "I wasn't possessed. But someone did get in my head. Not a being. It was almost like I was controlled the same way we can control. I don't know who did it, but I couldn't tell you even if I did. It's like a force wouldn't let me."

I put my fork down. "What did the voice tell you?"

"That paranormals were the superior race. That I was the

strongest and that I had to stay at the top and make things ready."

"For what?"

Fear spread in his eyes. I'd never seen that look in him before, and it unsettled me. "For what's to come. I was to help remake the world into one dominated by magic. I couldn't be swayed by it. The voice was telling me I should do the things I did to assert my strength."

Had he really heard a voice from some other paranormal or was this deeper? "Do you have a family history of mental illness?"

He furrowed his brows together and dropped his lids. "No. I'm not schizophrenic."

I nodded slowly, not sure I fully believed him. "Okay, then someone placed a spell on you."

He frowned. "Who? For what purpose?"

I shrugged. "That's beyond me. It could be someone in Silver Spring or a place you visited. Maybe these masters the Fae spoke about are doing this. Caused this. And they're coming for us because we're a threat."

He sat back and grinned at me.

"That's not the reaction I expected. You should be upset. Someone could be using you. I'm not sure my magic is strong enough to break whatever spell is over you."

"If I'm free of this spell, do I get a shot with you again? Let me prove to you that I'm actually a good guy."

I rolled my eyes. "You aren't focused at all. Someone could have dropped a mind-control spell on you, ironically, and you don't seem to be concerned." I looked away, think-ing. "Maybe that's part of the spell, too." I looked back at him. "And no, you have no shot. I'm Erik's mate."

"And my soulmate," he countered. "We never had our fair shot. We could be each other's greatest love." His large, light-brown eyes looked almost sincere and threatened to pull me in. Somehow those eyes were filled with a mix of sadness, hope, and love all in one. It was as if I could feel what he was feeling. This was new but not surprising. If we could hurt and feel the pain we caused each other, we could also feel any emotions we had for each other. Right now, I felt love. His love for me, to be more exact.

"Phillip... "

He grabbed my hand and kissed it. "Thank you for helping me. Let me help you."

I slowly pulled my hand away. "Help me, how? The only thing I want is to go back home and you can't help with that."

⁓

*P*hillip cooked for me again the next morning. Tea, scrambled eggs, toast, and slices of ham. He liked making big breakfasts because he missed lunch most times.

He looked up and smiled at me as he filled two plates with food. "Morning."

"Good morning," I replied evenly. He gave me a plate of food and a cup of tea and I sat down at the small circular kitchen table, saying, "Looks good, thank you."

He nodded and sat across from me. We started eating in silence.

"About your spell," he started. "I'm not cured, Amina. I want to lie, and say that I am, but I can't. So, I guess in that sense, it did work."

"What do you mean? My spell didn't help at all?" I was horrified to think that I could have lost the challenge then. I leaned in towards him and saw wet marks on his face. No, he was lying. "Have you been crying again?"

He swore and wiped at his face. "No, I just finished washing my face."

I twisted my lips in disbelief.

"Look, your spell helped some. Except for this watery eye side effect. For anyone else, it'd work perfectly. You

222

partially helped me but whoever did this to me is beyond my powers. Unfortunately, your spell didn't break the control. But it did help weaken it. I still feel tightness around the edges of my mind that I can't shake, but the voice is gone. And I won't do things that go against my character anymore. Like, rip out a person's tongue when they piss me off. Or confine someone I care about." He looked over to me, and his large, brown eyes were sorrowful; like he had let me down. "I'm not going to be that monster anymore. I promise you that."

I took a deep breath. "Watery eye side effects aside, it's okay to admit that it's upsetting to think about all the bad you've done. I'd cry too. Hopefully, the man you truly are is not one that maims or kills people."

"I never was. And I want to right things with everyone I hurt, including you. Maybe with your help, we can find a full cure for whatever darkness is in me." He reached across the table and grabbed my hand again.

I pulled my hand away. "Phillip, I can't give you what you want."

"You care about me, *Corazon.*" A slight smile played on his lips. "If you didn't, you wouldn't have cared enough to try to help me. I know I have a lot to atone for. Let me try. Let me show you who I really am."

With Phillip changed now, it wouldn't be so easy to hate him. I knew now that magic had made him someone he wasn't, like Mae had always said. It made things more complicated for me. I had fallen in love with Erik, but I did wonder. If Phillip had been in real life, who he'd been in my dreams, would I have made the same decision?

I got up and walked to the counter, pouring myself a glass of water to break up the moment. That question didn't matter. I couldn't, didn't want to, turn my back on Erik. "I just did that to make my life easier, is all. Don't worry about proving anything to me. Focus on all the others you hurt."

I heard him rise, and walk behind me. I turned and he was right in front of me. "You're too close."

He paused and searched my eyes.

I huffed. "What are you looking for?"

There was a slight lift at one corner of his mouth that made him seem innocent. "You haven't been telling me the truth."

I turned away from him and faced the sink again.

He balanced his hands on the counter, his arms on either side of mine. "You can lie to yourself but not to me. You feel something for me." I could feel his warm breath on my neck and it sent an involuntary shiver down my spine. I shut my eyes tightly, embarrassed that his nearness had caused that reaction in me.

"It doesn't matter," I stated.

"It does matter. I was a good man before, Amina. Let me show you that."

I turned around to face him, which was a mistake because locking eyes with him was like falling into his soul. As corny as that sounded, he just captured me.

He reached up and grazed my cheek with the back of his hand. His touch was like a feather on my skin and I lowered my eyelids slightly, enjoying the sensation.

"Amina, I know you don't want to hear this but—"

We heard a knock at the door.

I jumped and pushed away from him, racing to the entrance. I was thankful for the interruption.

I swung open the door, not looking through the peephole first like I normally did.

Ed stood at the entrance with a wide grin on his face.

Had he seen us? I hadn't done anything wrong. What was I nervous about?

"I've got some good news," he began. "I might have found someone who can help you get home."

CHAPTER 20

$\mathcal{E}$d paused and looked between Phillip, who was standing behind me, and myself. "Did I interrupt something?" he asked, his already wide grin somehow broadening.

"No," I replied.

"Yes," Phillip countered.

Ed shook his head and walked in. "You two should just have sex already and get past all this awkwardness. Works for me every time."

"I don't see how that's true," I muttered, closing the door behind him. "So, who's this person that can help us?"

"As you know, we've kept our eyes and ears open to any magic users who might be able to aid you in your return home. Well, on a bartering mission, we learned of a super powerful witch who asked about you two. Brilliant, right?"

"She asked about us, specifically?" I questioned.

Ed nodded. "By name."

"How do they know she's really powerful?" Phillip asked, crossing his arms, a mask of skepticism all over his face. Magic was magic to a non-gifted human. People often said someone was powerful, and when we met up with them, there was nothing high-level about them on the paranormal scale. "Or that this isn't a set up?"

Good point. Phillip may have been a jackass but he was a smart jackass.

Ed furrowed his brows as he scratched his chin. "I don't know. This came from one of you magics. I spoke to an elf lad I typically work with. He vouched for the witch. My mate said she can do impossible things and that she'd been doing this before the world changed." Ed turned to me with a smirk. "Amina, do you want to go? We can leave Phillip here. If he doesn't mind me stealing his girl from him, that is."

Before I could protest, Phillip spoke up. "Where is this witch?"

Ed gave a chuckle. "West of here in Galway. About a two-hour drive, longer due to road issues."

"When can we go?" I asked.

Ed shrugged. "How does now sound?"

~

The drive to Galway was uneventful. Since Ed and his people had come this way many times, they knew what roads to avoid due to the supernatural and road obstructions.

We drove into the city, past restaurants, bed and break-fasts, and quaint, little shops sitting on cobblestoned, pedestrian streets near a seaside promenade. The area was clean and well maintained. There were no other cars on the road. Most of the people we spotted were either walking or riding bikes and horses.

Ed stopped in front of a public house and opened the car door.

I frowned and got out. "We're meeting her at a pub?"

Phillip opened the door to the front passenger seat and exited. "This town is still functioning?"

Ed nodded. "For the most part. They keep it warded, but we received access some time ago. Permission was already granted for you two. A lot of magics live here. If they like city life, that is, and being under a ruler. They've got some wizard mayor who runs the place like a dictatorship, but people don't seem to mind. Suppose it's better than being out on your own and not having all the comforts that a magic city can bring."

"It's as good as Silver Spring," Phillip said, looking around.

"Except bigger," I added, exiting the car. It had to be at least twice the size, maybe three times. Of course, not every part was filled with citizens, but for purposes of the new world, this was a big city. Ireland was a small country, so it made sense that the survivors of the Sickness and the paranormal humans would find it easier to come together.

We walked towards the pub, and Ed opened the door. "This place has excellent food. I'd advise getting your fill."

Phillip leaned into me. "We should leave the Dublin village and come here."

I glanced sideways at him. I could already see the wheels turning in his head. He would come here and run the place. "I thought my spell was supposed to make you a kinder person."

He smirked. "It was supposed to bring me peace and happiness. Moving here would do that."

I scowled at him. I'd grown comfortable in Ed's village. I liked the people. I wasn't interested in moving unless it was to go home.

Phillip chuckled. "I kid. It's two hours away. We can visit anytime. What else do we have to do?"

I squinted my eyes at him and walked inside the restaurant. What was this 'we' he kept talking about? He could live here without me. In fact, I liked the idea of that.

Ed paused, looking around the pub. The space was a

typical Irish pub with heavy, dark-wood furniture, and various memorabilia on the wall. It wasn't especially crowded yet; it was only a little after 11 a.m. "I see them," Ed said and started walking.

We followed him through the space to a booth in the far-right corner, near a large window.

A man with brown hair, appearing to be in his mid-twenties, sat across from an older woman with long, straight, white hair that went past her shoulders. The woman, who was maybe in her late 70s or early 80s, was in great shape and regal looking, with wise, blue eyes under heavy lids and red, slightly-upturned lips. She peered over at Phillip and me with interest.

"Hey, Ivan, this is Phillip and Amina, the witches I told you about," Ed announced.

"Oh, they're much more than witches," the woman said, smiling.

Ivan slid down, and I took a seat next to him.

"Hi, pleasure to meet you," he said, eyes wide. His eyes were icy blue, with a black ring around the perimeter of the iris. His ears were large and pointed, and he was of slightly shorter than average height.

I held out my hand, and he shook it eagerly, giving my arm a workout. He did the same with Phillip, who looked at me with questioning eyes.

"It's very exciting to meet actual soulmates," Ivan exclaimed. He waved his hand towards the woman. "This is Liz. She's a very gifted witch. She knows everything."

Phillip sat down in a chair facing the booth, and Ed slid into the space next to Liz.

"I hardly know everything," Liz stated, chuckling. She looked at us. "Ivan filled me in on your predicament. So did Annie Mae."

Shock rocked me. "Wait, you spoke to Mae? *Our* Mae?"

She nodded. "Yes, older black lady, right?"

"Yes."

"She's been contacting me in my dreams for weeks now. She kept mentioning soulmates but I didn't know who she was talking about. I knew of the existence of magical soulmates but I didn't know of any myself. I asked for her to give me names, but she said she couldn't. She said I had to help the soulmates; that you would need a teacher. But since she couldn't tell me who you were or where you were, there wasn't much I could do. Then here you are!" She rested her chin on a hand, elbow balanced on the table. "Mae told me about this awful bad that's coming. I've done some sight spells, and I've seen some horrors of what's to come as well."

"If that is the case, Ms. Mae is one smart cookie."

"That she is," Ed stated, crossing his arms.

I cocked an eyebrow and side-eyed him. "How do you know?"

"Before we got attacked by those Fae, I had a dream about an older black woman, with short hair. She told me to stay with you two and go wherever you go. That I was meant to do good and be a part of what's to come. She also told me she'd make me bread pudding when I come to visit her. I have a feeling it'd be good."

"If you two can communicate with her, then can you tell her where we are?"

"She doesn't know where I am, and I tried to tell her in my dreams, but I don't think she understood what I was saying. As soon as I said the words 'Ireland' or 'Dublin' or anything associated with this area, it was as if she didn't understand what I was saying. I was hoping from my accent she'd figure it out."

I dropped my shoulders, disappointed. "Your accent is pretty clear. If no one has come it's because something is preventing her from hearing your accent. Or maybe they're here and just can't find us. It's a small country, but it would still take time to search."

Liz tapped the table with her finger nails. "This doesn't mean you won't find your way home. You still have hidden potential to tap into. This, I can help you with. I can help you both tap into that soulmate magic you possess." She sat back, looking at us all. "Magic was always here. If you looked for it, you would find it in the Pre-World."

"How did it grow?"

"Dearie, that is what I have been trying to find out for the past nine years. It was definitely purposeful. And there are so many types of magic in this world to understand until I get to the big answer."

"What are all the magical types?"

"Do we want a lesson with alcohol?" Liz asked with raised eyebrows.

Ed shifted to get up. "Woman after my own heart. I'll get a pitcher."

"No need."

Before our eyes, a bottle of whiskey materialized on the table with five short glasses.

Phillip reached for a glass. "I really think we should revisit that discussion about moving here."

"*You* can move here," I muttered.

"I'd like to move here, too," Ed said as he poured the drinks.

"Or we can find out the spell and do this ourselves," I stated, taking a glass.

"I'll share that and more," Liz replied.

The five of us clinked glasses, and then the lesson began.

"To begin, every magical category has subsets. The category of witch also includes warlocks, wizards, and mages. And witches vary within that. There are light witches, dark witches, and those in between. Then we have the Weres or Lycans, as I prefer to call them. The common werewolf, for example. This also includes your shapeshifter. Next, are your vampires and also succubi and incubi. Who am I missing?" She tapped her chin.

"Me!" Ivan exclaimed, his eyes practically twinkling.

Liz nodded slowly. "Yes, sweetheart, the Mythics. That is quite a large category to the outside world, but they are not the same. Elves, Fairies, Dwarfs, Trolls, Gargoyles. And there are light and dark within all of those. You also have Orcs, Goblins, Gremlins, and Demons."

This much I knew, but I never turned down a magic 101 lesson, especially from an elder who knew of magic from the Pre-World. Although there was one category I'd always wondered about, and it remained the most mysterious in my research. "What about Angels?"

"Right, that would be the final group. If there are Demons, there must be Angels. Everything has balance. Ghosts are the in-between."

"So, there is a God?" I was never super religious before, but I did believe.

Liz tilted her head, and her eyes softened. "Sweetheart, there is a God. There are many gods. The magic not only changed people, it brought beings into our view that we did not see before. There were gods who were resting, but are now awakened. And not all of them mean well for humans. Soulmates are meant to combat the more powerful evils out there. We can set up a schedule for when you visit me, so that I may teach you all that I know."

"What will it cost us?" Phillip asked, leaning his elbows on the table.

Liz gave a slow shrug. "You help me heal some people. That'd be enough. I'm not as young as I used to be, and healing takes a lot of energy."

"We can do that," I said eagerly.

We made a schedule for visits, ordered lunch, and had a few more drinks. Liz continued to share more information about magic, moving past the basics. I was surprised to learn that nine years in, there were still things I didn't know. Magic was ever changing and resources were always updating as it became more normalized. My spirits were renewed. I would learn all that Liz knew, make it home, and become magically wiser for it. This banishment would not be for nothing.

Before we left the pub, wanting to get home before the creatures of the night arose, Liz called me back to talk to her. She asked the men to go ahead outside while she had a brief word.

I sat back down in the booth and faced her. "What's wrong?"

"Do you love him?" Liz asked, eyes neutral.

I raised my eyebrows. "Who? Phillip? No. I have someone back home."

"Well, he certainly loves you," Liz replied with a knowing smile. "Soulmates don't come often. Ones who love each other, even less. You can be the ultimate good or the ultimate evil. Cause the greatest movement for the world or destroy mankind. Suppressing magic prevented that from happening, but now that magic is back fully, you two can be quite dangerous. At your full power, people may fear what you can do or they may come to worship you. Neither should be what you want, but it will be hard to ignore. That power will try to consume you. You must fight it."

"Why are you only telling me this and not Phillip?"

"Because you and I both know that Phillip is compromised. He's bespelled. I can feel that."

Crap, I'd really hoped he was lying about my spell not working. "I tried to help him with another spell."

"That is only a Band-Aid, my dear. You must break the spell, but you aren't strong enough yet. The type of dark control over him is beyond my powers. However, his love for you will help. That love's a power on its own. Whoever put the spell on him couldn't overcome that part."

"But why did they do this to him in the first place?"

"I suspect they hoped it would break you up, which would make you weaker and less of a challenge. Love is the key, my dear. It is the soulmate's greatest power. If you loved Phillip, you could break that magic hold on him, and you both would become stronger. No matter what I teach you, without that love, you will never reach your full potential. Yes, you will be formidable without it, but you will be so much more with it."

I swallowed what felt like a lump of coal in my throat. I truly wasn't interested in sacrificing my emotional happiness for him, but there was the greater good to think of. Still, that seemed not only unfair but problematic to have to force someone to be with another. "I don't think I have it in me to be any friendlier to him than I already am. I'm just so tired." Couldn't just being acquaintances be enough? Maybe even frenemies?

Liz gave a slow nod. "I can sense that. You must come to terms with your own emotions as well. Things have been very challenging for you. You can't continue to shoulder it all on your own. You might not be under a curse, but you are still battling your own darkness. Phillip could help."

I shook my head. "I don't need him."

"Then you will fail, and all will be lost." She frowned briefly before softening her face. "Give love a chance, dearie."

I let out an exaggerated sigh. "What type of love?"

"That is for you to find out." Liz reached over and patted my hand, then sat back with a smirk. "He is a handsome man, isn't he?"

CHAPTER 21

Several weeks passed, and we were still in Ireland. I had such high expectations that Liz would be able to connect with Mae again, but she didn't. If Phillip and I were special, why couldn't we break this damn magic?

Each day, I got up and helped wherever I could. Then in the afternoons, I practiced my magic and the soulmate connection. There were no more Fae attacks, and I could only assume it was because the town proved themselves to be quite formidable or perhaps the Fae really didn't want to kill Phillip and me. However, I suffered no delusions that they would not be back, stronger than ever. And so we prepared. Strengthening our physical and magical wards, defensive and offensive moves. Every man, woman, and child in the village who was able to fight would be prepared.

Four days a week, Phillip and I met with Liz, learned her knowledge, and practiced our magic. She'd been slow to share on our soulmate magic, first giving us aid in reaching our own full potentials as life mages; although, she liked to call us earth mages because we controlled anything living and growing.

We were on week three of our practice when Liz finally

taught us of our bonding magic in the living room of her small attached cottage. "Soulmate magic is tricky. You can only pull from that particular magic when the other soulmate is near. It's possible that because you are part of The Six, you are strong enough to use your soulmate magic even when Phillip is not around, Mina. And with you being an alpha's mate, there are even more possibilities. It's quite exciting."

She found it exciting; I found it overwhelming.

"I don't know the specifics of soulmate magic. It's really too mysterious. However, I know it is a form of binding magic. Similar to becoming a mate for a Lycan or a consort for a vampire. And anytime you bind with another person, you make your magic foundation stronger," she explained.

"How do people bind?" I asked.

"Many ways," Liz began. "You can become a mate of a were, marry someone, blood-bond with a vampire, become a familiar to a witch, or become bonded through another magical spell. When you combine with someone you are bonded to, you can become one on many levels, depending on the strength of the bond or the other person. You, Amina, have two bonds. You could actually have a tri-bond, and through you, your were-mate and Phillip are also connected and can use each other's magic."

Phillip folded his arms and rolled his eyes. "Fun."

"Or it could cancel everything out, which would explain why you aren't as strong as you think you should be for soulmates," Liz stated with a shrug, sitting down on her living room couch.

"So, you're saying her being mated with another man could be hindering us?"

Of course, he'd see it that way. Still, he could be right. Damn.

Liz touched her cheek, eyes narrowing in thought. "I've never encountered a person with two bonds."

"So how do we get strong enough to be undefeatable?" Phillip asked. "We are stuck with this fairy curse we can't break, which was cast by someone who shouldn't be stronger than us. Ghosts attacked us in a building that was warded. A crazy dude nearly took the both of us out. If it wasn't for a human's arrow, Amina would be gone. I couldn't save her on my own. We can do amazing things like mind- and body-control, but clearly, we should be able to do more."

"You aren't working together," Liz replied, sitting back. "On your own, up against a being immune to mind or body control, you aren't these all-powerful beings. You could be, in theory, easily defeated. Stop fighting your bond. Your bond boosts your powers."

I sighed. "So, how do we stop fighting it?"

"You should have sex," she replied with a light shrug.

I slouched in my chair. Why?

"I like that plan; let's do that," Phillip said eagerly, turning towards me in his chair with an excited face.

"There's no way in hell. How else do we connect? Can I just give him a hug?"

"You have to accept each other into your lives. It can be emotional or physical—" Phillip coughed at that "—you can open your hearts to each other. Touch each other. Fully feel the power simmering between you both. Don't fight whatever you feel. Sit and close your eyes. Feel it and let it in," Liz said, sounding like a hippie.

I didn't want to let anything from Phillip in but I also didn't know of other options.

She made us sit down on the couch and told us to face each other and hold hands.

"Close your eyes. Clear your mind and focus on the touch of each other's hands and the feel of your skin," Liz stated, getting up.

I did as instructed, and fought not to respond to the contact with Phillip. Despite us living together, we'd maintained our space. Touching him now, holding hands, took me back to the first time we met. Our attraction had been out of control then and I felt a tinge of that feeling again from his touch. His hands were large and strong and I felt safe. That felt wrong in my head. He wasn't a safe person.

A heat simmered in my palm and spread farther up my arm and through my shoulder. It continued over my back, relaxing the tight muscles and aches.

"Place a hand over each other's heart," Liz instructed.

I glared at Phillip, but he kept his hand respectfully above my breast.

"Focus on the rise and fall of the chest. The feel of the heartbeat under your fingers." Liz's voice began to sound soothing, like a yoga instructor.

I focused, as Liz instructed, on the feel of Phillip's chest rising and falling under my fingers. The warmth continued to spread throughout my body. I felt like I was getting the world's best invisible massage. My shoulders slouched, and my body felt weightless and free. This wasn't the same as when magic first awoke in me. This felt like the next stage. Like a continuation. Nothing in me hurt or ached. There wasn't the itchiness that sometimes came with the use of magic.

I yawned but felt energized; like I could run several miles. I actually wanted to run, and I hated running. My mind felt cloudy, as if I was high on some magical drug, and I swayed slightly. A giggle unexpectedly escaped my lips. Phillip chuckled in return.

"Open your eyes," Liz stated.

I opened them and stared into Phillip's face. He gazed back at me with a sleepy grin, and I opened my mouth and let out a silent gasp. His eyes, which were once a lighter brown, were now a beautiful violet color.

"Your eyes... " he whispered.

Had my eyes changed as well? I stupidly touched my face as if that would give me the answer. Man, I was out of it.

He squeezed my hand, and the look in his eyes were wonder-filled. He mouthed the words, "I love you."

I wanted to tense up and resist his words... but I couldn't. I couldn't think of the cruel Phillip who was under a control I could only dampen. I thought of the Phillip who had saved me from that prison and shown nothing but kindness to me and others since being in Dublin. Against my better judgement, I continued to let the magic in. Soon an all-encompassing peace wrapped around me, and I welcomed it. I wanted to hug him, hold him in my arms, and feel his heartbeat.

Liz let out a little yelp, and I looked over to her. Except something was different. She seemed shorter. Well, that couldn't be right.

"Whoa, this is new," Phillip announced, looking down.

I moved around on my invisible cloud of peace and suddenly realized that the reason I felt so floaty was because I was indeed floating. We were actually levitating two feet above the sofa. I kicked my feet in a panic. "How do we get down?" I cried, looking to Liz.

She just shook her head, a hand over her mouth.

I wiggled as if that motion would twist me down to the couch. Surprisingly, it didn't work.

Phillip chuckled, and I gave him angry eyes. "I'm glad this is so amusing to you."

"We're only up two feet; it's not like we're hanging off the ceiling." He looked all too amused, his eyes twinkling and his lips in a smirk.

"Well, do you know how to get down, then? Because being stuck even one foot above the ground can be problematic. Maybe if I... " I trailed off and let go of his hand.

Instantly, we plopped down on the couch.

Phillip lowered his eyebrows and frowned in disappointment.

Liz clapped her hands. "My dearies, I believe you have
just magically bonded yourselves. You'll only grow stronger
from here."

I nodded, rubbing my hands together. I felt oddly cold
now that Phillip and I weren't touching. I blew on my
fingers.

Phillip reached out and grabbed my hands again and my
freezing fingertips instantly warmed. Thankfully, we didn't
start floating again.

"We can't hold hands all day," I grumbled.

Phillip smiled and then blew on my hands before
releasing them. This time they didn't grow cold.

I suspiciously looked down at my hands then back up at
him. "Magic?"

"Actually, no, just my breath."

I squinted my eyes and he threw his hands up in surrender. "No, seriously. Looks like I have the stuff to keep you
warm." He gave me a wink that made my stomach clench
ever so slightly.

I was really starting to hate my body right now. It was
betraying me today. We had to leave Ireland fast.

~

I knew it was a dream as soon as I opened my eyes.

I was back in Silver Spring in the Japanese
restaurant I first visited for Phillip's welcome party. I recall
liking it, finding the dark-gray walls, dim lighting, and black
furniture sexy. I sat on a couch in the lounge side of the
restaurant, close to the bar. I wore a black, low-cut blouse
and tight, dark jeans, with open-toed, red stilettos. This was
my go-to outfit when I went out, back before the world went

to crap. A sense of familiarity and homesickness washed over me concurrently.

I turned to my left and found Phillip beside me, looking down at himself. He had on a charcoal-gray, well-tailored, three-piece suit.

Phillip looked up at me and raised an eyebrow.

"Why are you here?" I asked.

He shook his head slowly. "I don't know, you tell me, *mi corazón*," he replied with a slight smile.

I looked down, noticing for the first time that we were holding hands. I raised my eyebrows, shocked, yet I didn't move my hand away. I liked touching him. Liked feeling his warmth. I didn't understand how I was feeling.

I looked back up at him, admiring his handsome features. He looked amazing, as always, in anything tailored. Like some male model in a magazine. The jacket fell nicely over his broad shoulders and muscular arms. I wanted him to wrap those arms around me.

He bit his lower lip, as if he knew what I was thinking. "You look beautiful. As always. Why are we here?"

I let go of his hand and sat down in a loveseat near the DJ booth. Why was he asking me? Surely, this was his doing.

Phillip sat down beside me. "Did I say something wrong?"

I shook my head, lips tight. I inhaled deeply and instantly regretted it, as I caught a significant whiff of his scent, sandalwood mixed with vanilla. It was mesmerizing to me, and I leaned in closer to him without thinking.

"You're being weird," he said, his face a mixture of curiosity and amusement.

I was less focused on his face and more narrowed in on his lips. Had they always been that full and soft looking?

I stared into his eyes and became mesmerized. Was this some sort of magic? I was sure I leaned even closer to him because my hand found its way on his thigh. He licked his lips, and my attention focused back on his mouth. I remembered our kiss when we first met, and a fizzle of delight bubbled in my stomach. I recalled enjoying that kiss, and a craving grew in me.

"Amina, you are very close. Well beyond the western standards of personal spa—"

He didn't get to finish his sentence before I leaned into him and placed my lips on his. I kissed him as if it would be my last. He gave a momentary yelp of surprise before returning the energy of the kiss and encouraging me. Somehow, I had moved from beside him to on top of him, straddling him.

He moaned in my mouth, or perhaps he was trying to say something, I couldn't tell. Not that he tried to push me away. I nipped and sucked at his lower lip. How had I forgotten how silky his lips felt? The taste of him was like sweet butter, and I kissed him harder. His hands moved to my back, and he pressed me closer to him. I could feel his excitement between my legs and I lowered onto him.

"Amina," Phillip said in a hoarse voice as my lips moved to his neck.

I knew that he was saying words, but I was having trouble hearing them. I ground down harder onto him, wanting to feel more.

"Amina," he said again, tightening his grip on my back.

I pulled back from him slightly. "Phillip, what is the problem? Isn't this what you wanted?" I asked before moving to kiss him again.

Phillip grabbed my face and kept me at bay. "But is it what *you* want?"

I frowned. "I wouldn't be sitting on you if it weren't. Have you changed your mind?"

"It's not that I've changed my mind. I am in love with you, but you are not in love with me. Right now, you are confused. Probably because of the binding magic. It would be wrong of me to take advantage of that." He gave me a sad smile and ran the palm of his hand down the side of my face. It sent a pleasant shiver through me.

"I want this." I kissed him again, savoring the taste of his lips.

I felt Phillip take his hands away from my back. He placed them on my thighs and lifted me off him.

I sighed in frustration. "What is the problem?"

"This is a dream. A dream that I did not cause."

I rolled my eyes. "You're saying *I* brought us here?"

He nodded with a smile. "Seems you finally got control of dream communication. I'm proud of you."

No, if I had the power to summon a dream then he would be the last person I would dream up. Phillip was lying. Plus, I didn't feel like myself. I would never do this with Phillip. "I don't recall summoning this dream. So how could we be here?"

"I know I didn't call us here. Maybe this is just your subconscious, then. It could be you're having some sort of feelings for me, and this is a place to explore that without the consequences of real life. I honestly don't know. If I did this, I'd have no problem admitting it."

I shook my head and settled in a seated position next to Phillip. A wave of guilt, lust, and confusion came crashing over me. Had I really caused this? Phillip was right, he'd never lied about dream walking before.

"I love Erik," I said, more to myself than Phillip.

I turned from him. What was wrong with me? Instead of trying to pull Erik into my dreams, I was foolishly using my gifts to be with a man I now saw all the time. If I stayed here any longer, would I lose Erik and myself?

CHAPTER 22

*U*ntil I could control this soulmate connection, I had to separate from Phillip before I did something I'd regret in real life. The dream was mortifying enough. Sure, I could pretend that he was really behind the dream, but he couldn't control my actions. That was always all me.

The next morning, I got out of bed, hoping to avoid Phillip. I crept through the narrow hallway and, as some sort of cosmic joke, walked right into Phillip. I let out a yelp.

"Sorry, didn't mean to scare you," he said with a sheepish grin. He had on loose pajama bottoms and no shirt. It was the first time I'd seen his bare chest, and he was more in shape than I'd imagined. He had defined pecs, a hard stomach, and muscular arms. Was he this damn toned before?

Who cares, Amina. I had to get out of there. I felt like an animal in heat. "I'm moving out," I blurted out before I could think.

Phillip scrunched his face, lips turned down. "What? Why?" He took a step closer, and I slid away to head back to my room.

"We need to focus on those fairies coming back. We're

clearly stronger now, with the bond. We can't get off focus. I just think we need to keep things platonic. Opening that bond was a problematic distraction."

Phillip cocked an eyebrow. "I don't see that the two have to be mutually exclusive. So, you having a hard time controlling yourself around me? Just give in. Plus, the fairies haven't been back in a while. Maybe we actually scared them away."

I rolled my eyes. "You're smarter than that. You know them being quiet is just them being up to something. We need to stay far from distraction. We can never get too comfortable. If you moved to Galway, it would be easier for us both. I can see you during our sessions with Liz."

Phillip opened his mouth to protest but then closed it again. I turned and stopped in my tracks as I heard the sound of a loud alarm, soon followed by gunshots. There then came a pounding at the door. I raced down the steps, Phillip on my heels.

I swung open the front door and a local villager, a young woman named Tara, stood at the door with wide, brown eyes beneath strawberry-blonde bangs. "There's something at the gate," she said in a strained voice.

I didn't ask what, just threw on boots at the door and grabbed my coat. I heard Phillip whisper a spell behind me and when I turned slightly to him, he was appropriately clothed for the December weather.

We raced to the gates of the wall. Since being here Phillip and I had helped build the wall taller and stronger with our magic. I couldn't imagine anything breaking through. I hadn't even felt anyone attacking the ward. Was this the Fae again?

As we approached the wall, we heard growing sounds of gunfire, shouts, and cries. We stopped at the tower and a guard looked down, then tapped the shoulder of a man with red hair, Ed.

He waved us up. "I'm getting tired of this shite," he yelled.

Phillip grabbed my hand, and before I knew it, we were at the top of the tower, standing with Ed, Mercy, and the other villager.

I looked down and saw several of the villagers on the ground in front of the wall, battling the Fae, who were smaller in number than the last attack. That was probably because they had backup with them this time. Besides the Fae, the town's folk were fighting what looked like a forest closing in on the village from all sides. Thick vines grew from the dirt in front of us and surrounded the town in a ring of wiggling, thorny greenery. The town's people chopped at weeds climbing up the wall with axes.

Then there were trees. The trees were walking on their roots.

"Man-killing plants," Phillip surmised.

Killing wasn't a strong enough description for what we were witnessing. It was more like a supernatural slaughtering. I saw a wiggling vine wrap around a man's leg and rip it off. I next saw a tree bend forward and wrap its branches tightly around a woman. Her body began to meld with the tree, her skin taking on the texture and color of the bark. Her hair hardened, and eyes dulled as the tree absorbed more of her body. She screamed in soul-stirring agony, but we could do nothing to help. I tried to stop the tree with my powers, but there was a magic over it, much like a ward. It seemed whoever set the tree to attack had protected it, and even my earth magic could not pierce the ward.

Villagers shot at the tree, careful to avoid the remains of the woman, but the bullets did nothing. A man holding a blowtorch aimed it at the tree, and fired and that seemed to stop the tree from moving. However, it was too late for the woman; she was gone. They hacked at the tree in hopes of finding her inside. Blood poured through the slices in the tree, but no human body showed through. I didn't have to wait to know they would find nothing. The tree had digested her. I felt nauseous. I'd have nightmares about this forever.

"How can plants come from fuckin' nowhere?" Ed asked.

In between the madness, monstrous Fae attacked the villagers, teleporting and reappearing on the grounds in front of the town.

The ground rumbled and broke apart in several areas. More large vines sprouted from the earth, except these vines seemed different than the ones the villagers were battling. The leaves were thicker, football-sized, and linked to heavy, rope-like vines.

Far off movement caught my attention to the left. A vine struck out and wrapped around the arms and waist of a man with an axe, squeezing him. He dropped the axe, crying out in agony.

I teleported to the ground in front of the man. I balled my fist, and the plant crumbled and broke apart around the man. "Are you okay?"

"I think my arms are broken," he said in a cracked voice.

I held my hands out and whispered a healing spell, pouring my magic into him.

I felt a gust of wind behind me and turned to see a tall woman with a light brown complexion that looked unlike the other Fae. However, she wasn't a villager. She had long, silky, brown reddish hair and topaz-colored eyes that made me sure she was Fae.

"If that plant had bit you, you would be dead. The bite is very poisonous," she said with concerned eyes. She sounded American.

I looked down to the ground and saw a decaying vine. The head of the vine looked like a Venus flytrap, but it too was now browned and crumbled.

She is the enemy, I thought; *why would she care?*

"Did you do that?" I asked her.

She nodded.

"Why'd you save me?"

She looked away from me back at the fighting. "You can't die."

"Because your masters want Phillip and I to live?"

She looked back at me with a frown. "I have no master." She said the last word like it tasted bitter and I didn't blame her. That word to a person of color had different meaning.

However, it was the word the pink-eyed fairy had used.

She continued. "No, it's because you're part of The Six, and we need you.

Surprise rocked me. "What? How did you know? What's your name?"

She turned sharply to her right. "Francesca. I've got to go."

"Wait!" I cried, but she disappeared before my eyes.

I turned slightly, looking around for her, and saw one of the football-sized leaves split apart in the middle, revealing several rows of miniature razor-sharp teeth. A vined tongue shot out of the mouth-like hole and wrapped around Phillip's arm as he successfully fought off a male fairy. I moved to help, but a sword came down on the green tongue, splitting it apart.

Mercy appeared, letting out a warrior cry as she continued to chop at the plant. Another plant came from behind, her but she spun around, taking it down in one swift motion with her sword. She was human, I knew, but she had a strength that rivaled many-a paranormal.

"Thanks, Mer— Aww shit," Phillip swore, looking behind me.

I turned around and saw a man walking towards us with determination. The plants and Fae parted around him as he moved towards us.

This was the guy who'd nearly kicked our asses back in the city. Somehow, he'd found us. He threw out his hand, fingers curved, and Phillip gagged, clawing at his throat.

I ran forward to block Phillip from the man and threw my hands out in front of me. The ground shook and broke apart under the feet of the man, who opened his fist, letting Phillip go.

He looked at me with cold, unbothered eyes, and I was reminded of how calm his demeanor was last time. It was as if nothing concerned him. He was dressed well again, this time in a tailored, navy-blue suit under a long, tan peacoat. The man did not appear battle ready; more like he was about to head into his job on Wall Street.

Someone shot at him, and he wiped the oncoming bullet away from his face as if it were a fly.

I raised my hands in the air to show surrender. Not that I was really planning to do that. I just wanted to get this fighting to stop so we could get them out of here and away from the villagers. "I get it. You want us to submit. Can we talk about this? What did we do?"

He tilted his head to the side, eyes narrowing in suspicion. "You really know nothing?"

I shook my head quickly.

I guess he believed we were clueless because he looked up heavenward and sighed. "Honestly, I don't want to kill either of you."

Phillip stood beside me. "Then why'd you just try to send me to my maker?" He grunted, rubbing his neck.

"It is what I am required to do. Rather, I am required to subdue you," the man replied, his deep-brown eyes cool.

Well, that was cryptic. "What's your name?" Maybe if I could establish a bond, we could work from there.

"Ahmed. You are Amina and he is Phillip."

"Ahmed, why are you required to kill us?"

He looked at me but didn't respond.

"Can we have a momentary truce where you just answer some questions, and then, when we've talked, you can go back to trying to subdue us or whatever? If you call off these plants and Fae, our people will fall back. This fight is just about the three of us. No one else needs to get involved."

Ahmed's face remained unreadable, but seconds later, he nodded. "I am willing."

He snapped his fingers, and all our living greenery disappeared. They didn't retreat back into the ground; they just went away into a smoky nothingness.

Ahmed looked to the confused Fae around him. "Return to your realm. I have it from here," he ordered.

A male fairy with a bald head stepped forward. "Misandre said we should—"

"Listen to me," Ahmed stated sternly. "If I require your assistance, I know how to reach you quickly. I do not believe we need to continue the killing of these humans. We are only after the mates, and here they are. They cannot defeat me. Leave."

Well, that was mighty confident of him. We were working up to giving him a proper ass kicking. Hopefully.

The Fae looked at one another but soon disappeared into nothingness like the plants.

Ahmed looked back at us. "I will not have much time before they return."

I turned to the crowd of people who were looking around in confusion. "Everyone," I shouted. "It's okay. We're just going to talk. You can go back to your day. Thank you."

The crowd didn't move.

"We're not leaving you here with this bloke, darlin'. Sorry," Ed shouted back, walking up to stand beside Phillip.

"He's right," Mercy said, appearing beside me. "He called the plants that killed our friends. I'd like to chop his head off."

Phillip raised a hand to quiet her. "Mercy, love, hold that thought. How about some of you stand at a distance? The rest can go."

Ed nodded and asked the villagers to go back behind the

wall. Ed and Mercy remained with a few other villagers, their hands poised and ready on their weapons.

Phillip clapped his hands, and a burst of red surrounded the three of us in a glowing circle.

"A ward?" Ahmed asked with a curious look.

"A sign of good faith, since you called off your green goons. We put up a ward so you won't get jumped," Phillip explained. "It also protects what you say from eavesdroppers."

Ahmed nodded. "Thoughtful."

Okay enough with kind act. This guy was not our friend. "What are you?"

He looked at me and smiled. His smile was actually quite pleasant. He was handsome, in a distinguished sort of way. "Human. I'm Iranian, to be more specific." He paused. "But I suppose you mean my gift. Jinn."

"You're a genie?" Phillip questioned, an eyebrow raised.

Ahmed seemed to bristle at the word. "That would be the Western interpretation."

I felt silly asking this question as my knowledge of Jinn was pretty superficial. "Do you grant wishes?"

"Is that why you're here?" Phillip questioned. "Someone rubbed the lamp you live in, and one of their wishes was to kill us?"

Ahmed made a noise of annoyance. "I don't live in a lamp, but I can be trapped in an object if I do not fulfill the wishes." He clasped his hands behind his back and began to pace within the confines of the ward. "One day, I was teaching Middle Eastern History at Oxford, and the next I was this new being. I never knew I had an object that was tied to me."

"How'd whoever get your lamp?" I asked.

He shrugged. "They had someone break into my house, I suppose. The lamp appeared one day but I didn't realize its significance until it was too late."

"Who is 'they?'"

"The ones who have wanted you since they learned of your existence. You aren't easy to kill and they certainly don't yet have the strength to do anything against you themselves."

"And 'they' would be?"

"The first soulmates."

I really wanted some dramatic music to follow that announcement because this was huge. My mind raced with questions.

"So, the first soulmates want us dead?" Phillip asked. "What'd we ever do to them? They want top gun; they can have it."

"I don't know what they want," Ahmed replied. "They have been asleep for centuries and only awoke when magic came back. I believe there can only be one set of soulmates at a time. At the very least only one set with full strength. They tried to keep you apart but—"

"We met in our dreams," Phillip cut in.

Ahmed nodded. "Everything that you have gone through is due to them. Amina, your imprisonment. Phillip, your altered mind, which I cannot change. They were all wishes that I granted. Another was that I withhold their identities and location. And yet another was to have you subdued. The unseelie, or dark Fae, who attacked you are separate from me but are followers of the soulmates."

If he had been behind my imprisonment was he around for David coming back from Hell? "Wait a minute. You were the asshole behind getting Charles and me kidnapped? Did you help David escape hell so he could kill my brother?"

Ahmed bowed his head. "I apologize for what I was made to do regarding your imprisonment. If you survive this ordeal, I will be indebted to you. However, I played no role in bringing back a being from the underworld. I suspect the original soulmates had someone do such a thing. Their powers are limited right now, in part because of you both.

They need followers to grow in strength. Therefore, many of the acts against you were not done directly by them."

"Why wouldn't their first wish be to kill us, instead of going through all of this?" Phillip pushed.

"I cannot explain why they did not immediately want you gone. I'm not sure they want you gone now. I don't know all of their motives. They aren't exactly confiding in me. I am an unwilling party to their plans. And they do have plans. They also have many followers who will keep coming for you."

"Where are they?" I asked. "These original soulmates?"

Ahmed shook his head. "Only one is moving. The other is still confined to their land of origin. That one does not have the strength to move. All of their energy went to the other first, who still isn't at their full strength. You take them on now, and you would possibly defeat them, but that window is just about to close. I can tell you nothing specific of their locations, except you being away from home is highly ideal to them. Your support is fractured, and your friends are focused more on where you both are than preparing for any impending war or what the mobile soul-mate is up to."

"What are they?" Phillip asked. "Witches, like us?"

Ahmed stopped pacing. "No. They are something much older."

"Like?" Phillip asked impatiently.

Ahmed began to pace again. "That would be tied to their identities, which I cannot share."

This information was helpful but it was not enough. "How are we supposed to fight them? We were told there is a great evil coming and that humans will shift again. Are the soulmates behind that?"

Ahmed stopped pacing once more and faced me. "I do not know. I simply know that they see you as a threat to any plans they may have."

Phillip made a disgruntled noise, clearly as agitated as I

was. "I don't get something. Why'd it take so long for them to find us, if they know where we are all the time?"

Ahmed cocked a brow, face still unreadable. I wished I had such a great poker face. "You ask me questions I don't know the full answers to. They are not at full strength. They are not ready for battle. And I cannot say they always knew where you both were. I certainly lost you."

"How'd you find us again?" I asked. "And why'd it take so long? Ireland is a small country, and with half the population gone, it shouldn't have been that difficult."

"One of our followers, a witch, was finally able to locate you. That's when the Fae first attacked you. You proved a bit much for them that first time. To your second point, I was not in a hurry to get to you." He smiled, looking at us both. "The soulmates never gave me a time limit to finding you. I'm sure partly because they aren't strong enough to subdue you yet."

I raised an eyebrow. "You don't really want to do this?"

He gave another shrug. "I am prolonging it. Jinn or not, all this death and destruction weighs on my soul. I was never a deeply religious man, but I wonder if what I am would matter to Allah." A brief look of sadness washed over his neutral face, and he looked away, appearing deep in thought.

I nodded slowly. "I've had similar thoughts." I sighed. I didn't want to fight or kill this man. He was as much a victim in all of this as us.

"If you have no other questions, I suppose we must get to it." He looked at us quizzically. "You have no other questions, correct?"

By his look, I felt that we should have more to say. "What if we offer to get your lamp if you hold off on trying to kill us?"

Ahmed tilted his head. "How would you find such a thing? You don't even know where she is."

I hadn't thought that far but I was quick enough on my

feet. He'd already dropped an important clue by saying we didn't know where *she* was. "So, one of the soulmates is female, and she has the lamp?"

He raised his eyebrows but said nothing. I'd take that as a yes. Clever man, giving away a hint indirectly. Of course, that only remotely helped. She could be anywhere in the world.

"I'm assuming if you did agree to this deal, you wouldn't have much time to give us. Your Soulmates are going to be patient for only so long," I continued. "But unfortunately, we're subject to a fairy curse that won't let us teleport out of this country. We haven't been home in months. And trust me, we've tried everything. And even if we could leave, we'd need some type of hint on how to find your lamp."

Ahmed crossed his arms and narrowed his eyes in thought. "You are soulmates, and as such, you can tackle any form of magic. One benefit of soulmate magic, and what helps you find your mate, is being able to sense and tap into many forms of magic. That magic isn't strong, but being able to harness even just a little can be helpful. Like getting you home from a banishment. You just have to focus on the form of magic. I can help you with that."

"How do we know which magic is what?" I asked. My mind was spinning. He was essentially telling us that we had the sparkly shoes all along to get home. We just needed to find the equivalent to clicking our heels.

"Your witch magic works in various ways, correct?"

We nodded eagerly.

"You use spells, potions, and you sometimes just think of something, and it happens. I've seen that. So, think of the magic that you want in your mind." He pointed to his head. "Then when you do, break your curse with that magic. With your powers combined, this should be doable. I'll give you two weeks. You should make quick work of finding my lamp. The next time I see you, I might have to kill you. That would be a shame, as I would greatly like to know the new soul-mates. If you're going to be successful with finding my lamp, you must return home."

I frowned. "I'm confused. What about the location of the la—"

Phillip touched my arm. He whispered, "It's in the States with the female soulmate."

Ahmed did not acknowledge him and instead dissipated into a cloud of smoke.

CHAPTER 23

Phillip snapped his fingers and dropped the ward.

I then walked over to the others and recapped what we'd discussed.

"Do you trust him?" Mercy asked, folding her arms. "How do you know he won't double-cross you and just try to kill you once he gets the lamp back?"

That thought had crossed my mind. However, Phillip said, "Yes, I trust him."

His easy trust was perplexing. He rarely trusted anything. "Why are you so sure that he will abide by his word?"

"I did a truth-seeking spell when he was calling off his plant goons," Phillip answered with an indifferent shrug.

"Well, aren't you smart?"

Phillip looked over his shoulder and winked at me. "I think he's a good man. I also think we need as many powerful allies as possible. These soulmates have their followers already; we need supporters too. He told us how to go back. We should try it."

"So, it's time for us to go to America now?" Ed asked.

I gave a curt nod. "Yes but, wait, you're coming, Ed?"

"Bloody right, I am! I've never been to America, so why not go on a free holiday?"

"Who's going to run the show while you're gone?"

"I have a second that I trust and Mercy will keep everyone in line too, right, darlin'?" He asked, tilting his head to the woman.

She gave him a glare. "Don't call me darlin'. And yes, nothing to worry about here. After we've mourned our dead, you can go. Time to stop these arseholes from hurting anyone else," She said with a sour face.

I nodded and looked to Phillip. "Let's go tomorrow."

He gave me a weak smile. "I was thinking I should stay behind."

"With me?" Mercy asked with an overly-delighted grin.

Phillip gave her an uncomfortable smile. "I guess?" he asked more than said.

Mercy put her sword in the sheath hanging from her belt hook. "Yea! Stay with me. Let Mina leave alone. She doesn't need you, as long as you don't die. It's okay!" she exclaimed, bouncing.

"Well, then you'd have to take good care of him, love," Ed said with a wink.

Mercy smiled wickedly. "Oh, that wouldn't be a problem."

I cocked an eyebrow and looked at Phillip. "You sure you want to stay?"

He gave an embarrassed cough. "Yes. Yes, I'm staying."

"I thought we both had to do the magic together to get back."

He ran his hand over his face. "I need time, Amina."

I sighed but held in my growing annoyance with a tight voice. "We've had plenty of time. I need you to come back, Phillip. You have to help us find the lamp and other stuff I'm too tired to think about right now. We only have two weeks before that Jinn comes back and kills us. And, yes, I know you can help from here, but you have to redeem yourself.

Look, Phillip, if people in Silver Spring are going to believe us about this threat and that we are the new soulmates, they have to see us together. We can, together, heal the people you've maimed."

"He maimed folks?" Ed muttered. We'd told him some of how Phillip used to be but not the full details.

"He's so hardcore," Mercy whispered in awe, gazing at Phillip with a look of longing.

Her turn-ons were disturbing.

"Phillip, let's go back to the house and talk this over. It's freezing out here, and we're beyond the ward."

Ed wave a hand in front of his face. "Take your time with the decision. If you have the power, you can go home any time. Maybe after people aren't so mad at Phil, here, for being a massive psycho."

Phillip rolled his eyes and crossed his arms.

I barred my teeth in annoyance. I was done placating Phillip. "I don't want to take my time. This isn't a hard decision for me," I stated. "No offense, I really have come to like you guys and this place. Even though the sun seems to want to stay out of sight. But I have a brother, friends, a gu—"

"Who's probably with someone else. You think after all this time, he's still pining for you?" Phillip asked, his eyes darkening.

"If you want me to hate you, then keep saying things like that. Besides, it's not just about Erik and the others. We have a mission. We have to get ready for these beings coming for us, and we can't do it well here."

"We've done well so far."

"It's called luck. Not to mention, some of Ed's people have lost their lives helping us. We can't keep putting them in danger. We have to leave here. As long as either of us remains, it'll be no good for them."

Phillip looked away from me. "I need time. Please don't hate me."

I turned my back on him. "Whether I hate you is entirely up to you."

~

*P*hillip was resistant to talking about returning for the rest of the day. The next morning, I discovered that he'd left early to do who-knows-what around town. I'd gone past worried, to fuming. Here we finally had a way to get home, and he was dragging his feet.

When he finally returned home that evening, I was livid. I met him at the door and kicked him in the shin.

He leaned over, cursing and rubbing his leg.

"You are an asshole. Silly me, for thinking you were getting better," I yelled. "I want to go home, damn it!"

He frowned and limped to the kitchen, sitting down at the small table.

"I like it here," he said quietly.

"It's cold here."

"It's cold there, too. It's called winter."

"People love you there, Phillip. Without you controlling them, they liked you. Yes, you're feeling shameful about what you did. So, atone. Don't hide. That's not sexy."

At the mention of 'sexy,' he seemed to perk up. "So, if I returned, you'd find me sexy? Just like you did in your dream?" He gave me a devilish grin.

I instantly wished I hadn't said the word. I slumped into a chair across from him. "Phillip Leal, if you don't help me get us home, I will hate you forever."

He shook his head. "No, I don't think that's true. I think you care about me more than you want to admit. You can't hate me. And that scares you. It scares you that you're starting to have feelings for me."

"I have zero feelings for you, you crazy person. The binding got me all confused, is all."

His grin widened. "No, you think that if you continue to stay here with me, you might fall for me in real life. Maybe do something you really regret."

I got up. "A dream from my subconscious where we made out doesn't mean I don't care about Erik anymore. I just got a little confused. And we had just bonded. It won't happen again."

Phillip sighed and slowly stood up. "Can't blame me for trying."

"So, are you coming back with me or not? I don't think I have the power to get back without you, Phillip."

"If I don't help you, you'll hate me?" His eyes seemed genuinely saddened.

"It would make things strained between us. Which we don't need as soulmates to fight off this big bad coming."

He looked up at the ceiling. I could see the internal struggle on his face.

"For you, *mi corazón*, I will return," he said in a quiet voice, still avoiding my eyes.

I blinked several times in surprise. I'd honestly thought he'd put up more of a fight. "Just like that? You've changed your mind?"

He nodded. "Everything you're saying is right. Our happy home couldn't last too long." He looked over to me and gave a smile so sad I almost felt bad for him. Almost. "Let's go face the music."

"Thank you."

~

I looked to Phillip. "If this doesn't work for us, I'm going to be so embarrassed," I said. We'd said our goodbyes. I'd even gone to visit Andy. He tried to drown Phillip again, but I think he really was just playing around. Of course, Phillip didn't see it that way and threatened to blow the sea creature up. We had one last lesson from Liz, made several potions that the villagers could use for future healing, and made our way to the backyard of our cottage to leave.

Mercy and Liz stood with Phillip, Ed, and I to see us off. Mercy clung to Phillip, wrapping one of her arms around his like a loving girlfriend. He stood stiffly, seemingly afraid to move away.

"Don't be a stranger to us, dearies," Liz stated. "Next time you come here, you won't be stuck, so don't be scared of visiting."

"I'm not," Phillip replied, giving Liz a tight hug. "I might be back sooner than you think." He winked at her, and the older woman smiled coyly, waving a dismissive hand at him.

She then turned to me. "There's a friendly fairy that you met. You'll see her again."

"How'd you know about Francesca?" I asked with wide eyes.

"I just do."

"Who is she? Why did she help me?"

"She's on our side. Tell Felix to watch out for her."

"What does he have to do with this?"

Liz leaned in and hugged me. "Everything. He's a special man, just like the rest of The Six."

"Do you know what he is?"

"I have my theories. Nothing is coincidence. However, I need to keep it to myself for now."

I nodded and turned to Phillip, who was being captured in what looked like an air-depleting hug by Mercy.

"You ready, partner?"

He gave me eyes that seemed to scream for help, but I only chuckled in response. "I guess."

I gave him a curt nod then held out my hands to both men. "Okay, let's do this."

Mercy reluctantly let go of Phillip and backed away from us.

The three of us locked hands, and Phillip and I closed our eyes. I focused my mind's eye on the Fae and what I'd seen them do. I thought of Lisa and her magic in action. My fingers itched, and I tightened my grip. I heard Ed wince, and I relaxed my fingers. The itch grew up my arm, and it felt like thousands of ants were covering my body. I wanted to drop and roll back and forth on the ground but resisted the urge and bit my lip tightly. I tasted blood. I itched so badly I didn't even feel the pain. This was worse than when I became Erik's mate.

A thick wetness rolled down my cheeks and onto my lips and neck.

"You both are bleeding from the nose, ears, and eyes, mates," Ed said, a note of concern in his voice. "Perhaps you'd better stop."

"No," I replied in a strained voice, gritting my teeth as a throbbing ache attached to the base of my skull.

I sucked in a deep breath and focused on the fairy magic. The blue and ice of the Fae. I would have some of it and form something new.

I opened my eyes and looked at Phillip; his newly purple eyes glowed, and I assumed mine did the same.

"Fairy magic hurts like hell. Let's break this damn curse," he said in an exasperated voice.

Once we had fairy magic infused with our own, breaking the curse was easy. Well, not easy, but doable. We chanted a curse-breaking spell. It took some time, but I refused to lose faith. I wasn't going through this pain for nothing. Soon, we began to rise, levitating a few inches off the ground.

"Bloody hell," Ed cried out.

Now we were getting somewhere.

Moments later, the world around us started to dissipate. The scenery changed and nothing but a white space remained. However, this too went away as streets and familiar buildings filled our visions. We saw the blurry movements of human shapes pass us by. Long streaks of color followed their movements, and then those streaks shortened as space and time caught up with us, to display people walking normally around us.

The scenery was fully formed.

We were now in the town center of our Silver Spring community.

We were back.

CHAPTER 24

I looked around the town. Everything appeared the same. There were the shops and restaurants that surrounded us on both sides of the cobblestone street. The entertainment street still had the stage on the right side near the center. Only, I hoped whoever was running the show while Phillip was out wasn't holding public disfigurements.

A few townsfolk slowed their walking and passed us with curious eyes until recognition took hold, and they stopped. I think I heard a few gasps.

"They're back," whispered one older lady with a look of shock on her face.

I vaguely recognized some of the people in the crowd. It was the middle of the day, I think, and most people would be working.

"Amina?" I heard a female voice call behind me.

I spun around and spotted a tall woman with very long, wavy, brown hair. She was bundled up in a puffy coat and walked over to us, her eyes wide and mouth hanging open in shock. Grace Sarin.

"Grace!" I exclaimed and gave her a tight hug when she reached us. She looked over to Phillip and paused.

Phillip gave her a wave, and she waved back with a confused expression.

Grace frowned and looked at me.

"We're friends now. He was bespelled. I broke it, kind of," I explained, knowing she'd need more than that quick recap. I turned to Ed. "This is our friend, Ed, from Ireland."

She nodded at him. "Hi, Ed from Ireland. I'm Grace from America," she replied before turning back to me. "We were wondering where Lisa sent you. It's been nearly three months! And you're back!"

I nodded. "So, who's in charge?"

"Seth runs things now."

I shivered. "Crap."

"How'd that happen?" Phillip questioned.

"He had the power," she said matter-of-factly.

Ed leaned in. "I don't mean to cut into this reunion, but a crowd is growing. Is there somewhere we can go?

"I'm assuming my place is no longer mine," Phillip said.

Grace glanced at him. "No, it isn't. Seth and the pack took over your whole building."

"Of course, they did," he muttered.

"They said it had the best housing."

I didn't care about housing right now. "Where's Erik?"

She glanced over at me with a smile. "He's the sheriff. So, I guess he'd be in the police station now."

I knew where that was. About half a mile away. I turned to the others.

Phillip looked down the street. "Go. Ed and I will go pay my friend Seth a visit."

There was an edge of steel to his voice, and I had a fear that the old Phillip might seep back in. I looked at Ed. "Keep him on the up and up and watch his back."

Ed grinned. "Always, darlin'."

I nodded. "Grace, can you gather everyone and tell them to meet at Faith's in two hours?" I looked at my watch. "And by everyone, I mean Mae, Bill, Felix, and Charles. Tell Charles to bring Chelsea. Also, get Carter... and Lisa. And Phillip, you and Ed come too."

Grace nodded with wide eyes.

"Wait!" Grace called. "You might want to wipe the blood off of your face."

In all my excitement, I hadn't thought about how I looked. I pointed to her. "Thank you."

I whispered a cleansing spell, hovering my hands over my face. I turned to Grace, and she gave me a thumbs-up.

"See you guys in two hours," I stated before turning and walking away. I wanted to teleport to the station, but the strength it took to get back from Ireland was too much. I'd used the last bit of magical energy I had for now to clean myself up. I would just walk. Fast.

Once I reached the station, I walked in and saw the lone receptionist sitting at the center counter reading a book. In a small town filled with paranormals and led by a crazy person, crime was not a huge issue.

"Excuse me," I asked the middle-aged woman behind the desk. "Betty, right? Is Erik here?"

She looked up with open-mouth shock. "Amina?" She stood up and put her book down. "Oh my! You're back!" She seemed genuinely excited to see me. She moved around the counter and raced over to give me a hug.

I accepted her embrace, although we had never been on hugging terms before.

"It's good seeing you again." I tightened my smile, expectantly.

She opened her eyes wide. "Oh, right, Erik. He went to investigate a spousal abuse issue. Horrible thing. Between two vampires. She beat the hell out of that man." She shook her head. "I can get Erik on the walkie-talkie. Tell him to come back. He shouldn't be far."

"That'd be great, Betty."

"You can wait in his office. It's the big room against the back wall behind me. Oh, he's going to be over the moon. I'm so happy you're back. He was no good without you. Poor thing. But he's going to be all better now."

I squinted my eyes. "What do you mean, no good?"

She paused and opened her mouth as if she were caught spilling a secret. "Oh, dear. I run my mouth too much. Let me call him, and you guys can talk. Now that you're back, everything's going to be just fine. Go on and wait in the back. He shouldn't be long, honey."

I sighed and walked to the back of the open space, passing several vacant desks and some closed-door rooms off to the side. I opened the office door and took a seat at the long, oak desk stationed in front of a large window.

Suddenly, I became nervous. I hadn't seen him in months, and it wasn't like we were together all that long before. What if he'd fallen out of love? It would serve me right. I thought, guiltily, of my dream world kiss with Phillip. Was it cheating if it was in a dream and I was led by my subconscious? Should I confess to Erik if the kiss did count?

My mind raced, and I got sickened by the thought that I would be coming back less than innocent and looking like a sweaty mess. I ran to the bathroom a few doors down and looked in the mirror. I took off my peacoat and sighed, unsatisfied. I had on a basic blue sweater and jeans, with the same red Converse sneakers that I'd had on when I was banished. My curly hair was piled on top of my head in a loose ponytail. I had no makeup on. Ed's village wasn't so advanced that they'd had their own beauty store. I could have glamoured myself with magic, but it always made me look overdone, and I was still magically exhausted with the energy it'd taken to get back.

I proceeded to spend the next fifteen minutes forcing myself not to vomit up nerves or run away. Why was I so nervous? I wasn't some love-sick teenager. However, I couldn't ignore the nagging doubt that maybe he wouldn't be that excited to see me. Maybe he wouldn't feel the same after all this time.

When I heard fast footsteps growing closer, my heart decided to jump to my throat. I tightened my stomach muscles in nervous anticipation.

Suddenly, the door swung open. I didn't turn. I was too scared. I was being ridiculous.

"Mina?" I heard him ask more than say. It was as if he wasn't sure he could believe what he was seeing.

I finally decided to get myself together and stood up to face him. When I laid eyes on him, I was slightly in shock. He didn't look like he had when I'd left him or what I'd seen in my dream. His beard was back, and his hair was longer. He was also paler and thinner, with slightly sunken- cheeks. Dark circles rested under his eyes. Somehow, he looked like he had aged. I wanted to cry.

"Erik," I cried and ran to him, wrapping my arms around his back.

He held me tightly and I squeezed him. We stood that way for a while, relaxing in the feel of each other. I didn't want to move or let him go.

Eventually, he kissed the top of my head. "I can't believe you're here," he whispered in a choked voice.

"Yep, I finally made it back." I smiled into his chest and my tears dampened his shirt.

He moved me back and stared at me. Silently, Erik cupped my face in his hands. Still gazing at me with eyes filled with a mixture of joy and exhaustion, he kissed me.

His lips felt nice on mine, like a soft blanket. It felt good and somehow, I felt stronger. I didn't want to move away from him but he leaned back and now his eyes seemed to glow as if energized.

"I love you," I said. Finally.

He leaned in and kissed me harder this time. "We're going to need to go back to my place," he whispered in my ear.

Erik drove us back to the pack high-rise, whisked me past a desk attendant, who waved an open-mouth hello at us, and into the elevator. We ended up one floor down from the penthouse.

I looked around the open apartment space, walking past the foyer. There were floor-to-ceiling windows to the right, behind the sofa and dinette set, and dark, hardwood floors laid under heavy, high-end furniture. To my left, the open kitchen held stainless-steel appliances and dark, granite counters. I veered down the hallway past the kitchen. I passed an untouched spare bedroom before entering his suite, which was complete with bathroom. It wasn't as neat as the spare but it was still nice with a walk-in closet and another wall of windows.

"Look at number three, coming up in the world," I observed. I turned back to him before flopping down on the edge of his unmade bed. "You look good."

"No, I don't," he said, sitting beside me.

"You look fine. Lost a few pounds. You've been eating, right? Did food get scarce here?"

He chuckled. "Hardly. We're doing well. Farm's growing. I just haven't had time to eat that much."

I scrunched up my face. "There's always time to eat. You're a were. You have to eat a lot."

"Weres don't fare well being away from their mates. I didn't take care of myself."

"So, my being gone hurt you? Even with the dream and telepathic communication? It wasn't enough?" I frowned, feeling a wave of guilt.

He gave a look of irritation. "None of this was your fault, Mina. After the shared dream, it got harder for me. Talking to you when you were in battle helped a little, but we couldn't get to you any other time. I worried about you. If I could have seen you in a dream again, it would have been better, but it was a fluke we even met the one time."

"I was beginning to think it didn't really happen. I'm sorry I couldn't link back again." I tilted my head, a confusing thought entering my mind. "Why didn't I feel any worse?"

"You probably didn't feel any different because you aren't were. Or you were with Phillip, your soulmate, so you had another mate to pull strength from."

I grimaced, the guilt hitting me even harder. There, I'd been kissing his enemy in my dreams and here, Erik had been getting sick.

Erik pulled me to him, wrapping an arm around me, and I laid my head on his shoulder. He gave a deep inhale, sniffing me in. "I missed your smell," he whispered.

"I'll have a magic scent made, so you can have my smell with you anytime I'm not around."

"I can't figure out why you think I'll let you go anywhere," he said with a possessive growl. "I have handcuffs, and I don't mind using them."

I looked up to him and caught his mischievous eyes. "We'll have to explore what that looks like later," I laughed.

I heard a faint meow from somewhere in the apartment. "Did I just hear a cat?" I asked, giving Erik a quizzical look. Seconds later, I saw a familiar little gray kitten trot into the bedroom and hop on the bed.

"Poppy!" I cried, patting my lap. The kitten jumped on me and head-butted my stomach, demanding to be petted. I glanced over to Erik with a wide smile as I scratched her head. "You kept her."

He grinned. "I didn't have a choice. She wouldn't leave my side after you disappeared. Charles told me her name, and me and Pops have been roommates since." He leaned over and scratched the kitten's back. Poppy pushed her butt into the air, lavishing the attention we were giving her.

"I can't believe a cat wanted to hang around a werejackal."

"Shayla said she is your familiar."

I pondered that. Not every witch had or needed a familiar. It certainly helped to make one stronger. They worked as amplifiers, and I'd take any power I could get, especially from one as cute as this kitten. "Thank you for keeping her."

"It wasn't a problem. She helped me as well. I was lost for a while." He leaned in and kissed my shoulder. "Keeping her around helped me keep having faith that you'd come back to me. I admit, sometimes I didn't think you would. All sorts of things ran in my mind. You were banished away with a man who I knew had feelings for you and who was your soulmate. I gave up."

I'd felt the same way with Erik being here alone with a pack full of women wanting him but tried my best not to obsess about it with all that was happening. I'd pictured different women knocking on his door every night with casseroles and steaks because he was a carnivore, trying to soothe his broken heart as time went on. It didn't help that he looked like he'd lost a loved one. I imagined that very time a woman saw those sad, hazel eyes, she would run to the kitchen and come over with a plate of food and a short skirt. "Well, it looks like I came back just in time," I looked up at him with a wide grin.

He smiled down at me. "Far too late for my taste," he stated before leaning forward and kissing me again.

His hands slid down to my waist and under my shirt. The heat of his skin sent a welcome tremor through my body. Poppy, appearing to sense the situation or perhaps not wanting to get crushed, jumped off my lap and took off out of the room.

"Smart kitty," he said into my mouth.

I laughed and felt the curve of his mouth over mine as he laughed as well. Before I could finish, he'd moved me to my back and leaned in to kiss me again. I wrapped my arms around his neck, pressing him to me, and our kiss deepened.

His tongue danced with mine, and I moaned softly, moving a hand through his hair. I nipped his lower lip and took in the taste of his mouth. A growl escaped deep from his chest, and he moved his lips to the base of my neck and onto my collarbone.

A spark of warmth spread over me. My hands went under his black T-shirt and ran the length of his back. My fingers lightly brushed his smooth skin and played along his muscles, which bunched as he balanced on his arms above me.

He unsnapped my bra before moving his fingers under the fabric and onto my skin. At his touch, something tightened below my stomach, and I gasped as the heat deepened. He lifted my T-shirt over my head, and his own shirt followed soon after.

I touched his face, and he pulled away. I frowned. His eyes were no longer the human hazel but the jackal orange.

"What's wrong?" I asked. "Is it close to the full moon?"

"No. It's just that... this could hurt you, and I don't want that," he said in a heavy voice.

At first, I didn't understand. Then Seth's words from months ago played in my mind. Weres were stronger than other humans, even humans with magic. Mated Weres were even stronger. Erik exhibited great control our previous times together, but I had no idea what being intimate would be like with him as my mate. He was probably thinking that he would break me. The thought both amused and horrified me. I didn't want a shattered pelvis behind this, but I also didn't think I was that weak, since I was still paranormal.

I looked at his worried eyes. Such controlled restraint behind them. "You aren't going to hurt me, Erik. You wouldn't do that to me." And if he did, I'd have to find some magical workaround. Maybe I could make my bones out of steel, like some comic book hero. I wondered if I really could do that.

I wasn't used to Erik looking uncertain. Even when he was battling to the death for the spot of third, he'd seemed confident. However, now his jackal eyes were pained and I began to wonder if I should tell him never mind. Yet, I didn't want to. I wanted him.

"It's okay," I whispered.

He leaned back and looked at me silently one last time. When he it seemed he believed I would be fine, he moved to take off the rest of our clothes.

He looked me over, balancing on his hands above me, and suddenly I felt self-conscious despite the fact that he'd seen me before. I wasn't nearly as toned as he was, with his muscular arms, chest, and hard stomach. I crossed my arms over my stomach. He shook his head and gave me a lazy smile before uncrossing my arms and moving into me. I wrapped my legs around his waist, moving with his rhythm. We continued like this, his movements shifting between slow and deliberate to fast and hard. But he was always in control. I felt no pain, only absolute pleasure as he moved.

I locked eyes with Erik, and he smiled again, touching my cheek with the palm of his hand. I returned his smile, and we continued moving together until I screamed out in an explosive release. He quickened his pace and soon followed, letting out what I could only describe as a howl.

I stifled a giggle. He looked down at me with a quizzical look before leaning over and kissing my collarbone. He rocked into me again and again, and I arched my back in an uncontrolled release. Twice in a row. That was new for me.

"How do you feel?" he asked.

"Amazing," I replied. It was the truth. I felt as if I'd had the world's best massage. My arms and legs felt limp, but I was relaxed.

He turned my face to him and kissed me again. "I love you."

"You better," I cracked.

Content, I closed my eyes and fell asleep.

One hour later, I awoke to a throbbing pain between my legs. I looked beneath my covers and saw that my inner thighs and pelvis area were already a mass of black and blue. I bent over and put on my jeans, wincing at the dull ache. I grabbed the rest of my clothes and hobbled to the bathroom, where I whispered a spell of healing. If Erik knew about the bruising, he'd have a fit and there was nothing he could do anyway.

I hadn't felt pain during and since I could heal myself, I figured I'd be okay. I walked out of the bathroom and found Erik awake and sitting on the edge of the bed.

"Everything okay?" Erik asked with a grin on his face.

He looked so innocent, so happy. I didn't have the heart to tell him the truth.

I walked over to him and kissed him on the forehead. "Everything is wonderful."

"I just got a harassing call from your brother saying we're supposed to be at Faith's place right now, per your instructions. He mentioned something about CP time? What is that?"

I rolled my eyes. "He's right. I told everyone to meet and I lost track of time with you."

He gave me a cocky grin and wiggled his eyebrows. "Send them all home. We can catch up with them another time."

I shook my head. I really didn't want to leave the apartment, but if we didn't see the others, they'd just come here, led by my brother, and interrupt us anyway.

I sighed. "We have to meet the others. There's a lot to talk about."

CHAPTER 25

Faith lived in a high-rise, one-bedroom apartment overlooking additional farmland beyond the steel wall.

Upon seeing me at the door, Faith threw her hands in the air and cried out. "Yea!" she shouted before giving me a tight hug.

And thus, the hugfest commenced. When I saw Charles, I actually started to cry.

"Aww, sis, don't cry. You're gonna make me tear up, and my tears are pink, which disturbs me on many levels," he whispered as he wiped tears off my cheeks.

I nodded and sniffled back my tears. Then I made the mistake of looking over at Mae, who was wiping away tears of her own, and I started to tear up again.

"I need my hug," Felix announced, standing behind Charles.

Charles moved aside, and Felix moved in to give me a great, big bear hug, lifting me off of the ground.

I let out a yelp, and he put me down. "Glad you're back, Mina," he said with a wide grin.

I looked around at everyone and smiled. "It's so damn

good to see you all again," I announced. I narrowed my eyes, someone was missing. "Where's Lisa?"

"She's not one of us anymore, Mina," Faith stated, sitting on the arm of her dark-brown couch.

"She's one of The Six."

"She sent you away for almost three months," Felix chimed in.

"And I'd like to know why."

"She's back in Hagerstown," Erik said, standing beside me.

I shook my head. "Can we get her here? Please. I have to talk to her. Maybe we can work it all out." I wasn't really sure if we could, but if I was going to ask them to give Phillip a chance, I had to show that I could do the same for Lisa. Knowing that she was trying to bring me back helped. And I couldn't forget how she, along with the others, had helped me in the fight back in Ireland as well as healing Phillip.

Grace stood up. "I'll go get her. I can get a witch to teleport me there," she explained before heading out.

"I feel like we need a list to go over all the things we need to talk about," I said to the group.

Mae came from the eat-in kitchen with a large piece of cake on a plate. "Well, would you like some chocolate cake?"

I walked over and took the slice and fork she offered me with glee. I'd missed her cooking. Not so much what it did to my waistline, but I could indulge for a little while.

"I think we should first talk about Phillip," Mae stated as she took a seat at the glass dining room table, which opened up to the living room.

"Right," I said, reluctantly putting the cake down on the table. "The big bad that's coming had someone put a spell on him to make him go all psychopath. I did a spell to help with it, but it only worked up to a point. I'm not strong enough, yet. What I did do has seemed to make him better. He's a different person."

Charles swore as he leaned against a wall in the living area. "So, you want us to forgive him for all the shit he's done?"

I had to be careful of how I worded things. I was speaking to a crowd who hadn't been through the last few months with me. They wouldn't understand so easily. "I'm saying we have to look at things with an open mind. Something very bad is coming and we need help."

"He killed the man I loved," Chelsea spat.

I sat beside her at the dinette table and grabbed her hand. I didn't want to downplay anything. What Phillip had done was monstrous. I could not imagine that Phillip being under a curse would make her change her feelings about him.

"I'm not saying we have to be his friend or fully trust him. I'm saying let's have a truce and see where things go from there."

"He's going to want to be back in power, and then he's going to be his old self again," Faith stated, anger simmering in her voice.

I looked over to her from across the table. I understood her anger. Phillip wasn't an easy sell and I did feel a little icky having to defend him. "He won't go back to his old self. I won't let that happen."

"For all we know, he could just be pretending. He's no stranger to that. He could still be the man he was."

Charles shook his head. "There are things you don't know about him, sis."

Crap, what else had he done? Phillip was really going to make this hard for me. We heard a knock at the door, and Faith rose to answer it. Moments later, Ed and Phillip appeared.

I got up and did an introduction of Ed, who greeted the solemn group, remaining by Phillip's side.

"I've filled them in on what happened to you but not everything," I explained to Phillip.

"Look," Phillip began, stepping forward. "I know none of you are just going to accept me overnight. I'm only asking for a chance to atone for what I've done."

Before I could even see him rise, Charles raced across the room at vampiric speed and knocked Phillip to the ground, pummeling him with his fists. Ed reached down to pull him off but Charles knocked him back, either with his vampire strength or witch magic; I couldn't tell. Charles moved in a blur.

Ed fell back against Felix, who stopped him from falling to the floor.

Charles continued to punch Phillip. No one else moved to stop him. Mae and Bill cried for him to stop, but my brother was in his own zone. Phillip was barely fighting back. He could have stopped him with magic, yet he did not. At that this rate, Charles would kill him.

"Stop it, Charles," I shouted. I itched to use my powers to end the senseless beating but that would make me no better than how Phillip used to be. I would not abuse my powers and make anyone my puppet. "Please, Charles!"

Charles slowed down his punches before stopping altogether and then got up. He looked over to me, baring his fangs in an eerie smile. "Only because you said please. And I'd like to know why you think he's worth saving."

No one said a word. Ed moved to help Phillip to his feet. His face was bloody, and Mae rushed to him with a napkin in her hands. With all of the paranormals in this room, Phillip could easily be healed. He took the napkin but politely waved Bill off when the med mage approached him for healing.

"I know you don't like him, but you assaulted him without provocation!" I shouted.

Charles threw out his hands. "Really? How about for sentencing Felix to blindness, killing Chelsea's boyfriend, and locking you up when you fought to defend Felix? And because he locked you up, I had to break you out, which turned out to get me killed and turned into a vampire?"

Ugh, my brother knew how to build a case. I'd have to give another perspective. "So, you think you dying was Phillip's fault? David was the one who stabbed you. Phillip tried to heal you. David would have come for me regardless of where I was."

"What did he do to you?" Chelsea said, face sorrowful.

"Nothing, Chelsea. I'm just being reasonable." I dropped my shoulders, trying not to feel defeated so early. I knew this would be a hard task. "We weren't going to get anywhere if you continued to hit him, Charles. He wasn't even fighting back."

"That fucking asshole must have you brainwashed," Charles spat. "Got you thinking that he's a victim in all of this. He's not!"

"I get it. No one is totally innocent here."

Faith scooted her chair back. "Fine, if Phillip is your BFF now, did he tell you he's also Blake's consort? They've probably been communicating with each other all this time."

My heart momentarily stopped at the shock. I turned to him. "What? Phillip, is that right?"

Phillip looked over to me, eyes neutral. "Yes, Blake and I are consorts. We became so before the challenge. But she couldn't help me anymore than your bond with Erik could when we were banished. I definitely couldn't borrow powers, which, thanks for telling me about that," he replied with a hurt look.

I bit my lip, holding on to my anger. Suddenly, what little trust I had in him started to waiver. This was not a good time for that, as I was currently trying to convince everyone to join forces with him for the greater good.

"Guess you guys aren't such BFFs," Felix said in a loud whisper.

"If we can't kill him, then put him in a coma. Forever," Faith stated. "There, that's a way you can make it up to us."

"Sounds good to me," Charles said.

Ed took a step forward, lifting an index finger . "Look, mates, I don't know the lot of you, but from what I'm hearing, Phil was a real shithead, to put it mildly. I understand your positions, but if you were under a spell, would you want to be forever judged by actions you couldn't control? I know I, for one, have a less than presentable past. I'm glad I was able to still be a part of a town where I can do some good, and Phillip's done some amazing things for my village."

"Maybe you should take him back there with you, then," Charles grumbled.

I shot him a death look that he ignored.

Erik tilted his head, accessing Ed. "Did you kill anyone? Ed, is it? Before the world changed."

"No, but it was dumb luck that I didn't. I wasn't a good man, and I didn't have a spell to blame." Ed looked around at the group. "Now, I know I'm only human. So, what could I possibly share? But we have some serious bad coming. We've had to fight some of it twice already, and it's nothing to scoff at. We're lucky we survived. This infighting won't do us any good. Like it or not, these two are soulmates, and they are pretty damn strong. The things I've seen them do... Miracles. Even in this day and age, they are still doing things I've never seen before. And they don't ask for anything in return."

"So, you weren't all just on one long vacation while you were gone?" Felix asked with big innocent eyes.

My mind was buzzing with all that was going on. I was exhausted, emotional, and really just overwhelmed. I started laughing.

Phillip looked over to me with wide eyes and then started to join me in laughter.

"What the hell's going on?" Erik growled.

I looked at him, and my chuckling died down as I caught

his angry face. "Just so you all know, since Lisa banished us, yes, we made friends and explored Ireland. We also fought ghosts, got attacked twice by a Jinn, and battled an army of dark Fae and man-eating plants. We also trained hard under a very powerful witch who communicated with Mae. And before you ask, she couldn't get us to return home either."

"Mina," Erik said, grabbing my hand.

"There were no piña coladas or beaches. Moral of the story is, we've been through a lot. I know you guys think he's a heartless, cruel, insidious, selfish, self-centered, arrogant, monstrous, psychotic—"

"Is there an end here?" Phillip asked in a low voice.

"—despicable person who deserves horrible things done to him, such as maiming, putting him in a coma, giving him a lobotomy, taking away his magic—"

Phillip raised a hand. "Quick question, why are you giving them suggestions?"

I ignored him and continued. "And even though he may have deserved all of that—"

"Giving me a lobotomy seems to go beyond what's fair, but okay."

I spoke louder. "Even though he may have deserved all of that, he isn't actually the person he was when we left. Since being in Ireland, Phillip has done good."

"The whole time?" Charles countered. "He didn't try to control folk?'

"I did a little, in the beginning, when I was still fully under the curse," Phillip stated, looking down as he pressed a hand into his bruised face and wincing.

Ed turned slightly to him. "What's that now, mate?"

Phillip nodded, actually looking apologetic. "When we first met, I thought you wouldn't let us into your village, so I magically influenced you. I was a piece of shit in the beginning. I should have said something when I recovered, but I was... I was scared."

I frowned, both strangely sad for Phillip and proud that he'd admitted such weakness in front of everyone. I looked over to Ed, who sat motionless as if pondering his words. His face betrayed no emotion, which was not uncommon for Ed. He was a teddy bear at heart, but his poker face would keep you on the edge of your seat if you had to deliver bad news. You weren't sure if he would pat you on the head and say it was okay or punch you in the face and curse you out.

"He cried about all of the bad things he'd done while under the curse," I stated.

Phillip raised his eyebrows in surprise. "It was actually a watery eye condition that was ongoing."

I tilted my head at him and twisted my lips.

"Other people might call it crying. Fine, I had crying fits about what I did." He shook his head and looked away from the group.

Finally, Ed sighed. "Were you using your powers the whole time?"

Phillip shook his head, turning back to Ed. "No, I stopped soon after. Amina made me. Then I wanted to."

Ed looked to me, and I nodded.

"So, it's all sorted out, then," Ed replied with a sniff. "All's forgiven. Mercy did cut you when she first met you. So, I suppose we're even."

"Who is she? I like her," Faith cracked.

"How about we compromise?" I asked the group.

Erik scoffed, looking away. "Are you crazy?"

"Clearly," Charles said. "What did you do to my sister?!" He glared over at Phillip, fists balled, ready to pounce again.

"I can't hear any more of this," Chelsea said. She got up and left the apartment.

I needed to talk to her. I didn't want to lose my friend because of Phillip. I had to get her to understand the bigger problem we had to face.

Phillip pushed away from the wall. Blood caked around

his nostrils and the corner of his lips, which were already swollen, along with his right eye. In less than a minute, my brother had really done a number on him. "The compromise will be that I prove to you all through my actions that I am not the man I was before. If I do something reminiscent of my previous actions, then you may put me in a coma. I'll also heal everyone I've hurt."

Silence followed from the group as they pondered his offer.

"I think that what Phillip is proposing makes sense," Bill said in a quiet voice.

Bill rarely spoke, but when he did, like Mae, people listened. The medical mage got up and walked to the center of the room. "What spell is this that Phillip is under?"

"We were told that our true enemies were the cause of what happened to Phillip," I stated. I then went on to recount all that Ahmed and the Fae had told us. "This was all part of their plan. It was either to weaken our bond or make us easier to control. They want followers. Especially strong ones. We can't let them win."

"Well, then it stands," Bill announced. "We will allow Phillip to show what kind of person he is. We are not in a position to waste resources. We don't know how many followers these soulmates have, but we must not underestimate them. We must convince more people that danger is coming and put aside our differences for the greater good. At least for now."

"This is bullshit," Faith muttered, and Charles let out a series of expletives from his corner of the room.

"You all hate me," Phillip began. "I don't blame you. I will accept full responsibility for my previous actions. Spell or no spell, I did these things. Perhaps if I were a better man, I wouldn't have succumbed to that curse. If you need to hit me, Charles, or anyone else here, I get it. You can. You can hate me forever. But we've also got to focus on the bigger picture. The Fae are formidable, and we only have a small window where fighting the first soulmates would be easier. We have to focus on finding them before they get stronger. If any of you want to talk, I'm willing. Any time. I'll be moving into the witch complex, so you can find me there," Phillip stated, crossing his arms. "For now."

I could already see the wheels turning in his head of how he'd regain control of the town. Hopefully, he'd do so in a way that didn't involve controlling minds and cutting off limbs, or else he'd be in a permanent dream state.

Another knock at the door. Faith went to answer it, and seconds later, Grace appeared with Lisa.

She looked the same; thin and petite, except her hair was deep red now. She gave me a sad smile before speaking. "I'm so sorry, Amina. I really am," she said in a soft voice.

She actually sounded sincere. Lisa looked to Phillip. "I'm sorry to you, too," she said.

I narrowed my eyes. Now, that was odd.

"Why are you apologizing to him?" I asked.

She looked back at me. "I've told the others, so this is not new to them, but you need to understand why I did what I did for anything to make sense. I was visited by a fairy I knew, some time ago after the trial. She asked me to come with her to the fairy realm and since I thought Charles was really dead, what did I have to lose?"

"You could have said goodbye," I stated, keeping my voice even. "We spent a long time looking for you."

Lisa sighed. "My friend assured me that she told Felix before we left."

Felix shrugged sheepishly. "I don't remember seeing the woman until after Lisa came back. You all know by now my mind gets messed up without a moment's notice. I'm sorry."

"I should have been the one to say goodbye, but—" Lisa looked to Charles, who didn't look back at her. He stared stoically at the wall in front of him. Something was off here. I really *had* missed a lot. "I was really in pain at the time, Mina. I wasn't thinking clearly. And then in the fairy world, I didn't think I was there so long. Maybe a couple of weeks. When I came back, I learned I had been gone for months. Fairy time is very different."

"Yeah, we know," Ed said gruffly.

I tilted my head back towards Ed. "That's Ed. We met him on our forced voyage. Ed's town was terrorized by Fae a few times."

"I'm sorry for anything my people have done. Although we are few, we are not all the same." Lisa started, "While I was in the fairy world, we talked about the evil coming. We discussed the danger of soulmates. When magic ruled, soulmates came about every few generations. They often started good, but that level of power always mutated into something awful. Some soulmates did some pretty bad things. I mentioned to the Fae that you and Phillip were soulmates," Lisa went on. "They already knew and were very concerned. Fae make it a habit to know such things. They can even predict pairings. When the magic mostly went away, they stopped predicting. During the time of little magic, soulmates were of no importance to the Fae. Until the two of you. At first, they couldn't figure out the importance of knowing who you were. For the Fae to be alerted to a new soulmate pairing seemed odd when there was no magic. They followed you. They knew about the kind of humans you were." Lisa looked to Phillip. "Then the magic came back, and everything became clear. When I explained your behavior to the Fae, it was very concerning to them because they didn't believe that was your true character. They knew you were bespelled."

It would have been nice for the Fae to clue us in a little earlier but that had never been their style. Still, if the others knew the truth about Phillip, why were they acting like they were hearing it for the first time? "I'm going to assume Lisa told you all this already. Why do you still hate him?"

"Don't be mad at them," Lisa stated.

Erik stuffed his hands in his pocket and gave a disinterested shrug. It was clear he was still pissed. "We have to see it all for ourselves. Make sure his magic isn't influencing you both."

"Well, does Phillip smell or feel like he did before?" I asked Erik. He'd been unsettled before when we first came to Silver Spring but wasn't able to pinpoint the smell of dark magic to Phillip alone.

Erik scrunched his face and looked away. "He has B.O. but other than that, I don't smell dark magic." Oh, he was being petty Erik today. I kind of liked it.

Phillip looked up to the ceiling and rolled his eyes.

Felix stretched his hands above his head. "I don't get a bad feeling either. Okay, well, that's something, right?"

Mae and Bill said, "Yes." The others answered with shrugs and twisted lips. Seems they just didn't want to give Phillip the benefit of the doubt.

I shook my head and turned to Lisa. "So, if you knew that Phillip was cursed, why did you send us away?" This is what I really wanted to know beyond anything else. How could someone I called a friend turn her back on me?

Lisa gave me a sad smile. "I was told by a Seelie Fae Queen that it was the only way to stop Phillip from doing more harm and to strengthen your soulmate bond without any distractions."

"So, you sent us away for me to focus on healing Phillip and having us bond? You couldn't tell me first?"

Lisa sighed. "There wasn't time. To be honest, I didn't want to do it." She walked over to me and grabbed my hands. "You're like my best friend now. I thought we should just lock Phillip up in fairy world where he couldn't harm anyone. But the other Fae made me afraid of the evil to come." She looked to Phillip. "You really have the Fairy Queen I was with to thank. She's the one who actually came up with the plan. And she said you, Amina, were needed to help heal him, so he couldn't go alone. In all truthfulness, if I hadn't done this, someone else would have."

Phillip gave a tilt of his head. "So, how long were we supposed to be gone?"

"We were thinking a month, maybe a little over. We figured you both would find common ground quickly without any distractions, which would open you up to being healed."

Although that made sense, why did they let so much time past? "So then why are we only *now* getting back? And of our own accord? Phillip was helped around two months in."

"Because I couldn't get you back. Some other magic was preventing me from doing so."

"So, someone hijacked your spell?" Phillip asked.

Lisa nodded. "We were thinking maybe there was another type of magic that enforced the spell."

"But we used fairy magic to get back," I explained.

Her green eyes squinted in suspicion. "You found some Fae to help you?"

I lifted my hair off my neck, looking down as I thought about the right words to share. Talking about how we worked out our soulmate magic would open ups some doors I didn't care to touch. "Not exactly. While we were in banishment," I gave her a pointed look. "Phillip and I were able to work on our soulmate magic, once we stopped hating each other, that is."

"What did that entail?" Erik asked, arms crossed.

The stupid hand-holding, levitating, eye-color change, and dream kiss all flashed in my mind. I broke into a slight sweat in my armpits, wondering if Erik could read my mind. How could I explain this all to him and make it seem as innocent as I wanted it to be?

"Opening our magic up to each other instead of working against each other like we had been doing for the challenge," Phillip cut in to explain. "It's as simple as that. Once we stopped fighting each other, we got stronger."

I gave Phillip a grateful nod. He really was becoming less irritating. I really was nervous he was going to make it seem more sordid than it was. Erik looked to me; eyes inquisitive. "Tell me more later," he said more than asked.

I raised my eyebrows and smiled, hoping I didn't look as guilty as I felt. That was going to be a fun conversation. "Of course. So, Lisa, why didn't you just come to Ireland and get us then?" I asked, quickly changing the subject.

Lisa shook her head. "We didn't know where you went. I sent you away but had the destination removed from my memory by the Fae Queen. It was better to make sure you stayed away if I didn't know where you were. Amina, I can't apologize to you enough," Lisa said. "You've been nothing but good to me. You saved my life. I just... I just didn't know what else to do. I knew Phillip had to be stopped and that we couldn't hurt him or you'd be hurt."

I looked at her without speaking. For almost three months, I had hated her. Even with her very sound explanation, I wasn't sure I was ready to forget. I had put trust in her that I had not in Phillip. Her sending me away without discussion felt more like a betrayal of a family member than Phillip's behavior. With him, perhaps, I might have always been a little leery. At least, for a while. I didn't want to be suspicious of her, and yet, now I felt I had to be. It was upsetting.

However, I had more important things to focus on at the moment. I needed to find a genie lamp.

CHAPTER 26

"By the way, I was wondering, whatever happened to Phillip's animal he raised in the challenge?" I asked. It was probably the wrong time to find out if I was as powerful as Phillip as I was hoping I was, but it had always been on my mind.

Erik's walkie-talkie went off and he picked it up to answer it.

Phillip nodded. "Yeah, I raised a puppy."

I looked around at the others. "Did anyone keep it like Erik did Poppy, my kitty?"

Faith snorted. "No."

Erik turned back to the group. "I've gotta go. Some idiot is causing a riot at the hospital. People are acting more and more like nut cases," he surmised. He looked over at me. "I won't be long. You going to be okay?"

"I'll come with you. I can help," I said, not really wanting to leave his side so soon after reuniting with him.

"It's too dangerous." He walked over to me.

I opened my mouth to protest, but he kissed me hard. "I love you. I won't be gone long." He then turned and walked out, giving Phillip a solid stare.

Phillip rolled his shoulders. "What happened to my dog?" he asked, his voice tight.

"Well, Chelsea killed it. Drank it dry," Faith replied in an unaffected tone.

I raised my eyebrows in shocked horror. "What?"

Faith nodded. "Yeah, your friend is hardcore. Phillip, watch your back."

Ed scratched his head, brows furrowed. "Who kills a dog?"

"It was a puppy," Phillip muttered, shaking his head.

Chelsea drank the blood of a familiar. More importantly, she'd murdered a puppy. That was beyond unsettling. I added this to the growing list of things I'd have to resolve.

~

*W*alking back to Erik's place, my mind still raced with my to-do list. Calm down, Chelsea. See what was going on with Charles, jumping to violence was never his thing. Find the genie lamp. Find possible, female original soulmate. Get rid of Seth as head of the town. Gain supporters against the original soulmates and big bad that was coming. I'm sure I was missing something, but that seemed enough for now.

"Amina! Is that you? I heard you were back!" Cried a voice I was not too pleased to hear.

Raya.

I turned and faced the pretty werewolf. News certainly traveled fast in a town the size of a small college.

Raya gave me a tight smile. I did the same. We weren't friends and wouldn't be hugging.

"I guess I'll be seeing you at the party Saturday?" she asked, crossing her arms.

"What party?" I asked with a raised eyebrow.

"For you and Phillip, of course."

I frowned. "I've only been back a few hours and there's already a party?" I did not have time for this. I had a lamp to find before a Jinn came and set me on fire.

She shrugged. "We have nothing else to do on a Saturday night. It's not like we're getting any new movies or going out for wine tastings."

I smirked. "Is that what you used to do on a Saturday night, before? Pretty tame for someone who'd been in their early twenties, then."

She smiled, showing me her wolf teeth in an anything-but--friendly way. "I was just suggesting something I thought was more your speed. I was more of a dive-bar or live-music person. Kind of like Erik."

I squinted my eyes at her. "Well, nice talking to you," I replied and turned away.

She walked up beside me. "I'm going the same way. Back to the pack apartment."

I nodded, and we walked together in awkward silence.

"So, how was it being with Phillip all that time? You hated each other when you left, and now you're going to have a party together. I'm assuming you've called a truce?"

I really was in no mood to chit-chat with Raya, and it was clear to me that she was fishing for information. I'd give her just enough to shut her up. "Yep, we called a truce. He promised not to be an ass anymore, and I promised not to keep trying to hurt him. All's well that ends well."

We reached the front of the apartment, and I climbed the steps and opened the door. Raya followed me through.

"That's really impressive that the two of you were able to make amends. Is that all that happened? Three months is a long time for two attractive people to be together." She gave me a sideways glance.

"Thank you for calling me attractive. That was really sweet of you." I pressed the elevator button. "Well, I'm going to Erik's now." The elevator doors opened. "What floor are you?" I pressed Erik's floor number, and my hand hovered over the numbers waiting for her to tell me her floor.

"Actually, I'm going there too. I left something at his place the other night."

I dropped my hand and balled it into a fist.

What.

The.

Hell?

I wanted to twist her head off. I actually envisioned doing it, which was dangerous because had I really meant to do such a thing, her head would be rolling on the elevator floor by now.

Calm down, Amina; maybe it was a pack leadership meeting that Erik was hosting, and she'd left her hat there. Yeah, that's what happened, I told myself.

I didn't say anything as we headed up on the elevator and walked what felt like an exceptionally long way to Erik's place. I opened the door with a key he'd given me and walked inside.

"Honey, I'm home," I announced. Not my style to make such an announcement but the petty in me wanted to play.

Erik walked from the bedroom hallway. "Hey, Mina."

"We have a guest," I said pleasantly. I would keep my cool. I would not let her get to me.

He looked at Raya and then me. "Hey," he said in a tone that sounded more like a question.

"Hey, yourself," Raya said. She touched his arm as she moved past him. It was brief, but it was enough to annoy me.

"What are you doing here?" Erik asked.

"Left something in your bedroom."

She walked back to his room without waiting for an invitation, as if she was used to being there.

I tightened my lips together and walked past Erik to the spare room, closing the door. I sat down on the bed and crossed my legs, yoga style, resting my hands on my thighs. I wasn't sure I had the right to be angry, but I was. Raya was in his room. At this point, the whole left-a-hat-behind theory was probably not the case. He'd been with Raya for who knows how long and here I was, spoiling things for her. At this point, she'd probably been with him longer than I had.

I felt sick. Perhaps I was being a bit hypocritical. I'd made out with Phillip in the dream world. What right did I have to be indignant about Erik doing the same with Raya? However, I thought my make out session was just the result of a subconscious dream. That was my excuse. What was Erik's? That he thought I was gone and wouldn't come back or ever find out? Did that make it worse or better?

I was beginning to second guess my decisions. I needed to focus on finding the lamp, and here I was pouting in my room, jealous. This was what I had wanted to avoid before. I was too emotional, and it was a distraction that could cost us all.

A few minutes later, I heard a knock at the door, and then it opened. Erik appeared, not waiting for me to answer. I turned my head away and felt him sit down on the bed. I stiffened, moving forward to the edge of the bed, but he wrapped an arm over my stomach and held me tight to him.

"You're not going away from me again," he whispered in my ear. "You already said you love me, so it's too late."

"Of all the people," I began. "Maybe you should just go be with her. It's what she wants. You have feelings for her."

"Is that what you want? So you can go to Phillip?" His voice sounded stiff and bitter.

"No. But you were with her. Do you love her?"

"I wasn't with her. She used my bathroom because the other one was occupied when I hosted a pack meeting for some of the canid Weres. She left her scarf. Yes, she wants something more. She wanted to be my mate; to help me when you were gone."

"Help you? How?"

"I wasn't doing so great being apart from you so early in our bond. If she'd broken it by becoming my new mate, I would have... recovered."

"What exactly happened to you?"

He didn't respond for a long moment.

"Tell me, Erik."

He wrapped his legs on either side of mine and rested his forehead to the back of my head. "You ever been addicted to anything?"

"Candy."

He chuckled, and I elbowed him. "Don't laugh at me. Sugar addiction is a real thing."

"Fine, Mina. How'd you feel when you cut back on candy?"

"Irritable."

"Well, that's what it was like for me. Only worse. It was like I was suffering from drug withdrawal. I got pretty sick."

"Erik, I left you to suffer. I'm so sorry." I could understand Raya being so bold as to try to become his mate if it meant healing him. My mind raced with images of Erik in despair and weakened. Meanwhile, I'd been only getting stronger. I felt worse than crap. This man deserved better. "Why didn't you let her help you?"

"Because I didn't love her." He kissed my shoulder. "Are you in love with him?"

Was he serious with that question? "Absolutely not."

"I wouldn't be surprised. It's been so long. And you both seem to be getting along now."

"We're friends. Nothing more."

"The same with Raya. I don't want anyone but you." He gave me a light squeeze before taking in a deep breath. Inhaling, I assumed, my scent as he used to do before. It didn't freak me out and even comforted me.

"Mae. She told me to be patient and that I'd see you again. I tried to keep the faith, but it was hard."

"It was hard for me too."

"But the way that he looks at you... "

My stomach tightened. I had to be completely honest about my soulmate bonding. It was now or never. "Erik, I need to tell you something."

I felt him stiffen. "Yes?"

"The bonding magic between Phillip and I made us closer. We had a teacher that we practiced with, and she was really the one that stated that we had to be nicer to each other to get to full strength. By that time, Phillip and I were in a better place with each other. So, we just thought good thoughts, held hands, and we levitated. I mean, not super high, but we can float! And then our magic just burst through. Our eyes even change, like yours do. I get purple eyes." I paused, waiting for a reaction from Erik before I went any further.

"Interesting," he replied.

Well, that wasn't helpful at all. *Okay, be strong, Amina. You've come this far.*

"But then I had a weird dream where Phillip and I made out," I said in a rushed sentence. "I woke up in shock. Phillip and I never kissed or anything while over there."

Erik didn't say anything for a long moment. "So, your subconscious mind really wants to be with Phillip."

I shook my head quickly. "No! Not at all. It was a just a reaction to opening our bond. I haven't had a dream like that since. I don't want Phillip. I only want you. I have a better handle on this bonding magic now."

"Does Phillip? I'm sure he got off on that."

I stroked his arm around me, glad it was still there and that I hadn't run him off. "Doesn't matter what he thinks. I make my own decisions."

"As long as you know I don't share. I'll make sure Phillip knows that, too. I don't want him coming near you."

I let out a deep sigh. "Fine, as long as you tell Raya the same."

I'd figure out a way to keep my promise. Staying away from Phillip was my only option, but we were soulmates. We had to work together to fight what was coming.

How could I control my soulmate connection and keep the man I loved?

CHAPTER 27

I spent the next week searching for the lamp and officially moving back to Silver Spring to stay with Erik. I did secret searches in Faith's, Lisa's, and Felix's places, looking for the lamp. I didn't find anything, but I was hoping I wouldn't anyway. They were part of the Six, so it wouldn't make sense that they'd be an original soulmate, but I wanted to rule all my friends out first.

I went into every home I could think of like it was a full-time job but was failing miserably at my new gig. One week left, and I'd be meeting my maker if something didn't happen quickly for me.

I'd found out, through Ed, that Phillip was also searching for the lamp. Phillip tried to reach out to me on several occasions, but I'd blocked him from my mind and pretended I was too busy when he came to the pack apartment. I was staying in Erik's home; there was no way I'd disrespect him by talking to Phillip.

The welcome back party that Saturday was held at a former wine bar that I didn't recall being open the last time I was in town. It seemed to be turned into one of the fancier establishments, which fit the occasion, as this party was another pseudo-sophisticated event.

I put on a strapless, maroon gown I picked up in one of the few boutiques back in Hagerstown with credits I'd earned from teaching before I was banished. The store was filled with clothing collected during scavenging and a few newly designed items. I was pretty sure my dress was from the prior decade, but it fit me well. The one lovely thing about the apocalypse was that no one was worried about setting trends, so people would wear clothes from any era they wanted, and no one cared.

I swept my curly hair to one side of my head and held it in place with bobby pins I'd scored some time ago. I did myself up in my limited amount of makeup, then threw on some black heels and a peacoat since it was winter. Although, I had every intention of teleporting directly inside the place, since the temperature was ranging in the single-digit degrees at night. We weren't even halfway into the winter, and I was certain it was set to get colder as the pattern had become in the last several years.

The restaurant was semi-light inside, with light wood floors, wooden tables and chairs pushed near the wall, a marble bar countertop, and deep-brown walls holding black-and-white photo artwork. Recessed lighting lit the space, and a DJ, near the left front corner of the room, played a rotation of music from various genres and decades. Waitresses and waiters walked around the space with trays of finger foods and drinks.

Erik stood beside me, dressed nicely in a pair of tailored navy-blue pants, a white button-down shirt, and a matching navy-blue jacket. His hair was slicked back, and his beard was trimmed and neat. He looked amazingly healthy, compared to just a few days ago. The dark circles under his eyes were lighter, almost gone, and he had the coloring back to his skin.

A tinge of guilt reminded me that I had been the cause of him looking like he was coming off a week-long bender while I hadn't suffered physically at all.

Erik leaned into me. "I really want to take that dress off of you," he whispered. "I plan to cut this reunion short."

"Aww, that's the sweetest thing you've ever said to me," I cracked.

I spotted Faith and Grace near the wall to the right, talking to each other and looking very cozy. Faith moved a strand of hair out of Grace's eyes. Interesting.

I turned to see that Shayla, Henry, Ed, Felix, and Lisa sat far off at a booth chatting.

Raya and Carter walked over to us before we could make our way to our friends.

Carter gave me a tight hug and Raya gave the slightest of nods.

"Amina, will I see you at the pack run tonight?" She asked, then slapped her forehead. "Oh, that's right, you're not a were. Never mind. Erik will have to leave you behind."

I glanced at Erik.

"It's a full moon tonight. But I'm not going with the pack," he replied with a smile, grabbing my hand and squeezing it.

I leaned in to him. "You're third in command. You have to run with your pack."

I shook his head quickly like an upset child. "I'm not leaving you." His voice had a finality to it and was full of authority. However, he wasn't the boss of me.

"I could ride a bicycle beside you all and keep up," I offered with a grin.

Carter let out a chuckle. "We can make that happen."

Erik gave a grunt of laughter. "I'd like to see that but for some reason, I don't think that'd be safe."

I rubbed his arm. I felt bad enough making him sick. I wouldn't let him miss a run. "Go with your pack. I'll be home, waiting for you. I promise I won't leave."

"Your honeybun won't leave you behind again," Carter cut in with an amused look on his face. "We'll lock her in the pack apartment and keep a shapeshifter on watch."

I shrugged and looked at Erik with wide, blinking eyes. "I've been confined to an apartment before. I'm a pro now."

Erik growled but said nothing more. "Maybe. I'll let you know," he said before moving us on to the others.

"Where's my brother and Phillip?" I asked, looking around as I sat down next to Ed.

At the mention of Phillip, Erik let go of my hand. "Going to the bar, want anything?"

I asked for wine, if it was available, and Ed asked for another beer.

"Haven't seen either, yet," Faith answered. "Charles usually shows up to places late."

Erik came back a few minutes later and stood to my left. He put a beer down on the table and slid it over to Ed, who gave him a nod. Then he passed me a glass of red wine.

"Your brother is at the bar," Erik stated. "With Blake."

I raised an eyebrow. "How chummy are they?"

"Very," Lisa spat. She shook her head and looked towards the bar.

I followed her gaze and squinted my eyes as I watched Blake grab Charles' arm and give his bicep a squeeze. What the hell was going on?

The world I left had changed, and I had too many things to focus on. I suddenly remembered the state I'd left Charles in. He hadn't been coping well with being a vampire, but I had to remember that nearly three months had passed. Surely, that was enough time for him to get a better handle on things. Yet, I couldn't ignore a nagging feeling that him being a mage and vampire made him a prime target for those who wanted to exploit him. Blake, who was chummy with Seth, being one of those people.

"Dear God," I muttered. "How'd you let that happen while I was gone?"

Erik gave me an exaggerated sorrowful look. "I'm sorry, Mina. I was busy trying to find my mate and stop myself from going loupe. Charles' love life somehow fell off my list of important things."

I slapped him playfully on his chest, and he held my hand to him before leaning into my right ear. "Don't leave me again," he whispered. He touched his forehead to mine.

My heart pinched at his words and the pain within his tone. I would do all I could to make sure he never worried about that. "I'll never leave you."

"You guys are giving me gas," Faith cracked. "Glad to see you two together."

"Me too. Well, I guess I'll just add finding out about this Charles and Blake thing to my growing list," I muttered. I was slightly saddened that Charles and Lisa were no longer together and hoped Blake was only a temporary rebound.

The rest of the evening went by smoothly. As midnight approached, the Weres left to go on their moonlight run. Erik had our group of friends all but swear a blood oath on keeping an eye on me. He refused to leave unless Faith and Grace agreed to stay in the apartment until he returned.

Upon entering Erik's apartment, Faith flopped down on the couch and Grace sat, daintily, beside her. "I'm so glad you're back, Mina," Faith said. "Erik was a grizzly bear while you were gone."

Grace nodded in agreement.

I frowned. "Erik mentioned fighting to keep from going loupe. He was exaggerating, right?"

Faith bared her teeth and raised her brows. "Only slightly. He wasn't eating. He was snapping at everyone. He got in a bar fight with a gargoyle dude. Almost started a war between the gargoyles and their allies, versus the Weres with that one. I thought he'd kill Lisa."

Grace clasped her hands together and brought them to her chest. "It's so beautiful how much he loves you." Leave it to our resident Disney princess to focus on the bright side. The siren seemed to set herself on a positivity autopilot.

"Raya tried to break our bond and become his mate. To save him."

Faith rolled her eyes. "That bitch."

Grace patted Faith on the knee. "Luckily, you have such a loyal man," Grace said with a wistful smile on her face.

"I sort of feel bad for befriending Phillip."

"And yet, you've changed him for the better."

Faith snorted. "Is he going to stay that way, now that Mina's back with Erik?"

Grace's eyes widened. "How long can your spell last? Especially, if you can't go near Phillip."

"Good question," I replied with a shrug. "I was hoping forever. At least until we can really break it." I wasn't prepared for the possibility that my spell could wear off and no longer work. We were accepting Phillip into our inner circle. If he went bad again or even became a follower of the first soulmates, we'd all be in big trouble.

I left Faith and Grace to chat in the living room while I went to my bedroom to change into leggings and an oversized top.

I sat down on the bed, feeling tired from the day's events. There were so many things I missed about the Pre-world. One of them was the spa. It'd always been a good, if temporary, stress reliever. "I would love a massage," I whispered to myself.

"I can help you with that," came a voice.

I turned, and Phillip was suddenly beside me. I let out a yelp. He reached out and grabbed my hand, and before I could pull it back, we were being whisked away to a different setting.

"What the hell!" I shouted as I looked around. We were no longer in Erik's spare bedroom but in an apartment living room.

"We're in my new place. I was debating kicking the pack out of my apartment building, but I got a penthouse, and it's just as nice," Phillip replied with a shrug. "Anyway, I just needed to get a moment with you."

I took my hand back. "Phillip, we don't need to do anything to call attention to ourselves. Erik's already on edge because of how close we've gotten. And if Grace and Faith find I'm gone, they are going to get Erik, and he will flip the hell out."

He sat down on the arm of the couch. He did not seem bothered, unsurprisingly. "How's the search for the lamp going? I've come up with nothing. I still have to get to Seth's and Blake's places somehow. Although we know the soulmate in the States is female, it could be any one of Seth's sister wives."

He wanted to talk about non-relationship things. I would allow it for just a few minutes since it was relevant. Then I'd have to get the hell out of here.

"That would certainly explain their complacency. For one of them, it could all just be a ploy. And the female soulmate may not actually be in this area like you believe. Maybe you're reading too much into Ahmed's words."

He bit his lip, pondering my response. "He couldn't tell us directly, but I know he was trying to give us hints. He said we needed to return home, and he made a point of mentioning how our friends would be focused on finding us rather than what the mobile soulmate was up to. Why would they have a role at all in finding what she was up to if she weren't nearby?"

I scratched my head and looked up. He had a point. "Okay, so if she was nearby and our friend's attention wasn't focused so much on finding us, then they would pay more attention to anything *off* around them. However, as long as we were away, they would be ignoring signs or clues that focus them on any impending threats."

"Exactly. That's what Ahmed was getting at. It's why I believe the soulmate is closer than we think. If she were in another country, it wouldn't matter if we were here or not because we wouldn't know what they were up to. But if the soulmate is here or close to here, we would be cognizant of strange things going on."

I tilted my head from side to side, not as sure. "That's a big assumption."

He leaned forward, resting his forearms on his thighs. "You got anything better?"

I shook my head. "No, nor do I want to ignore that line of thinking. Better that we at least rule it out."

"Exactly. Look, Amina, I need your help with something." His eyes grew serious.

Oh no, that didn't sound good. "What is it?"

"I want to heal the people I've maimed. I'm talking about the ones who have lost limbs, eyes, tongues. I can't regrow that sort of thing on my own."

I nodded and smiled. "I'm not sure if our power can let us bring body parts back even together, but we raised animals from the dead and cured blindness before we even joined, so... I'll go on this healing campaign with you."

He sat upright, giving me a supposedly innocent look. "*Corazon*, it's not like... I can't lie to you, can I?"

I shook my head. "Help everyone you can, Phillip. I'll help any time you need me to. After we find the lamp, that is because if we don't, none of this matters."

He grinned, and there was something more than platonic affection sliding across his eyes. My hand ached to touch him, but I crossed my arms instead, disturbed by my reaction. He still had that pull over me. I'd have to set a time limit when it came to being around Phillip.

"I need to get back before Erik finds out I'm gone and goes apeshit."

Phillip nodded. "It kills me."

"What does?"

He looked into my eyes, searching them. I wasn't sure what he was looking for but I hoped it wasn't encouraging. "Seeing you with him."

I couldn't help him feel any better about that. His feelings weren't foremost here. "Phillip... He was in pain without me. I feel like shit."

"So, you're going to stay with him to save his life?"

I rubbed my forehead. I so didn't want to have this discussion with Phillip. I didn't need to prove my love of Erik to him, yet here I was, doing just that. "I'm staying with him because I love him. Nothing changed."

"If we were together in Ireland longer, we would have—"

I raised my hands in front of me to stop him. "We don't need to talk about that. We were roommates for three months, and that's it."

Phillip stood up. "Is it that easy for you? I'm in love with you, Amina. I know you love me too. I know it." He balled his fist and looked away from me.

I felt bad. Just a tad. I thought of our time in the past three months. In time, I believed I could have fallen in love with him. Now, all I wanted to do was forget my months with Phillip and keep it as platonic as possible. I still loved Erik.

Suddenly, a heavy sinking feeling weighed on my chest, and I struggled to let out a relaxed breath. Tears welled in the corner of my eyes. I fell onto the couch, my legs going weak. A heaviness of depression engulfed me, suffocating me. What was wrong with me?

"I don't feel right," I gasped, confused at the sudden change in my emotions.

Phillip moved over to me and wrapped me in a hug. "I'm doing this to you. You're feeling how I feel. I'm sorry."

What in the world? "How?"

"It's part of our bond."

I pushed away from him. "You projected your feelings onto me? You can do that?" How I continued to underestimate Phillip was confounding to me. He was never still. He would always be ahead of me, because he would constantly be on a quest to reach his full magical potential.

"I'm sorry, Amina. I wasn't thinking." He ran his hand across his face and turned from me. "I can't help myself when it comes to you." He balled his hands into fists by his side again, holding in something I could only feel. Frustration, anguish, anger.

I tentatively placed a hand on his shoulder. I wanted to be mad but I also felt sympathy. Could it be the bond? "You can't use your magic on me, Phillip. I care about you, but I don't want to be controlled or guilted into anything. I know you didn't mean this, but you have to gain better control. You have a goal now, to take back the town and make it better than it was before. You should focus on that. Along with finding the whole lamp and fighting the bad soulmates thing."

"I can do all of that better with you," he said, voice soft.

"I'll still be here."

"But you won't be mine."

I looked up into his eyes. I shouldn't have done that. Those eyes, full of emotion and tenderness, were what had trapped me in the first place. I shook my head and looked away. I couldn't be with him. As much as Phillip affected me, my love for Erik was too strong. Apart or together, Erik stirred my soul. I would never be Phillip's.

Phillip sighed and nodded as if understanding everything I hadn't said.

He looked towards his living room windows. "Tell him I'm sorry about whisking you away."

"He won't know."

"Of course, he will." Phillip smiled. It didn't reach his eyes. Those were still sad.

CHAPTER 28

*A*s I feared, Grace and Faith knew I'd been missing and had freaked out. Luckily, I found them before they went to alert Erik and company, who were still frolicking outside the border, hunting down bunnies or something. Although I told Phillip Erik wouldn't know, I knew better. I just didn't want it to be his problem. I would take the hit. One way or another, I'd have to explain to Erik that Phillip and I had to work together in some capacity to fight the first soulmates. We just had to figure out a way that was less sneaky and more open, even if it pissed off Erik. Sneaking behind his back just made things worse.

Unsurprisingly, before I could even say a word, Erik could smell Phillip on me when he returned. Damn, those were nostrils!

"He came over?" He thundered.

Faith and Grace quickly exited, and I unsuccessfully tried to follow.

"He actually just teleported me away."

Erik punched a wall and I winced at the new dent that formed. "I'll rip his throat out!"

I needed to get him to simmer down. "That might kill

me," I replied, heading to Erik's bedroom. "I'm stronger, but not sure if I would survive his death."

He followed me. "Then I will rip his arm off."

"No need for such violence." I sat on his bed and patted the space beside me.

It was winter, but all Erik had on was a pair of sweatpants he'd grabbed from a clothing pile the weres put beside a designated tree. This way, they wouldn't return to the town naked after shifting back to human.

"You aren't taking this seriously, Mina. I lost you. I can't let that happen again."

It wouldn't happen again but I needed him not to pop a blood vessel with anger. I wanted him to trust me. He didn't have to worry about Phillip. I held out a hand to him. "It's not going to, Erik. I'm never leaving you. I am more powerful now. And I can handle Phillip."

"I could beat him into a coma."

I snorted. "That moon sure does bring out the violence in you."

He narrowed his eyes at me, not speaking.

"It's almost 3 a.m. Can we just let it go and go to bed? Nothing happened. He asked me to help him heal the people he maimed, and I agreed."

I scooted back on the bed and got under the covers. Under the blanket, I removed my leggings and panties and threw them onto the floor. I then took off my T-shirt and tossed it aside as well.

"Are you going to stay standing there angry or join me under the covers?" I gave him a naughty smile.

He titled his head and considered me before taking off his sweats in a blur and joining me.

$\backsim$

I woke up a little before 7 a.m. in the winter darkness. I shivered, my skin feeling like ice. Erik ran very hot, and he liked to keep the apartment set on Arctic. I ran the other way and thought we'd come to a compromise. Apparently, in his fit at my short disappearance, he'd turned the heat on low, and I'd forgotten to adjust it. Lying next to him was like lying next to a space heater, but separating from him left me with a miserable coldness.

I scooted to the edge of the bed but soon felt Erik's arm tighten around my stomach, pulling me back to him. I tried to lift his arm, but he felt like a boulder.

"I'm just going to get a glass of water, babe," I whispered, turning slightly to Erik.

His eyes were still closed but he was frowning.

"I'll be right back. You can time me."

His frown remained, but eventually, he lifted his arm. I turned fully to him and kissed his forehead before picking up my clothes off the floor and throwing them on, socks and all. I needed gloves and a scarf to walk around inside.

I went to the thermostat in the hallway and turned the heat up before going to the kitchen. I grabbed a glass out of the dark, wooden cabinet above the sink and turned on the faucet; hovering my glass under it to fill with water. I did a two-step at the sink to turn up my body heat.

A cold breeze lifted the hair on the back of my neck, and I spun around, seeing nothing. It felt like a blast of air conditioner had just shot out of the vent. How could that be? I'd just turned up the heat. Maybe I'd turned on the air conditioner instead?

I turned the faucet off and placed the glass on the counter, intending to rectify the temperature battle, when I heard a noise. Something small fell in the living room. It sounded like a book falling on the carpet. I walked out of the kitchen, passed the dining room, and entered the living room space. I surveyed the floor but didn't see anything out of the ordinary. I walked over to the balcony sliding glass doors and peeked behind the vertical blinds, looking out at the quiet town.

I narrowed my eyes as I looked down at a dark mass hovering under a streetlight in the parking lot. It looked like a human silhouette, except it was floating and was the color of charcoal, like a shadow that refused to hide from the light. A prickly heat stabbed at my limbs and fear seized me. It was no shadow. I thought back to my first night in Ireland in the abandoned apartment and stood back.

Something brushed against my ankle and I yelped, spinning around. I looked down and saw my furry, gray kitten. I bent over and picked up Poppy.

"You scared me, kitty," I whispered. I leaned forward and peeked out of the blinds again but the blurry figure was gone. "What the hell is going on?"

"Amina," called a male voice.

I spun around, thinking it was Erik, although it didn't quite sound like him. The voice was deeper and croaking.

I saw nothing. At least nothing at first glance. But as I took a step away from the balcony sliding doors, I saw the dark outline of what was possibly a male figure sitting, no, crouching in the leather chair facing me near the entrance of the living room.

"Erik?" I squeaked.

The figure slowly shook its head.

Poppy hissed in my arms.

The thing clearly wasn't Erik but a girl standing in the dark had to ask. It was a shadow really, perhaps the same one from outside. It had a humanoid shape but was very thin, with long limbs. Its twig-like arms seemed to go past its boney knees. I couldn't see any features. No eyes, nose or mouth. It didn't have hair or any clothes on. It was as if I were looking at the black skeleton of some alien creature.

The prickly sweat crept under my arms and I took a step back. The thing that clearly wasn't Erik unfolded itself from the chair and stood up. It was tall, so very tall. Maybe eight feet or more, as there wasn't much room from the top of its head and the ceiling. I'd seen many things in the past several years, but this was new. I was facing a lot of new things recently.

"Aaaammiiiinaaaa," it croaked again.

It had no mouth. How the hell was it calling my name? How the hell was it seeing me?

It moved towards me in an awkward walk. Like a baby just learning to take its first steps. In theory, I could outrun it, but it was standing between me and the front entrance. That was assuming it wasn't some incorporeal being or ghost that could teleport, which I suspected it was. It struggled on towards me, arms now raised out as if reaching for me.

Poppy dug her little claws in my arm, and the pain brought me back from my frozen fear.

I let out a horrified scream, shouting Erik's name and teleporting to the outside of the apartment.

I stood in the parking lot in my sock-covered feet, shivering in the cold dark. It had to be at most, ten degrees out. Poppy snuggled closer to me, bumping her head against my neck.

"Poppy, I gotta leave you out here and go kill a monster. That doesn't seem like a ghost," I whispered.

"It wasn't," Phillip said beside me, looking up at my apartment.

I jumped away from him. He looked over to me with an expression of concern. He was dressed only in sweatpants and a long-sleeved T-shirt. He also did a two-step in bare feet.

"Where'd you come from? How'd you know something was in the apartment?" I asked.

"I felt your fear. Like last time," he replied. "Did you leave—"

"Hold my cat," I demanded. I gave Poppy to Phillip and teleported, bravely, back into Erik's apartment bedroom.

But Erik wasn't there. I heard a growl and ran out of the bedroom to the living room.

I saw Erik's bare back as he clawed at the giant shadow creature with his now-inhuman jackal claws. His claws connected with the creature and vivid, red slashes appeared across its thin torso. It belted out an ear-splitting screech before back-handing Erik, who sailed across the room towards me.

I threw out my hand and magically pinned the creature to the floor. It struggled against my invisible hold.

Erik scrambled to his feet and charged at the monster again. He pounced on it, tearing into the creature. He tore into the blackness with his talons with a superhuman speed, like the blades of a fan, not giving the creature time to react. Its cries continued.

I heard pounding on the door and telepathically opened it to keep an eye on Erik. Phillip appeared with Poppy, as well as Carter and a couple other pack members.

"Something broke in," I explained before turning back to Erik. I clapped my hands, and the room became illuminated with the light fixtures.

I stared down at Erik, who had stopped clawing. There was nothing but a thick puddle of black goo in front of him now. It was also splattered over the furniture and his body. He stood up and turned to us. A gash crossed his chest, from his left shoulder to his right hip. His hands were dripping in the thick, black liquid as if he'd been playing in it.

"I think he got it," Carter stated, breaking the silence. "Whatever it was."

I looked around. There wasn't a body. No black skeleton.

All that remained was the black goo. Had it escaped? Dematerialized, somehow?

"It melted or something," Erik explained, breathing hard.

"How'd something get in if this place is warded?" Phillip asked. I turned to him. Poppy, the traitorous cat, was snuggled in his arms.

"Good question," I stated.

Erik nodded, crossing his arms over his bare chest. He only had a pair of boxer-shorts on, but he still looked like a Roman gladiator ready to fight. "The building and the town are warded."

He was right. That something was still able to get in was very disturbing. Unless someone let it in. "Clearly, this thing was stronger than the ward here. I've got to put up a new one around the town." One that not just anyone could break.

"I can help with that," Phillip said.

"It knew my name."

He rubbed his chin, nodding slightly. "Just like the creature in Dublin knew mine."

"Something's coming for me."

Carter turned to the growing crowd. "We've handled it, folks. Go back to your apartments. We will put up a stronger ward around the apartment and the town within the hour."

People slowly piled out of the apartment, exchanging worried glances, but they did not question the second in command.

"Why would something be coming for you?" Carter asked, hands on his hips. He was dressed only in black sweatpants and was very muscular. Did all the pack members live at the gym, or did they just get all beefcake when they became weres?

Back to his question. At this stage, I was growing enemies by the moment. Apparently being strong soulmates made us a target. "A big bad is coming, and said big bad knows that we are threats. It came for Phillip in the form of a dark spell.

It's coming for me as some sort of shadow creature. I've never heard of or seen anything like this." I looked down at the black mess. "I thought it was a ghost, but we can't physically fight ghosts. We'd have to use magic or prayer."

He walked over to the goo and peered down at it. "And yet, Erik fought him like an animal."

"It reeks of dark magic," Erik said, grimacing and looking down at his hands.

Phillip looked over to him and wrinkled his nose. "Yes, you smell like burned death. Someone summoned this."

I wasn't as familiar with summoning. My basic understanding was that a summoning mage, warlock, or witch, could bring forth creatures from other worlds. The only other worlds I knew of were Heaven, Hell, and, most recently, Fairyland A.K.A. Fae World. "Could this have come from hell? Could someone have summoned something from hell to kill me? Like they did with David?" I asked in a slightly-panicked voice.

Phillip tilted his head from side to side. "Possibly. Or somewhere else. We have no idea what magic worlds exist. A conjuring mage could have done this as well. They could have even made up this creature from their own minds. Whatever it is and whoever brought it, they are very powerful. They broke our wards."

Whatever was coming for us was growing in strength. I had to find that lamp. We needed to find the original soulmates and take them down before they killed us all.

I turned to Erik. "I'm going with Phillip to strengthen the wards on the town and both of our apartment buildings. I can come back and do a cleaning spell for all of this."

He nodded. "Go. We have some witches on retainer who can clean this up. Don't be gone long." He glanced over to Phillip.

"I'll make sure she's safe," Phillip replied with a curt nod.

Erik gave a nod back.

That was probably as friendly as I'd ever seen them. Progress.

After I got fully dressed, Phillip and I proceeded to spend almost an hour in the cold warding the town with every bit of strength we had. By the time I returned to Erik's, I was glad he had a cleanup crew because I had no power to do anything, not even make a candle flame flicker.

Once I entered the apartment, I saw that it was not only sparkling clean but much warmer. I walked to Erik's bedroom, finding him asleep on top of the covers. He had a new pair of sweatpants on and was still shirtless, except he was clean, and the gash on his chest was gone. I could only assume one of the witches had healed him. Left to his own were healing; there would be a scar. A silly pang of jealousy erupted from me as I pictured some witch placing her or his hands over his uncovered chest.

"He was there for you, tonight. That's why he showed up, right? He felt you in danger?" Erik said in a low voice, his eyes covered by his forearm.

"So were you."

"I heard you scream my name."

I sat down beside him. "You didn't need to. You'd have known, just like Phillip did. And I'd know if you were in danger. We just need to hone in on our mate magic. And we can do that regardless of Phillip. I can even learn a way to reduce my connection to Phillip, so that he doesn't know everything I do. I spoke to a witch back in Ireland. She showed me how."

Liz hadn't had much time to go over that magic because I didn't want Phillip to know. I didn't want to hurt his feelings. However, Liz was adamant that I needed to learn how to shut the bonding magic on and off. Unlike Mae, she was still very nervous about Phillip. While she wanted us to bond our magic, even if that meant through sex, she thought I should remain cautious of Phillip.

"He saved you before," Erik said, more than asked.

"Yes, but—"

He put up his hand to stop me. "If he can help protect you when I'm not around, then I guess I can deal with your friendship with him."

There was some confusion here. I was no damsel and his role was not to take care of me. "You do realize, babe, that I don't need protecting. I have power and stuff."

"I know that. I just... I get worries."

I rubbed his arm. The skin was so smooth I wanted to bite it. *Focus, Amina.* "So, do I, but you have to have faith. You have to just let me be who I am meant to be. I'm more than someone you or Phillip need to watch over. I'm a bad-ass, remember?"

"I'm a fool for forgetting."

I lay back, leaning on an elbow. I moved his arm away from his eyes and looked at him, smiling. He looked back at me, and returned my smile and that simple grin stole my heart. Again.

He touched my cheek, rubbing a thumb back and forth. "Those eyes."

"I just used a lot of power. They're my magic eyes," I replied in a playful whisper.

He laughed, and the deep bass was delicious to my ears. "They're beautiful."

I wondered if he would still think that when he found out Phillip had the same eyes.

CHAPTER 29

Once we confirmed that Seth, his sister wives, and Raya were at the pub, a usual Sunday activity for many pack members, Phillip and I teleported into their apartments and began to search. I went straight to Raya's, and Phillip went to Seth's.

I really hoped Raya had the lamp. Finding out she was really an original soulmate would make her a formidable enemy. That would suck, but I didn't like her already, so it wouldn't be any bother.

I walked around her one-bedroom apartment, sensing for magic. She was a slob. Her kitchen sink was stacked with dishes, pots, and pans. Her bathroom needed a good scrubbing, and her bed was unmade.

I felt no magic anywhere, but that didn't mean she didn't have the lamp. I checked in every space I could imagine a genie lamp fitting. Nothing. I could sense no cloaking magic to make it invisible. Of course, it could be a magic beyond my capabilities. I couldn't take these beings for granted. They'd broken wards. In sum, I was searching, but I couldn't say for sure that any place I'd already looked was actually cleared. We didn't even know for certain that the soulmate or the lamp were in Silver Spring. They could be in Florida, for all we knew.

I had to assume that Ahmed literally meant that our need to return home was because the lamp was literally home in Silver Spring or Hagerstown.

We left the pack apartment in defeat.

"We still have tons more here to check and more in Hagerstown that I haven't gotten to," I sighed. "This is going to take forever. We need to tell the others. I'm getting stalked by summoned beings; I don't have time to waste."

Phillip walked up beside me, hands in his pockets. "We have to be careful who we tell, including your friends. I wish a location spell would have worked. It pains me to say, but maybe Erik can help."

So we went and got help. Telling Erik the truth wasn't an easy ordeal. He was naturally pissed that I had withheld the information. His eyes went all jackal, and I threatened to teleport out of Phillip's apartment and leave town, which only made him angrier.

Erik cleared his throat and crossed his arms. "I assume since you are sharing the full story with me now, you trust that I'm not a cohort of these first soulmates," he replied in a gruff voice.

I clasped my hands in front of my face in a show of apology. I really hated when Erik was pissed with me. Especially if I deserved it. "I believed you weren't before. I mean, you're my mate. But after the Lisa banishment thing and Ahmed's warning, we still had to play it smart. Can you forgive me, Erik? We can't win this without you."

He looked away from me. "As long as you aren't hiding anything else. We are a pair here. It's not just you and Phillip against the world."

I nodded quickly. "No more secrets. I promise."

He glared at me for a moment, and I stood my ground, not squirming. He was an alpha but I was no beta. Finally, he gave me a curt nod before speaking again. "Besides this Ahmed guy, is there anything else I need to know?" he asked, looking at Phillip.

I tilted my head. Why was he just looking at Phillip? "I've already told you everything,"

He shrugged. "In case you've forgotten something."

I sighed. He was still pissed. Phillip looked at me with a careful smile. "Tell him what he thinks I didn't tell him."

Phillip sat down on the other end of his couch from me and rested an ankle over a knee. "I'm sure Amina has told you everything you need to know. We believe that the lamp and one of the soulmates is in America, most likely in this state. The other one is confined to his country of origin and not yet mobile or something. Neither one is at full power, but if they get to that level, they might be impossible to beat. If we can find the lamp, we can learn more about the OGs from Ahmed, who will no longer be beholden to them. If we learn more about them, we can find the soulmates now and defeat them before they get to be too powerful and that window is quickly closing."

"So, how do we find the lamp?" Erik asked, face still full of irritation.

Phillip threw his hands out to the side dramatically. "Well, I had an idea that I think might work. We tap into genie magic."

I frowned. "What?"

"Just as we did with the fairy magic to get home. We do the same for genie magic. We can't do a normal locator spell to find older paranormals, like Fae and Jinn, but if we tap into their magic, we might be able to locate the lamp. We tapped into Fae magic, and it took us to where Lisa was, which was here in Silver Spring. Ahmed was cryptic in his explanation on how we got home. We just made assumptions. As soulmates, we can tap into other magic just enough to break wards and possibly locate things."

"How do we tap into Jinn magic? I only knew fairy magic because of Lisa and our fight with the Fae. I didn't get enough information from Ahmed to know anything about his magic. I wouldn't even be able to know what it looks like in my mind or feels like."

Phillip gave a toothy grin. "I focused on Ahmed's magic the two times we met. The way that I fight is to know my enemy so that I know how to attack. When I first met Ahmed, my focus was to see what he was. I thought he was a witch, so I fought him the wrong way and lost."

This guy was so damn smart. I really needed to level up. "You knew how to feel magic forms back then?"

He sighed. "Amina, I know a lot. I'm in a town full of magic that I helped run. I was in a better position than you to get those skills, so don't be upset with me."

I was more upset at myself for not thinking of it before but he didn't need to know that. "I'm upset because you didn't tell me."

"At the time, we weren't on the best of terms, and it didn't cross my mind after. Then Liz came and showed you how."

I looked away. The more time I spent around him, the more it was clear that I was not at his level. It was depressing but I would do better. "You would have won the challenge."

"You don't know that, *mi cora—*" Phillip looked to Erik, who was on the verge of a growl. "Sorry, Amina."

One point to Phillip for actually making an effort. More Progress.

"So, what does Jinn magic look like?" I asked, attempting to stir past this tense moment.

"Orange. And it feels hot. Much hotter than witch magic."

I nodded slowly, trying to picture it in my mind. I threw out my hand to him. "All right then, let's get to it." I looked to Erik. "We might look like we're hemorrhaging, but we won't be."

"Unless we are," Phillip cut in. I glared at him, and he

shrugged. "Jinn magic is older than Fae magic, or so I've heard. It might be tougher. So, Erik, make sure we don't die. Pull us out if things get too rough."

Erik looked over at me with concerned eyes. "I don't like this."

"We can't play it safe anymore, Erik. This is bigger than David and that prison. You don't know Ahmed. He is coming for us, and we have less than a week left to find the lamp," I stated. "And he is formidable. And if this scary soulmate from afar can come at us now, imagine what will happen when he gets the strength to leave where he's stuck. As soon as he bonds with his mate, we are done. None of us are ready right now. We don't have the knowledge. They have the upper hand. Ahmed can help us with that."

"Or he'll just kill us," Phillip cut in with a nonchalant tone. "So, we should get started."

Erik nodded his head. "I'm pulling you out if things go south. And I'll decide what that looks like."

I sighed. "Fair enough."

I looked to Phillip, and we clasped hands. Closing my eyes, I focused on Ahmed's face. He was framed in gold and looked almost saintly. My mind searched for the magic of the Jinn. A blanket of heat fell over me. It wasn't comfortable, and I began to sweat. My hands were hot and clammy in Phillips' and I lifted my elbows uncomfortably to air out the sweat forming in my armpits. This was not cute. In fact, it was stifling. I could barely breathe, and I opened my mouth to take in air.

I heard Erik's movement around me and the opening of the balcony glass doors. Soon, a cold breeze washed over me, but it was a momentary relief as the heat latched onto it and covered me again. I felt weak and nauseous. I swooned a bit and then felt arms around me, holding me upright. Erik. My breath quickened, and sweat dripped from my hairline into my eyes.

And then I saw it.

It was not what I expected.

Phillip erupted in laughter.

It was a lamp. An actual lamp. I expected it to look like what I'd seen in cartoons. This was a lamp I would find on my grandmother's side table, back in the day. The lamp was antique looking. It had a golden, circular base with black etchings of people and what I assumed were spirits. The lampshade was made of what appeared to be stained glass with various colors swirling around it.

We'd been looking for the wrong thing this whole time. Luckily, we hadn't been searching for long. I looked past the lamp to the background. It was in a small, dark space, surrounded by boxes. A closet. I looked to a small shoebox. It was the brand name of a company that used to sell expensive, red-bottomed heels, so most likely, the space belonged to a female. That was a tiny bit helpful. We still needed to know where this closet existed.

A stream of dim light shone through the cracked closet door. I peered through with my mind's eye and saw a bedroom. The light came from a window. In front of the window was a bed. It was neatly made, in purple satin sheets. A beige teddy bear sat between the numerous pillows on the bed. I couldn't see anything else. I'd have to search more of the house to find out where this was. Right now, I was sitting from the point of view of a lamp in a closet, and this wouldn't do. We were never going to find—

"I know this place," Phillip stated in a whisper.

I opened my eyes and raised my eyebrows. "Huh?"

He opened his eyes and looked at me, his eyebrows connecting in a frown. "I've been there. I know that room."

"Whose is it?"

"Blake's."

CHAPTER 30

"Let me get this straight," Charles began. "You had to find a genie lamp to get some dude to help you fight these original soulmates who seem to be all powerful. You found the lamp using your soulmate abilities, and it's in Blake's apartment. Now you think she's one of the original soulmates?"

We were piled in Erik's apartment. This time it was only The Six, Phillip, Ed, and Mae. The only people we knew were cleared from being possible soulmates or followers.

I nodded. "Well, yeah, that's it in a nutshell. We snuck in and grabbed it."

Charles snorted. "You mean you broke into her apartment and stole from her. You committed a crime."

I poked out my lip. I didn't feel guilty. Not really. "Yeah, well, something like that but it wasn't hers in the first place."

"So, you believe."

I huffed. My little brother had a point. We were just going off Ahmed's words but what else did we have?

"I don't think it's her," Phillip said, his back to us as he looked out of the balcony glass doors.

"I'm actually going to agree with him," Charles said, face

in amazement as he looked around at the group. "Blake's a good person. Sis, she doesn't care for Erik that much. She's been Team Phillip all this time. We argued about it a lot."

Erik pffted. "Not surprised."

"The point I was going to make is that if she were a soulmate who wants to destroy you, why would she want you and Phillip together? You're weaker apart."

"But they don't just want to destroy them," Felix said in a quiet voice. "They want them to submit. Isn't that right?"

"Here's a crazy idea, how about we ask Blake?" Faith put forth, sitting on the arm of the couch. "You think it's her, but you're letting her run free?"

"Do we want to play the hand that we know?" I asked. "Are we ready for that fight?"

She shrugged. "Can we afford to wait? They broke our wards and manifested a monster to come hurt you. They're only getting more powerful as time goes on. Let's get it all out in the open while they aren't at the top of their game. We've been strengthening our powers. Now's the time."

Mae stood up and walked to the center of the room. "My dears, we could speculate all night, but we won't know the truth. We know someone who might," she pointed to the antique lamp we'd swiped from Blake's apartment, now sitting on the coffee table.

We all looked at it.

Felix leaned towards it. "So, what do we do? Rub it?"

I leaned forward and gave it a rub. Nothing. I rubbed it again from various angles and sides. I rubbed it three times. Then seven. The numbers were random. I had no idea, beyond what I'd seen in *Aladdin*. Still, nothing.

"In horror movies, if you say the guy's name three times, he shows up," Felix offered. "It's usually to a mirror, but if you look at the lamp and say dude's name, maybe it might work the same."

I gave him a long blink, then sighed and turned to the lamp. "Ahmed, Ahmed, Ahmed," I stated.

Not a thing.

"You gotta touch it when you say it," Felix added. He gave me a confident head nod.

I was pretty certain that his love of horror movies was clouding his thoughts, but I didn't have a better idea.

I sighed again and touched the lamp. "Ahmed, Ahmed, Ahmed."

We waited a few seconds for a cloud of smoke to appear and a dapper man to show up through said smoke. Nothing.

"Maybe it's not the right lamp after all," I heard Lisa whisper.

I was getting annoyed now. "Well, then who the hell's lamp is it?"

"It could be—"

"Mine," said a male with an accent of Middle Eastern and English.

He stood next to Mae as if he'd been there the whole time. No smoke. No materializing. He was just there. As usual, he was well dressed in a three-piece suit. Mae turned to him, not frightened by his sudden appearance.

"Apologies for the delay. For the record, you only have to touch the lamp and say my name once," he explained. Ahmed looked down at the lamp. "I see you were able to complete your task. I am most grateful." He leaned towards the lamp, but it disappeared before he could get any closer.

I frowned and shot up off of the couch.

"Not so fast," Phillip announced. He was now holding the lamp. "Didn't want you to just take the lamp and bounce. Your credibility isn't the best, what with you bringing man-eating plant life to kill the townsfolk in Ireland."

"With all the trouble Amina and Phillip brought, it doesn't sound like any of us are going to be welcome in Ireland," Felix muttered.

I couldn't say I disagreed. Ed's people were certainly better off without us. We'd brought fighting to them on several occasions. I had to help them in some significant way beyond our healing potions.

"I am very remorseful of that incident, but as I have explained, I did not have control," Ahmed replied.

Phillip shook his head. "Still, it doesn't look so good on you. Trust me, I know about doing wrong when it's out of my control. We have to prove ourselves to gain credibility again. So, we helped you, now you have to help us, and then you get your lamp back."

"Phillip," I said.

"Gotta be smart."

Ahmed looked at him with a cocked eyebrow. "I see. You want help defeating the original soulmates," he replied, clasping his hands behind his back. "What would you like to know?"

"Everything, my dear," Mae responded, giving him a gentle smile.

Ahmed nodded to her. "I will tell you all. We must use our time wisely."

"Is Blake the female mate?" Charles asked, his face looked visibly pained. I could imagine he was struggling with the idea that his new girlfriend was some great evil.

Ahmed turned to him. "I don't know for sure. I've never seen the female soulmate. I've only communicated with her telepathically. It's the same with all of their followers. Your friend's domicile could simply be the place the lamp was hidden, and she has no connection to the soulmates."

I hadn't thought of that. Crap, that made this even more complicated.

He put a finger to his lips. "But she could also be the soulmate, and you are now in grave danger. Either way, I'd leave nothing for chance. They plan as we speak, and once the male soulmate is able to move freely, he will leave his current location."

"He?" Faith asked.

"The male half of the original soulmate pairing."

"Where will he be going? Here?"

Ahmed shrugged. "I'm quite sure he will visit here. But this is not one of his bases. He'll be going to Baltimore, as it is the closest base to you."

That couldn't be true. Most of the city was destroyed by the war against the zombies and ghouls several years ago. Then again, it would be the perfect place to hide a base. "Nothing's in Baltimore. Well, nothing organized. There are a few small communities rebuilding but nothing established like a government town or this place. "

Faith shifted back in her seat. "That's not exactly true, Amina," Faith stated, looking at me with wide eyes. "A lot has happened in the almost three months you were gone. There is a section of Baltimore that we've heard interesting tales about. We haven't found it, though; maybe it's cloaked. It's supposedly full of just paranormals like here and it's doing pretty well. That might be a soulmate locale."

Ahmed nodded. "It's a town run by an ally of the original soulmates. One full of warriors."

"Are you telling me we have the soulmates' army less than an hour from here?" Phillip asked, taking a step forward.

Ahmed frowned. "Baltimore is only but one of their armies." He looked around the room. "You all have no idea?"

"How many followers do they have?" Faith asked. "What are we looking at here?"

"There are nearly a thousand people in this Baltimore town."

"That's less than our size here in Silver Spring. Then we also have Hagerstown," Erik surmised.

"That's just in Baltimore. They have followers all over the world. Although the Baltimore base is their largest."

"How'd they gain that kind of following?" Charles asked, leaning forward. "It's just two people. Paranormal or not."

Ahmed folded his arms across his chest and began to slowly pace. "They can get access to people without leaving their room, and I don't mean through the Internet. Imagine being able to gain power over a stranger in another country. They were powerful enough to entrap me. Not just anyone can control a Jinn without serious repercussions. And as they gain followers who do their dirty work, they get more control any and everywhere. The world is their proverbial playground."

Well, then that meant we had to do some talking as well. Make our own deals. "Maybe we could go to Baltimore and talk to the liaison there who is running the place. That person could reach out to the soulmates."

"Tell us about the guy over at the Baltimore base." Erik cut in.

"The Baltimore town is run by an elf named Joo-won," Ahmed replied.

"I'm assuming this Joo-won isn't a good elf?" I asked.

Ahmed furrowed his brow. I'd take that as a yes. "I've only met him once. He is... indifferent. Very difficult to judge. The best way to describe him would be cold. But he is very powerful. He should be neutral, but the soulmates must have enticed him with something."

Faith swore under her breath. "Why would anyone want to follow these people?"

"Maybe that's a question we can ask Joo-won when we meet him," I stated.

"And if he causes any trouble, we can take him. We're the Six."

Ahmed turned to her, a brow raised. "He will kill you. Elves are challenging to kill, and he is the strongest I've encountered. He is calculating. The best way to handle him is to match his wit. His greatest weakness is his arrogance."

If the soulmates had a large following, there had to be layers to their organizing. Something we could penetrate. "Do the soulmates have an inner circle?"

Ahmed looked over to me and smiled. "Smart question, and yes, they do."

"Who are they?" Phillip questioned.

"I just told you of Joo-won. You and Amina met the fairy in Ireland. Misandre is her name. She's quite old. Very sadistic. You wouldn't want to be captured by her."

"She was hard to fight. She almost killed Phillip," I recalled.

Ahmed nodded. "Then there is the demon king."

Charles slapped his forehead. "Fuck. A demon king?"

"I don't know much about Alister. I only saw him in passing, and I recall feeling like my soul was withering away, for lack of a better description. It was extremely unpleasant."

This would not be a cake walk. Not that I expected anything less. We'd be fighting their allies before we got to the big bad boss, like some death match video game.

Faith ran a hand through her hair, her face looking determined. "So, fine, three badies. A fairy, an elf, and a demon."

"Correct," Ahmed replied. He smiled at Faith, and she nodded back at him. "Of course, you must count in all their followers as well."

"Damn it," Faith cursed. "Forgot about that."

"We could turn the elf. I hope, since he's neutral," Lisa stated with nervous eyes. "Maybe make him an offer he can't refuse?"

Ahmed looked around the room. "Are you sure you want to involve yourselves? They aren't after you, if you don't stand in their way. A war is coming between the paranormals and regular humans, as well as any sympathizers."

Erik rubbed his hands together as if preparing to fight right then. "Well, we aren't going to sit back and let innocent humans die just because they don't have powers."

"We've got human friends," I added. I thought of Ed, Mercy, Joanie, and the others back in Hagerstown and Dublin.

I looked to Phillip, and he nodded. "And these soulmates probably know this, which is why they're coming for us."

Ahmed nodded. "So, I suppose you have an army of your own to build."

He was right. We had to gather supporters. How we were going to get enough people to prepare for a war that most didn't even know was coming was the first problem to tackle.

I leaned towards Ahmed. "Tell us everything you know about these soulmates and how we can take them out."

If you enjoyed this book please leave a review on Amazon and Goodreads!

What happened to Lisa in the Fae realm and the others while Amina was banished? Find out in Mystic Realms, A Paranormal World Novella.

C.C. is originally from Baltimore, Maryland and has actively written fiction since the age of eleven. She's an avid "chick lit" reader and urban fantasy fan. During her days, she works in Civil Rights for the federal government. In her free time, she sings karaoke, travels the globe and watches too much TV... when she's not writing, of course.

For more information on C.C. Solomon, her books and her lifestyle and travel blog, check out www.ccsolomon.com.

Subscribe to her newsletter so you don't miss any swag, giveaways and free stories! https://bit.ly/3iBVhEI

You can also reach C.C. at the following social media sites:

www.ingramcontent.com/pod-product-compliance
Lightning Source LLC
Chambersburg PA
CBHW031615100726
47898CB00006B/1804